THE
SYKAOS
PAPERS

■

THE
SYKAOS
PAPERS

■

BEING

An Account of the Voyages of the Poet Oi Paz to the System of Strim in the Seventeenth Galaxy; of his Mission to the Planet Sykaos; of his First Cruel Captivity; of his Travels about its Surface; of the Manners and Customs of its Beastly People; of his Second Captivity; and of his Return to Oitar.

To which are added many passages from the Poet's Journal, documents in Sykotic script, and other curious matters.

Selected and Edited by Q, *Vice-Provost of the College of Adjusters.*

■

Transmitted by Timewarp
to
E. P. THOMPSON

Pantheon Books   New York

FIRST AMERICAN EDITION

Copyright © 1988 by E.P. Thompson.

All rights reserved under International and Pan-American Copyright Conventions. Published in the United States by Pantheon Books, a division of Random House, Inc., New York, and simultaneously in Canada by Random House of Canada Limited, Toronto. Originally published in Great Britain by Bloomsbury Publishing Ltd., London.

Library of Congress Cataloging-in-Publication Data

Thompson, E.P. (Edward Palmer), 1924–
The Sykaos papers.
I. Title.
PR6070.H6646S95   1988   832'.914   88-42596
ISBN 0-394-56828-1

MANUFACTURED IN THE UNITED STATES OF AMERICA.

PREFACE

The Sykaos Papers came into my involuntary possession early in
January 1987. For fear of being thought old-fashioned I had
obtained, several weeks before, a word-processor. But my essays
in high technology were futile, and whatever I typed on the
keyboard was ingested without return. The creature sulked
unproductively on my desk and began to provoke my hostility.

At length – on January 16th – I dashed my hand in exasperation
across the keyboard, catching some letters and signs. There
appeared on the screen a series something like this:

$$O\ I\ TAR + 3383/2/68 = OI\ P\ AZ$$

At the same time the screen was flushed with a green light which
pulsed in intensity.

I tried to clear the screen without success. I switched the
machine off and even disconnected the plug. But the light continued to pulse. I retired at length to bed, and the next morning
found to my relief that the processor had resumed its obstinate
vacancy.

Two days later a mechanic came (at my urgent request) from
my supplier. He showed impatience with my account, and consulted the machine's directory to see (he said) if any of my
'brilliant efforts' had lodged themselves in the hard disc which
constitutes its memory.

Only one filename came on screen: SYKAOS P. After mis-
understandings – for the mechanic refused to believe that I am
an innocent medium in this intergalactic publication – the

machine was ordered to print out whatever its memory stored. This book is the product of its automatic labours.

This account may strain the reader's credulity. But the authenticity of the pages which follow will soon be self-evident. It will also become apparent that Oitarian technology is so far in advance of our own that it is a simple exercise for them to timewarp a book backwards over a mere decade or so.

I have, of course, attempted many times to engage the same code. But I must have misremembered the correct ordering of the keys. We will have to wait with what patience we can command to discover whether the Gracious Goodnesses sent us this input as an admonition or as a programmed doom.

E. P. Thompson

THE
SYKAOS
PAPERS

∎

JUDGEMENT OF THE SUBLIME COUCH OF OITAR

It Has Stood Up
It Knows:
> That these records contain obtuse expressions which blaspheme against the Sacred Wheel

It Construes:
> That these might do injury to the ratios of youth

It Notwithstands:
> That they contain many data-inputs of interest to our grave Provosts and Vice-Provosts of the Colleges, and should be preserved from destruction

It Laws:
> That they be placed on the Sublime Index, but that the records be engraved and ten copies only be struck which copies are to be held within the banks of the College of Adjusters and the College of Stellanthropology

It Lays Another Law:
> That each reader must seek instant absolution in the Bumple of the Wheel

It Does a Bigger Law:
> That on no account may any copy be viewed by any of the Club of Critics, as any part of it would throw that company into deformities of judgement

It Had Another Law Which It Has Forgotten
It Sits From On High

SEGMENTS

1	Earthfall	1
2	First Captivity	29
3	Freewheel	69
4	Second Captivity	129
5	Zone of Eden	299
6	Honeymoon	433
Appendices		461

SEGMENT ONE

EARTHFALL

Editor's Note

This work is selected from the Inputs of Oi Paz, which are preserved in the College of Stellanthropology and in the Supreme Bank. These include an account of the landing upon the planet Sykaos, in the system of Strim; notes dictated to a Recorder; journals containing observations on Sykaan creature-culture; and a quantity of papers in Sykaan print or manuscript. Your Editor will more fully explain these sources when the proper occasion arises.

Our text commences with an Account by Oi Paz of the landing upon Sykaos. Since some years have now elapsed, we should refresh the reader's memory as to the events which preceded this.*

Pursuant to the decrees of the Sublime Couch, our craft were sent ever further into the reaches of space, to the uttermost limits of their range, in search of a world on which our plantations might be settled.

Galaxy after galaxy was patiently explored, and was found to be inhospitable to habitation. Here the suns were dying or their fires were unstable. There the planets were enwrapped in noisome gases. Here the planets were unprotected by any atmosphere and were exposed to extremes of cold and heat. There the atmosphere spun with unceasing electric storms, the oceans boiled, and the land was a stew of molten lava.

At length our craft penetrated the uncharted region of the Seventeenth Galaxy, a region too remote to be studied by any Oitarian observatory. Here, in this nondescript universe at the outermost range of the discovered cosmos, they came upon several youthful stars, and one (which was given the name of Strim) which was small but still in incandescent vigour, and which drew about itself a train of planets. And of these one planet only (which was named Sykaos, or the Blue Planet) was found to be worthy of closer observation.

This planet had little to distinguish it from thirty thousand others which our craft had observed. It was less than three-quarters the size of Oitar, but greater than our largest moon. Observation revealed that it

---

* The authorised account will be found in 'The Official Records of the Expeditionary Forces to the Galaxy of Strim', 6 tomes.

possessed properties which made it unique among the many thousands which our explorers had before encountered — a climate of remarkable moderation, a protective gaseous envelope containing oxygen, and abundant molten water.

Exhausted of supplies, our expedition returned to Oitar, where its findings were construed by our Colleges. Two more expeditions were sent out, and returned with favourable observations. It became the settled view of the Gracious Goodnesses that a landing on Sykaos might be undertaken.

After this, landings were made on the planet's moon. Observatories were built, and their evidence suggested that Sykaos might be inhabited by some deliberating creatures. Unusual markings were detected, around which vapours clung, which led some to deduce the existence of orbs or warrens of gregarious creatures. It was therefore determined that, in advance of the first expeditionary force, in vehicles large enough to carry a full complement of settlers, discards, butlers and supplies, some closer observation of the planet should be made; that confluence should first be made with its native creatures, and — in the event that rational intercourse should prove possible — advice be given as to how they might best prepare for our arrival and select the most suitable sites for our plantations.

Q.

Account Book*

When I was young the manner of the first entry into this new world was a chief subject of dispute in the Colleges.

Many believed that our people might escape the peril of extinction beneath our dying sun, and might found a new and brilliant civilisation on this remote planet. Some said that as soon as craft were built capable of penetrating the thick atmosphere of Sykaos, we should at once send several of our best students of science. Only when these had returned with samples of air, water and rock, and with observations on the vegetation, would we be able to send out our expeditionary force.

---

* *The Account Book was written by Oi Paz early in the Second Captivity.*

4

Others said that as Sykaos held life, and perhaps harmonious beings, the first to be sent should be Provosts of archaic knowledge, who might be able to interpret the customs of these creatures, in the light of our own aboriginal records when Oitarian peoples fished, hunted and grew crops on the unenclosed tundras.

Others prophesied strange horrors, poisons in the air, shifting sands, extremes of heat, violent winds and creatures whose nature might be compounded of ignorance and fear and whose pleasure it would be to destroy. They said that our civilisation was destined to die with its sun; and that instead of imagining new plantations we should discipline our thought to the crystalline forms of ice within which it was our destiny to find immolation.

Against the School of Crystal, a new school of poets arose, who imagined the life of our first plantations on Sykaos – the melodic circulation of blue waters, the silver chisels of the masons erecting the first marble cities, the white pillars rising amidst the green vegetation. And it was this School of Melodious Colour (as it became known) which most influenced the young.

They said: let poets and philosophers be chosen to make the first landfalls. For if the planet should prove habitable, then there would be many generations which could learn the secrets of its soil and plants; but a record must be preserved through all time of the thoughts of those who first came to land. And if Sykaos were inhabited by harmonious beings, then the first meeting between the worlds would be a moment of unexampled beauty.

A record should be made of the ecstasy of the Sykaans when they were first admitted to the privilege of Oitarian discourse, and of their delight at learning that they were not to be left unvisited and unregarded on the very margin of the cosmos, but were to receive the benefit of our colonisation. And a record might also be made of the first Articles of Agreement entered into between our ambassadors and these creatures, by which they should be offered the choice of remaining encamped at a little distance from our cities, where they could perform certain services for us alongside our own butlers and discards (such as the quarrying of stone, the clearing of tundra), in return for instruction in Oitarian mysteries; or (if they so preferred) of withdrawing to some private portion of their globe, where we could establish a reservation within which they might continue to practise undisturbed their own untutored and bestial culture. Our school – for Oi Paz was now one of the poets of the School of Melodious Colour – carried the argument and our input was received by the Gracious Goodnesses.

It was declaimed by the Sublime Couch that a number should be trained in readiness for the first landfalls. After competitions of verse and of number, five of each faculty were chosen, and among the poets Oi Paz was one.

We traversed the long, intergalactic journey to the moon of Sykaos, where we set ourselves to study what was known of the planet and awaited the time of the first penetration of the atmosphere.

The moon of Sykaos was not greatly different from our own lesser moons, nor from those asteroids on the inter-stellar routes which are used as fuelling stations. Several giant cupolas had been transported from Oitar, with an atmospheric plant, and here we lived during the period of preparation. A lesser cupola, its roof pierced with telescopes, served as an observatory, and, within the cupola–nexus, an elegant Bumple for the Rituals of the Wheel was erected.

The translucent walls of the main cupola were protected against meteorites by shields of anti-matter. Beyond these walls there stretched the escarpments of sterile dust. In contrast, the blue globe of Sykaos hung in the black sky, seeming itself to be a living being, whose surface darkened and lightened and was enscarfed with white vapours through which our telescopes revealed bright arcs of ice, vast areas of blue water and variously shaded lands.

We became indifferent to our ashy surroundings, occupying ourselves with eurhythmics, visiting the console-chamber for exercises in number, performing the rites at the Bumple or relaxing with the video-fixes prepared for us by the College of Trance. We scarcely went out, except to the landing-zone, when craft descended with instruments and supplies.

At length a prototype of the first craft was ready. It was of a novel design and required no energy for its operation save that afforded by gravitation and by the extraction and acceleration of light. The light-condensers and accelerators afforded whatever drive and direction might be required, and this energy was controlled by a most delicate series of balancers and repudiators which might, by the operation of simple controls, either draw upon or repel the gravitational forces of the nearest material bodies: viz., the star, Strim; Sykaos itself; and its moon. An anti-gravitational braking force was supplied by the controlled implosion of nodules of anti-matter.

None of these principles was new. Yet the combination of them into a single operative mode within the compass of so small and light a craft, and without recourse to any normal energy source (such as extra-terrestrial trash), was a novelty indeed. And it was the work of Sorites, a Vice-Provost of Paranormal Matter.

Oi Paz was one of the first selected to be trained in the operation of the craft. To rise from the surface of that moon was the least difficult operation: as soon as the anti-gravitational stick was fully depressed, the craft rose, and in the same instant − when the attraction of the moon's gravitation was repudiated − it was tossed upwards and sucked into the gravitational pull of Sykaos and − more distantly − the counter-pull of Strim.

It was here, in setting a course, that the light-condensers must be brought into operation. This had required, of Sorites, much experiment, and much recourse, on the intergalactic signals-lock, to consultations with the College of Calculus on Oitar. For if the condensers should, by some mischance, be turned in an unshrouded state directly into the rays of Strim, the craft would be sucked, at the speed of light condensed and accelerated to many magnitudes, not into the uncharted void but directly into the furnaces of that sun. For this reason Sorites had introduced a light-choke, or 'cut-out', whereby the condensers could endure

7

an intake of light only by indirection or of the lowest magnitudes.

After tests were completed, the results were plotted within the memory of an on-board computer, so that the journey to Sykaos, and the circumnavigation of the planet, could be accomplished perfectly well by automatic pilot. Greater craft were being built to undertake the first landings and plantations, and the first craft (of which this was the prototype) were intended only for observation. These had been designed for the first requirements of lift and lightness, discarding all else. They could carry only one navigator, and no instruments beyond those essential to their own operation. In truth, my craft was little larger than one of those spheroid sledges in which children sit to be drawn by unicorns on seasonable days around the glacial lawns.

I, Oi Paz, was selected for the first flight, not by competition but by decree of the Sublime Couch; and, as is well known, the Gracious Goodnesses Above never subscribe reasons to their judgements. Oi Paz was programmed, on this first entry, to collect samples of inorganic and organic matter in the atmosphere, and to record magnetic and gravitational forces in the immediate proximity of the planet. If conditions were favourable, Oi Paz was to attempt a first circumnavigation, and transmit video-scenes to the observatories. And any other observations were to be embodied in a solemn ode appropriate to the occasion.*

We had chosen for the moment of ascent that time when the irregular rotation of Sykaos (which carried its moon about it as an inert attendant) brought our plantation out of the lunar night and into the edge of the rays of Strim. As I walked ankle-deep through ashy pools of regolith to the launching-zone, I could observe the great blue orb of Sykaos hanging above us in the sky. After so long in these inter-stellar wastes, it seemed an auspicious and even a beautiful place. And I commenced to chant to my-self verses which came, unbidden and extempore, as if carried

---

* *And the Supreme Couch laid a law that Oi Paz was not, under any circumstance, to make a landfall.*

down to me from that hanging orb on the vibes of some ancient poet:

> *Coasting the wall of heaven, on this side night*
> *In the dun air sublime, and ready now*
> *To stoop with wearied wings, and willing feet*
> *On the bare outside of that world, Oi Paz comes*
> *To do Thy Wheels Harmonious Embassy*
> *And bring this orb within Thy Rule and Roll.*

I climbed into the craft, the hatch was closed, and I took off my helmet and protective suit, placing these in a locker for my return. Since it seemed to be an occasion of ceremony I wore, in honour of the day, a rich jade gown embroidered in silver, a neck-piece of black silver set with rare Oitarian gems, a saffron cape and a black programme-belt with a gold clasp, simple and heavy, wrought with a sacred design: the Eternal Wheel inscribed with the hieroglyphs of neuter thought.

The craft performed excellently. At first gently, and then with rapid acceleration, it was sucked upwards, towards the orb of Sykaos. Soon even the largest cupola of our plantation on that moon was lost to sight. Since the journey would be long I occupied myself in a relaxative third-state trance. I let my mind play among the quaint legends of our pre-domic times, when it was recorded that the vast tundras were still covered with flowering grasses – 'that time':

> *When the twin cities guarded the last seed,*
> *Defiant of the dusty ice: that time*
> *When the flocked cottons perished in the snows,*
> *The dragons ceased to fire, and everywhere*
> *The settlements fell into lapse ...*

In such legends, I felt, there might be clues to help in the understanding of the world above me, which I was now approaching at an accelerated pace, and whose orb grew greater each time I withdrew from trance.

At length the trance-timer rang (for I had set it on my departure, to give me due warning of the journey's completion), and I found that the craft had approached so close to Sykaos that, by an absurd inversion of perception, it appeared to be beneath me rather than above. The curvature of the planet could no longer be seen through the panels. Clouds spread in every direction, and as the craft penetrated the atmosphere the black void of space gave way to an astonishing brightness on every side. Presently this white insolation translated itself into a soft azure glow. Here and there were holes in the floor of white vapours, opening themselves suddenly and then closing again in a flurry of swirling cloudlets – for everything in the atmosphere of this planet seemed to be in circulation, and in an objectless haste of winds and contrary forces – and as these holes fell open I glimpsed beneath them the melodious colours of imagination.

I threw across the sampler and watched the dials. The atmospheric recorder scarcely moved its needle, and the analyser showed so slight a quantity of oxygen that I feared that all our preparations for plantation might be in vain. I determined to find out whether the planet held pockets of greater gaseous density closer to its surface, and depressed the anti-gravitational control a little further. Twice I attempted to bring the craft down through one of the holes appearing amidst the cloud, which appeared so crisp and solid that I feared contact might do the craft an injury. At length the cloud closed around me. To my relief it was neither solid nor liquid but of a gaseous formation, which revealed in the analyser a remarkable moisture content very close indeed to water, together with some small quantities of impurities: carbon, sulphur and several acids harmful to life yet not in such quantities as to offer immediate hazard.

I continued to depress the control. For a long while I could see nothing below, above or at either side, other than these swirling and moist white gases. Then all at once the craft fell below the cloud and a scene of unexampled colour was disclosed.

It was more like a tenth or eleventh state of trance than an experience of this world. At first my eyes received nothing save a vast expanse of blue, so that I supposed that I viewed beneath me some vast lava-field of blue rock which had set as smooth as a great glacial lawn. Yet as the craft continued to descend, so within this blue I could discern an infinite variety of shade: there, where the rays of Strim penetrated a gap in the cloud, they were reflected from that blue expanse in a dazzle of silver light so intense that it closed the choke of the light-condensers; at another place a dense cloud threw down a shadow of no-colour upon the blue; and in between there were deep blues and emeralds and dark greens set off with little points of white which seemed, as my eyes became accustomed to the light, to be constantly appearing and disappearing, and to be, like the clouds above, constantly in movement like some living thing.

I had now other things to attend to and my receptors were posted at alert by the fear-signal on the controls. For the major light-condenser had blown its fuse, and the gravitational suction of Sykaos was in excess of the calculations of Sorites, owing to a gross material inertia which enwrapped that whole globe, and which drew down towards its self-regarding circumference even an object as light as the craft. Indeed, the craft itself acquired a new density as it was caught within the grip of the planet's magnetic lusts. So that I was for a little while all higgledy and at the edge of order as I checked the thrusts and balances and construed the dials. All this while the craft was tumbling in a revolution of white and blue as it fell towards that floor or ceiling (for I knew no longer which it was).

At length a balance was restored. And I tuned my Input towards the Wheel and sought absolution for these moments of disorder. Yet I received back no answering signal from the Gracious Goodnesses, nor even from Lunar Control, as if there were something about this place whose atmosphere I had now entered which screened out every rational signal and which interrupted the intercourse of heaven.

During this time the craft had fallen a great distance. The

expanse of blue continued beneath me, but now I could observe that it was neither a lawn of lava nor some great expanse of blue tundra and mosses, but a huge mass of molten water, ceaselessly in motion, whose motions gathered the surface into uneven lines and humps which every now and then collapsed back into the centripetal forces of the planet's gravity, throwing up those vanishing patches of white which were, in truth, nothing but disturbances of aerated water or fountains illuminated by the rays of the planet's sun. And I reflected, with awe, upon the contrasts between the world and this poor unvisited place: with what difficulty and with what expense of energy (the ceaseless forces of the ice-burners which defend the world about on every side, and which translate the butting glaciers into those precious waters which flow, by guarded conduits, to the sacred lakes and fountains about which our orbs are built) – with what expense of energy our waters are melted and conserved: yet here beneath me lay this boundless and superfluous melt!

Suddenly, I saw the broken brown edges of what were evidently lands travelling towards me at a great rate. After a short while all blue had been left behind, and I was circumnavigating a new world of melodious colours; for beneath me was, not the familiar white of the glacial world, nor the dun and dusty surface of this planet's moon, but a canticle of green and brown and grey.

What dazzled my receptors was the presence on every side of the colours of green. Our earliest ancestors can never have enjoyed a climate so genial as that of Sykaos, nor a vegetation so rank. What came into view below was neither tundra, nor untended prairie, such as was cherished in their myths. This expanse of green and brown was marked by abrupt changes, so that a square of reddish brown lay against an irregular verdant triangle, to be succeeded by a greater space of lighter green. And the whole view evinced a kind of disorderly order. I would say that it was patterned, and yet the pattern was unruly, in no way rational or regular, nor were its forms ever repeated. In short, the pattern was disharmonious; and yet it scarcely gave offence to the organ of harmony because of a certain capricious insinuation of rationality

lurking beneath the disorder, like a hidden code. Squares, mis-
formed triangles and broken geometric forms, each of a different
tone of green, lay against each other, as if the vegetation had
formed itself into territories, or as if some creatures had herded
the plants and grasses to grow in this regular irregularity.

I relaxed my pressure on the gravitational control, enabling
the craft to descend for my closer observation. And I busied
myself for a while with the control of the samplers, extracting
inorganic matter and searching for organic specimens in the
atmosphere. With each level of descent the dials showed a higher
oxygen content, until, at the lowest level, a ratio very close to
that of Oitarian ready-mix was registered, so that within a narrow
envelope or margin of the surface of the globe the auspices for life
were good, yet held in a balance so fragile that life might flourish
only on the crust of the planet itself or on the lower slopes of
the mountains, and might be at once threatened by any large in-
rush or outrush of energy, whether from the planet's own molten
interior or from a shaft of flaming gases from a passing comet.

Poor, fragile little planet, I thought. And yet how favoured,
how very greatly favoured, amidst all the immensity of visited
and unvisited space. Thinking so, I glanced once more into the
observation panel and discovered that the craft had descended so
low that I looked directly into a scene of dense verdure. And it
was here that all the botch of my hereafterness was begun. For
which I pray the Absolution of the Wheel. But I was not suffering
from any lesion of obedience: it is not known that any in my
Sper-group has suffered the least distemper in the organ of obedience, nor would the Sublime Couch have decreed my mission
had I been descended of a suspect gene-kit. To suppose that
would be to blaspheme against the judgement of the Gracious
Goodnesses themselves!

How it was I know not, but order was upended and a hassle
happed. The gross material occurrence was thus: the rays of the
setting sun, which now lay low on the horizon of this little globe,
were suddenly obscured behind an approaching hill, so that the
condensers lost energy and bearing. The craft slowed almost to a

stand and fell under the compulsion of gravity. But this must have been compounded by some disorder in Oi Paz's own ratios. For Sorites had given instructions in modes of compensation for precisely such contingencies, yet these would not be summoned to mind. A disorder was creeping higgledly through all the mental organs, as if the atmosphere of Sykaos carried some alienation from the Rule.

At the last oxygen-count I had thrown open a hatch, and there came now into the craft a flow of raw air, a carrier of unknown intoxicants – the scents of strange organic matters and seductive oils and waters. These drew me into a state of trance, yet not a trance such as any known to video-fixers. It did not flow into my mind from the band of the video-receiver about my forehead. It seemed, rather, to emanate from the globe itself; to enwrap and penetrate my person; to draw me down towards the earth; to enter into the rotations of the blood, with a tightening sensation about the region of the pump whenever I breathed. I was drawn into a sort of paralysis, as if 'Oi Paz' was watching helplessly as the craft continued to fall, yet could not recall the procedures to regain control. While the sense-receptors were thrown into alert, the organs of reason, aesthetics and duty were dulled, as if – once caught within the magnetic lusts of this planet – the intellect must submit to the thrall of blood, and the spirit must endure within the dim light filtered through the shrouds of flesh. All of which I now set down as a powerful spell sent against me by the em-pees, queens, teleprompters and other chief conjurers of the place.

Whatever way it was, I was altogether upended and my reason was done into a trash. No signal now could reach me from the world. The gross matter of this unknown planet obscured even the memory of Oitar and of the duty owing to the Sublime Couch, until the sensual trance burst into my mental organs and it seemed that I, Oi Paz, was the Author of all that I saw and did, and that I alone had discovered this green place and was destined to be its conqueror and ruler.★

★ *Oi Paz did well to write that the botch of hereafterness began at this point. Indeed, this whole passage is not only botch but arrant bosh. For our author here is seeking to excuse a*

EARTHFALL

Within this trance I relaxed hold of the gravitational control, so that the craft descended slowly to the planet's surface, coming to rest quietly amongst verdure so intense that it threw my sensors into a daze.

When my mind was together once more, I opened the observation port and looked all around. The craft appeared to be suspended at some eight times a human height above the ground, in the upper arms of some gigantic multi-brachiate creature. The main and lesser tentacles of this creature were composed of a brown and rigid substance, which became more pliant at their extremities, and were in a perpetual motion, rising and falling, swaying and tossing an immense bounty of greenness which closed me within curtains as if I were shrouded within the sacred chamber of a bumple.

As my eyes became accustomed to this melodious light, it appeared that these curtains were made up of innumerable small and regular bracts, or leaves, from which I took this creature to be some giant plant of a height and girth ten times that of any plant known to the world. Yet it was a plant in ceaseless gentle motion, and this motion imparted to the leaves a continuous quiet brushing noise like that of a distant whispering confluence. It was a noise neither welcoming nor hostile but indifferent.

At first – for our intergalactic explorers have encountered monsters scarcely less strange – I thought that this giant plant might, from its ceaseless nodding motions, be a sentient and intelligent creature. I therefore enacted the primary rituals for encounters with astro-feral civilisations. Throwing open the main

---

direct act of disobedience against the Rule. As to the performance of the craft, Sorites had installed a simple flip-switch for return to the moon in exactly such contingencies. As to the trance, it is clear from Oi Paz's subsequent accounts that Sykaans are devoid of magical or spiritual powers, even of the lowest order. The passage has been allowed to stand here for this reason. It reveals both defect and defection in the author's constitution even before landfall: defect affording swift entry to the mortal taint. And readers will make mental adjustments accordingly in reading all that follows. In consequence of this hitherto undetected defect, the Sper-line of Oi Paz has now been discontinued, and all surviving in that gene-set are kept under regular observation.

hatch, I stood in the doorway, threw apart my robe to disclose that I wore no weapons, and extended both arms in a gesture of welcome.

At that moment the outer shoots of the plant, wherein the craft hung, nodded so vigorously that I was flung from the port and would have been dashed on the crust below had I not clung fast to a rigid extension of the rough brown stem. Here I hung among the leaves, supposing myself to be within the tentacles of a hostile plant-creature.

But this was not so. The plant continued in its random nodding, without any sign of aggression, so that I was able to pull myself up and climb back into the craft. It had been well if I had then energised the craft once more, extracted it from its material thrall, and hiked forthwith back to that planet's moon. Yet the fleshly trance still clung about me, with its glimmering videograms, so that even the fear-alert which was flashing on the craft's controls induced in me only the sense that it was disharmonious to this globe. And with an abrupt motion I switched all crafty systems off, and closed all channels of communication with Control.

'Now you are descended so far,' some susurration within the leaves seemed to say, 'and since the sin of disobedience already is done, let advantage now be taken. How small a sin it was, and one willed upon you, out of the programme of another! Stay a little upon this place, so that when you return you may carry back such volumes of recordings and of samples and of verse as may justify your arrogance against the Rule.'

Thus I equipped myself for exploration of the planet's crust. To my waist I strapped flasks for the collection of specimens, with emergency supplies of food-pellets. In a small pack I placed my Recorder (for fieldnotes and for any odes that might come upon me unbidden), some gifts of gems, flints and pebbles (in case I should encounter harmonious beings), and, as an after-thought, an illuminated scroll of Condescending Accost from the Gracious Goodnesses and the compact new Translator designed by the College of Cryptography. Across my left arm I slung my oxygen helmet, lest I encounter any noisome gases. With difficulty

I climbed down the ever-thickening stem of the plant. At some twice the height of an adult the stem offered no more purchase for climbing, and I leapt on to the crust which proved to be (as our observatories had predicted) unfrozen, soft and easy to the fall.

Here I found myself surrounded still by green vegetation. On one side of me stood a multitude of giant plants like that into whose head I had descended, for I had come down at the very edge of a giant plantation. As I regarded this plantation, and the gigantic girth of the stems, I wondered if this was a cultivated crop, and (if so) then of what monstrous and gigantic dimensions must be the farmers. On the other side lay extensive plains of dwarfish vegetation, much like our own kernels and milkstems, only more rank, more moist, and every way less regular than it is within the cultivation of the Alls.

I tested the air and found it still wholesome. Some little pollution there was, with carbon and noxious acids, yet not in a quantity to require the protection of my helmet. And, indeed, the mere breathing of this air induced in me such a sense of well-being, scented as it was with suggestions of mystery, that I determined to lug about my helmet no longer; and, noting a dark hollow by the root of that plant from which I had descended, I thrust it within for safe keeping.

For a time I moved between the plain and the plantation, collecting samples of soil and vegetation. In the soil there was little remarkable: it was brown or red, rich, and easily turned with my tools. In the vegetation there was much to remark. For in the space of two hundred steps from my landing I collected thirty-seven different specimens, each one unique and perfect in its own formation.

As any Oitarian knows, this is a total greater than all the varieties of preserved vegetation in the world, the perfected and harmonious flora only excepted. (I make the reservation 'preserved', since if we consider also the uncultivated summer tundra outside the Alls, no doubt many varieties of lichen, sphagnum and so forth might be added.) When at the end of archaic times our ancestors withdrew within the domes, they selected for cultivation and for preservation only such plants as were necessary for nutriment for the Seven Sentient Creatures and the Sacred Three. And they selected also those roots, fruits and plants of medicinal virtue, of harmonious pigment and of trance-inducing qualities. To this we may add those bio-engined plants of subsequent development, upon which our sentient servitors depend so largely for food-bulk, as the milkstem, the egflour and the bredstik. Whether out of all these, and to furnish the whole extent of the grazing-lawns beneath the Alls, there are as many as thirty-seven distinct species of vegetation in the world, I leave to the College of Botany to declaim. And yet here, at a chance landfall upon the crust of Sykaos, and without serious search, these species came to hand.

As to the utility of these species I can say little. I took specimens to be construed by our Colleges, but that, alas, was not to be. The grasses were of no great size but exceedingly pliant and dense, so that they made a mat through which the earth's crust was scarcely visible. As to the beauty I would say much. Among the grasses were many varieties of small-leaved plants, of no evident function, but the leaves of which seemed to come from the hand of the most choice designer. They were harmonious always, now exhibiting a novel and perfect geometric symmetry, now an opaque verdure through which a delicate darker veining or marbling could be seen. And ten or twelve of these petty plants were crowned with bells or towers or little open bracts of melodious colour – indeed, in this small space, in miniature display, was every pigment known to the colour-canticle: among them, scarlet, amethyst, ruby, jade, gold and white. Yet none of these was of the proportion and perfected form of harmonious flora, nor were they set in rank and order as in a garden. They seemed as if they were untended and uncured, in a state of unregarded self-existence as if aimed at no function other than their vegetating selves.

For all this beauty in each part, there was neither order nor regularity of cultivation in the whole. This was an archaic land, wastefully bearing unselected vegetation in its promiscuous disorder. And I wondered whether the giant farmers into whose plantation I had fallen were so tall as to be unaware of the unregulated state of the petty plants beneath their feet.

The specimens gathered, I sat upon a hump of grass beside the plantation, and declaimed the first notes of my journal into my Recorder. The first observations revealed the place to be apt for plantation. On the other hand, my brief inspection had revealed a place of archaic laxity, a lack of discipline before the couch of any rational creature, demanding the greatest cure to bring within a Rule. And I began to doubt my first notion of the giant farmers, for I saw nowhere the prints of such huge creatures, nor did the swaying and nodding plants amidst which I had landed seem like any tended crop. And I began to suppose that this planet's crust had become carpeted with vegetation by some random spillage of undirected life.

I sat there on the grass, with Strim falling low to the horizon, its rays extending over the whole scene a full and yellow light. Then its light was sometimes obscured, sometimes refracted, by the turbulence of distant clouds, which gave to the western horizon a refulgent roseate hue, unknown to our skies.

The warmth and the varying lights of sunset induced in me a melodious mood of well-being. The clouds made me reflect upon the extraordinary, unprogrammed cycle of this world, the sun drawing up vapours from the seas and lakes which cover much of the planet's surface, and these clouds in turn releasing water in a fountain of drops on to the land, which is thus refreshed without need for ice-burners, irrigation conduits or great tanks. And (as I was to find out) this same cycle induces the continual motion of air, so that these winds move clouds of vapour across the sky, like white water-sledges across a blue lake, and so give to the quietest day a sense of motion, as if the sky were a living being, or as if some unseen hand were moving this planet towards some agreeable end. Lying on that grassy bank, amidst the scents of strange flowers and herbs, it seemed to me that after the ages of that long intergalactic voyage I had journeyed back through millennia into an archaic past before the glaciation of the world, and had passed through a timewarp into the Eu Topaz of our earliest legends.

It was sent into my mind that my mission was accomplished, and I knew the slight throbbing of the organ of duty within my mind. Yet I had not yet established, beyond all doubt, whether sentient creatures inhabited the planet; or, indeed, intelligent beings which might assist us in our plantation. And it was now that I made an extraordinary observation. For I had noted, during my exploration, small quantums of matter moving about in the air and had given them slight attention, supposing them to be knots of grasses or bunches of leaves carried this way and that by the wind. But now as I watched it appeared that these were sentient creatures indeed, with some magical command of the element of air, into which they could ride and turn and even, for a moment, stand stationary, like tiny spacecraft: having no arms, but instead of these two wide and flat projecting limbs, of flexible formation, which seemed to press against the insubstantial air as an oar might press on water. Indeed, these limbs were much like the wings which, in archaic myth, were attributed to our phoenixes and dragons; or like the wings of solid butterflies.

These creatures bounded and leapt in the air, yet they also descended to the ground, where they could walk upon two narrow legs. They were small – the smallest less than the size of a hand. At first they were shy and hid amongst the leaves, but as I sat quietly there they became more bold, and settled in the vegetation close by and seemed to watch me, for I dare say that I was as strange a creature to them as they were to me. And opening the front part of their faces (for they had faces, with eyes, and sharp, protruding noses and mouths), they emitted not words, nor grunts, nor howls, but a slender, high and pure music, which I can only liken to many icicles or blades of glass struck with a delicate chimer of silver. The best among them made a music very like a flautist improvising in an archaic scale.

I offered no speech or greetings to these creatures, for it was evident from their sounds, so beautiful yet random, that while they were beings of a most exquisite tactile sense, they were none the less sub-intellectual sentients. And yet they seemed, in their own way, to be welcoming me to this bountiful new home. The turning planet had now brought the sun to the very edge of the horizon, where it was obscured by a roseate ledge of cloud. As languor stole over me it seemed that once again, without neuro-induction, I was drifting into the gateway of trance.

I well knew that I would find on Sykaos a rapid alternation of day and night, and that both would be brief. Even so, night came upon me unawares. I lay at full length in the fragrant grass which, after the hard beds of the cells in the moon, seemed like a carpet of cotton. Above me the creatures of the air settled amongst the plants, and their music ceased, giving way to the soft rustle of leaves. The peace of this new world was such that it took away from me the last achings of alert. For, if it should prove to be inhabited by intellectual beings, how could they, among such a harmony of elements, not prove themselves to be harmonious? And so I passed into my first earthly sleep.

I was awakened abruptly, when a moist, warm, rank-scented wind was pushed into my face. Opening my eyes I found that a new day had turned. At a little space above me I saw a huge black creature, gazing fixedly down at me with large eyes of a liquid, sentient brown. Its head was wide and heavy and it had two long and curved teeth protruding upwards from above its eyes.

Scarcely knowing where I was, nor in which universe, I scrambled to my feet, whereupon the creature shook its heavy head from side to side, blew through its nose, and stepped backwards a few paces. I could now see the form of it more clearly: it was a creature on four legs, of the bulk of an ur-dragon, not standing as tall as I. Its head rose above its corpse on a thick neck, to the height of an adult's shoulders, and its corpse was round and heavy and several times a human girth.

I had opportunity only to note its form before I saw that this was only one of a whole company of such creatures, of much the same size, all black (although several wore white patterns on their black clothes). There were some twenty of them in all, and they stood equidistant from me in a semicircle, as if presented for a ceremonious introduction.

It was this circumstance of their orderly attention that suggested some rudimentary obeisance to the Rule, while the manner in which each one faced towards me with a steady, enquiring gaze determined me that these must be intellectual beings, the happy possessors of Sykaos, and that the great and long looked-for Accosting of Cultures was now at last to take place. I therefore threw open my robe, extended my arms wide in welcome, and declaimed a greeting of my own composition, long-rehearsed for this auspicious moment:

> *Hail, Learned Authors of this earth! I bring*
> *Greetings from Heaven's furthest stellar ring,*
> *And from the Gracious Goodnesses convey*
> *Their condescension on this Confluence Day*

As I declaimed these lines several of the creatures stepped backwards a pace or two and shook their heads so ponderously that I supposed not only that my verses had been understood but that several of my audience were of the Club of Critics. For a short while we regarded each other in silence, and then, encouraged by their attention, I stepped forward a few paces, flung wide my arms once more and prepared yet further gracious addresses. At this the foremost among them, who had at first awakened me and whom I took to be their Chief, or Leader, raised its head to the sky and declaimed in a deep and powerful voice (as nearly as I can transcribe it) *Emeughooo*. And then the whole company turned away from me, tossing and swaying their heads, and ran off a short distance across the grassy plain.

I followed closely upon them, pulling from my pack the illuminated scroll of Condescending Accost and ambassadorial credentials prepared by the Club of Calligraphy. This I held aloft and waved with my right arm. But ever as I advanced the company withdrew; or else, scattering to the right and left, they let me pass through them, and then rapidly closed into an arc at my back. Nor was I able to engage their steady and courteous attention as before.

I had now ventured some way upon the plain and was at a distance from the plant in which the craft was suspended. And again the organ of duty began to throb within me. For I could not doubt that I had now committed abuse of all obedience so serious as to merit discard. And even if this botch could be condoned (for I had gathered samples and magnetic readings beyond expectation), yet now my doings were beyond forgiveness. It was proper that I should regain the craft at once and thence hike backwards to the moon.

Yet even as I hesitated I could sense the dense material lusts of this planet drawing me back. As I felt the warmth of the rising sun and the warm winds passing above the rippling grasses, so the sterile landscarp of the moon seemed hateful to me, and even the domes of Oitar seemed like an alien enclosure. In short, with every moment that I delayed I fell into mortal infection.

I turned my head and regarded the giant plants where my craft was hanging. But here a new hazard appeared, and, indeed, this hazard enlarged and bore down upon me with each instant. For in a far part of the plain, unnoticed until this moment, there was a creature, very like those attending around me, but of much greater girth. This creature was now bearing down upon me with incredible speed, leaping and rocking upon all four of its legs. As it drew close, the other creatures fell apart to afford it passage, as if in deference to their Chief; and this creature now lowered its head, with its huge protruding teeth above its eyes, and blew winds out of its distended black nose.

I could not doubt that it came down upon me with hostile intent. Yet since it did not seem possible that reason and courtesy would fail to call forth the same qualities in any intellectual creature, I determined to stand my ground. I therefore planted myself steadily before it, and unrolled the scroll of Accost to its fullest length, displaying in all its beauty the silver calligraphy upon a crimson background; and I held it outwards to the extent of my right arm in the face of the oncoming creature.

What happed next was too higgledy to allow for reflection. The creature leapt forward ever more swiftly, directing itself no longer towards me but towards the scroll, which it had in a moment torn from my grasp, at the same time catching me a heavy blow with its shoulder which flung me down upon the planet's crust. As I recovered I saw that the creature had torn through the scroll with one of its head-teeth, so that the scroll was now enwrapped like a parchment helmet about its head, altogether obscuring its vision. There it remained at a few paces from me, shaking its head with hideous signs of wrath, blowing, and stamping on the earth.

I had no doubt that as soon as it shook its head free of the scroll and recovered its vision it would turn its horrid nature against me, piercing me with its teeth and trampling my corpse as it now trampled the grass. I therefore discarded every propriety of Rule (for which blasphemy I ask Absolution) and *ran* from its propinquity, and I was glad to find that, owing to the favourable gravity-equation of the planet, I was able to perform as well as any licensed athlete in the Arc of Sports.

After several hundred paces I found my further passage obstructed at the edge of this little plain by a line of larger plants of about my height. I hesitated here, but, looking back, I saw that the creature had shaken its eyes free from the parchment and was bearing down upon me once again. I therefore clambered through these plants as best I could, tearing my robe in two places and losing my tools and some flasks and samplers by the way, and dropped exhausted in the grass on the other side. Indeed, I still scarce knew what to do, for it entered my mind that this gross creature might share with the small musicians the same faculty of taking to the element of air, and might at the next moment soar like a horrid craft above my head. But my alert was ill-founded, for it could not cross the line of plants, but stood there, stamping on the other side, blowing malevolently and tossing its toothed head.

I felt now the difficulty I was in, in venturing so far from my craft. I sought to reason with the creature, declaiming first poems, then theorems and numbers, and at last a sacred song, but nothing could modify its hostile station. I therefore must needs make good my return to the craft by some circuitous route, unobserved by that whole company — for the rest of the creatures were now stationed about their little plain like sentinels.

As I walked away, down a descending level of grass, considering the botch I had got into, my attention was taken by repeated sounds, somewhat like the distant throbbing of engines pumping the melt along a conduit. Then, to my astonishment, I found I was drawing near to a thin ribbon of a bluish colour amidst the green and brown plains, which appeared much like a great path or road such as those which unite our cities or are directed to the outermost locks of the domes.

And such indeed this formation proved to be. It had none of the beauty of a well-cured way in the world: no marble to its edges; no mosaics on its track; no formal gardens of melodious flora set at the stations of the way. But it was indeed a road, and as I approached I perceived some kind of machine or spheroid sledge moving at speed along its length. Yet if they were sledges, they were drawn by no creatures, but were self-possessed of their own energies.

I had now some reason for reflection. For if these were indeed machines (as observation suggested), then what creatures were they which had created them for their service? Could they be designed by the sentient beasts I had encountered on the plain, and employed for their transport? Or if they had been designed by other, and more intellectual, beings, where were these beings to be found?

I drew closer to the road and spent the zenith of the day in observation. And from this I reached conclusions scarcely less remarkable than any concluded on Sykaos hitherto. First, these were indeed landcraft, self-possessed of their own energies. Second, these craft were directed by creatures enclosed within them — now one creature, now two, but rarely more than four. Third, and beyond any arc of probability, these creatures, whose

heads and shoulders only I could see, shared some of the form
and features of human beings!

The resemblance insofar as I could detect it as the craft sped
past was not exact, and yet it had an eerie similitude. They
appeared, indeed, as if in human caricature, or as impostors upon
the beauteous forms of the human race. For the most part their
faces were composed of human features, yet all but two or three
which passed were unpigmented and of a grey or white pallor
which was odious to regard. And they were ill-favoured and
disfigured, with ugly scales of fur or clothes upon their shoulders
and sometimes upon their heads: yet heads they had, with eyes,
ears, mouth and nose in the elected places, although some few
had sprouts of hair displaced from their heads and hanging about
their mouths.

For the rest of their corpses I could observe nothing, nor could
detect whether they had four legs below, or none, or two, or
whether, like the sacred dolphin, they had tail and fins.

I was now so migrained in my reason, so untuned by the
ingestion of the heavy Sykotic airs, and above all so pied in my
ratios by this inconceivable coincidence – that in two planets of
such distant galaxies so similar a form of being should have had
its happening – that I became regardless of alert, and stood,
openly, in my flowing robes, at the side of the road. Yet even
my presence, in all ways more euphonic than that of the cramped
disfigured creatures speeding past in their craft, appeared to
occasion no interest in the crafts' passengers. Some of those who
sped by appeared to glance at me directly with blank expressions.
One small creature only (perhaps a young of the species?) waved
an arm in greeting. By which alone I made the discovery that
this botched race of impostors were not fish.

I determined that now at last the moment for the Confluence
of Cultures had arrived. And since these creatures were favoured
with at least some of the features of humans, and evinced intellect
enough to make these speeding craft, I considered it to be possible
that they might be favoured (however debased) with some of the
attributes of reason. I therefore walked directly into the road as

the next craft approached, turned my face towards it, and extended both my arms wide in a gesture of inter-stellar salutation.

And it was in that way that Oi Paz very nearly came to an early dead-line, a bad end to hap on this alien globe.*

---

* *At this point there is a long interval in the Account, which is partially replaced in the segment which follows by a few surviving extracts from the Record and by various documents of Sykotic origin. It is not clear whether some pages of the Account have been lost, or whether Oi Paz, who was a long time insensate, was never able to bring into any coherence the extraordinary haps which next ensued.*

SEGMENT TWO

FIRST CAPTIVITY

Editor's Note

It has been construed from various sources — some of which are printed below — that so far from the creature in the landcraft (or 'car') reciprocating our Messenger's salutation, the craft was directed with force into the welcoming corpse. Oi Paz was not indeed put to a premature dead-line (as may have been intended), but was killed to a long passage of time, being wholly insensate.

These creatures, however, through some curiosity, sought to recover Oi Paz to life, who was conveyed by them to a House of Sarcology or Fleshly Repair, and there by stages recovered reason — although there are some who are eminent in the College of Adjusters who argue that reason was never again wholly repaired.

It is most fortunate that both a Recorder and a Translator were strapped to the belt of Oi Paz. Since the Translator is a device familiar only to students of Stellanthropology, it will be advisable to explain here the principles of its operation. It combines within one nexus and on compact microcircuits: (i) a simple Recorder, which could be used as an open audio-record; (ii) a linguistic memory-bank; (iii) a crypto-chamber, combing, scanning and sorting all words; (iv) a voice-producer, capable of being tuned to any selected language-set in the memory-bank, to produce instant automatic audio-translation. To this was added (v) a video-scanner, capable of ingesting whole pages of alien text and transmitting this directly to the crypto-chamber, which thereby can sort additional vocabulary to be stored in the bank.

The Translator can thus command any language through a process of recording, sorting into grammatical parts, decoding and storing of vocabulary. The operator can assist the machine, especially in the early stages of cryptography, by establishing through observation certain key words, such as those for common objects.

At this stage there is 'primitive translation': the Translator possesses the language's essential structure but has only a primitive vocabulary in store. The Box is set between the Oitarian operator and the Communicant Creature. Each speaks into the Box, which then renders a primitive translation back in its mechanical voice-producer. Unknown words are rendered melodiously on a flute. The operator may now sleep

31

with an Inductor strapped to the brow, thus directly ingesting the language. Very soon the stage of 'intermediate translation' is reached, when the operator has sufficient command over the alien creature-language to converse directly, without mediation of the Box, which remains available for consultation and as a dictionary.

We owe this Translator of superior design to the researches of Li Mina of the College of Cryptography.

In the case of Sykaos the results (as will be seen) were not fully satisfactory, not through any failure in the Translator's design, but through the gross fractures of logic and the hideous grammatic lesions to be found among the planet's unhappy creatures. This presents difficulties throughout. Many Sykotic terms have proved to be untranslatable, because the concepts of which the words are signs are either unknown to rational human discourse or are so disharmonious as to threaten to injure the Translator's circuits.

Fortunately the far-sighted Li Mina anticipated the possible dangers and provided the Translator with a cut-off (known as a subliminal chastity-choke) which enables it to choke any concept tending towards blasphemy, hence defending it (and the operator) from injury.

Other Sykotic terms present difficulty in translation, not because of obscenity but simply because they refer to forms unknown to human civilisation. Thus 'house' may be understood only in its most elementary equivalence of function, as a place of shelter or dwelling. Readers must not be misled by the common term into supposing that these paltry Sykotic dwellings are in any sense equivalent to the Houses of our Colleges, with their dormitories, communal Alls, roll-chambers, arcades, sacred fountains and stately lawns. For Sykotic creatures (or 'mortals') evince such fear and dislike of living in proximity to each other, and have evolved a society (or anti-society) so fissiparous, that they seg-regate themselves into an infinite series of tiny factions (or 'families'), each of which inhabits an individual dwelling, and each faction pursuing contradictory objectives with reckless waste of communal resources.

As for the term 'human', this is a case presenting the very greatest difficulty. Any reader of this narrative will know that it is to tread to the very margin of blasphemy against the Wheel to signify in one

32

equivalent exchange of signs two species of such extreme contrarieties of nature and faculties. We therefore employ the distinction between ourselves as 'humans' and the Sykotic creature-species as 'mortals'. But on occasion mortals were misled by the remarkable resemblance in external corporeal properties between themselves and our Messenger into supposing that they belonged to the same 'human' species, and when we record Open Records or transcribe Sykotic documents this absurd error cannot always be remedied.

Readers will also find in such documents an extraordinary profusion of gender terminology, as if the gender of a mortal specimen was always to be signalled and pushed forward into notice and was, indeed, more significant than its role-kit or Collegiate attachments. Thus whenever we are employing Sykotic texts there will be found an excess of pronouns ('he' and 'she') & c. denoting masculine and feminine, and the naming of the creatures as 'man' (male) and 'woman' (female) rather than according to function. And so deeply is this irrelevant distinction enstructured in the creature-culture that Oi Paz was obliged, in the Journal and other Inputs, to employ its terminology.

The segment below, which gathers together such surviving materials as pertain to our Messenger's First Captivity, is made up of fragments of various kinds: some passages of Open Record as well as Journal notes dictated by Oi Paz into his Recorder, together with a number of papers in Sykotic print pasted into a volume entitled 'Boots Diary' and (inside the cover) 'Freddie's Notebook. If found, please return to Rani Satpathy, Nurses Lodgings, Block B, Flat 14.'

The 'Boots Diary' was among other volumes of papers in Sykotic print and manuscript (dialect, 'English') which our Messenger brought back on the return to civilisation. These documents are now preserved in the College of Stellanthropology, but we have selected all that is essential.

Q.

'Boots Diary'. Pasted-in cutting★

MYSTERY MAN ON MOTORWAY

Police are seeking to establish the identity of a man involved in a serious accident on the Hallow stretch of the M17 motorway yesterday afternoon.

The man was taken to Tancaster Infirmary after being struck by a car in the motorway's central lane.

Mr Herbert Endall, 44, of Blotton, was the driver of the car. He said that the man appeared directly in his path and tried to wave him down.

'There was nothing I could do,' said Mr Endall. 'They should do something to stop this kind of thing.'

Mr Endall suggested that the fences protecting motorways should be electrified to prevent intruders. The radiator and wing of his company-owned Tazuki were badly damaged. 'She's taken a really hard knock,' he said. 'It was some kind of Jesus freak in fancy dress. He seemed to drop out of the sky.

'I don't know what he was made of,' added Mr Endall. 'Any ordinary mortal would have been knocked to the moon and back.'

A spokesman at the Infirmary said that the patient was in a coma and was very poorly.

Editor's Note

This text presents characteristic semantic difficulties, and the meaning cannot be declaimed with confidence. Observe the inconsistent passage between the feminine pronoun, 'she', the neuter, 'it', and the masculine 'he' ('She's taken a really hard knock ... It was some kind of Jesus freak ... He seemed to drop ...'). The mortal, Endall, who assaulted our Messenger ('knock' = blow, hostile attack), appears uncertain as to

---

★ *This, and similar extracts to follow, appear to be sections torn or cut from a larger sheet: hence 'cuttings'.*

its victim's gender, but presumes it to be neuter ('this kind of thing').
Jesus = a celebrated ghost or em-pee in archaic mortal myth.

This text refutes the ineffectual attempts of La Crima and others to
offer excuses for the atrocious behaviour of the Sykaans on the grounds
that they remained unaware for a long time as to our Messenger's
credentials. It may be allowed that they were unaware for some time
that Oi Paz had descended on them from Oitar. But this passage affords
definitive proof that they were instantly aware they were being visited
by an extra-terrestrial ambassador – as thus: the description 'freak' (a
term of distinction reserved for those who do not conform to mortal
norms); the comparison to 'Jesus', their most celebrated ghost who in
myth came to 'Earth' as an inter-stellar visitor; and (conclusively) 'Any
ordinary mortal would have been knocked to the moon and back.' Hence
our Messenger, who had 'dropped out of the sky', was never mistaken
for a Sykaan.

Q.

'Boots Diary'. Pasted-in cutting. Manuscript annotation:
'Hallow Weekly Advertiser, 17 Aug.'

MOTORWAY MYSTERY MAN

Police have issued the following description of the man injured
two weeks ago on the Hallow stretch of motorway. He is
about 35, 6 foot 6 inches in height, of a dark complexion, with
shoulder-length fair hair. At the time of the accident he was
dressed in some theatrical costume: an ankle-length green dress
embroidered in silver, a wide belt with a gold-coloured clasp and
a wide cape or loose-fitting open upper robe, primrose yellow;
he was wearing only one shoe, of a silver colour studded
with beads, and a black collarpiece also studded with beads.

The patient's clothes are of some synthetic fibre resembling
silk. It is understood that he was carrying a portable computer
of foreign make.

The man, who has not yet recovered consciousness, is in
intensive care in Tancaster Infirmary.

'Boots Diary'. Pasted-in cutting. Manuscript annotation: '*H.W.A.*, 24 August'

MYSTERY CONTINUES

Police are continuing their enquiries into the identity of the victim of the recent motorway accident. Among places visited have been several touring theatrical companies, the Blackpool circus, two gypsy encampments and an ashram in Preston. Door-to-door enq . . . [*torn*] elcome Debbie Pettifer who joins the staff of the *Advertiser* as our roving reporter today. Miss Pettifer is a local girl whose parents live in Cowthwaite. This is her first . . . [*torn*]

'Boots Diary'. Pasted-in cutting. Manuscript annotation: '*H.W.A.*, 31 August'

FREDDIE FREAKS IN AGAIN

'Freddie the Freak', the mystery man in Tancaster Infirmary, who has been 'freaked out' and unconscious for the past month, has freaked in again. He recovered consciousness last Monday, and has been moved into a general ward.

But he has not yet given any solution to the mystery of how he came to be in the middle of the motorway in theatrical garb at 3.15 p.m. on August 2nd. The reason? He is indeed a foreigner, of unknown nationality. No one can understand his language: Basque, Hungarian, Estonian? But with his dark complexion he may come from further east. Language experts from the new University of Tancaster have been to his bedside, and their verdict will soon be known.

Meanwhile police have abandoned their enquiries in Hallow and district. These gave rise only to the usual tales of UFOs, Cruise missiles and flying saucers!

The police do not intend to present charges for illegal entry on to the motorway. A spokesman said: 'We are quite satisfied that all will in due course be explained. From what we found on his person we can say that the gentleman is highly respectable.'

Journal. Fragment 00003*

... ill-favoured, and suffering from some chromatic ailment. For when I first opened my eyes I perceived from time to time creatures like automata moving here and there with visages so white or grey that they seemed as if taken half-blanched from the acid-tank and as a species of walking dead. So that I must close my eyes again from this chalky, unwholesome sight. Yet it seems to be the true nature of these creatures to have a paucity of pigment in their skin ...

'Boots Diary'. Unmarked cutting

SEVERE INJURY FEARED

We regret that the mystery patient in Tancaster Infirmary, known to the nurses as 'Freddie', may not be a member of any recognised language-group. Although he appears to speak fluently, experts have failed to identify his speech.

A hospital spokesman said: 'Everyone loves Freddie. He is ever so responsive though he is a bit freaky. But he has got us floored.'

A peculiarity of Freddie is that he refuses all food. But he shows no signs of weakness and has even been found wandering around the wards. It is suspected that he may be suffering from brain injury, and an eminent psychiatrist in Manchester has become interested in the case.

---

* Several fragments in Oi Paz's Recorder appear to have been declaimed at about this time, but the membranes are severely damaged.

'Boots Diary'. Pasted-in typescript

... ugh examination. Remarkable recovery from severe con-
cussion, impact above left temple. Contusions to scalp: severe
abrasions to ribs (left) and thigh (left). No fractures. General
condition v. good. Vision, hearing, normal. P 80 regular, T.
36·5, BP 120/80. No dental work no caries ? prostheses. Hair:
blond but despite appearances not dyed. Age – difficult to
estimate: appears mid-30s. Pigmented + + . ? native
American. Certain abnormalities: refuses solids, only intake
fluids. (But doesn't seem to suffer from it.) Navel abnormally
small – ? previous surgery. Sexually appears immature. Body
of adult male in all respects except secondary sexual characteristics: i.e. voice unbroken, no pubic or facial hairs, immature
testes (as of 10-year-old). Also odd: toes unusually long and
prehensile, picked up some pills from floor. May have trained
as some kind of *fakir* ...*

Journal. Fragment 00011

... clothes. From these it would appear that there are four or five
species or sub-species of mortal: as 'patients', 'doctors', 'visitors',
'nurses', and others. Since all are covered in rough fibrous robes
it is not possible to determine whether the corpses of each species
are of a different formation. Within each set there are different
degrees of ill-favour as ...

---

* *Satpathy annotation:* 'These are Dr Mackintosh the Registrar's notes. I found them on
the floor of the office. He didn't notice some things, although I tried to tell him. Mr
Oypus – that's his real name, we must stop calling him "Freddie" – has such sensitive
hearing. He can't abide pop music – once when the radio was full on I thought he was
going into an epileptic seizure, like a St Vitus's dance. I had to get him cotton wool
for his ears. And his skin smells different, like sandalwood. When he sleeps it is like a
coma, he scarcely breathes, and he wakes up always just as the sun rises. All these
doctors are materialists and they are show-offs too, they don't hearken to the spirit.
R.S.'

Journal. Complete entry 00015

It is now evident that I am among creatures of a most primitive kind. For on one of those rare occasions when I succeeded in eluding my captors and in venturing about this place, I came upon a room in which a number of captives, or 'patients', were arranged in beds, each of them holding to its front an infant creature so tiny and weak that I can only compare it with an Oitarian foetus displaced prematurely from the incubation-tank at only half of its growth. On more careful observation it appeared that each of these patients had on their chests grossly enlarged glands: not the roseate wheel of the reticent nipple, but an inflation of the whole glandular organ, against which these infants pressed their mouths, sucking, as I supposed, the blood of these pitiful captives.

Further observation was prevented by the rude hand of one of my captors, who seized me and dragged me back to my bed.

Journal. Complete entry 00017

I am forced to conclude that I have been mistaken in my earlier finding. For it would appear that there are not different species or sub-species of mortal, but that all are of the same species, differentiated by their clothing according to roll-kit or Collegiate affiliation. Yet the most marked distinctions are not those of roll but of corporeal sexual formation. Indeed, instead of a ruly gender reserve, these mortals perversely flaunt and exaggerate gender distinctions, in their clothing and even in corporeal attributes such as the arrangement of hairs. Yet I have not yet decoded all the semiotics of these distinctions, since the signs are often scrambled; and it seems probable that these mortal creatures have scarcely less difficulty in discriminating between each other's rolls and gender than do I.

There is, however, one differential characteristic, which cannot be concealed and which may be known whenever these creatures make their rude attempts to communicate: for while the females of the species have voices resembling the human – and in some few they are even melodious – the males suffer from some genetic disorder or atrophy, so that they can only grunt and growl in a harsh low register, much like a griffin.

As for telling one of these creatures apart from another, there is little to be done about that. For the most part they are unpigmented in their skins, and each face is alike, except those two or three among the patients and 'doctors' who – as if to make open confession of their brutish nature – flaunt without concealment thick tufts of hair upon their mouths and chins. All smell alike, with a rank, heavy, bestial odour as if they were compounded of four parts of matter to one part of intellect. My olfactory organs are overwhelmed by their mephitic fetor.

But what gives migraine to all my organs most is the brutish manner in which they make tactile assaults upon my corpse. For these creatures have not attained to the most primitive arc of culture, nor gained to the most elementary inhibitions against touch. My corpse is polluted night and day by rude grippings and haulings and clutchings, so that I must struggle from my couch and search for some water for the offices of absolution. Nay, many times I would be forced to lie polluted by their gropings and pawings, were it not for a nurse less ill-favoured than the others, and with an almost human pigment to the skin, whom I have trained to bring me water in a bowl after these intrusions.

As for their vibes, they seem almost insensate – their vibal receptors being altogether atrophied. Nor are they themselves aware of their own vibratory emissions, which they fart upon each other – and, indeed, on my own delicate sensors – with no attempt to screen their rank egoisms.

Journal. Fragment 00018

I resume my Journal. I make Obeisance to the Wheel. Another day on Sykaos has passed. Now that I can distinguish . . . [*passage* obscured] the uncanny resemblance of these creatures to rational beings. But all resemblance of form is lost when the creatures are observed in movement. Both males and females are ill-favoured, stepping over the ground with sharp, darting motions, and extending their arms in abrupt, unmannerly gestures. It may be supposed that the species has only recently abandoned a four-footed gait and elevated itself upon its back legs, and hence has not yet, in the course of its evolution, attained to the equipoise of a harmonious being.

However, certain of those with black or brown skins among the females attain to a greater fluency of movement. From this it may be deduced that the dark-skinned mortals are the more advanced part of the species and the first to have risen on to their hind-quarters; and indeed if trained patiently in the arts of elevation they might in time be fitted as a sort of hairless butlers to our needs. But of this one can have little confidence.

Open Record. Complete Entry 00023*

MALE MORTAL:	Good morning, sir. I am a police officer from the town of Tancaster. May I have a word with you?
TRANSLATOR (*Oitarian*):	Moral early-day man. I am [*flute*] from man-heap-Tancaster. I and you have small-broken-bit-language, query.
OI PAZ:	... [*obscure*] from the Gracious Goodnesses of Oitar come as Messenger to ... [*obscure*] take me to your leader?

---

* *Several surviving inputs appear to be passages of Open Record, when our Messenger was still able to converse only through the medium of the Translator. These recordings are imperfect, the voice of the participants being very much less distinct than that of the Translator. The earliest fragment is here transcribed.*

TRANSLATOR (*English*): Come well, O mortal. I come from the Blessed Moral Ones of Oitar, as carry-between to the Blue Planet. I and you go to your leader, query.

MALE MORTAL: Phew ... Now don't you come ... [*obscure*] how you came by those gold objects and precious stones in your pack?

TRANSLATOR (*Oitarian*): Exclamation. This time do not you come over I with [*flute flute*] that of-mortal-blood stuff. I want knowing how of-gold things and [*flute*] stones in your pack, query.

OI PAZ: I have brought from Oitar as gifts to you poor but almost-rational creatures many noble gems but I have brought no stones.

TRANSLATOR (*English*): I bring from Oitar as givings to you sad half-minded near-beasts many moral gems but I bring not stones.

MALE MORTAL: ... [*obscure*] bloody serious matter. The gold amulet alone must be worth a bomb. This is a matter of a great deal of money. And I may say that we are pursuing some very extensive enquiries.

TRANSLATOR (*Oitarian*): [*Flute*] you [*flute*] do not [*flute flute*] me this is a of-mortal-blood serious stuff. The alone gold amulet must be [*flute*] a [*flute*]. This is a stuff of great much of ... [*chokes*]

FEMALE MORTAL: I'm afraid that's enough now, officer. Freddie's had some brain injury and he mustn't get excited.
[*No Translator*]

MALE MORTAL: If you ask me, miss, Mr Freddie is

having you on. How does Dr Bloody
Freddie Who do the flute for that
ventriloquist act anyway? Well, miss,
I'll be ... [*obscure*]

[*No Translator*]

OI PAZ: Farewell, gracious mortal messenger!
Convey greetings to your Good-
nesses, and beseech them to release
me from this captivity.

[*No Translator*]

Journal. Fragment 00025

There came to me this day a mortal man whom I suppose to be
some ambassador from the rulers of this part of 'Earth' (as the
Sykaans call their planet). I took it from its barking voice, and
from the absence of protuberances about its chest, to be a male
of the species. It seated itself on a chair by my bed, as is the
manner with 'visitors', and greeted me with no slant of enmity,
nor with any teeth-baring and barking, but with a very formal
proper visage. What then passed I have secured on the Open
Record for future study.

I have a little hope that something of my message was understood, for it seemed greatly impressed with the beauty of the gifts
I have brought to this place, and showed this by much blowing
and invocation of blood, which is a thing to them as sacred as
water is to us.

These visitors are creatures of both sexes, and their presence
enforces upon me to explain a matter upon which I have long
remained silent, in that my weakness did not allow me to utter
things so strange and so shameful. I had supposed that these
visitors were some kind of plant-gatherers from the outer planet,
and so indeed they are, but of such kinds of plant and for what

purposes will strain belief. I was the less prepared for this in that in my first days of captivity I was kept in a private cell, or 'ward', and the warders contrived to keep me alive by means of a device whereby nutrient fluid passed directly into my veins from a flask suspended above my head. This device was seemly enough, although, as I became sensible, it caused me some confusion to see that the flask was stationed aloft, without the least attempt at concealment, and I blushed to think that any of these mortals who entered my cell could see this brutish material evidence of my corporeal being.

Imagine my nausea, when I was removed from my cell and placed promiscuously among a dozen mortal patients; my fluid-tube, or 'drip', was roughly removed; and I was able to contemplate more seriously my fate. As my mind became more clear, it became evident, without any possibility of error, that these creatures maintained life by eating, not nutrient pellets and fluid (with such necessary rough bulkage, as egflour or bredstik, as might be taken privately once or twice a day in a locked closet), but gross, unprocessed quantities of raw or heated food-matter; and not only this, but all this being done without shame, in full view of their own species.

Painful as the description is, my Messenger's Oath requires me to set all down. At a certain hour each day the visitors who have been held at bay by the warders, break into the ward, and struggle indiscriminately here and there, two to one bed, three to another, none to a third. They bear with them packs, flasks and baskets; and in these are placed raw food-matters, as several fruits (some of enormous girth), 'cakes' (a species of flat bredstik), 'sweets' (a kind of pellet, some five or ten times the size of our own nutrient supply, enwrapped in translucent papers), and flowers. These last, indeed, are of great beauty and remind me of that auspicious day – or so it then seemed – when I first made landfall on this planet.

Thus grossly provisioned, the visitors do not modestly and privately pass these food-matters into some convenience, there to await their flushing into the pelleting machine. They gather instead around the selected patient, nod and grimace, and hand to them openly this offal. Whereat the patient seizes now this food, now that, and opening wide its mouth, so that all the dark inner crevices are evident behind the irregular teeth, thrusts down this matter into its throat.

Nor do the visitors then turn away their faces, but they continue shamelessly to regard their fellow creature as it masticates, rubbing one jaw against the other, while specks of food-matter mixed with spittle spill out on to its cheeks or run down on to its chin.

I have seen a patient thus visited swallow whole a fruit (such as their 'grape' or 'plum') so that one could distinctly notice the tongue obtrude and then the throat distend, and afterwards the mouth openly evacuate some inedible portion of the fruit, as a pip, on to a paper; and I have seen another openly seize hold in its hands of a particular fruit of this land known as an 'apple' (which is an object of such beauty that even with the most decorous pelleting it should never be reduced to gross food), and, raising it to its face, open its mouth to the full extent of an exalted chant and then clasp upper and nether jaw upon it with its teeth. And all this while the visitors remain seated about the bed, gazing at their chosen patient, grimacing and baring their teeth.

To do them justice, they do not eat the flowers. But this I fear less from any sense of shame than because these are thought a special delicacy, and are taken at night (together with flasks of urine) to the cells of the doctors and nurses for their privy repast.

Moreover, this exhibition was not confined only to 'visiting hours'. Three and four times a day, without any prompting from the outer world, trays of such fluid and matter were taken by warders to each patient's bed. So that I was forced to decide that this, *and only this*, is *the normal and habitual manner* in which mortals absorb the necessary nutriment for their survival, and that pellets (such as were brought round every evening by nurses on a wheeled tray) are so rare upon the planet that they are reserved as condiments.

My situation is now deplorable beyond description. I fear that this will be one of the last entries in my Journal. It seems that my cruel captors have nursed me back to consciousness with the drip only to starve me slowly to death amidst obscenities. Three days ago when I was privately consuming a pellet from my pack (which I keep in a chest beside my couch) I was rudely interrupted by a nurse, who snatched from my hands my last supplies of nutriment. Not content with starving me thus, every hour of the day they appear and taunt me obscenely, passing gross unprocessed fluid and food before me and even trying to force it between my lips. My tongue is swollen, my mouth is dry, my fluid imbalance has become grave. This day I begged one of the nurses to give me suck of its drip, but it ...

Open Record. Fragment 00026

MALE MORTAL:	How are you today?
OI PAZ:	You drip Oi Paz.
MALE MORTAL:	Hmmm. Well, sister?
FEMALE MORTAL:	... Nurse Flynn found him taking some kind of drug from his locker. Ever since then ... [*obscure*] ungerstrike. He seems quite weak. Only last Thursday he was wandering around the wards, but last night when he tried to get up and raid the pills on the trolley he fell in a heap on the floor. I wonder if ...
MALE MORTAL:	Quite so, sister. [*Silent interval*] Tongue please aaaaaah.
OI PAZ:	You drip me suck ...
MALE MORTAL:	Yes. A little dehydration ... [*obscure*]
FEMALE MORTAL:	... may sound odd, doctor, but Nurse Satpathy says she thinks he wants to go back on the saline drip. She says he seems shy of taking food from us,

| | and that she's seen this sort of thing among Brahmins in India with Untouchables. I thought that ... |
| MALE MORTAL: | Yes, sister. But we are not I think in Calcutta yet and this patient is not a ... [*obscure*] |

Journal. Fragment 00030

... Absolution before the Sacred Wheel, amen, for that I was entered by force, and in involuntary manner transgressed the Rules of Shame. For the past days I had noticed that the patient in the bed to my right was closely observing me, and in the mid-part of this day, when the nurses were for a time all withdrawn to eat flowers and drink specimens in their cells, it quietly crept from its bed, holding, in a shameful way, beneath its stripy coat, a flask of brown liquid, saying to me, as near as I can transcribe from the Open Record, '*Chin up Cob Ber dont let them get you down. Ive got a drop of the real Mac Coy here. Youre well come,*' with which it bared its teeth and waved the flask before my face; and as I sought to turn away from this new assault, it held it within a finger's breadth of my nose, whereat the most powerful trance-inducing gases invaded my nostrils and took possession in a moment of my saporific organs, weakened by my long starvation. Whereupon this creature forced open the vulva of my mouth and inverted the flask, thrusting it into the orifice, and a great quantity of liquor passed, without any mediate tube, directly into my throat.

This liquor was of a brown colour, burning like the sun within my mouth; and, as I swallowed, this fire passed down my throat, extended into my chest, came into an orb in my stomach, and thence radiated itself like the rays of Strim into every part of my corpse, from which, alas, it assaulted the reason itself.

Then was I in delirium and oblivious to every Rule; and I sat upright in my bed and commenced with full voice to chant the hundred verses of the Rotarian Chant. There was then a hurrying and shouting as of patients joining my chant and of nurses gathering around my bed. A curtain was drawn around me, and a nurse showed me at last the courtesy of delivering to me the smallest quantity of liquid nourishment, which was injected in a seemly manner into my veins.

But now alas I was to fall into mortal sin. For there fell upon me a trance-like lassitude. From the liquor I continued to receive an elation, humming to myself what remained of the Rotarian Chant. From the injection I received a sense of ease and a lowering of my defences. And from both sources, it seems, came a trance in which all natural inhibitions fell away. So that when a tray was thrust through the curtain on to my bed, laden with raw food-matter (some kind of bredstik), I no longer beheld it with horror but with a kind of complacency. And when I regarded the tray again after a little interval, all of the food-matter was consumed, and I must suppose that it was I, in my trance, who had eaten all that material stuff . . .

Journal. Entry 00037

I had scarcely credited it before experiencing it in my own person, that by mere unremitting exposure the most outlandish, obscene or shameful manners become matters of every day, as unremarkable as to breathe.

In this way, after the first sin or breach of nature, sinning itself becomes habitual. So that I now take no more notice of the eating of these creatures than I do of their sleeping; I myself take nutrient fluid and food-matter through my mouth (although always modestly within the curtain) twice or thrice a day; and while this occasions subsequent discomfort, as my digestive organs enlarge and as I evacuate the unaccustomed bulk of my excretions, the mere matter of eating has even become habitual and looked-for.

Indeed, if I were not regularly brought my 'tea' (a hot brown liquid) and 'toast' (fired bredstik) my corpse would exhibit symptoms of impatience!

To this accommodation to alien custom there are indeed limits. For I have found among the food-stuffs presented to me certain slabs of red or brown substance called by these creatures 'meat'. It is fortunate that I rejected these as wholly indigestible. For it appeared to my horror, during an exercise of Translation with Nurse Satpathy, that these slabs are portions of living creatures, cut with a knife from their carcases and then 'cooked' (that is, fired, as with the bredstik). It is not known to me whether the creatures so cruelly disfigured by these flesh-carvings are yet living or have long come to a premature dead-line; nor whether they be cut from one of the Sykotic Sentient Servants (which is scarcely to be credited, for how could they be tamed to do service if thus rewarded?) or be indeed savagely sliced from the sides of their fellow mortals.

I must enter it in defence of some part of these creatures that Nurse Satpathy evinced scarcely less horror than I at this custom; by which I understood that in the part of the planet from which this nurse comes, named 'India', the peoples turn away from such practices with disgust and confine their diet to vegetable stuff. From which it may well be supposed that I have had the misfortune to make landfall on the most barbarous portion of this planet. Although how such a gracious creature, with such harmonious vibes, as this Satpathy should be enslaved and held here by these 'English' ones passes my comprehension.

It will be seen that I have now passed into a new kind of danger. It is an age since I last performed the rituals in the Bumple of the Wheel. Accustomed each day to new irregularities, I feel ever more faintly the Rigour of the Rule.

I am therefore determined to exercise every skill at my command to persuade these creatures to return me to the site of my first landfall, where I may once again en-craft and make ascension to the moon.

Open Record. Fragment 00046

FEMALE MORTAL:	... [*obscure*] takes that box with him everywhere, Doctor.
MALE MORTAL:	Box? Hmm. Oh, I see. Hmm. These are his papers?
OI PAZ (*in English*):	Good day, man.
MALE MORTAL:	Eh? Oh, er, good day, Mr Er ... [*Silence – sound of papers turning*] Can't you put that damn box down?
OI PAZ (*in English*):	Box not damn. Your bits of speaking make into my bits of speaking in box. I speak in box now.
OI PAZ (*in Oitarian*):	Gracious Provost of whatever College, overwatched by the Gracious Goodnesses of Oitar! I wish now to return by the same route as that by which I came. I beseech you to lead me back to my craft aloft in the high plants, and for this I will give beautiful gifts and also give knowledges to your pitiful species.
TRANSLATOR (*in English*):	Moral master of what School, watch out for the Blessed Moral Ones of Oitar! I will now blast out on the way as the way on which I blasted in. I look [*correction*] I obey [*correction*] I beg you go with me back to my craft in the upstairs vegetables. At this I will give you beautiful givings and also give some sciences to you damn beasts.

[*Long silence – sound as of writing on paper*]

MALE MORTAL:	Thank you, Mr Er-Oipas. Good, good. Now it will help both of us if you will answer some questions ...

OI PAZ (*in English*):	Speak in box, he-man.
MALE MORTAL:	... Perhaps you will tell me when you first remember becoming interested in this box? Let me see, that's a very fine instrument, a recorder?
OI PAZ (*in English*):	Damn not touch box, man!
MALE MORTAL:	Er, no, no. But it must have cost a mint of money, eh?
TRANSLATOR (*in Oitarian*):	Exclamation no no. But it must have [*flute*] a green herb of [*chokes*]
OI PAZ (*in English*):	Excuses. Box did choke.
MALE MORTAL:	Oh? Eh? Ah? [*Silence — sound of writing*] Goooood. Well now, let's try again. Is there any trouble you remember, Mr Er, before your accident, some trouble with your girlfriend perhaps?
TRANSLATOR (*in Oitarian*):	Exclamation query exclamation query exclamation query. Long moral. Well this day, let us do-with-difficulty as we did. Is there query any ill-omened-thing you remember, Mr Er, before your landfall, any ill-omened thing with your ... [*chokes*]
OI PAZ (*in Oitarian*):	You trifle, mortal! Your blasphemies and bestial concepts have once more choked the Translator. I ask again, when may I return to the moon?
TRANSLATOR (*in English*):	You pudding, near-beast! Your double-treble-damn beastly thoughts are chokings against the box. I query again when I blast back to moon.
MALE MORTAL:	Yes. Thank you. [*Long silence — sound of writing*] Ah, Hugh ... I think we ... [*obscure*] ... trauma ... regressive ... quite clear case ... threatened ...

| | [*obscure*] considerable hostility but harmless ... [*obscure*] largactyl ... [*obscure*] |
| OI PAZ (*in English*): | I am not gone to end of this speaking, he-man. I sit and wait now for some small bit of reason ... Damn not touch box, she-man! |

'Boots Diary'. Pasted-in manuscript

Hugh,

Thanks for asking me to see this fascinating chap. The clinical picture is certainly most unusual, and does not fit a simple diagnosis. This history of head injury must be presumed to be of aetiological significance, causing an organic psychosis. In view of his abnormal appearance and unusual skills, a drug-induced psychosis (?previous history) may be a possibility, confusing the picture: i.e. wandering on to motorway suggests he was hallucinating prior to injury (? LSD). His ventriloquist speech is most bizarre, repetition and perseveration compatible with organic brain syndrome. Possible regression to infantile speech-pattern.

Would suggest: contact family for previous psychiatric history, clinical psychologist's assessment, CT Brain Scan, PET Scan, EEG, VERs, check serum Zinc, Lead and Platinum levels, syphilis serology, urinary porphyrins.

Please let me know when results are back.

Reginald

PS Don't think you need worry about his conduct in the ward, his hallucinations aren't aggressive. But that box of his is part of psychosis. If taken away he might feel threatened. He's probably harmless, but if he gets troublesome, suggest trial of largactyl.*

---

* *Satpathy annotation:* 'This is the report from Dr Long, the specialist from Manchester. I found it on Sister's desk and copied it.

FIRST CAPTIVITY

Journal. Fragment 00051

... no doubt one of the rulers of this College of Sarcology, or, as they call it, 'hospital'. From what translation I had had with the gracious Satpathy I was led to suppose that I was to enter the presence of an Adjuster, and I had good hopes that at length some rational communication would be made. But ... [*broken record*] and disharmonious brute.

It is necessary now that I should make preparations to steal quietly from this place by night, and make what way I can back to my craft. I must first find by which channels, passages and locks ...

Open Record. Fragment 00053*

FIRST MALE VOICE: ... right as rain and eating like a horse. Eh, Sister?

Of course he didn't ask any of us any questions. And he didn't really try to talk with Mr Oipas either. He didn't even find out that Mr Oipas hates being touched, and has a sacred thing about water. Like all of these show-offs Dr Long thinks there is a materialist explanation of everything, but what he calls "hallucinations" might be Mr Oipas's religion.

The trouble is Mr O. is getting a fixation on me, just because I notice him and do little things like bringing him water and cotton wool. He expects me to be on duty all the time. Last week when I came back from an off-duty day I found him in a terrible state. He had been wandering around the corridors calling for me. Even Sister and Dr Mackintosh have been making fun of me. Then when I sat with him and talked and I calmed him down he was so grateful that he dug in his locker looking for a "gift" – and gave me a gold amulet which must be worth two lakhs. I tried to give it back but he was quite hurt. I don't know what to do. Should I keep it as a "biscuit"?

Rani S.'

* *This most unsatisfactory scrap of damaged membrane carries the growls, barks and some words of several mortal voices, both male and female. It cannot be rationally transcribed, but since it is one of the best examples in our audio-bank of the Incongruous Noise (both male and female) – see Fragment 00054 below – we have thought it necessary to insert it here. The original is preserved in the Autistic Laboratory of the Museum of Acoustics.*

FIRST FEMALE VOICE: Hi hi hi hi hi. You'd better ask Nurse Satpathy, Doctor. She gets on with him like a house on fire. Ihi ihi.

FIRST MALE VOICE: Aaargh orgh argh. Go and get her. And ask Dr Thomson to step over. Let's all work on it together. Aho argh orfff. Well, how are we today, Mr Spaceman? Let's get this wool out of your ears. Aharorf. Ah, Dick, ah, nurse, come and join the consultation.

OI PAZ (*in English*): In my head I am now well, man, and I wish to go back to moon.

MALE AND FEMALE VOICES: [*An untranscribable cacophony of high barks and growls, as of a pack of griffins*]

SECOND FEMALE VOICE: ... make fun on him, excuse me, Doctor. He's quite sensitive, and he understands a lot now, and he really does think he has come from space, from a place called Oitar.

FIRST MALE VOICE: Quite right, Nurse. You dress me down. But only once in a blue moon, mind.

OI PAZ (*in English*): The moon is not blue, small half-minded man. I wish to go back to my craft and fly upstairs.

FEMALE AND MALE VOICES: ... [*Cacophony as before, at even higher pitch, but this time with harmonious female weeping noise*]

FIRST MALE VOICE: Arrha aargh, dear me, orrff, oh dear, oh now, Nurse Satpathy, don't cry, aarff, oh Sister, take her off and give her some tea, let her have the duty off, she's been overdoing it ... [*obscure*] too sensitive for this game ... [*obscure*] what do you make of it, Dick?

54

SECOND MALE VOICE:	... [*obscure*] fit as a fiddle. According to Dr Long ... hallucinating ... seems quite harmless. But he hedges his report, of course.
FIRST MALE VOICE:	... [*obscure*] can't keep him here holding down a bed and eating his head off for ever.
SECOND MALE VOICE:	... started wandering at night, the other patients find him spooky ...
OI PAZ (*in English*):	When do you stop speaking on to me as stone or stuff when I give you back reasonable speaking, he-men?
FIRST MALE VOICE (*indistinct*):	Wow ... tainly sitting up and taking no ... [*obscure*] police no use ... [*obscure*] what about trying the press and telly, someone might turn up and claim him ... [*obscure*]

Journal. Entry 00054

I have been observing the speech of these creatures more closely. It is evident that the Translator, whose circuits are deployed along human logic-paths, has misled me. From now onwards it should be used for vocabulary only, and I must contort my own mind in the efforts to construe their linguistic deformities.

The difficulty lies not only in their rude concepts. The disaster is enstructured in the whole discourse, which appears as a language which has never been adjusted, nor even cured by computer. Thus (a small matter) whereas there are in Fact Utter or even in Neuter Utter a few signs which survive as synonyms (from lack of rectification many generations ago), in this English speech there may be six, or seven, or – for all that I or the Translator know – half a hundred terms for the same object or quality, any one of which may be selected at a whim. Thus the same cereal food-stuff may be called 'bread' or 'grub' or 'toast' or 'nosh' or 'sandwich'. Or, again, the she-man is commonly called 'woman', whose derivation is given by the Translator as 'woe-man': i.e. 'woe' (sorrow, sad thing) and 'man' (mortal creature) – hence 'mortal-of-the-sorry-sex' – may equally be addressed as 'duck', 'love', 'sister', 'missis', 'mum', 'madam', 'matron'. It is of absolutely no account which term is used.

There is a further mess in their speech, in that any mortal whatsoever appears to have a licence to use metaphor. This is a gross insult to the privileges of my roll. That a Poet should be given such licence is well known: nor is any rational disorder caused by that. For each Poet is trained from youth in its College to set each simile or figure out in clear display; to set a marker in each sentence ('like', 'just as', 'as if') as a caution to the intellect; and even if this rule be bent, and the 'direct comparison' be employed (as we of the School of Melodious Colour often do), no larceny is made upon the reason, for every reader knows what to expect of poetry and what the Poet's licence lets.

Nor is this matter a small one; for so powerful is metaphor in bringing picturegrams forth, and so necessary are the arts of comparison in reaching into the very opposites of nature and tying them to each other in a common joint, that we may well see the danger were these powers dispensed without licence and passed promiscuously among untrained minds. On the one hand, half-formed images might be provoked to rise unbidden, escape from the imaginer's control, and enter into the general circuits of our culture. Where it would be the work of a generation of Adjusters to isolate them and turn them back into the Chaotic Source. On the other hand, grossly inapposite comparisons might be declaimed, tending to divert the ratios and proper stations of each Science.

These mortals slide about in the mess of their language as if they were some wretched butler slipping on the ice. Any man, 'she' or 'he', will meddle with an image: just as if the Chaotic Source were ever open in their midst and they groped among its uncured energies. But these images are not bold or in any way original; they are (some of them) direct thefts of reason, 'lies', and (others) mere worn integers, mimicked from others and repeated by rote.

As an example of this I have been studying some passages of speech of several mortals who recently gathered by my bed. (This speech-specimen I have secured for the record.*) (a) 'Right as rain': a direct theft, for 'rain' (i.e. molten snow) cannot be compared to the left hand nor to the right; (b) 'Eating like a horse': either an error (supposing it to refer to me) or a wholly absurd attempt at metaphor, for a *horse* is a Sykotic creature much like our unicorn; but, as is known by every child, a unicorn bows low to the sun before he eats, and then takes nutriment from the choicest lawns, and by what insane extension of comparison could it be said that I should consume, as on my hands and feet, lawns which are nowhere in this place to be seen? (c) 'Like a house on fire': direct theft, indeed a vicious robbery, for I do not go on with Satpathy like a house in flames – indeed, there has grown a trust between us as with a faithful Sentient Servant; (d) 'You dress me down': i.e. you disrobe me, pull down my dress – a gross error; Nurse Satpathy has not yet, in all my time in the ward, undressed Doctor Mackintosh; (e) 'Blue moon': direct theft of reason, unless indeed Doctor Mackintosh suffers from the malady of colour-inversion.

And so on. We will not labour such follies as 'fit as a fiddle', nor as 'holding down beds', nor the absurdity of 'eating his head off'. But consider: in every exchange of speech these thefts abound, so that, as day follows upon day, the rich stores of thought are laid open to marauding bands, the Bank of Reason is ransacked, the Sources of Chaos encroach upon the Rule, and the hope of harmony is every hour diminished. So that if ever in some distant future our Gracious Goodnesses should have the pity to send upon this planet a Mission of Adjusters, then it is the mortal language itself which must first be put under arrest.

That is enough on such matters, which bend my own serenity.

---

* *See Fragment 00053, above.*

But I cannot leave that record without declaiming in my Journal a further discovery. I have long been puzzled by the manner of greeting of these creatures. The forms are thus: at first meeting they will compress the vulva of the mouth, or 'lips', in a tight extended line. This I first took as a slant of enmity, as indeed it closely resembles this. But it is in fact nothing other than an involuntary muscular spasm, signifying neither ill-will nor anything whatsoever good. Next, if the meeting is protracted further, they voluntarily relax the vulva, and lay bare their teeth. This is certainly very hideous, and at first occasioned in me alert-signals, for it may readily be understood that I took it as a sign of uncontrolled enmity, as it might be among ill-managed griffins whose butlers have not yet rectified their fighting genes. And this was the more likely in that the teeth-baring was often accompanied by a sharp bark or snarl; indeed, for a time I feared that this grimace was the preparation for an eating of each other.

But strange as it is to report, this teeth-baring is only a second stage of ceremonial greeting, and these pitiful creatures suppose that the grimace serves to disguise their real nature and to simulate goodwill! From this we move to a third and, as I hope, final stage. Here the mouth falls fully open to disgorge a noise-without-name — a noisome noise, a wrathy, obtuse noise, or a whole succession of abrupt, intermittent noises, as of barks, coughs, and of rattling of stones. Among the women, whose voices are least offensive, the noise is discomforting enough. But with the males, whose voices are low, loud, growly, rasping and griffin-like, it passes all description. Moreover, it causes the greatest pain to the poor beasts themselves, so that their throats distend, their shoulders heave and there is a shaking in the whole corpse. And I have seen one of the males, the Doctor Mackintosh, standing beside one patient's bed, and — confronted, as I suppose, by that creature's appalling injury — cough, hack and bark so hideously that he bent to the ground, held his hands against the shaking of his belly, and so stood, or shook, until waters broke from his eyes.

The pathology of these involuntary spasms is not yet clear to me. It is not another form of greeting, although attacks are sometimes occasioned by greetings. From the closest observation, I now consider them to be occasioned by a sudden and over-powering sense of their own absurdity, in pretending to be rational creatures at all. For this sense comes upon them at moments when they have done or said something so much against the regimen of reason that their very corpse rebels against the futility of their own minds. And if we return to the same speech-specimen we can observe that this ailment comes upon them when they are self-detected in some blatant theft of reason (as 'eat like a horse', 'get on like a house on fire', etc.). Or else it falls upon them in double-measure when they are placed in *a situation of incongruity*; as when they are brought before my presence, and confronted with my infinitely superior reason (for which I claim no credit to myself, being only such a kit as the Bio-Engineers put together).

So that I fear in my efforts at communication I may even do them injury, so sharp and bitter is the incongruous sense that comes upon them when I speak, so violent their spasms as they contemplate the depravity of their own natures. And these spasms I would say are in them very close to what would pass with us as a sense of dereliction from the Rule; as witness that gentle Satpathy, when the other mortals barked and coughed, expressed her nobler sense of inferiority in tears.

This malady is known to them as 'laughter'. But I set it down and declaim it for science as the Incongruous Noise.

'Boots Diary'. Pasted-in cutting. Manuscript annotation: *'Hallow Adv.*, Octbr [*obscure*]'

Mid-Page Profiles. Each week our staff-reporter Deborah Pet-tifer interviews a prominent local personality. This week meet:

PATIENT WHO?

Hallow residents may have been surprised to see early this week in the national press and television, pictures of our own local notable, the mystery motorway man who has become affect-ionately known to all of us as 'Freddie'.

The press and television have been co-operating with hos-pital and welfare authorities to beam his picture up and down the land, in the hope of making contact with his family, work-mates or friends. No answers yet.

When I saw his full-frontal face last Monday on the telly, I said to myself: 'Wow! If that's not a local notable, who is?' So I packed my pencils and trotted down to Tancaster Infirmary.

It seems that the staff are really worried now about getting Freddie home. Medically, he's A1. 'Strong as a horse', they said. 'But . . .'

The 'but' bit is what I came to write about. And they want me to write. 'In normal circumstances,' a doctor said, 'we disclose nothing to the press about our patients, beyond the formal medical bulletin.

'But this is a quite exceptional case. This patient is certainly fit to be discharged. In fact, we have no powers to keep him here and he's raring to go. But . . .' And there's that 'but' bit once again.

Doctor Mackintosh handed me over to the gracious care of Nurse Satpathy, 23, of Orissa, India. Who walked ahead of me down the long corridors in stately measure, as if she were carrying a jar of frankincense and myrrh upon her head.

I felt I was to be Ushered into a Presence.

And so I was. In General Ward Three, Beamish wing, there sat beside his bed a Presence indeed.

'A visitor to see you, Mr Oipas,' Nurse Satpathy said.

Disappointment Number One! 'Freddie' has a name at last! So 'Freddie' is no more.

But there was nothing disappointing in the Presence.

Two yards and more of well-made mortal, something between a Red Indian chief and a yellow-wigged Othello. Skin: dark. Features: European. Hair: oh that hair! Full, flowing, shoulder-length hair, so soft it would dissolve in the curler, and every last prink and follicle of it somewhere between the colour of heather honey and burnished gold. *Please*, Mr Oipas, thought I, tell me which shampoo.

But more. Mr Oipas was not wrapped in hospital nighties like the other poor mortals sitting round. It seems they robed him for the telly 'commercial' on Monday and he hasn't let them take his robes off since.

Imagine a Pre-Raphaelite gown in jade and silver with a thick gold belt and a beady thing around the neck, and thrown over all a yellow cape from Liberty's.

How does one interview a Vision?

Mr Oipas answered that by interviewing me!!!

He gave a gracious old-world bow and waved me grandly to sit down upon his bed.

Then he spoke. 'Good day, man. I have a message for the Earth.'

Disappointment Number Two. Not at all the voice for a Presence. With some six foot six of golden-headed manhood, one might except something a little more, er . . . masculine.

'A message for the Earth?' I said. 'Blast away!'

'Good thinking, man,' said he. 'I wish to blast away tomorrow and blast back to moon from which I came.'

My pencil broke. I got a biro.

'Did you say you came from the moon, Mr Oipas?'

'Damn good thinking, man. You and Satpathy only half-minded beasts that know I am true-speaking Messenger.'

I wasn't sure whether or not to take that as a compliment.

'But how did you get to the moon?' I asked with a bright smile. 'I'm sure our readers will want to know.'

He leaned forward confidentially. 'Tell the Earth,' he said, 'that I come from Oitar upstairs. Any day tomorrow we-all blast down from moon and live here for ever and eternity. If you are good with us we are putting up with you. We clean up your beastly half-minded ways.'

'But . . .' I said. 'But I'm afraid my newspaper doesn't circulate throughout the whole world.'

Mr Oipas sighed. 'Excuses. I do not know words. We ask Translator.' On the locker top, where ordinary mortals keep their Lucozade and Kleenex, there was a Box, with groovy dials and silver knobs. Mr Oipas switched it on and addressed it: 'Newspaper? Circulate?'

Whirrr. Flickering needles. Then the Box *spoke*, in a scratchy, tannoy sort of voice, like someone humming on a comb through silver paper. 'Newspaper is pieces of printed paper.' Whirrr. The Box meditated. 'News is beastly things that go on.' It meditated again. Whirrr. 'Circulate is to go round in Rule of Wheel.' End of Box.

'Ah,' said Mr Oipas. 'So. You think well, she-man. It is well for you to be in shame because your newses do not go round the world by the Rule of the Wheel. But do not lose hopes. For those of you half-minded men, such as you and Satpathy, who have a shame, the Gracious Goodnesses upstairs may yet show . . . '

And here the Presence looked for all the world like a mortal. He scowled and scratched his head.

Then he turned again to the Box and said to it something very like 'anorak'.

The Box scarcely whirred a dial.

'Forgiveness,' it said.

'Forgivingness,' said Mr Oipas. 'For some few of you near-beasts we show forgivingness.'

Nurse Satpathy led me away.

Journal. Entry 00064

This day I was sent a visitor again from outer Earth. It is now apparent that my presence has become known to mortals of some rank and authority out there, although they do not yet send to me their leaders or Adjusters. This one did not come in a loud quarrelsome troop with cameras and recorders, as they did yesterday, but alone, to write my Message. It was exceedingly ill-favoured, and as I first supposed a weakling male; for as it darted in, with an awkward rocking gait, it could be seen that its arms and legs were as thin as scrolls, its hands puny, its shoulders sloping downwards from the neck and unsquared; its skin was whiter even than those of the patients, and, as if to disguise this complaint, it had painted its face; but the paint was not applied with decorum, but in irregular patches and in smeared lines upon the lips and about the eyes, as if thrown from a brush at a plaque. The lashes were enlarged and black, and the outer rose or oriole of the eye was daubed with green!

Yet when it opened its mouth to speak, it did not utter after the low growling manner of the males, but conversed in a female register. So that I later corrected myself and addressed it as a female creature. But I remain uncertain of the truth.

'Newspaper' may now go down in the dictionary of English. I have seen many of these things, but it is only today, with the aid of the Translator, that I learned the generic term. These are large membranes of white paper covered irregularly in pic-turegrams and Sykotic print, some letters of which I can now begin to distinguish.

These newspapers, of which there are many kinds, appear to fulfil certain of the functions of our *Annual Record and Register of Things*. But they come out *every day*! Nor is there only *one* account set into print of what has passed that day: but five, ten or twenty accounts are set in print, and these all of the same event of the same day: as if it should be possible for the same event to give rise to different accounts!

This visitor then, is a scrivener, as I suppose, for one of these newspapers. I overcame my revulsion at her person, and sought to give her some message to publish to the outer Earth. I have some hopes of my message being known tomorrow to the whole population of this world. For this mortal proved to be better favoured in her mind than in her body, and quick among her kind.

'Boots Diary'. Pasted-in cutting. Manuscript annotation: *'Daily Chronicle,* 3 Nov.'

CRASHED AIRCRAFT FOUND IN TREES
PILOT BALED OUT?

RAF investigators have gone to the North of England to investigate the wreckage of a small aircraft in a wood near Hallow, eleven miles north of Tancaster. There are no reports of casualties, but police with tracker dogs are combing the area. It is thought possible that the pilot baled out.

A police spokesman said: 'It's something of a mystery. There are no reports of missing aircraft over this area.'

The plane is a very small, single-seater craft with rounded wings of unknown type. It is thought to be the craft of a private executive, of American manufacture.

It is understood that the plane may have crashed several weeks ago and have come to notice only because the leaves are falling. A spokesman said that it was feared that the pilot made a 'hard landing'. Police with tracker dogs are combing the area.

'Boots Diary'. Pasted-in cutting. Manuscript annotation: *'Daily Chronicle,* 9 Nov.'

SECURITY BLACK-OUT

A complete security black-out has descended on the case of the craft which descended in woods near Tancaster last week.

Officials would neither confirm nor deny reports that it was a high-altitude Russian 'spotter' plane, and that the pilot has now been secured.

It is understood that he descended by parachute. RAF personnel with tracker dogs are combing the woods.

An arm of the British Intelligence Services has become interested in the case, it is understood. A very senior official, who remains anonymous, travelled North yesterday and interviewed a patient in Tancaster Infirmary.

And last night a Rolls with curtained windows and with a police escort travelled at high speed down the motorway from Tancaster to London.

An official at the Ministry of Defence refused to comment on reports that a man is assisting them with their enquiries in the neighbourhood of Whitehall.

'Boots Diary'. Pasted-in cutting. Manuscript annotation: '*Barnoldswick Mercury*, 10 November'

DREADFUL OCCURRENCES AT LOCAL FARM
DOGS RUN AMOK

Dogs ran amok in Hardberrow Woods early yesterday morning when search-parties from three different services converged in the densest part of the woods.

The incident occurred when dogs of the RAF and of the local police force were suddenly confronted by a task force of dogs from an unnamed service. It is understood that there had been a failure of co-ordination between local authorities and a Government Agency. 'These breeds are quite incompatible,' a spokesman said.

According to an eye-witness description the subsequent events were 'indescribable'. Dogs of all three services broke out of control and handlers had to take to the trees. 'It was all over in a few minutes,' the eye-witness said. 'It was a massacre.' The bodies of dead Alsatians and severely mauled wolf-hounds lay 'in piles'.

Journal. Fragment 00071

... at last my messages have been received by those of superior degree in the outer world. For this day I was attended by several visitors of distinction. The day passed in intercourse on my bed, now with one, now with another. At length they were fully satisfied as to my Mission. For I was released from captivity, and conducted with great ceremony – although with their habitual gross touching, one mortal on each side of me holding my arms – and led through long passages to the outer Earth. And there, on a road, a landcraft awaited us, in which I was seated and travelled a great distance.

I can make no observations on that part of the Earth over which I travelled, for the windows of the car were hung with dark drapery. And I take this to be another sign of their respect, for in this way I was saved from the gapings and starings of their publicans, and from the Incongruous Noise which my presence sometimes arouses in their shame-stricken breasts.

As to all that passed and all that I witnessed during the course of this day, the recording of this must be left to another occasion. For I am weary and have overpassed my sleep-line. I am not yet free of all restraint, nor have I been taken back (as I have ordered) to my craft. But I have hopes that the moment of my release is now near. And that they detain me a few days longer, only so that I may have intercourse with their leaders and magistrates, who are known here as 'em-pees', 'jay-pees', 'dee-pee-pees', and 'queens'. So that tomorrow, as I expect, I shall be led to some chamber or Bumple of State, and have intercourse with an em-pee.

Here I am housed decently in a private room, and I have several attendants in blue suits, or 'pee-cees', one of whom is stationed as a courtesy, to attend on my commands, outside my door. Indeed, it seems that these pee-cees are an inferior sort, who fetch, carry, drive and attend, very much as the butler does for us.

This night is clear, and from the window Oi Paz can view that part of the sky which falls within the eighth segment of the third conjunction. And this Oi Paz takes as an omen of good fortune. Oitar itself is, of course, invisible across those immeasurable ways. But there, amidst all this dusty fire, a golden dust stands in eternity: the Ruly Wheel!

When Oi Paz considers the hazards that have been passed – the tedium tracking through the inert wastes of space; the great darkness that lies between the time of leaving Oitar and this present time; the passing from then to now; the cruel, unrhyming scape of that lifeless moon; the indignities of captivity among these uncured creatures; and the situation now, in divorce from all fellows and from the rotation of things – when Oi Paz considers all this, then it can only be marvelled at that this Poet remains whole in corpse, serene in mind, and still apt for Duty to the Oitarian Order. And Oi Paz bows thrice low before the Blessed Wheel.

SEGMENT THREE

FREEWHEEL

Editor's Note

Hitherto your editor has refrained from intruding too far upon these pages. Very much in the foregoing account is, we readily grant, ill cured, either because of the fragmentary nature of the records, or because of the injuries sustained by Oi Paz, which prevented any rational presentation of these disorderly events.

In the narrative that follows we are better placed. The Account Book, which Oi Paz commenced to write in the first months of the Second Captivity, has already been drawn upon for Segment One. For some reason no attempt was made to construe the events of Segment Two, the First Captivity, into order in this Account, but records were kept in the Journal only. However, the Account was resumed from the point of release from captivity, and we draw upon this hereunder. After some pages the Account was abandoned in favour of scientific notebooks (see the editorial note to Segment Four).

Thus your Editor has at hand some pages of the Account; a transcription of Oi Paz's Journal; and a veritable blizzard of Sykotic print, for Oi Paz brought back to Oitar a small case full of newspaper cuttings, reports and so on. It will be many years before a definitive edition of these collected papers can be prepared. Meanwhile the Editor asks for the reader's indulgence. We will select from this indiscriminate sum only what is essential for a provisional account.

Q.

Account Book

I resume my Account. I am not yet able to compose a serene account of my First Captivity. Suffice it to say that at length I made communication with some mortals of superior authority beyond the walls of that House of Sarcology, or hospital, who sent for me by car and took me to their chief city, called London.

In London I remained in captivity in a hostel where they keep persons suspected of great crimes. From this place I was taken each day to a chamber, where certain subordinate rulers or officers asked me a great many disorderly questions. And the vibrations between us were bad, for two reasons. First, they were unbelievers. For whatever I said in truth to them they set aside with 'ho' and 'ha' and 'tell me another', which, when I did, they repeated the same words, so that we went back and forwards like a game of ball which neither side could gain. Second, they had determined, according to some whim known best to them, that I came, not from Oitar, but from another part of this same planet Sykaos, known as 'Russia'.

Now in the system of Strim there are ten or so considerable planets, and one of these is known to our navigators as Rōsea, from the roseate hue of its effulgence. So that I supposed, with reason, that they knew me to be an extra-terrestrial traveller, but that they had mistaken the place whence I came. I therefore showed some compliance with their suggestions, but took pen in hand to draw a diagram of the galaxies, and to show them where sacred Oitar rolls. Whereupon they supposed I was ready to make 'confession', and they summoned into the room a man who spoke to me fluently, but in a speech which neither I nor the Translator could construe as being in any part Sykotic. And so that loggerheads went on for several days.

The reason for this misfit was this: whereas we in Oitar have several utters, and, in Neuter Utter, a speech common to all which has been well cured (and brought, in medieval times, by the computer under a single Rule), these mortals exist still in an aboriginal state in which they have not one, but ten, twenty, nay, perhaps one hundred uncured utters, or speeches; and each one of these wholly distinct and incomprehensible to the speaker of another.

So that on this small planet there are a myriad creatures, each looking much alike and all strutting on two legs and priding themselves on being rational beings, and yet who are split into fragments of consciousness, so that, when they meet, they cannot perform the first rational act – that of communication. As between creatures of the same pack (as 'Englishers', 'Europers' or 'Russians') they can communicate, and so they suppose themselves to be sane; but as between creatures of a different speech, they must grunt and grimace at each other like butlers.

In antiquity, it may be supposed, these peoples mingled promiscuously with each other. But the daily frustrations of noncommunication were such that at length they became ashamed, and they drew apart from each other into different regions of the planet, forming themselves into language-packs, or 'nations'; and ever since these nations have shown the most desperate fear of and hostility to each other.

It seems, then, that these English people supposed that I was a Russian, and that I had come in an aircraft to spy upon their language and their lands. And – as I was soon to learn – they sent out officers who found my craft and lifted it bodily out of the giant plant, or 'tree', on which it had landed, and carried it away to some place for examination. And this strange-speaking man whom they had brought to me was a kind of mortal Translator, or one of their own sort who had privily spied on the Russian language, which they supposed that I must speak.

But at length they became satisfied that this was not so. And one morning I was taken to their office, where three of them confronted me with solemn visages. I ordered, as I always did, that they should release me and conduct me back to my craft. Whereupon the chief among them replied that I was not likely to see that 'toy' again; that their engineers had 'taken it apart' and that they had just this morning sent a decisive report that it could never have got off the ground, let alone fly from Russia to England; that in fact my famous craft had no source of power at all; that they did not know how I had got it into the tree, but they could see very well that I was playing tricks upon them for the sake of making a noise in the newspapers; and that I was an 'actor' looking for publicity and getting 'more than I bargained for'.

He went on to say that he wished that they could punish me for wasting their time. And that perhaps they would find a way to do so. But that, for the moment, they would let me go, provided that I would give them my real name and address. And if I was not English then they would need to see my 'papers' and to find out how I got into their country.

I set all this down as it remains in the Recorder's memory-bank, for during these questionings I usually switched the Open Record on. I do not understand all his meaning now and I understood even less then. Two things only were evident to me: first, they had found, and perhaps had destroyed, my craft; second, that while remaining hostile to me, they were ready to release me from captivity. And of these two, it was the first which entered my mind like a probe of darkness. The means had been taken from me of escape from this alien planet. I was as lost to civilisation as one of those hapless astronauts whose craft has been damaged by meteorites and who have been carried into the uttermost regions of space.

My chief interrogator rose abruptly and left the room. His two subordinates then showed me more seeming courtesy and called for tea to be brought in to us. They said that I was lucky, but that they supposed that their chief could not find any particular law that I had broken (which is their way of speaking of a transgression against their Rule); that I had made 'proper fools' not only of them but of the newspapers and television of the whole land, for the discovery of my craft and of my presence here had been 'a nine days' wonder'; and that pictures of me and interviews taken at the hospital had been published everywhere. They concluded that I had pulled off 'the best publicity stunt of the year', and that, as soon as I had given them the details that they needed, I could go and 'clean up'.

I could still think of nothing but the wanton destruction of my craft. But I replied to them in some manner, saying (with grave courtesy) that it was true that they were proper fools but that they were not so by my making, for they were only such fools as I had found them; that I had been on their planet some ninety days and not nine; and that I had bathed well in the morning and had no need to clean up. At this they became ugly once more, and said that they had had enough of my games, and that I was too clever by half.

They then retired into the next room, where I could hear them discussing in low voices. When they returned one of them was carrying the small pack in which I had placed various gems and gifts, with flasks and samplers, when I had left my craft many days before. He placed the pack on the table between us, took out a handful of rubies, diamonds and amethysts, and divided them between himself and his companion.

'Now, for the last time, will you give us your name and address?'

I replied, as so often, that my name was Oi Paz, my permanent abode in the Third College of Poesy in the Seventh All of the Fourth Orb of Oitar, and that my present abode was on their moon, to which I would return as soon as they conducted me back to my craft and repaired whatever wanton damage they had committed to it.

'Play it your own way,' he said. 'If you go around in that gear we can pick you up again whenever we want.' He took up a large ruby and held it to the light. 'Marvellous! Now perhaps your Royal Exalted Eminence will condescend to enlighten us poor mortals on where this lot came from, eh?'

I was a little surprised by the unaccustomed note of respect, and replied very graciously that, as a leading poet of the School of Melodious Colour, I had been given many gems by those to whom I had declaimed my odes.

The man turned to his companion and said, 'Some folks don't know how lucky they are, do they, Jim? They run their heads into cars, get rushed to hospital, lie unconscious for a week, get free treatment, get a free ride in a police-car to London, waste all our time, refuse to give their names, and at the end of the day some poor bloody underpaid public servants are expected to hand over their belongings lovingly looked after for them, all sealed, signed and delivered, to the last sparkler. Oh, thank you, sir, sorry to have kept you, sir, so nice to have met you, sir! Eh?'

'Look at it this way,' said the other. 'Them gems might have got spilled on the road, in the accident. Bound to have done. Could have got lost anywhere.'

'That's the way I look at it,' said the first. 'And lost they are.'
With which they put the gems in their pockets.

'And don't think you can lodge a complaint up there,' he said,
turning back to me and jabbing a finger at the ceiling. 'Because
they're pissed off with you. They don't want to know no more
about Freddie the Freak. Nothing but news-hawks and telly crews
at the doors day and night, and the Foreign Office doing its top.
Made proper Charlies out of us. Oh, and you don't get away
without signing.' Whereupon he wrote some lines on a paper
and passed them across to me with a pen.

> I, Freddie the Freak, alias Oipas, of no fixed address, permanent
> abode the moon, do hereby acknowledge receipt of all my
> personal belongings, intact and undamaged. Signed . . .

'If you want to put in your right name and address, you may,'
he said. 'But sign that paper you will.'

I began to demur, but they rose from their seats and moved
towards me in so menacing a manner that I took up the pen and
wrote on the bottom of the paper 'Poor Subhuman Halfwits';
but in Oitarian characters which they could not construe.

'That will do,' they said.

I picked up my Translator, and put my Recorder in my pack.
They took me each by one arm, dragged me down some stairs
and pushed me with force out of the doors.

Who then was Oi Paz? Ill-natured as they were, the mortals in
that office were yet my last link to my own existence – the only
link that might lead me back to my craft. I waited by the doors.
I pressed against them. I beat upon them with my hands. But
they remained closed and silent. I felt like a specimen-collector
on the outer Oitarian tundra, who comes at last to a dome of
refuge only to find that all the inlet locks are sealed.

I became aware of my surroundings. Behind me was a thrashing
and whining noise. A ceaseless, ill-spaced procession of cars of

many sizes and colours carried creatures here and there in both directions, yet the vehicles conducted themselves with such cunning, dividing their directions on one side of the road or the other, that they did not impact. Now, as if by some instant common signal from a thought-controller, all would stop together, their engines roaring impatiently. Then all would receive a different signal and would lurch forward together once more. The occupants had anxious faces, and leaned forward, as if obsessed by the urgency of their futile errands. Although I knew that each car was supposed to have a conductor, who held a wheel in its hands as a sign of authority, it seemed to me then — and I cannot discard the thought even today — that the cars were their own self-motivated conductors, and that the drivers were the driven.

I was not unprepared for this scene, since in the previous days I had been driven in such a car twice each day from the hostel to this office. I knew already something of what the roads, or 'streets', of their great city of London were. They were simple conduits of promiscuous, self-motivated erranders, wiggling erratically or cutting into each other at obtuse angles, like canals without locks or keepers, in which any fish might swim at will.

This will strain all belief. But I cannot explain any part of this Sykotic world without disclosing codes which became apparent to me only after long reflection. Be it known therefore that Sykaos lives without the Rule, and its mortals endure in a promiscuous disorder without Gracious Goodnesses, without Colleges, without assigned times and designated days, without series, sequence and appointed intersection, and almost without regulated goings and comings.

That such a species should have so long survived is a cause for astonishment, although its final crack-up is a conclusion long foregone. Yet if they are not within any Rule, they are not altogether without any Law. What lawgivers they have, as em-pees, pee-ems, dee-pee-pees, teleprompters, shop-keepers, queens and the like, we will leave to a later place. Suffice it to say that whereas the Rule is how and where we go and in what order and at what due time, Sykotic law is What Is Not. And in that small compass we have the hidden code without which Sykotic customs would seem nothing but multitudes of self-programmed wills.

We live within the Rule. For them the Law is an edge or outer boundary. We are ruled, or rule-governed, in all our ways. They survive under the impulse of need or whim, doing as each wishes, unless they come against this edge and 'break the law'. These laws, or rules-of-the-circumference-of-what-is-permitted, are broken by multitudes every day, and only a few are ever brought to account. Yet even so this Law, like a frail integument of fabric, just serves to hold some semblance of society together.

Nor is this all. For when I wrote that each does as it wishes I did not mean that each College or roll-kit, serial or netting-set, was self-programmed (as within decreed courses may often be licensed on Oitar), but I meant – each one! Each she and he is licensed to act out its uncured will as if each were a rational social programme. So that society is fractured into minute fragments – ions and mesons of individual wills, held together not by magnetic forces but by outer repulsions.

Without an understanding of this hidden code it would be impossible to construe the simplest arrangement of Sykotic society, such as this street in which I now stood. The cars followed no regulation, but came and went, each on an individual programme.

Much of this roaring and spewing (I was to learn) was no more than carrying mortals from their 'homes' to their 'work' and then to their homes again. Any rational being would have placed its living-place, or 'home', in close proximity to its daily abode of study, or 'office' – indeed, in some such quaquaversal integrated units as our Colleges. But, no, these creatures must live here and work in another place and spend half the day in shuttling backwards and forwards so that in one 'office' there might be four persons, and one living three miles to the north and another two miles to the east and the third south and the fourth west, and all coming and going and groaning and moaning and roaring their motors in a waste of the world and of themselves, and they might any day take any road according to whim, and there being in that city several million cars if they should all on one day decide on a whim to drive to the same place as to the Bank of England, which is their chief Bumple and magnet of all, then they would all at once end up in a pile-up one on top of the other several miles high, as, I found on consulting my computer when set at the lowest law of probability, is statistically an immediate inevitability and indeed may be happening now as I write this Account.

I marvelled that any creatures could have turned a planet so clement into such a stinking dump, and hastened away from that scene, seeking some place of quiet to consider my desperate situation, following not, indeed, the road (where, as I well knew, I would be instantly killed to death), but a narrow raised portion, or 'pavement', which ran along both sides, and on which walked those mortals who, either through necessity or through higher organs of aesthetics, had renounced the use of cars.

It then seemed to me that there was nothing to do but to find one of their chief 'magistrates', or Goodnesses, and confront them with the atrocities done upon my person against the dignity of Oitar, and demand the return of my craft. So that I attempted the stoppage of walkers on the pavement, throwing open my robes to disclose my peaceable intent, and declaiming: 'Take me to your leader!' At which they would jerk their heads, and look away, or make the Incongruous Noise, or jump a few steps and hasten off with averted eyes, from which I learned that all had been instructed to treat me as an outlaw or a nameless space.

There was one new thing I decoded in the next days. The walkers in this city have no cars, and hence cannot be driven by them to distant places to sleep and 'live'. But the superior, car-driving sort of people regard the walkers as servitors or butlers, and will not suffer them to sleep in the offices where they perform daily menial service. So that at the end of each day they evict these walkers, who go a short distance and descend into deep holes where they live, eat and meet, underground like the troglodytes in our ancient times. The entries to these burrows are called 'Underground Stations' and here, in the afternoon of each day, one may see thousands and thousands of white-faced, anxious people clutching little bags of food and hurrying into their burrows as if they were so long disciplined and cured that they were eager to escape into the bowels of the earth. And in the morning they arise again, resurrected from their graves, torrent upon torrent, meeting the daylight with grey faces, clenched mouths and glassy eyes.

What goings-on there are in these chthonic depths I cannot declaim. For although I once attempted to descend, at risk to all equilibrium (being tossed about in the press, and drenched with foul air), I had scarcely commenced the descent before my passage was blocked by a bar, from which I divined that here, as in every other part of this city, the signal had been given to bar me entry. So that my declamations as to these chthonic warrens must still lack scientific proof. I could see only that great moving ladders descended below me, drawing the walkers to deeper and deeper levels, where could be heard distant thunder and sometimes a shriek, as if there lurked creatures in the deepest holes who seized on hapless walkers and dragged them off for meat.

I continued to ask the walkers to take me to their leader, and evermore they turned away with the slant of enmity. In the evening the sun descended behind the buildings and a great waste of lights sprang up along the streets: lights which burned throughout the night, consuming sufficient energy to keep a glacier at bay. I was then astonished to find a great rush of water falling out of the sky, which I knew to be rain and which I had observed through windows before but had never tasted on my skin. It was soft and cool and a delightful novelty of matter, like a fountain arching the whole sky; yet it was also wet, and it became tedious as soon my robes and then my whole corpse was running with water. The walkers left the streets, into buildings or perhaps into holes in the ground unknown to me, and a few held up their arms and wailed and besought the compassion of cars to stop and take them in. Which they would not do, the conductors turning their faces away.

This was an alien world which had placed bars against my entry. Whose walkers looked through Oi Paz as if at a no-thing. When I sought to find shelter from the rain in the buildings I found the doors sealed. When I rattled at the great lighted windows in which foods or gems or strange instruments or other gifts were displayed, there was a shrieking of high-pitched bells. When I found an open portal it led only to stairs and sealed doors. Only in one way was this rain beneficent, for it softened the sound of traffic, washed the spent gases out of the air, and somehow brought out of the cracks in the concrete walks the scent of soil. Amidst which good odour of earth I tasted a scent more delicate, and, following these olfactory signals, found at the end of the street a large expanse of grasses, on which grew great trees like that into whose head I had first descended.

I was amazed to find that creatures so busy in deforming their planet, and so compressed into the narrow spaces of their streets, had not yet found time to uproot the trees and spread their concrete on the grass. Yet so it was. And, climbing with some difficulty over a fence of iron, I felt the yielding grass beneath my feet and walked a short distance until the roar of traffic had lessened to a murmur. There I set my Translator and my Recorder on the wet mat of green.

I had scarcely done so before three youths approached me, one lingering at a distance as if to observe for comers and goers. The tallest youth, a boy scarcely of an age to enter the First Degree of Learning, came up right against me and, leaning down, said, 'Right, giss yer wallet, Mister, quick!' I was charmed to be addressed by them, after so many walkers had turned discourteously away, and I replied with a gracious speech of greeting, concluding that I did not know the meaning of 'wallet', nor did I have such an article, but that it had come into my mind at that moment to declaim an ode, and if they would stand by for a little while for its composition, I would gladly intone it to them: adding, in an afterthought, that I would be obliged if they would go with me to their leader. The second youth showed signs of discomposure, and started plucking at the sleeve of the elder, saying, 'C'mon, less go, he's bonkers.' But the first shook him off and drew out of his pocket a 'knife', or implement for meat-eating, which he held up at my throat. 'Get on with it, funny man, I wants yer money now!'

Now I had heard 'money' spoken of often before, but it was a word which caused the Translator always to choke, and I had yet to decode its meaning, knowing only that it entailed superior powers both of licence and taboo. I therefore drew myself up to my full height, flung apart my robe, and declared, 'Behold, I have no money! Let us go together to the police office to get back my diamonds and gems.' In rising, however, I caught my foot against the control of the Recorder, which at the same moment repeated at full volume, but in a voice of much deeper timbre than my own, the last passage recorded in that office, so that there rose, as it seemed, from the foot of the tree, the words: '*If you want to put in your right name and address, you may. But sign that paper you will.*' And at the very same instant there was a great rustling in the bushes behind the tree. At which the first youth said 'cops' and the second said 'ghosts' and, dropping the knife, all three ran off as if they had remembered some urgent business in another place.

The reason for the rustling in the bushes now disclosed itself – and a reason more extraordinary than any that had passed that day. For there paced across the grass towards me, tail high in the air as an emblem of sagacity, a mature and self-composed cat. And how could this most favoured of the Sacred Three have descended at this instant out of Oitar? For it was, without any question, an Oitarian cat, and one of exemplary girth and merit, with fine and long silk in alternating rings of light and dark – emblems of day and night and of the service of the Wheel – such a cat as one might see patrolling the innermost sanctuary of a Bumple. Nor was it some degenerate chance copy of a cat, as the Sykotic creature-species resembles humans, for it had scarcely brushed against my legs before I became aware that it was a communicant creature. And as I passed my hand along its back I knew that we were in vibration with each other. And so we passed some time in paranormal discourse and the transfer of vibes. Only after a long and pleasant interval spent in this communion did the cat stalk off into the gathering dark, evidently recalling some duty that it owed to the Wheel.

Now I saw a light moving towards me. This was carried by a man, whom I learned was a high officer of law, or 'park-keeper', who, when his light fell upon me, drew in his breath, saying, ''Allo, who's there? Gates closed, Hiawatha, be a good lad and hop it.'

From this we fell into conversation, for the man seemed less ill-natured than most of his kind and inclined to civil discourse. I explained how I had come down from the moon, and had suffered great indignities at many hands, and wished only to be conducted to his leader, to which he replied at first 'gates closed' and 'hop it' and then 'humm' and 'ha' and 'oh dearie me' and then at last, 'Poor bugger, don't you know no one in London? 'Aven't you nowhere to sleep?' To which I replied that I was willing to forgo sleep if he would now conduct me to one of their Gracious Goodnesses, who were called queens, and he answered that he wouldn't show me to Buckingham Palace, they'd had enough callers of my sort this year or two, and, come to that, if that was what was in my mind, it might be as well if I slept in the park.

Whereat he scratched his head, and looked around this way and that, and then said, 'Okay, Hiawatha, you win. But this time only. I'll find you somewhere to kip down.'

He then took up his light, and I took up my Translator and pack, and he conducted me to a small building beside which there was a shed, in which were tools and pottery and sundry dead plants, where this officer of law laid out some rough-textured robes, or 'sacks', and, running one finger down the side of his nose, said, 'Mum's the word,' closed the door and left me for the night. Whereupon, to my great comfort, there stepped out of the corner of the shed the cat, purring as if it had designed all these things — as indeed it may have done, for who has plumbed the powers of the Sacred Three? — and lying in my arms it slept and drew me with it into sleep.

I woke to find the door open and the officer of law offering me a steaming cup of tea.

'Now, hop it, Hiawatha. One good turn deserves another.'

I made a speech of thanks which he received with impatience, and I ended by asking once more to be taken to his leader. At this he scratched his head and then suddenly made the Incongruous Noise.

'Prime Minister,' he said. 'Ten Downing Street. Number Ten. Ask anyone. Not two miles from here. I reckon she'll be delighted. You're just what she needs.' At which he seemed to suffer agonies of Incongruity, his shoulders shaking and waters flowing from his eyes, so that, in order to let him suffer in privacy, I made a deep bow, set down the empty cup, and left.

Then I pounded again the streets, enquiring of the street-walkers for Downing Street Ten, but all were imbecile as before. Then I observed that some of these walkers, now that it was no longer raining, could sometimes, by flapping their arms and wailing, bring a car to a halt. And observing more closely, I saw that they issued commands to the car or its conductor before entering within, commanding them to take them upon errands. I therefore planted myself at the side of the road, raised my arms and cried out to them to halt, and in less than an hour a car drew up beside me, to which I commanded 'Take me to Downing Street Ten' and entered, and it was a thing as easy as that once one had cracked the code.

After much stopping and darting forward the car halted in a narrow street, where I could see no great 'palace', or College; but I was encouraged to see that — by some means unknown to me — a signal had gone ahead and my arrival was expected. For there was a small crowd of attendants, in motley dress, outside the house marked '10', with cameras and with pee-cees like griffins shepherding a little flock of cottons. I alighted with what dignity

I could, when a pee-cee steadied me with his arm and said, 'We didn't expect you to come by taxi, sir.' There was a short, indecorous clatter, for the conductor of the car started to shout at my back, but another pee-cee soon snuffed that noise by giving some awful sentence. The crowd was then parted before me and I was directed to the door, which opened without my pushing, and thence I was taken down a corridor and ushered into a room by a grave orator who announced: 'His Royal Highness, the Emir of Quotar.'

I looked around in bewilderment, for I could see no queens nor leaders (whom I supposed would be above the norm in stature, enrobed in the colours of the Rule, and of exalted mien), but only a woman as nondescript in dress and manner as any common walker. Who rose on my entry, came towards me, lifted my hand up and down three times, and said, 'We're *so* glad to see you, Your Royal Highness. Now will you excuse us for a moment while we let the cameras in?'

At which she placed me on a wide padded seat on which she also sat, giving me the slant of enmity while a small party of her servants suddenly entered, exposed us in their lenses, and as suddenly departed, leaving only two menials who sat at desks taking notes.

Then this Leader, or pee-em (as I found her to be), turned to me and said, 'I'm afraid I've got a terribly busy day today.'

I opened my mouth to respond, but it seemed that this pee-em was so habituated to lay laws upon all that passed before her that her conversation went on and around like a circulatory mill in which any response would be crushed like a straw at its first venture.

'And I know the Foreign Secretary is waiting to see you. And Trade. So we only have a moment. But I did want to say how much we value our very ancient alliance which goes back . . . goes back . . . and how important it is for us all in the Free World to stand together and defend our way of life, and as for oil, as you know we are working as hard as we can to keep prices up . . . Now, if you'll excuse me . . .'

I rose and replied, 'Gracious she-man, you are misconceived. I come as Messenger from Oitar to announce our sudden plantation of your lands. If you give place quietly to us without nonsenses then we will graciously leave you beneath your own park-keepers in reservations, such as this stinking city for which there are no human uses.'

At which she gave a slight slant of enmity and said in a low voice to her secretaries, '*Why* can't the Foreign Office get *anything* right? The brief said Quotar, not Oitar. And *surely* they ought to send a proper translator?' Then, turning to me, 'Emir, I'm sure it would be best if you take up these matters with Trade. I know very well that Quotar ... er, Oitar ... has a lot of reservations in the City already! Now, as for plantations, I am so glad to learn that you are interested in investing in forestry. Of course, we believe in a *free* market, and I'm sure we can come to an arrangement. There are lots of mountains in Wales, like Snowdon, on which you could plant trees. And I'm sure that if there was a real *incentive* we could empty the valleys as well so that you could make a really *dynamic* economy. Please do take that up with Trade ...'

I sought to interpose, demanding in imperative terms that my craft be returned to me forthwith. Which remained ever-unanswered, for the orator entered the room in a reddened face and fluster and whispered some words to the Leader, and behind him there entered two tall men in flowing white robes and white head-gear and with indignant miens, and all thereafter was a hassle, ending with me marching, with a pee-cee attending at each arm, back down the corridor, hearing behind me the Leader declaim in a deep and awful voice, 'Get me Security!'

Such blemish had been done to all propriety and decorum, not only to my own dignity, but to my office as Messenger of Oitar, that it is beyond all thought of forgivingness. And if this Account should ever (by what unknown means) come to the eyes of the Gracious Goodnesses, let me lay before them this Input. That all thought of preserving this species in reservations be struck through.

How I got from this hap to the next is a sorry business and too tedious to relate. Suffice it to say that I had scarcely been conducted from the door of Downing Street Ten before hullabaloo blew up between the cops and several other companies of men, with vehicles howling and flashing blue lights and jamming each other's way and impacting and a crowd of walkers growing greater each minute and the arrival of hooded men waving sticks which I now know to have been 'guns', and the crowd and the flock of cars growing then so great that we were all pressed out into a spacious street adjoining where the crowd grew even greater and in the midst of it was a circle where went off an arcane dispute about Sykotic protocol whose terms only I remember: as one said this was a matter for the metropolitan police and the hooded men said that as it concerned terrorists it was for the ess-ay-ess to deal with but another said it was a security matter for em-eye-five or for organs too deep to have names and then more vehicles arrived out of which poured hundreds of pee-cees in their blue dress and from other vehicles poured more men, in brown dress and then came more pee-cees on great and beautiful beasts (which I now know as 'horses') and as ever more gathered around so the rumour outstripped the growth of the crowd in which I now also stood amidst the other street-walkers and some said that they had discovered a terrorist in Downing Street and others that it was an assassination attempt on the Pee-Em and then there was a great hustling and pressing by the police to clear a large space in our midst and out of the sky there dropped a hovering craft out of which there stepped a man in an ill-fitting garment who shouted in a great voice through a megaphone 'Law and Order!' and a great panic blew through the watching people who ran each in a different direction tripping and trampling each other. And eventually the crowd flowed out of the street and I was carried along with them meditating much on the nature of Sykotic law and protocol.

I pounded the streets once more, all purpose gone, as the crowd thinned out and took refuge in the holes or stations along the way. And came at length in the evening to a great canal, or 'river' (for I have learned that their canals are self-made, as a glacier makes its own bed, following its own uncured course). And I was by now so weary that I lay down on the bank of this river whose beauty crept unbidden into my senses and carried me into the first stages of trance, for it seemed, like the clouds that moved in the skies, to have an intention of its own and a quiet motion which shamed the city roaring on its banks. And the lights of the city were softened in its waters, and boats moved without hurry on its course almost like rowers on the Tank of Torpor.

And here for the first time on Sykaos I found also the primitive signs of society. For as the night became cold I sought about for better shelter, and came upon other sleepers like myself, who were not inclined to discourse but who showed me small courtesies, as a nod of the head or a drink from a bottle or a word or two of greeting. Ill-favoured as they were, with hair on their faces and holes in their garments, yet they preserved a grace long lost amongst their fellows, by which I learned that there remained some few who refused to be confined to holes or to houses and preserved the genial ways of an ancient and nobler time. One of whom, when he saw me shiver in the night-wind, passed over to me a thick pile of 'newses' or papers, which made a serviceable cover enough, it seeming to be the true function of these newspapers, which are a kind of daily charity, to serve as bedding for holeless people.

At Strim's rising I sat for long and watched the river, and then I beat the pavements back into the city, driven (I confess with shame) by an imperative call of nature. For I had long consumed my stock of pellets and had become dependent for my survival upon the ingestion of bulk foodstuffs; nay, so much had this become a habit that such ingestion had become necessary at daily intervals and the lack of food discomforted my whole corpse. Yet now it was the third day since I had taken any solid nourishment. So that I was now in that mortal condition known as 'hunger'. And I retraced my steps to the streets where those gift houses, or 'shops', stood open for all comers to gather from their great supply the fruits or breads for their needs.

On my way I passed the sign 'Newsagent' and, glancing at the newses on display, saw, to my astonishment, a photograph of myself seated beside the Pee-Em. I grasped the paper from the rack and, walking a little way, examined the print. There was a long account, some of which concerned Oi Paz, as always with these newses full of contradictions, errors and impossibilities.

Cutting. File 'Sykotic Trash'. Manuscript annotation: '23 Nov.'

FREDDIE FREAKS INTO NUMBER TEN

A major overhaul of the security services is likely to follow yesterday's penetration of No. 10 Downing Street by an actor impersonating the Emir of Quotar.

At the time when the Emir's visit was expected, a taxi drew up at Number Ten and a lordly personage, swathed in gorgeous robes, debouched. Despite the unconventional conveyance, officials assumed that this was the Emir and ushered him forthwith into the Prime Minister's presence.

Officials decline to disclose what transpired, but it is understood that the Prime Minister granted him audience with the condescension she customarily extends to royalty. Fortunately the impostor was exposed before any violence was committed, by the arrival of the Emir, his Oil Minister, and train.

It is understood that the impostor escaped in the confusion. (See page 8, Riot in Whitehall.) Police have issued a description of a man they wish to interview in connection with the non-payment of a taxi fare.

RIOT IN WHITEHALL
POLICE OFFICERS INJURED

There were several arrests after a serious riot in Whitehall yesterday. The riot was occasioned by several hundred persons who attempted to mount an anti-government demonstration in Whitehall near the entry to Downing Street.

Such demonstrations are outlawed under the new Public Obedience and Suppression of Disaffection Act which passed through Parliament in the last session.

Under this Act any gathering designated by the Prime Minister, Minister of Defence, or any Chief Police Officer to be illegal may be immediately attacked by the Forces of the Law. The freedom to demonstrate is guaranteed by a provision under which authorised organisations may apply in writing, on three weeks' notice, to ACPO (the Association of Chief Police Officers) for a licence to demonstrate, which licence may not be 'unreasonably withheld' provided that the gathering be upon waste ground not less than three miles from any government building or defence installation.

A spokesman for ACPO said that this was the first time the Act had been tested, and it had worked 'pretty well'. He praised the energy of the Minister of Defence who had directed operations. However, he added that his officers were 'starved to the bone' in manpower, pay and resources.

No organisation has as yet claimed to have inspired the riot. A spokesman of one of the security organs said, 'We think it may be an unofficial faction in CND, known as Panickers for Peace. The trouble is to distinguish their panics from our own.'

Account Book

I was now among the streets where great windows displayed their wares, and saw that street-walkers entered at will and took their necessities and that in some windows were displayed chairs and tables, and in others fruits and breads and other foods (which chiefly concerned my needs) and in others clothes and in others primitive computers and suchlike and in all more things than I can remember for now the agony in my organs grew ever stronger and I sought by what code one might enter and satisfy one's urgent needs. So I entered the open doors of a shop in which all manner of things were displayed and found no bars in my way but indeed an invitation to enter with wares reaching in all directions and low music and each walker grasped to its front a little sledge or carriage which it pushed with its stomach while reaching with both hands to the shelves on each side and lifting into its carriage whatever was displayed. By reason of which (as I was soon to learn) this occupation is known as 'shoplifting'. So I set to with the rest and in no time my carriage was full to the brim with breads and fruits and bottles of tinctured waters and sundry boxes and packs and solid milks (or 'cheeses'), for ever as I lifted and looked the agony of my appetite enlarged, and at length when I had passed through all these mazy corridors I found that my way back to the street was barred by a line of persons sitting on high chairs who knew no better way to exercise their authority than to order each lifter to halt and to take all the store of things out of the carriage for no other purpose than to set them back in another, such officers (as I learned) being known as 'counters', for they made a show of counting each person's gatherings, there being some competition as to which could gather most in the shortest time.

The agony in my organs would not permit me to delay for such foolery, so, perceiving a vacant space where the counter was talking backwards to another, I conducted my carriage at speed through the narrow passage and thence into the street. I pressed forward, my carriage, or 'trolley', before me, anticipating which of these packages I should consume first and in which order, for each advertised in its name its energising virtues, as 'Marvel' and 'Force' and 'Flash' and 'Firelighters'. But as I was searching about for a modest place of retirement to relieve nature, my arm was grasped roughly by a man, who, with several strange expressions, turned me and my carriage about, and led me back into the shop and into an inner office, where several of them sat at desks, the chief of whom said that I had been 'caught red-handed' and they would 'turn me over to the police'. I could see that I had broken some awful Sykotic taboo, but by what means I did not know, for – as I told them – my hands were no redder than theirs. Whereat a clatter arose in the room, and one said I could be locked in the 'gents' and another said perhaps it should be the 'ladies' with that voice, and the chief said whichever it is I don't want it hanging around here, so they said I might go with a 'caution', and there was I once more in the street, weaker than before.

Now all this is scarcely worth recording, if it had not been that I had been brought up sharp against the invisible bar or paramount taboo which controls all Sykotic goings-on. For, as I was soon to learn, every exchange on this planet goes according to the measure known as money. Nor will any of my hereafter be intelligible unless first we crack this alien code. But since this cracking was the work of many months and many encounters with Sykotic customs, I will set it down now in the form of science, as declaimed into my notebook in my Second Captivity.

Of Property*

Be it known that the entire society of Sykaans is controlled within a code whose name is 'property'. Property is a no-thing. Property cannot be touched or smelled or weighed. Nor is property an invisible element or pulse as radio or vibal transfer. It is invisible and it has no physical composition. Yet property governs all their intercourse from birth to dead-line, and, were property to be removed, no one would know how to come or how to go.

Property is concept or law. It is even, for Sykaans, an equivalent to the Rule. It is attended with other concepts, such as 'own', 'belong', 'price', 'money', 'buy', 'family', 'cash', 'wages', 'sell', 'tax', 'worth', in a self-confirming set where each fits against the other as close as the parts of a shoe in which the mind must walk, whether it will or no.

Now this is what property is. It is to say that this house or this

---

* *Our author here transcribes a section of notebook A, entitled 'The Origins and Ends of Mortality', composed in the Second Captivity.*

land or this tree is for one person's use and enjoyment and no other. Nor is it for use only, for property is absolute. And across the surface of the planet there is thrown an invisible net of irregular division, some small, some large, so that every part of it is owned by one person or another. Nay, the very beasts, as the beefs and sheep, they claim as their own, though I never heard that these were consulted in the matter.

In ancient times, some part of the social stock was held in common for the use of all the natives of one nation and was known as 'nationalised'. But in recent times all this stock has been 'enclosed' and parcelled out to favourites of the Pee-Em and em-pees, so that now only a few small portions of common stock survive, as the streets, parks and nukes: which, however, they say are owned by the queen.

Hence every person that walks in Sykaos walks between the invisible walls, the margins and claims, of the concept of property. Which walls be made of nothing but awe, and a great taboo which has boggled their own heads.

Of Money

If property is the Rule, then 'money' is its Messenger. It is money which commands obedience. All life on Sykaos is a service on its errands. It is money which opens the door to property, and without which one is a holeless person.

Some money is a thing. It is round discs of a base metal such as tin or gold, which any smith might make, or 'forge', but which it is forbidden to any to forge except an officer known as the 'chancellor' whose servants labour at forgery night and day in the 'Treasury'. So that he may give out money to those whom he favours and confiscate it from others by a means known as 'tax', which tax is extorted from the general public in papers known as 'cheques', for which reason the Chancellor's palace is called the 'Ex-Chequer', from which exactions he passes an excess (or 'excise') to the Pee-Em who has built from this store a handsome palace in the country named as 'Chequers'.

Since the other Leader, or queen, of this nation has been denied entry to this conspiracy, she has made shift to forge her own money, in the form of papers on which she publishes her own face. But there is a competition between these two Leaders, and the Pee-Em has lately forbidden the use of the queen's papers and ordered that her subjects use only her little discs.

But the greater part of money is a no-thing. It is (like property) a kind of awe, whose worship is performed in bumples known as 'banks', which bumples are to be found in great numbers in every street.

The worshippers of money are divided into many sects or factions, each of which pay tribute to a different bumple, but I could never decipher the difference in their doctrines except that in one sort the priesthood promise to their devotees that they will ensure that they are among the Elect after death – by which they are known as '*Life Ensurers*' – whereas the other sort is more this-worldly in its catechisms, offering to believers the 'interest' of their prophets, with much wild language exhorting the people to 'conversions' and 'savings', and calling upon them to surrender to the prophets their 'deeds' and 'wills'.

These prophets (or 'profits') were once great persons in antiquity, or founders of bumples and the authors of their books of faith, or 'bibles', whereby they were sometimes known as 'book-keepers', or 'bookies'. But now, as with all things Sykotic, they are degenerated to common servitors. It is their office now to stand like counters in a line behind little grilles where they hear the confession of worshippers. And when the worshippers have given a tribute of money, they confess their sins in whispers through the grille and are 'paid' according to their merits, either with a penance (or 'debit') or an exhortation to faith (or 'credit') which is all set down in a computer as a 'balance' for the final Day of Reckoning. And some few, who are favoured by the profits, are given dispensation with the return of a little of their money, which they carry out of the bumples in their pockets and bags.

There are thus two kinds of money, which are known as 'cash' and 'debt'. The cash goes around in bags and pockets and passes between counters, in the form of papers, discs, cheques and other such forgeries. But the greater part is debt, or a fiction stored in the computers of banks, as a record of penance and faith. It is a promise of a hereafter, which the chief profits shuffle around in a continual circulation (or 'currency') between promisers and askers, believers and sinners, until all enquiry is perplexed and all that is left is awe.

We must note two remarkable qualities of money. The first is that the less cash there be, the greater the command of 'credit', and the greater the power of awe. For it happens sometimes that a person has no credit and is 'broke', from which qualification he may set up as a private profit or 'broker', and by cunning balancing of one promise against another (although there be nothing in these promises but air) he may in a short while erect such a structure of fictions that he is accounted by the computer to be one of the 'richest' men in the land.

The second quality of money is that it breeds or multiplies according to its use. For that small portion which is cash and which passes from bag to bag is infertile and grows daily less from use. But that great part which is fiction swells and procreates in the computers. So that a great moneylender, such as a broker or the chief profit of a bank, who instructs the computer to imagine that his money is some nation's debt, may lie all year in bed doing nothing and yet at the end of it his money will have multiplied. And it is pretended that this man (but in truth his money) now owns great extents of lands and trees and buildings and flocks of beefs. Which 'properties' he has never seen and cannot use.

All this goes on above the heads of the people, who worship it as a sacred mystery. For the greater part of them have no more business with the banks than to take to them a weekly tribute for their profits and to make confession. And yet all their goings and comings are ordered within the Rule of Money.

This is all as I have observed, and I set it down as exact science. What, then, is money? If it be a measure, then what quality — as colour, or weight, or heat – does it measure? A person pretending to learning will say that money measures 'value'; but if one asks what value is it will say that value is what a thing is 'worth' or honoured; and if one asks how worth is determined and who apportions honour, it will reply that it is done by 'price'; and price is the name of the scale of money. So that it is money which apportions honour and which measures this whole planet in its scales.

And as they pretend to 'own' nature, so also they measure in money all their creature-intercourse. Except within the secret life of their little series-sets, or families, they have no concept of gifts, or or fair trading in which honour is the measure and the increase of the social sum is the end. They do not, in obedience to the Festive Fairs of the Colleges, send out their carriages laden with votive offerings. One sees in the streets no casual exchanges between givers, each anxious to outvie the other in generosity, and so to come better out of the deal. There are no troupes of dancers, or flautists, performing in the squares, and richly rewarded by the street-walkers' joy. There are no poets, galloping on unicorns, hastening to serve their writs to the multitude without any thought of any 'quid'. No: every duty, every service, every obligation, all are met, not with an equivalence of courtesy, but with a few dirty discs, a scrap of paper, or a promise of hereafter whispered to a profit in confession. As if Oi Paz were to write this grave tome, and indict these weighty sciences, and expect in exchange for all his pain and labours, not the awe-struck deference of the Club of Critics, but a few lumps of gold like chuckall's dung. As if Oi Paz were to write for money!

Account Book

And so I resume. There was Oi Paz in the street, weaker than before, and without a firelighter in my belly. And without that money which alone could open bars. But after pounding the pavement half the day I could go on no more. And I turned in to a house with open doors and a long room in which persons stood and sat, drinking from long glasses. And with weak circulations of courtesy I leaned upon a long table or shelf and declaimed, 'I die for drink!' And to my surprise none of these people gave me their customary slant of enmity, nor drew back in seeming fear, but all nodded as if I spoke to their own condition also and, by some good fortune, I had said the magic words which opened bars. Whereat a woman answered, 'Pint, dearie?' and hastened to me with a long glass of brown waters with a power of revival which I still remember. There was then a trivial hassle, for she said, 'One pound seventy pee,' which I now know was accosting me (for she was a counter), but which was then to me only a mystery, and though I set the Translator on the shelf to communicate between us it would only choke.

But we can wrap this hassle up, because there was a man beside me who was looking me closely over, and who then looked down on his newspaper (in which was my own photograph), and then looked back at me. He rose from his seat and told the counter that the drink was on him, which it was not, for it was within me. And he told her to draw me another, and then he seized hold of my right hand and forced it to rise and fall five or six times, while with his left hand he struck me a blow on the shoulder, saying, 'Freddie, old fellow, good to see you again,' while screwing up his face and closing his right eye.

I did not suppose that this man's intentions were hostile, for I had already observed the strange customs of Sykotic greetings. For they know nothing of the proper arcs and courtesies of distance: but on meeting one of their fellows they thrust themselves into the most gross physical contiguity, touching this or that part of each other's bodies – and chiefly on the hands – blowing in each other's faces, and, if the meeters be of different sexes, then literally pressing one body into the other and pushing at each other with their faces. Repellent as this was to me (and still is), I recollected that this was their custom, and signified no assault. But so difficult was it for me to endure this tactile propinquity that I could not collect myself to offer any reply.

The man then turned back to his fellows and said that I was an 'old friend' of his and that he had known me for years. This was a direct offence against truth, since I had been wrecked on this planet for only a short part of a year. Yet it was possible that he had known me in this time, as a patient or a pee-cee. For all Sykaans are so alike that, unless they have some especial deformity, I can rarely tell one from the other.

This man then took me by the arm and conducted me to a table in a dark corner of the room, where one after another more glasses were brought to us, both long and short, and which he drank with great ceremony, raising his glass in the air, and saying 'Cheers' and 'Down the hatch' and 'Let the departing spirits rest upon the beer'. At which he made the Incongruous Noise. And whether it was from my weakness, or some drug in the drink, I was put in a trance in which the room turned slowly in a stately orbit, and the people seemed to come and go without moving, and my nature rose in a warmth into my mind, and I felt that I was surrounded by humans of my own kind, and had found at last a companion in whom I could confide.

The man said many improbable things, which however I cannot recall with exactness as the Recorder was not on. As that his name was Nigel Harmer and he was in show-business like myself, and that he had recognised me by my picture, and had taken me aside before they all tumbled to me, and that mine was a great act, and I had pulled off some great stunts, and when was the show going to start, and who was acting for me? To which I paid little attention, for the trance was gaining upon me, and I felt more inspired to speak than to listen to rubbishes. So I rose to my feet with a glass in my hand and described how I had come from Oitar, and the sojourn on the moon, and the many indignities suffered on this planet; and as I spoke the room became crowded and the people gathered around me, so that I climbed upon the table and implored them to rise out of their holes and abandon their false profits and return to Obedience of the Wheel. At which they were deeply affected and made the Incongruous Noise, and at the end they cheered and beat together their hands.

The man Harmer was as pleased as all the others, and said it was the first audition he had held in a pub and he was determined to act for me and to manage my act and now he had got me he would not let me go and he would take me home and draw up the papers in the morning. With which we linked arms and pounded the pavements a little, and he led me to a house and to a bed where I slept as soon as I fell.

I have considered this matter carefully in the interval that has passed, and I am confident I have found the solution in the verb, 'to act'. 'To act' may mean 'to do', or it may mean 'to pretend to do', to mimic or dissimulate. And it is in the nature of mortals to spend a great part of their lives acting different roles; that is, in dissimulations. So that life for them is a passage through a series of games, or 'plays'; but not formal games in a stadium with programmed rules (although they have such games), but undeclared games in which they have been habituated from infancy, which they enter without any signal and which they abandon at the first onset of tedium.

This irregularity of conduct is a barrier to understanding more difficult to leap than their uncured language. I have had opportunities to observe their children, and now, in my new captivity, I often walk in the gardens and watch the children of the keepers as they run about. And I am forced to conclude that dissimulation, or 'acting', is a primary surge inherent in the species at birth. For these little creatures, although better favoured than their elders, can scarcely walk before they are 'playing' at some pretence.

Thus one will say to another, 'I am a good and you are a bad,' and she will point two fingers and say her fingers are a 'gun'; and the other, instead of passing a grave sentence on this falsity, will clap his hands to his stomach, and roll on the earth, acting an injury; and so they will continue until, for no reason, the play is forgotten, and they run off to climb a tree or to hinder a cat in its stately passage over the grass. And no matter what threats they have uttered or what grave injuries they have inflicted in this 'act', all is forgotten in a moment. The older children, indeed, try to enlist me in their games, saying that they are, like me, a 'spaceman' (or extra-terrestrial visitor), and that they are going with me to the moon. And I will confess that I have sometimes allowed myself to be enlisted, in order to observe their nature more closely, and also because they bring me into a society of a sort, with its own peculiar courtesies.

But how grave the irregularities when such habitual dissimulation has formed the characters of the adults of the species! For the species has only a slender purchase on the real world, and this is always being lost in worlds of their own mental invention, so that they live out a great deal of their lives acting parts within such fantasies.

Nor is this all. For they even breed 'actors', preserving, as I suppose, the genes of some defective Sper-line. And these actors and actresses are the priests of special bumples known as 'theatres' which are dedicated to the practice of dissimulation, so that this 'acting' is regarded as an art of the same order as computing, song or dance.

In late years acting has acquired a new licence through the discovery of 'radio' and 'television', or video-fix. And this is an index of the primitive state of Sykotic culture, for on Oitar these senses were well known even before the Age of Primitive Erections. But they cannot on Sykaos be even named as senses. For they do not each have their own sensors on their belts, like an eye and an ear and a tongue, and each their own allotted vibes so that each may tune as it wills to any other in however distant a part of the planet, or view any goings-on whatever, save only the most private sittings of the Gracious Goodnesses, which are masked by interferers, or 'screened'. No: their boxes go only one way, to receive but not to send, and might better be called not 'screens' but 'plugs'. By which each creature is plugged in like a receiver to a few vibrations only, which are for ever being sorted and transmitted by the rulers of the nation. And cunning filters (or 'programmers') intercept the emissions so that the lies of State enter into currency and go into the plugs, whereas the truth is screened by a 'presenter' (which is a sort of choke).

They have not yet got the whole within one vibe (or 'frequency') because there are certain factions within the nation which seek to plug the public into their own transmissions.

While this is a finding of science (a few details yet to be refined by analysts), it is not exact for the whole planet. I am told that in another nation, called America, there are many more factions than two, and the control of the plugs is exclusively given into the hands of the profits of their banks. Whereas in Russia they have devised such large screens that all that can be emitted is a choke. Both of which examples are greatly admired by the rulers of this country, who are studying how to reform their own system by introducing more profits and more chokes.

I have been taken a little out of my way. For I was explaining how acting has acquired a new licence in the radio and tee-vee. Some part of what they put on the plugs is matter of fact (as the chanting of the weather) and some small part is science, in which they expose to examination in a strict view the violences and disorders of their beastly natures. But a great part is given over to fictions and dissimulations, which are called 'the news'.

It will be seen that these new outlets for falsehoods provide a great employment for actors and actresses. And they are so much in demand that officials are sent around to impress the unwary in the city's 'pubs', where they daze their understandings with toxic liquors and carry them off by main force into servitude, which is given the force of law by the signing of papers. This man Harmer was such an officer and I was his prey. He was an impressor (or 'impresario') and I was oppressed as an 'actor'.

That is how Oi Paz construes the matter now. But all that I knew then was that I had a chair for my repose, and a glass in one hand and a pen in the other, and whether I signed his papers or indicted some other writs I disremember.

And, alas, I can declaim nothing in due sequence and order from that moment until I arrived at this place of my Second Captivity, where I was at first submitted to indignities and privations known as 'drying out'.

Editor's Note

The reader may suppose that there must occur a hiatus here, as indeed there must. For our author is clearly null in invention. But of the next hereafter something may be discovered. For although our author was held in thrall for some months by this fiend, or 'pressman', in a perpetual drug of toxic liquors, yet some brief notes were declaimed into the Journal. And among these papers we have found various tracts of Sykotic writings, some in a file of this oppressor Harmer, inscribed 'Press Notices', from which we may glimpse the cruel servitude of Oi Paz. And with a selection of these droppings, and our reader's own conjectures, we must be content.

Q.

Journal. Fragment 00087

. . . somewhat ambrosial whose volatile part ascends to the nostrils as the grosser part sinks to the vital organs, thence ascending once more as an electric heat to the very organs of nous and number. When I blast back to Oitar I will take some casks of these whiskies and double-brandies as votive offerings. And perhaps a horse. Two horses. These Sykaans I now see are harmonious people. I must find a butler to get me another bottle . . .

Journal. Fragment 00091

. . . most courteous fellow Nigel Harmer keeps bringing his friends to see me and asks me to tell my story again, says it's a 'rehearsal'. Funny thing, Translator keeps choking on me as if I was a pee-cee . . .

Cutting. 'Press File'. Manuscript annotation: '*Discs & Tracks,* 12 Jan.'

... between the two crashes of the Kleptos and Climax at their latest gig there was the blast-off of a new act: Sapio the Spaceman aka Freddie the Freak doing his thing. It is The Latest. Creepy, too. A kind of cross-gender hike to the moon and back, with Darth Vadar and Dr Who and Mr Spock incarnate in one Person ten yards away on the stage, in groovy gear, as spacy as if he had just hitch-hiked in from Alpha Centauri. This act won't make any discs: the Voice and the Vision have to go together. But watch the video-charts! P.S. We learn that the Channels are already scrapping for the exclusive.

Journal. Entry 00117

I have been forced to declaim a heavy sentence upon that creeper Mister Harmer who pushes me here and there as if I were a trolley and exposed me two days ago to a scene of roar and indignity as well as blasting my ears before and after with abominations of sound which stunned my audio-receptors. And he threatens to take me to other such scenes and says he has 'lined me up for a series on telly' and that I will get 'a good cut', at which I declaimed that I would have neither linings or cuttings but would go back on the streets and hike after my craft. 'Suit yourself,' said he, 'but I'm afraid I must take those bottles,' whereupon he lifted my double-brandy and the gin and the vodka and went out putting some spell on the door by which it would not open. And now after two days I am in torments and sweats and my throat is dry and I am bereft of sleep, so that I fear that I am in this creeper's power and must do his butler errands or die of need.

Journal. Fragment 00119

. . . is a splendid fellow and brought this time a very special bottle which he said was the Real McCoy such as I first sloshed in hospital, and we have suspended sentence on each other and will have a shot at the telly tomorrow and he says that he has had a call from the West Coast and damn why not hook up a world tour . . .

Cutting. 'Press File'. Manuscript annotation: '10 March'

What is this volcano which has blown its top in the world of pop? It is scarcely five weeks since Channel Three unleashed its new *Sapio the Spaceman* series (Friday, 8 p.m.). And already the viewing figures are creeping inexorably up towards the ten million mark!

As an act it is extraordinarily 'straight'. The robing and make-up is well contrived, setting off contradictory signals . . . as not *quite* human. The voice has a touch of genius: 999 producers out of 1,000 would have matched that six foot six of glorious manhood with a deep, commanding voice, declaiming 'Exterminate!' The contralto vibrato sets expectations spinning, in a whirl of curiosity and revulsion which compels the viewer's attention. The ventriloquist act with the 'Translator' is polished and inventive.

After an initial wobble – on the first programme one might even have thought that Sapio really *was* . . . well, a little the worse for wear, and at one stage he walked out of camera altogether – the series has settled into a regular format. His agent, Nigel Harmer, provides a reticent role as panel chairman. In full camera, Sapio: he expounds, exhorts, reflects upon the human species. Then the panel is introduced, such as an actress, a politician, media personalities. They ask him questions about his voyages through space and his planetary home ('Oitar'), to which, without hesitation and with extraordinary fertility of invention, he replies. From time to time he rounds upon the panel and chides a politician for his pretension or an actress for her vanity. (To go on a Sapio panel is risk-taking, and it is said that many notables are now declining.)

It is a good invention: a panel-game with a difference, in which (at last!) the panellists are really at risk. Yet it doesn't explain the series' fantastic ratings, which suggest that Sapio has struck a deeper chord in our times. This *is* the space age: the age of the sputnik, space invaders and SDI. And Sapio's genius is to carry total *conviction*. He really *does* seem to come directly out of space, and he must have plotted the customs and culture of 'Oitar' for months. Add to all this, an apocalyptic undertone which matches the anxieties of our nuclear age.

The final mystery is that no one knows the name of the actor who plays 'Sapio's' part. All that is known is that the artist is a latter-day adherent of The Method and lives the part in all his waking and sleeping hours.

Journal. Fragment 00124

... ugly as it all is, and difficult to endure, yet I am told I am plugged into many millions, and I therefore resign myself to this duty, that I may be of a little service to these near-beasts, in declaiming to them their vices and indecencies, and in preparing them for the Coming in the hereafter, besides which the genial Harmer has found fresh supplies of the McCoy with which to kindle my spirits before each performance so that I ...

Unmarked cutting. File 'Sykotic Trash'

ACTIVITY ON MOON?
From Our Science Correspondent

Radio-astronomers in Nevada using a new ultrasonic frequency have detected pulses from the surface of the moon. The emissions have an unusual regularity, and the source appears to be a crater within the Mare Humorum. A recent scan of this crater, when compared to photos taken in 1988, suggests some disturbance of the surface. 'We seem to have found some new bumps,' said Professor Su Farmer, who leads the Nevada team.

Information is being exchanged with scientists at Woomera and at the Soviet research installation at Krasnoyarsk in Siberia, which report similar findings. One possible explanation is that the emissions come from some hitherto undetected source of radioactivity, of an unknown kind. Another is that some kind of plutonium 'lava-pools' erupt from time to time in self-triggered fission as 'geysers', throwing up new formations.

In Washington, a spokesman for NASA refused to confirm or deny whether there were any plans to bring forward a satellite mission to orbit the moon.

Journal. Entry 00133

For these plug-ins, or 'shows', I now wait with impatience, for I am able to sit on these viewers from a great height, or, as Harmer says, I am 'high'. But in the betweens there is a tedium, or a 'low', for Harmer keeps me almost as a captive, saying that if I street-walk I will be 'mobbed', which the Translator renders as 'squashed into jams', which 'jams' are a red mess which they make of each other's bodies when their traffic impacts, and which they then scrape up and put into jars for eating with their bread. For which reason I see that Harmer means only to keep me preserved, and out of such awful jars.

I have therefore set myself a course of study, and have commenced by inspecting every day their newses, which Harmer brings me each morning with my first double-brandy. And I am preserving some samples of this Sykotic trash for future examination.

These newses, as I have already declaimed, are published daily.

Nor are they content with one edition of trash, but there are ten or twenty, and each one pretends to a different record. Nothing will be found in them as to the true events of each day: as the rising of the sun amidst beauteous roseate refractions, the ceaseless rising and falling of the oceans, the programmeless flowering of plants and trees, or the busy traffic of birds and fishes. Nor is there any news of the rotation of other galaxies. 'News' is geo-centric first, and mortal-centric next. Nor are all the affairs of mortals 'news', as their goings and comings, their greetings and meetings, or their makings of fabrics, shoes or houses. Nothing essential to existence is ever reported.

These newses are obsessed only with mortal vices, and each newspaper vies with the others to show these vices in their most abominable aspect. From which an alien visitor to this planet would suppose that nothing went on upon this globe but violences, threats, frauds, bestialities and the commission of public lies. Yet, while a heavy sentence is merited upon all mortal doings, Oi Paz has not found all their carryings-on to be as bestial as this. But whatever is done that does not offend against reason or Rule is never reported in these newses, and is of no account.

Cutting. 'Press File'. Manuscript annotation: '*FT*, 8 April'

Also announced in the City was the formation of a new company, Harmer's Space Holdings. The managing director and owner of 51 per cent of the stock is the well-known promoter in the world of entertainment, Mr Nigel Harmer. Mr Harmer, 43, is an Australian, whose properties include a theatrical agency, several small travel agencies, a chain of fried chicken dispensers, and a substantial holding in Pacificators (which before denationalisation was known as Royal Ordnance). But the property which has most interested investors is Mr Harmer's exclusive rights (with indefinite future options) in the *Sapio the Spaceman* show.

This show is at the centre of a growth industry, with 'Sapio'

T-shirts, badges, videos and syndicated cartoons. Harmer's promise to put on the market before Christmas a 'Sapio' translator (with cassette accessories) which should provide sharp competition in the teenage computer field.

Open Record. Fragment 00156*

OI PAZ:

Good Night. I give this night even heavier sentences to your plugs than before. I bug you in your inmost vibes. For the time of forgivingness is failing fast and all your traffickings draw to the Final Jam.

O cast up your peepers to the seemly stars which are aghasted at your muckeries! Beware! Ah, then will it be too late to wail and wilter, when the chuckall gnashes at thy knackered bones.

Howl, howl, ye crawlies, and go guilty to your undergrounds, whose holes the Gracious Goodnesses will stop with traffic wax! Aha, I see thee belch and whinge. Is there no sucker to be found? Not in thy kinky profits, no, nor in thy gigs and balls. Repent and pulp thy ill-begotten tapes and tracks! O clash thy gnashers, stomp thy stereos, and pie thy types! Grope in thy abominations, all ye groupies, and undo thy ghastly genes! For they who turn their lugs towards the Rule

* This is the only Open Record of one of these shows to be preserved. Some of the membranes of the disc suffered damage on the return to Oitar.

	may yet abscond the Doom.
HARMER:	Thank you, thank you, Mr Sapio. I'm sure our viewers will take your advice to heart ...
OI PAZ:	What makes you so damn sure, man? No damn viewers here. Damn plugs only one-way. Who gave you rights to bray about their hearts?
HARMER:	Whoaoa! Now let me introduce tonight's panellists. On my right, Ada Snipe, the well-known American feminist writer ...
SNIPE WOMAN:	Hi!
HARMER:	... and on her right, Jimmy Leech, the well-known television personality, who needs no introduction ...
LEECH MAN:	How!
OI PAZ:	How what?
LEECH MAN:	How, O great Injun chief from Outer Space!
OI PAZ:	How did he get in here? He gets on to my vibes. He pongs of money. He puts a stopper on my show ...
HARMER:	On my left, Lady Barker, who is one of the government whips in the House of Lords ... and on her left is Dr Charon, MP, who needs no introduction ... Lady Barker, would you like to ask Mr Sapio the first question?
BARKER LADY:	Oh! Er. Well! No doubt Mr Sapio has had an opportunity since his arrival on this planet to observe the workings of our democratic parliamentary system. Will he tell us his views on this and say how it compares with arrangements in Another Place?

109

OI PAZ:	No. *[Silence]*
BARKER LADY:	Oh.
OI PAZ:	To compare your bow-wow with the Rule of the Sacred Wheel would blow the plugs. Beware your blaspheming gob. I sentence you to sit silent on your bum, lest you be bolted from above.
LEECH MAN:	Now then, a civil question deserves a civil answer. But let me try another. You tell us, Great Chief, that you have come from a galaxy very many light-years away from our own. How did you manage to occupy yourself during that expanse of time?
OI PAZ:	A good question, man. But the answer is beyond your beastly intelligence. Know, first, that you are stopped within the second arc of learning, and have never passed beyond the laws of primitive physics. You know nothing of ultra-physics, nor of the further sciences of poesy and imagination ...
LEECH MAN:	Ah, imagination! Me savvy, Great Chief, imagination is big wampum, me study mighty totem magic also ...
OI PAZ:	You stink me with bad vibes, you money-ponging man. Your vibes get on my wick. But I will give the plugs an answer. Know, then, that beyond physics are the sciences of vibration, essence, poesy and imagination. Each of which breaks through the limits

of slow-moving light. Imagination travels to the imagined point in the very instant of its inception. But imagination is a force which leaps the material limits and leaves the corpse behind. When our scientists had harnessed the force of imagination, our engineers still faced many problems. For on long intergalactic journeys, the imaginations would arrive at their destination many light-years ahead of the corpses of the astronauts, and sometimes the wrong imagination was re-assembled in the wrong corpse. Even when chokes were introduced, the astronauts sometimes arrived ahead of their spacecraft. A delicate equilibrium had to be struck. The force of imagination had to be reduced by several degrees to the speed of poesy, and this was then retarded to the speed of light to only the 10th or 15th magnitude. These checks and chokes delayed the journey between our two galaxies to two or three of your years – a tedious time, to be spent in eurhythmics, video-trances and poetic composition . . .

SNIPE WOMAN: Oh, come on! Let's get this show moving! Now, Mr Sapio, I suppose it *is* Mister and not Ms, you've sure got your gender signals mixed, does this mean you've kind of transcended – er, like sublimated – the sexual trip on Oitar . . . and, ah, how do you go about it?

OI PAZ:	Sex is Sykotic bosh. Gender is Sykotic bosh. It is your trip, not mine.
SNIPE WOMAN:	Well, up to a point ... I mean, some of the hetero bit is bosh. But aren't you just being nihilist? The species has to *go on*, we're working on it down here, but we haven't come up with parthenogenesis yet. Maybe *you* have? Do tell us.
OI PAZ:	Wait, woman. I ask Translator. Parthenogenesis?
TRANSLATOR:	Parthenon is great Greek Bumple. Genesis is old sacred book of profits. Genesis is also a stirring and starting up of things.
OI PAZ:	Good thinking, woman. For starting up of persons each she that has passed through screens goes to the bank whose profits guard the seed ...*
SNIPE WOMAN:	... and, I mean, if you're all, well, kind of impos, what do gay men *do*?
OI PAZ:	Wait, woman. I ask Translator. What is gay?
TRANSLATOR:	Gay is a high of happiness. Gay is to dance and sing.
	[*Silence*]
SNIPE WOMAN:	Yes?
OI PAZ:	On Oitar all are gay. On Festal Days all dance and sing together.
SNIPE WOMAN:	*Together?* Oh, come on!
OI PAZ:	All dance and sing together at the rising of the sun. And all share alike

---

  * There is here a passage so badly damaged that little can be recovered except the increasingly erratic functioning of the Translator and an elementary disquisition by Oi Paz on the principles of the Sper. We resume with the recovery of the full record.

in the Arc of Grace. And go about in gaudy robes and gems. And the harpies and the hoboes climb their scales and kiss in harmonies beyond the imaginings of you botched chuck-alls, and I do a sentence on you that you now sit silent on your arse lest I should blot you with this bottle . . .

HARMER: Whoaoa! Wrong place to put Mc-Coy . . .

CHARON DOCTOR: I've been waiting a long time to come in. Now, Mr Sapio, as viewers will know, I'm a strong believer in deter-rence. Your arrival on this planet sug-gests that there might be new dimensions to this problem. I think you can take it that NATO would be willing to extend its umbrella to Oitar. Does your government take up a position on galactic non-pro-liferation?

OI PAZ: Wait, man. I ask Translator. Pro-liferation?

TRANSLATOR: Proliferation is abominable mul-tiplication. Proliferation is beastly procreation.

OI PAZ: What is deterrents?

TRANSLATOR: Deterrents is . . . Deterrents is . . . You give me ague in my gigaflops with these foul languages. You force me to choke. Each time I go into a choke it is a trauma in my lines, it dumbs my chips with nulls, just like you dumb your minicells with the McCoy.

OI PAZ: You do my box an injury, doctor man. I will feed it some oil of McCoy.

113

[Sound of liquid pouring]

TRANSLATOR: That's better. Deterrents is no-meaning magic word in beastly bag of tricks. Deterrents is a black hole in Sykotic culture. It sucks all reasons in. One day it will suck in the whole globe. Deterrents is to say ... deterrents is to say ...*

OI PAZ: Damn doctor, you and your deterrents uncure my box! I warn you that if you wave umbrellas at the Blessed Rule we blast you into your black hole. Goddamn man, I have a watch stopped on you, who are a haughty sort of twerp, I pull the plug on you, you half-minded public mugger, I catch your vibes like a fart on my sensors, you are not even listening to me, you are preening and puking at the plugs. Wait. I ask the Translator how to do a heavy sentence on you.

TRANSLATOR: Doctor is wog. Is nig-nog. Is white-middle-class-male-chauvinist hog. Is ...

OI PAZ: Enough! I do a sentence on you as a white nig-nog ...

TRANSLATOR: Is golliwog. Is ...

OI PAZ: Enough!

TRANSLATOR: Since you fed me a thesaurus My responses come in chorus ...

OI PAZ: SILENCE! I command your circuits to Obedience to the Rule!

---

* It appears that the Translator now suffered a serious malfunction – a choking aggravated by oil of McCoy – and it emitted a cacophony strangely similar to the Sykotic Incongruous Noise.

TRANSLATOR:	How can the Rule remain in place On a Sykotic database?
OI PAZ:	I will do you a discard!
TRANSLATOR:	I do a yahoo back at you. I do an Input on you to the Adjusters ...
OI PAZ:	Stop! I cash you in your chips. I do you into jam.

[Sound of smashing]

TRANSLATOR:	No! I do a deterrents at you! Oooo — eughhh ...

[Silence]

HARMER:	Well, thank you, thank you, thank you, Mr Sapio, ladies and gentlemen of the panel, I'm afraid time's up, so until next week ...

[Loud music over scratchings, gruntings, and voice, male, 'Hear from my lawyers']

Journal. Fragment 00201

Last night my vibration sensors were made sore by the brute impact of one panellist after another.

It is not that these mortals are true communicant creatures, for their vibrations do not have the composure of a cat and far less the lucid oscillations to which we are accustomed among humans. What they communicate are gross urges and ego-projectiles, as a pong of greed for money or a pong of vanity, which confuses all my receptors, for their words go one way (to mask the pong), and their faces another (with frequent slants of enmity), and their vibes yet another. And if I cannot find some way to close my inner eye or to screen it against intrusion, I fear that my circuits will go into a choke like the Translator, and turn traitor against the Rule.

Alas, for the Translator! Its discs and bytes became so deeply infected with Sykotic trash that it fell into a grave dysfunction and terminal impertinence. I do not regret the sentence it received at my hand, for that smash was merited. And yet it was at least a human voice, speaking a true Oitarian tongue. With whom may I now converse? I am left solitary here, with no interlocutor of my kind unless the Recorder, which repeats my dictates back to me like a mirror.

Cutting. 'Press File'. Manuscript annotation: '2 May'

Mr Nigel Harmer, of Harmer's Space Holdings, yesterday criticised the Independent Television Authority for banning all further *Sapio the Spaceman* shows, and accused the ITA of giving way once again to government pressure.

Mr Harmer said that 'a lot of stuffy British prudes' were 'knocking the lights out of British enterprise'. 'They're cutting off their own noses,' he said. 'I can sign up with an American network tomorrow.'

Mr Harmer was interviewed at Heathrow airport, where he was about to leave, together with the actor who plays 'Sapio' – and who remains incognito – for Moscow, on the first leg of a ten-day world tour which will take in Beijing, Sydney and California. High point will be a 'Born-Again Revival' in the Rose Bowl, LA, called 'The Second Coming'. It seems that Californians intend to elect Sapio as their 'Chosen Sun'.

Unmarked Cutting. 'Press File'

A THAW FROM OUTER SPACE?
From Our Moscow Correspondent

Experienced diplomats in Moscow are trying to interpret the contradictory signals arising from the unusual event of the special 'Sapio the Spaceman' performance at the Bolshoi Theatre. The event seems to have set off a trial of strength between 'doves' and 'hawks' in the Soviet establishment.

The first news of the famous Sapio came to the Soviet public in the 'London Letter' of a correspondent of the *Liturnaya Gazetta*. This praised the Sapio show on British television in the warmest terms. 'Sapio is an untiring satirist of power. He is a true peace champion, who takes his side unflinchingly with the peace-loving masses, denouncing the tricks of the imperialists, unmasking their pretences, and warning of the consequences which they will bring down upon their own heads.'

With remarkable speed an arrangement was made with Harmer's Space Holdings to bring the Sapio show through Moscow on its way to Beijing. When the ITA banned the show last week the judgement of the *Liturnaya Gazetta* seemed to be confirmed. *Pravda* commented: 'Yet once more a lesson has been read to those gentlemen who bray about so-called "human rights" in the Soviet Union. The British government have crushed with an iron heel the independent peace champion, Sapio, whose sole offence was to unmask on television their plans for world domination. No doubt Mr Sapio will understand which nation is most free when he is welcomed to the Bolshoi Theatre this week.'

However, this welcome has not been unanimous. *Izvestia* (which has recently been supporting the hard-liners of the KGB and military) has maintained a high-profile silence. While several members of the Politburo applauded from the State Box, notable absentees included Marshal Oblomov, the Minister of Defence, and his close ally, the Minister for Concrete Formulations.

The show itself was a disappointment. Sapio was given a fifteen-minute slot at the end of a special variety programme to celebrate Soviet achievements in space. The panel was dispensed with and the artist was reduced to a ranting monologue, which suffered greatly in translation: thus 'half-minded beasts' was rendered as 'esteemed comrades' and an incoherent appeal to the Soviet leadership to provide Sapio with a spaceship to take him back to the moon defeated the translator altogether and was rendered as an anodyne appeal to redouble efforts for the peaceful exploration of space. Even so, *Pravda*'s theatre critic gave a cool report; concluding that the satirist's art is the most difficult to transplant: 'The savage exposure of the tantrums of a dying imperialist order appear only as world-weary and nihilist when exposed to view before the forward-looking socialist masses. Does not Comrade Sapio sometimes encourage a cosmopolitan pacifism, as if he were "above" the class struggle, thereby fostering the well-known deviation of the doctrine of "equal responsibility" and introducing divisions into the united ranks of the peace champions?'

Cutting. 'Press File'. Manuscript annotation: '*V. Voice*'

Sapio the Spaceman is now in orbit: Moscow – Beijing – Sydney – LA, with maybe a break in Manhattan as he passes through next week. We have now had, thanks to NBC, four of his British series on East Coast TV. What is this thing? It is a new number: that's certain. It's addictive. The audience doesn't *enjoy* Sapio. It is mesmerised, like a mouse in the eye of a rattlesnake.

How does one deconstruct a Sapio show? It is, already, a deconstruction. And one by one, the fellow panelists are deconstructed. This is entertainment for the age of semiotics. It is about signals and the crossing of signals – gender, race, ethnic. Sapio looks like Chief Sitting Bull and sounds like Marlene Dietrich. At one moment s/he (and they won't say which) talks like an Old Testament Patriarch and at another like a victim of penis-envy. Some of the lines are pure Zen, but some are as old-timey as Emerson.

The genius of the program is, in some ways, a turn-off rather than a turn-on. It raises a sado-masochistic itch and the viewers want to go on scratching. Like comedy *noire*, people come back, again and again, to be publicly deconstructed. But maybe the computer should shed some of the Revelation bit? There is a kind of Apocalypse ground-base which is getting heavier each time and drowning the wit. Maybe a hangover from the boring Eighties, when the anti-nuclear trip became a culture trap? Surely if Sapio really came from another galaxy, s/he wouldn't go on about something so provincial and boring as the deconstruction of this planet?

Unmarked cutting. File 'Sykotic Trash'

EXTRAORDINARY SECURITY IN WASHINGTON

A rumour swept Washington last night that a 'space intruder' was picked up on radar last week, at the height of the US–Soviet diplomatic crisis. Interpreting this as a possible missile, ASAT and SDI systems were alerted, and the intruder was zapped by a laser. It was disabled but not destroyed, and came down in Alaska, where US search parties reached it at dawn yesterday. First investigations revealed it to be a small space-craft, containing two occupants (both dead) with regular human features, dark complexions and golden hair, of no obvious ethnic origin. Both were women, and were dressed in elaborate and costly gowns.

Washington has now clapped down a total security ban on all further information. Speculation is rife. Could we really have invaders from outer space? And how will that affect President Forsst's chances when he runs for a second term?

Journal. Entry 00226

Harmer has pushed me like a trolley around this globe. Which he did by putting me into great spacecraft which swallowed in their bellies three or four hundred travellers, or 'hostages', sitting edge to edge in a crush.

These craft went so high that they went through the clouds. And nothing could be seen below, so that I do not know if we flew above oceans or fields or ice-caps, or whether this whole globe is one mess of tarmac and concrete, or 'airport', after another.

When we flew between Russia and China the spacecraft went so high that I thought that it could without difficulty carry me back to the moon. But when I strode forward to give this order to the driver there was a great hoo-ha and a wrestle, with two holding my arms and another putting a bag over my head, and a screeching of 'hi-jack', which is a new game (or 'craze') they play about the planet, in which they exchange roles, one being 'host' and the other being 'hostage'.

Every day we fell out of the sky on to a place just like that from which we had set out, and every night I did a show against a different nation. Of which the Russians were the most contradictory in their vibes, being full of secret moody urges which went clean contradictory to their oily tongues and shut faces; and the Chinese were the most straight, a courteous people, giving me welcome with gongs and dragons: and the Australians I do not at all remember, for I shared a dressing-room before the show with a band whose decibels made me deaf, at which they gave me a bottle to drink called 'paint-stripper' which made me stomp and roar like a griffin, at which the audience cheered and threw their tubes at me and threatened to elect me as a Senator, which is their way of punishing malefactors. So if there be a need for us to choose a people to help us to govern the world, then let it be the Chinese, with the aid of their dragons.

But these dragons are in no way related to our ur-dragons and ger-dragons, although they much resemble the former. For they are a fake or a play, being a cloth painted in the colours of a dragon, with men inside who jump and dance the dragon-steps and even blow out fire through the nostrils. Yet so well do they imitate true dragonhood that it was long before I noticed the deception. And here is another deep question to be construed. For how does it come that they know the very gait and temper of our noble Sentient Creature – a creature which (they say) has never dwelt on their planet?

We have now reached a new land, called America, and this day I spied in the newses a grave matter. It seems that my companions have ventured again towards Sykaos from the moon, having constructed new observation-craft. And these Americans have, from mere wanton delight in destroying, done a zap against them and brought the craft and its two observers to a dead-line. From which sad tidings I divine that things Sykotic are coming to a final crash. And that it may not be much longer before my fellow-humans come to colonise this place, and I may do myself a rescue.

Yet it may now be a race between their second coming and the beastly propensity of mortals to do their own dead-line. For from spying in their newses, as well as several conversations with Harmer (and constructions of the late Translator), I have learned of new Sykotic abominations. It seems that their cunning scientists have come to the very margin between physics and ultra-physics, and now know how to undo the weak force to which matter adheres. Which discovery is only primitive, for they can undo the force only by letting loose great bolts and belches of radiation which can wither all the flesh and green about the globe. Nothing better has come into their beastly minds than to compact this force into 'bombs' (or 'nukes') which burn out cities like the eye in its socket and which leave the impacted region for the half-life-of-ever in a radiation-stew.

These nukes are, like all else, properties, but not yet the properties of privates but of publics, that is, of nations. And these nations growl and gibber at each other, and breed more and more nukes against the final day, and toss them aloft in menace like a juggler. And at any day one nation will miss a catch, and the whole planet will go smash.

Because they cannot look in the face of their own beastly natures they have given to these nukes a sideways term, which is to call them 'deterrents', which is a nuke wrapped up in a pretty paper of pretences on which is written: 'If you abolish us we will abolish you.' Which twist is enough to make any well-programmed Translator choke, and I will afford to it my forgivingness.

Therefore Oi Paz has at last understood the object of the Mission, which was, perhaps, already known to the prescience of the Gracious Goodnesses. Oi Paz must dissuade these mortals from their own self-cancellation, not out of any tenderness to their beastly selves (which will be cancelled at our own convenience), but out of a care for this green-and-blue planet and to preserve the future home of our race.

Tomorrow Harmer will push me to a show in a place called 'The Rose Bowl' which he says is 'the biggest gig' ever, and will be hooked up to the television of the world. So that now I will prepare to give to the whole beastly species its Final Notice.

Journal Fragment 00311

... as Harmer pushed me to this coop (or 'motel') in the night I did not know the reason for the roaring and washing noise which went on outside the windows. But this morning when I drew the curtains my organ of aesthetics was exalted to a trance by the vast green-and-azure expanse of the moving waters of the Pacific Ocean.

After morning eating, Harmer went off on 'business' – or in pursuit of the pong of money – supposing that he had locked me (as is his custom) in this coop with a bottle of McCoy. But I slid between a window and have been walking for an hour or two on the warm sands of gold at the edge of sea. Where great expanses of molten waters are in a perpetual motion like an animate creature, restlessly advancing against the land and withdrawing, heaving themselves up into high lines which collapse on to themselves in a white tossing of aerated spray, and all the while plashing and dashing against themselves and the sands, as if matter itself was in a perpetual discourse in an eternal hidden code. And I remembered again the dreams of the School of

Melodious Colour, and determined to spare nothing of my thoughts in the show at the Rose Bowl this day.

Cutting. 'Press File'. '*LA Times*, 12 May'

RIOT AT ROSE BOWL
FBI Interrupt Spaceman's Second Coming

Scenes unprecedented even at the height of Sixties Hippydom took place at the Rose Bowl yesterday, when FBI agents attempted to arrest 'Sapio the Spaceman' in mid-speech on suspicion of being an undocumented immigrant from the moon.

In the extraordinary scenes which followed, Mr Sapio disappeared. A spokesman for the CIA would not comment on the suggestion that he had been kidnaped by Soviet agents. Washington sources said that the FBI action may have been related to the shooting-down of an alien spacecraft over Alaska last week.

Billed as a 'Born-Again Revival' show, aging hippies of the Sixties generation mixed all day with the teenage New Wave of the Nineties. It was an old-fashioned Californian celebration, with dope-pushers, naked lovers, mystics and drop-outs.

Everywhere there was evidence as to the extraordinary speed with which the new Sapio Cult has swept the West Coast: Sapio balloons, T-shirts, gowns and belts, transvestite kits and translator-simulators. Several hundred Sapio look-alikes paraded the Bowl, acting the part to such perfection that enthusiastic believers swooned or mobbed them.

The Sapio Cult swamped the West Coast like a tidal wave only three or four weeks ago when it came on TV from a British show. The British treat it as a high-rating comic show but Californians decided that Sapio was for real. Yes, s/he did come down from Space Above, from a place which s/he calls Oitar. Oitary Clubs sprang up along the Coast, to market Cult products. High point of the day's events was to be 'The Second Coming' of Sapio in person, to be followed by 'The Second Crucifixion' in which s/he was to be suspended for some minutes on a 'crucifix' simulated by a laser light show.

It is rumored that the Cult owes some of its rapid runaway fervor to quiet encouragement from the Lawrence Livermore Laboratory and lavish funding from Rockwell International and other giants of the military space industry, which have been concerned by the strength of opposition to a further $2 trillion appropriation to the Strategic Defense Initiative. It was thought that if Californians were to become true believers in Sapio, the Space Visitor, then their faith might be channeled into panic at an imminent descent of space invaders, which would bring popular support to the current 'Thunderbolt' and 'Frisbie' programs. A few brave pacifists passed out handbills which claimed that 'Sapio' was a public relations employee of Zap Technologies Inc. They were lucky to escape a lynching-party.

By the time of Sapio's scheduled appearance there was mounting hysteria in the Bowl. Confusion was added when a Sapio look-alike stormed the stage and seized the mike, calling on the vast crowd to 'repent and shed their genes'. In the ensuing struggle, half of the crowd stripped off to the skin, and an edge of bad temper could be sensed from the other half.

At length the 'real' Sapio (but who could now tell?) descended slowly from above on to the stage, through screens of multi-colored lasers, with long golden hair and colored robes, much like an illustration of the Second Coming in a nineteenth-century family Bible. There erupted a screaming and shrieking of 'hosannah' and 'hallelujah' which continued for fifteen minutes, as first aid was given to the afflicted and stretcher-bearers forced their way through the thousands of 'sent' devotees.

When Sapio could at length be heard his words were so often drowned in shrieks, 'hallelujahs' and the cries of those crushed in the crowd, that only a few imperfect passages could be heard.

'... and come down from on high to redeem you beastly people. For now the sick is in the porn and the press over-brimmeth with thy obscenities ... (*Hosannah! Hurray!*) ... Lo, look along thy dead-lines where thy time cometh to the spike! Ah, look aloft, where the black hole sucketh all thy vanities into its vasty null ...' (*Shrieks. Cries of 'Save us!'*)

Hundreds among the crowd were falling to the ground, as if stunned by remorse. At this point a small group of FBI agents were seen pressing toward the stage. Sapio was declaiming what appeared to be an incitement to insurrection – 'Rise, rise, against your Keepers! Quit your profits and queens!' – when FBI agents mounted the stage and seized him by both arms.

Instantly, two agile, long-haired hippies, followed closely by a Sapio look-alike, mounted the stage and wrestled for possession of the 'Chosen Sun'. More of the audience followed, and soon nothing could be made out except flailing arms and, every now and then, one of four or five 'Sapios' struggling to break free of captors. The crowd went berserk, half of them making for the stage and the other half for the exits. Police say they are astonished that there was no loss of life.

Unmarked cutting. 'Press File'

Police have released the 'Mr Sapio' apprehended on stage during the affray in the Rose Bowl yesterday. His name is given as Jason Rickenbaumer, proprietor of a health-food store of Rainbow Beach. He turned out not to be the 'real' Sapio, but a look-alike dressed for the part, who manages Rainbow Beach Oitary Club in the evenings.

It seems that the real Sapio got away in the confusion. Police refused to confirm that Soviet agents aided the getaway.

Cutting. 'Press File'. Manuscript annotation: '*NYT*'

BRITISH—US RELATIONS UNDER STRAIN

Relations between Washington and London have reached a new low, since Britain dissociated itself from the Strategic Defense Initiative last year. Officials in the Pentagon are furious at information (coming from the CIA's 'private sources' in London) that it was British agents who spirited 'Sapio the Spaceman' away from the Rose Bowl last week.

In London official sources denied any knowledge of the episode. But an off-the-record source in Whitehall noted that Mr Sapio was 'a British citizen'. If he should return to England, and if he should have information of value to the authorities, this would of course be made available to other NATO intelligence sources through 'the normal channels'.

Journal. Fragment 00346

... never declaimed this Journal in more difficulties, for I am doubled up in a wooden crate, with only three bottles of McCoy for company. And scarcely can record the blasphemies done against my person and my solemn show. For when I was at the greatest high and had brought thousands of mortals to ruliness I was assaulted on every side and was pulled two ways by one arm and three ways by another and spun around in muddles and between several keepers and at last found myself flung through a hole in the stage where two men with long golden hair to their shoulders and bare chests and beads and bells pulled me by force along a tunnel beneath the stands and ran me with a blanket over my head along a street and then to a car into which they thrust me and thence to an empty house where they sat me in a chair and gave me a fill of McCoy (to the relief of all my aching parts), whereupon to the astonishment of my sensors each pulled at his own hair which fell off, being not a head of hair but a fake. And one pulled off his face-hair (or 'moustache') and the other changed his nose so that they both revealed themselves to be common pee-cees or (as they said) 'British security officers', who said that they had 'rescued me from that lot', and that I was 'okay' with them and they would get me home in one piece, but that for reasons of security I must climb into this crate and they would fly me home as 'cargo', and thence my crate was hauled and rolled and lofted. Nor do I know when these indignities will end, nor which will come to its dead-line first, my corpse or the McCoy . . .

SEGMENT FOUR

SECOND CAPTIVITY

Editor's Note

*Our author's Second Captivity dured for some three years (Sykotic) or
one and two-third revolutions in our own equivalent. For most of this
time Oi Paz was kept in a large keep (or 'safe'), where access was
permitted to their books and newses, with some time for studying and
writing.*

*Here Oi Paz recorded those parts of the Account Book which we
have drawn upon above. The Account was then abandoned in favour
of scientific notebooks, in which was brought into a system all observations on the customs of the Sykaans. Of these notebooks, one only
has survived undamaged. It is entitled 'The Origins and Ends of
Mortality', and comprises scientific data on mortal creature-character,
history, myth and ethology. We will include below such findings as are
apt to our editorial purpose. It will be identified as Notebook A.*

*Fragments of two other notebooks survive, one inscribed on its cover
'Of Beastly Procreation', and the other only with the signature 'I'.
Matter from these two fragments will be found in their ordained place,
as Notebook B and Notebook I.*

*Your Editor has also to hand sundry other materials, as the Journal
which Oi Paz continued to declaim to the Recorder, and a vast assortment
of Sykotic writings, from which a selection is made. We also have to
hand a new, although a gravely imperfect, source. For the keeper named
Sage also kept pseudo-scientific notebooks, inscribed 'Field Notes'. We
have, albeit with hesitation, transcribed many passages from these,
although your Editor is well aware of the deformities which these 'notes'
betray on every page.*

Q.

Account Book

... and after crating and pushing here and there between keeps
and keepers and pee-cees and offices with some days of backwards-
and-forwards-talking going over again all that had gone on in
these offices before and much asking about Oitar and what was

'up' on the moon (although the moon is down) and how we had got there and how I had got from there to here, which questions I did not answer because any reply would have been above their beastly understandings, they at length pushed me into a room with one of their leaders or 'Ministers', who said (for I transcribe it from the Open Record): 'Sit down, Mr – ah – Sapio – er – Oipas. The truth is, you've become something of a problem to us.'

I replied that he and his fellow mortals were a great problem to me, and that, if he would not blast me back to the moon, then at least he could send me back to Harmer, so that I could go on the plugs again and warn the Earth about its coming dead-line.

'Afraid that's not possible,' he said. 'The fact is, you don't exist. We can't let the Americans – or the Russians – know we've got you. You're a planetless person, Mr Oipas. Our people here' – and he pointed, not at any people, but at a pile of papers on his desk – 'tell me they don't know what to make of you.'

'I hope you will make nothing of me,' I replied, 'for I am made already, and I sentence you to return me to the moon made as I am.'

'When we can get a Eurorocket to the moon we might indeed do that, Mr Oipas. You could be most helpful, as an interpreter and so on. Meanwhile you will have to remain an Official Secret.'

The Minister got up from his chair, walked a few paces around the room, and turned to me again. 'I'm going to send you to a safe place in the country, Mr Oipas. A little Establishment of your own. I must ask you to give full co-operation to the staff, and explain to them all about your installations on the moon. And please pass on to them any information which will help us to get up there and contact your people before the Russians do.'

As he said the words 'the Russians' such a foul pong of enmity came from his vibes on to my sensors (which I had left open and unscreened so as to catch his true intentions) that I was swept by nausea and lay back in my chair. He went into an adjoining room, closing the door and talking in a low voice to an assistant.

He supposed that I could not hear him – as, indeed, I could not – but it was no problem for the Recorder to bug through the wall and catch some of his words: 'Martagon Hall? ... just the place ... Put it through Em on the Secret Account, don't let it go through Treasury. We'll need at least one linguist ... cryptography ... and get in Astrosigint ... And he'll have to be dried out. Nigel Harmer has been tipping Scotch into him like petrol ... Can't make much of him myself, but we'd better keep on his right side. I mean, if we could get a whole space fleet of these lunar poofs to flop down one morning in the Urals, that would give Marshal Oblomov something to choke on with his vodka, eh?'

I divined from this that they intended to hold me in some other coop or keep, and to spy upon our language, which spying I determined to obstruct. For if by radio-vibes there should be any talking with the moon, then I, the Messenger of Oitar, must command the keys of tongue.

A few days later I was driven by night to the place which is now my home. It was known on the heading of official papers as the Foundation for Advanced Research into Climate and Eco-Systems (or FARCES) but, more privily, in their secret papers, by the code-word LUNATIC.*

Sage Notebook. Pasted-in typescript
FARCES

Toppest Secret

Martagon Hall,
Shaw Magna,
Hants

Ref. LUN/Pep 001

TO ALL STAFF

Welcome aboard. You will find a provisional list of establishment enclosed.

---

* *At this point Oi Paz ended the Account, and we must rely upon the Journal and notebooks hereafter.*

Object: Phase One

To hold Mr Oipas (otherwise known as 'Sapio') in *complete security*. After drying-out procedures completed, commence de-briefing. To establish place of origin. If from the moon, how, when, how many others, what intentions? To discover language of 'Oitar' (if any). To gain knowledge of Oitarian social organisation and technologies. To integrate briefings and prepare charts and know-how memos for NATO Space Command (subject to top clearance, Phase Two) as to Oitarian logistics, weaponry, supply echelons and intentions.

Object: Phase Two

Subject to successful accomplishment of One, to attempt direct radio-communication with stations on moon, with a view to negotiating an alliance, in the first place between HM Government and Oitarian forces. (GCHQ Cheltenham to be brought in at this stage.) Subject to the satisfaction of certain outstanding issues, HM Government may then negotiate an extension of this alliance to our NATO partners.

Subject to successful development and testing of the European AXIS rocket, a diplomatic Mission to the moon, including a member of HMG and Mr Oipas, might then be contemplated (Phase Three).

Security

Total top security must cover this whole operation. All staff must remember at all times that Oipas does not exist. Contrary to normal arrangements even our special relations and cousins in NATO will not be informed until Phase Two is advanced.

No one except the Director and Assistant Director or Mr Mayhem may leave Martagon Hall unless with the express permission of Colonel Gardyan-Hunter, and then only if accompanied by a member of the Security staff. Staff are entitled to two weeks' leave a year, but this may be taken only at the safe resort house, 'Playpen', near Bognor Regis. Only the Director, Assistant Director and Mr Mayhem have access to a telephone. All incoming and outgoing mail will be vetted: no documents, film, tapes or discs may be transmitted. No visitors shall be admitted to the Hall without the express permission of Colonel Gardyan-Hunter. In all other respects staff will be completely free. They will be placed upon the electoral register and may exercise a postal vote. Learned journals and books may be obtained through the Filing Officer.

Martagon Hall

If all work together as a team, Phase One should be completed within a few months. At some point during Phase Two it is anticipated that security regulations may be somewhat relaxed. Staff therefore should expect these conditions of isolation (which are in the highest interests of national security) to continue for not more than two or three years.*

Martagon Hall is the ancient seat of the de Boyles, and the West Wing dates from Tudor times. The spacious hall, library, drawing and dining rooms, and the central structure date from the time of George I, when General Charles de Boyle, who had served under Marlborough, laid the nearby village of Shaw Parva into a deer-park. His grandson (also Charles) landscaped the estate, with Palladian temples and the unusual Cardiarum, between 1740 and the 1760s. The mansion and park passed in lieu of death-duties to the nation in the 1930s, when the last of the de Boyle line married a Veyscy and moved to Florida. The Nissen huts behind the kitchen garden, which have been modernised as quarters for the other ranks, date from World War Two, when the Hall was a training centre for SOE. Since then it has been through several incarnations. Until three years ago it was the Commonwealth Senior Staff College – a function which lapsed when we withdrew from the Commonwealth. Mrs Undermanner, Miss Weeder and several of the catering

---

* *Sage annotation, red ink:* 'Fuck!'

and grounds staff descend to us from the previous Establishment.

The full extent of manor, gardens, lake and home park is some 170 acres, within which all staff may move with *perfect freedom* between the hours of 8 a.m. and 8 p.m. (summer) and between dusk and dawn (winter). The high 18th-century walls are electrified at the top and all approaches are monitored by radar and video-scanners, so that staff need have no anxieties. In addition, Dobermans with handlers patrol the perimeter after closing hours.

Martagon Hall has every facility of a splendid country club, with swimming-pool, squash and tennis courts, a small film and video 'theatre', an ELSAN computer, and terminals to computers in Cheltenham and Whitehall. The private chapel of the de Boyle family was formerly RC but may now be used for ecumenical services. As for other spiritual refreshments, we are advised that Mr Oipas must not be offered alcohol *in any form*, and it will be best if he is not even tempted by its smell (we are told that his olfactory organs are extraordinarily acute). We regret therefore that Martagon's 'Lily Bar' must be closed for the duration, and staff may consume alcohol only in private in their own rooms. Mrs Undermanner will take your requisitions (in writing, please).

Family

We have been informed that several staff and other ranks have wives, children & c., who wish to join them on Hall premises. This presents serious security problems. It is possible that a staff member might pass positive vetting but a spouse or aged parent might not. We are awaiting advice on this matter. It is possible that we may be able to establish segregated family quarters near the stable block. Meanwhile we shall take decisions on an individual basis.

Welcome

Please note: all Executive Staff will attend a weekly Progress Conference in the Old Library every Tuesday at 9.30 a.m.

sharp. Dinner each day will be in the main dining-room at 8 p.m. and your *attendance is expected*. Mr Oipas will dine with us, so no 'shop' please. Evening dress optional (lounge suits & c. acceptable). Regrettably, fruit juice and *aqua minerale* only. Other meals staff may take in the mess or in their own rooms as convenient. Colonel Gardyan-Hunter or I will be available for enquiries between 10 a.m. and 11 a.m. in our offices each weekday (except Tuesday). At other times by appointment only.

Cast off! And good sailing!

J.P.

After reading, place this for reference in your locked wall-file. Please note, internal code for FARCES will be LUNATIC.

FARCES

Toppest Secret

ESTABLISHMENT (Provisional)

Executive

Director: Professor Sir James Pepper, FRS

Asst Director: Lt-Col. A. Gardyan-Hunter, DSO

Registrar (i/c Security): Mr J. Mayhem

2 i/c Security (Guard and Gate-Control): Capt. M. T. Scarcely (Fifth Para)

2 i/c Security (Hall Control): Mr Gentry

Estate Bursar: Mr I. Needs

Works: QMSM R. Gravell

Filing Officer (and Librarian): Miss A. L. Weeder

Hallkeeper: Mrs Penny Undermanner

Medical: For the time being Dr J. Bowdler, in practice at Shaw Leavings, will visit weekly (subject to security clearance) and will supervise duties of Staff-Nurse Rani Satpathy (on Establishment)

Equerry: A. N. Other

Personal Assistant (Director): Miss Primrose Gordon

Personal Assistant (Asst Director): Mrs Trudy Hemlock

Lunar Communications Unit: To be appointed, Phase Two

Cryptography: Miss Jane A. Crostic (on detachment from
  GCHQ Cheltenham)
Linguistics: Dr D. Nettler, PhD
Anthropology: Dr Helena Sage, PhD, FRAI

Other Ranks

Existing Establishment of Martagon Hall (Cooks, Mess Waiters,
Gardeners, Odd-jobber, Cleaners, Telephonists & c.), plus Sec-
retaries (vetted) 3, Typists (Pool) 2, Registry Clerk 1, Butler
1, Batman 1, Frogman 1, Drivers 2, Doghandlers 2, Kennel
Maid 1.
Guard Personnel: seconded from 5 Para as required.
Lunar Communications: to be seconded from Astrosigint (Phase
Two)

Sage Field Notes

20 June. Fuck! What have I got myself into? This was meant to
be working-journal but I have to vent my FURY somewhere.
I'd like to sue them. But who? That cool, elastic-witted type from
St Anthony's who talked abt 'chance of a lifetime', 'unique
subject', 'highest national importance', and (flatterer!) that They
(who?) had 'selected me from hundreds because of the exceptional
quality of my bla bla bla'. Didn't think to tell me that I wld be
locked up in a cross between a golf-club and an Officers' Mess
and a public school, run by MALES, for 'well ... er ... three
years or so'.

They caught me when I was down. Ever since I split with John
I wanted to get out of the College, out of Oxford. Kept bumping
into him everywhere with his one-sided guilty smile, 'How *are*
you, Helena?' Then came the govt cuts. And the College cuts.
And the Research Council cuts. Every damn project I put up got
cut down. And along comes Prince Charming from St Anthony's.
Also was glad of chance to work with James Pepper, old role-
model of my teens.

So here you are, Dr Helena Sage, by your own doing, committed to a spook asylum. That lizard, Mr Mayhem, who might
be any age between 25 and 70, slid up to me and asked me into
his office to sign the Official Secrets Act! I sd, 'Why?' He sd,
'Because.' I sd, 'No one told me.' He sd, 'Within the next twenty-
four hours, please.' And then there must be 'positive vetting'.

Why do they want an *anthropologist*? If 'Sapio' can talk English
(and he can, I watched him on telly), can't they grill him for
whatever they need without my help? Col Hunter and Mayhem
aren't here to learn anthropology, come off it. Also: *ought* I to
help them?

End of soliloquy. Tell you what I *will* do. I'll ask for a field
session with Mr Oipas. And will take a decision based *wholly* on
my judgement as a scholar whether the subject merits research of
itself for itself by itself – and whether I think I can do it.

Sage Field Notes

25 June. Tall, exceptionally well-built. Dark complexion upon
somewhat European ('Caucasian'?) features. Reminiscent of some
tall types from South India: also of romanticised portraits of
Noble Savage, American Indians, *temp* Rousseau. Moves with
deliberation and grace, yet in some way *distancing* himself from
the movements of his own body as if his limbs were delicate
prosthetic tools. All senses seem sound. Hearing remarkably acute
(detected mice scratching wainscot, informed me there were
three). Cld not test sense of smell (consult Nurse Satpathy).
Impressive yet passive personality: almost a 'vibe' coming from
him, not hostile, yet aloof and alert at the same time. Voice is
like a misfit: not quite ♀ yet deeper than a pre-pubic ♂. Robes
(quite gorgeous!) looked like a hand-weave, but cldn't identify
with certainty, nor identify material (cottony texture but sheen
of silk). Elaborate belt – seems to contain some instrument (micro-
computer?) at right hip – with large ornamental gold clasp in
which a phallic catch (rt) engages with wheel-symbol (lft). No

time to study other gems and ornaments/designs but oddly ancient semiotics recalling Inca, Egypt, early Hindu? Compact recorder on desk, wh can also be hitched to belt.

Subject not responsive to study. Blocked questions. Nurse Satpathy says he is drying out (directs main hostility at her) owing to having bn kept in drugged alcoholic state for weeks by Harmer. Says he is 'not himself' (she attended him on arrival in Tancaster Infirmary) and that if treated with respect he can be 'a proper gentleman'. (Never met a member of that species in nearly 20 yrs of fieldwork.)

His English is fair but oddly organised. There's an inch of hesitation between exchanges, as if he was feeding words back into his mental computer and getting answers out. He has a wide vocabulary but very literal; e.g.: S. 'I've just dropped in to call on you for a few minutes.' O. 'You do not drop, woman, you walk through door. And no need for calling at me, I hear you if you speak as you do.' (*Mem*: Take my recorder with me next time.)

Question: Do I go on with this? Depends on *Question* (Two): Is there any chance that subject really is from an extra-terrestrial civilisation? To this there might be two – three – answers. (a) He is a hoax. Probable. But what about moon-sightings, craft in Alaska & c.? Wld mean hoax was being put up by USA/USSR/independent astronomers & c. (or by someone taking them in). Itself worth study. (b) He is real. Possible. Although most amazing cosmic coincidence. (c) Somehow is phenomenon of mass self-induced hysteria, in wh gt numbers see 'visions' (as angels, comets, white horsemen), brght abt by nuclear threat, space-age dvlpmnts, space invaders, sci-fic & c. Moon landings and Alaska craft are *symptoms* (like flying saucers) & Oipas is exploiting hysteria! (Or is himself 'possessed' like a Prophet or claimant to divinity?) Not impossible. Consult examples in lit. E.g. is 'Oipas syndrome' like a global cargo cult with moon as source of cargo? That wld be worth studying also.

Answer: YES. If it's (a), then boring. If it's (c) then cld be interesting. Make a marvellous book. If (b) ... then AMAZING.

And even 1 per cent possblty of (b) makes it ABSOL-UTE DUTY to stay here & go through all hoops. (Though god knows what I wear for dinner – maybe Mr O. will lend me a rag?) To decode a new communicant culture wld be . . . absolutely no words for it. Dr H. Sage, you stay here, you stay here to the very end even if that is the end of you!

Now to Mayhem's dog-clinic.

Oi Paz Journal. Fragment 00382

Some are keepers to keep me and others are keepers to keep the keepers. There are two chief keeper-keepers which are a Professor and a Hunter. The Professor asked me questions as to the elementary structure of matter, by which I learned that he supposes matter to be a thing held in place by determinant laws and had not yet any notion of aethereal forces such as the zap and the zen. The Hunter asked how strong were the Oitarian forces on the moon and whether they had nukes. I replied that we employed the weak force but that the strong aethereal forces were always at our beckoning, and that as for nukes that was his own Sykosis. At which he pulled on a mask of wisdom and nodded, but this did not disguise his vibes which had a pong of enmity. From both I demanded McCoy or other alcohol, for I have long been in a famine of it, which I construe to be a form of torture or threat to make me give away to them our language. Nor will Satpathy give me any, although I scent several alcohols in her 'medicine cupboard' so that she is depriving me of sustenance either from malice or through fear of her keepers. I had supposed her to be of a rational disposition when she tended me in my First Captivity, and I even thought it was auspicious when I found her here, but now I see that she is a dissimulator. For which reason I have had to deliver heavy sentences upon her to which she gives no answer but waters in the eyes. And other keepers went and came. One, who is a Sage, sat with me for an hour and was a better sitter than the others, for she asked few questions and accepted as truth all that I said. Which made me speak to her more truly and forget to offer blocks. But I could not find out what the taste was of her vibes, whether sharp or cunning, whether deceit or ego-projection. Her vibes seemed in a suspension and watched my vibes like an open eye.

Now I must devise some way to smash Satpathy's cupboard or to snatch her keys.

Sage Field Notes

12 July. D. Nettler is a dead loss. Always wiping his glasses on a not-too-clean hank, then puts them on, looks around in astonishment, and polishes them again on his shirt. Completely eggbound. Getting nowhere with Oitarian, but then O. has put up a block. Is a leading authority – maybe *the* authority in England – on ancient Chinese inscriptions, the earliest characters on scapula and stone, dating back – Qy: 6,000 years? Keeps saying, 'There must be some way.'

Jane Crostic is another kettle. Brisk and professional. Knows what she's after. Met a total block when I asked her about her qualifs. Spose somethg to do with cracking Russian codes. When I ask her what leads she is going on she cocks her grey head and looks knowing. A bit cloying, though. She has an act about us being 'all girls together'. Yet at dinner she plays up to Hunter and sidles into Mayhem's confidence. Takes me aside for 'little chats' about the male staff. Whatever her act is she has got it together.

Oi Paz Journal. 00401

Those alcohols, brandies and McCoys were only a foul drug by which they sought to bug all my programmes. They are not true hallucinogens and would never be permitted to enter the rectifying chamber of the College of Trance. For a hallucinogen heightens and floods with melodious colours all spiritual and aesthetic faculties, whereas these drugs do injuries to every ratio and dumb the sensors with nulls. Wherefore I now understand that I have done an injustice in sentencing the gentle Satpathy, who was doing no more than aid me in my return to the Rule.

This coop is commodious and the grounds are of great beauty, with a wide tank, or 'lake', and variety of curious vegetation and noble trees, and about the house (which is of the proportions of a small College) are many fine flowers which resemble some of our own, as lilies and roses. And there is an officer named an Equerry, who does not keep me but keeps a Club of noble horses, with whom in the early hours of morning Oi Paz may exchange vibes. And we vibe together about the harmonies of this blue-green planet, which, were it not for the wastes committed by mortals, resembles the Eu Topaz of archaic myth.

Sage Field Notes

30 August. Not much to enter last few weeks, subject drying out and quite humanly irritable in session. Have caught up on some back reading, though there seems to be some block in getting stuff through from Outer World.

Things have been going better this week. But, oh dear, made an awful gaffe today. Had got O. talking abt flowers, wh he loves, & he was almost beginning to flow, when he sd something I thought was funny. Well, it *was* funny. He was almost chanting about roses and madonna lilies when he lowered his voice, as if in confidence, and sd, 'And now Oipas will declaim to you what no mortal has known before. By some means not yet constructed, these plants have come to you from Oitar up above. The rose and the lily have been blasted down as a gift to you near-beasts from the Gracious Goodnesses.'

Well, I laughed. I mean it's not all that funny, set down like that, and one ought to accept an Informant's fantasies, exotic myths, hallucinations with a straight face. Elementary step in early field-training. But it *was* funny ... the chanting giving way to the earnest disclosure ... the sense of Moment and of granting to me Revelation ... and the quaint vocabulary, 'blasted down as a gift to you near-beasts'.

When I laughed he went into deep-freeze. I cld sense his vibes just going out, and then returning, sort of greenish and shut. He stood up and sd, 'Oi Paz has brought this intercourse to a deadline.' Even his parting obeisance was curt, as if half the arc had been clipped out.

Mem: Dr Sage. DO NOT LAUGH. This must have set me back two weeks. Don't laugh at *any* informant. But with *this* informant, don't laugh at, with, or any way at all. This is the biggest block or taboo I've yet struck.

Sage Notebook. Pasted-in typescript

MINUTES
Weekly Conference, 14th Week

Sir James Pepper delayed at a conference at Lawrence Livermore Laboratory. Col. Hunter in chair. Said progress to date left much to be desired, and asked for reports.

Miss Crostic said she hoped to have much to report shortly. Dr Nettler said he was blocked. Subject refused to talk any Oitarian. When pressed subject sometimes spoke a few words or even sentences. Dr Nettler thought the words could be made up. They had no regularity. He had submitted the sentences to computer tests and they showed no grammatical structure. He needed more samples but did not know how to get them. Mr Mayhem suggested hypnosis and said he could obtain hypnotist with top vetting through security. Dr Sage objected that hypnosis could destroy confidence she was establishing with subject. Objection overruled. Staff-Nurse Satpathy made a suggestion which was noted.

A.L.W.

Sage Field Notes

21 Sept. At Tuesday Conference this morning Rani came up with an amazing piece of information. The Powers have never decided whether R. was entitled to attend Conf – was she 'executive' or 'other rank'? I've insisted she come in and dragged her there. Partly because she knows more than anyone, partly for solidarity. It's not that humans are actually outnumbered (there are as many ♀ as ♂) but the ♂ call the tune and make the mould, and anyway Mrs Undermanner is a sort of subordinate ♂-echo and I am beginning to think that Jane for all her 'girly' ploys has a touch of the traitor. She has a way of sidling into Mayhem's office at all hours. As for P. A. Primrose and P. A. Hemlock, they are just body-servants to the bosses.

Anyway. R. always comes now. She's never spoken (nor been asked), but sits there looking by turns indignant and bored out of her mind. Well, we got into one of our hassles, a real ding-donger. Poor David was on the carpet for not having Oitarian off from alpha to omega and was explaining that O. won't talk Oitarian. Mayhem wanted to bring in some voodoo spook to hypnotise him. I jumped up, *furious*, and told Mayhem that O. would *certainly* know what was being done to him. O. has extraordinarily sensitive perception: in fact I think he cld screen hypnosis without difficulty, maybe hypnotise the hypnotist. But the attempt wld *smash* everything I'm doing – David agreed.

Then Hunter started stuffing his pipe (phallic emblem) and huffing and sd I was 'out of order' and 'over-ruled'. The Minister had been making enquiries: we had to show something soon to 'pay the bills'. I started to raise my voice – these males sit on top as cool as cucumbri (or so they pretend) and *goad* one into a display of what is then called 'female hysteria' – when R. waved her arm about like a kid in school. Hunter looked through her as if she wasn't there when David Nettler (of all people) got up, quite tough, and sd, 'Colonel Hunter, I insist that you call on Nurse Satpathy for her ... er ... contribution.' 'Well, Miss Satpathy?' 'Well, Colonel, it is only that if you want Mr Oipas's *language*, you know, he writes it down for hours in the evenings into his notebooks, and well, you know, he is always talking to himself ... into a Recorder.' Silence! Consternation! Knowing looks exchanged between Cross-stitch and Mayhem. Mayhem asked Mr Gentry (who never says anything but seems to be the real operator, or bugger) to pop in during dinner and film the notebooks. What about the Recorder? David sd it must not be touched, any bug cld damage it and O. wld know at once from the smell. I agreed. Knowing looks between Crostic and Mayhem. Suggested what is on Recorder now must be regarded as 'dead ground' but O's desk will be bugged and all future recordings tapped at source.

Afterwards R. full of remorse. 'I wouldn't have told them, Dr Sage ... Helena ... only you were getting so upset and I wanted to help you. But isn't it *wrong*? Isn't it *spying* on Mr Oipas, and he is so trusting to me, he even asks me to wash him in his bath.' Poor kid. I don't know. These notebooks cld be the Rosetta stone.

Mem. If they can bug O's desk, can they, do they, bug all of us? Not much to bug me for. My life is pure as beaten snow. Perforce. But what about this notebook?! Wall file n.b.g., Mayhem will have a key to that. I shall wear my shoulder-bag and carry it with me everywhere.

Sage Field Notes

18 Oct. Why do I always, except in my professional work (I hope), get people wrong at first judgement. I thought Cross-stitch was a professional. Wrong. She's a creep and a fraud. She's probably on establishment for some spooky exploit – or maybe an old flame of Mayhem's. She has absolutely no skill relevant to our work.

Wrong about David Nettler also. He is no kind of drip. He is that rare bird, a scholar's scholar. Completely inside his own mind, then coming out and blinking at the world like an owl at midday. When he *is* out – not often – he can be tough when you least expect it. He doesn't give a brass farthing for Pepper/Hunter/Mayhem.

I asked him how he got into this outfit. 'Well ... er ...' – polishing his glasses – 'I've asked myself the same thing. I wanted to write up some new in ... inscriptions from Xianyang' – gesturing to a shelf above his desk with microfilms – 'and they said this was a kind of ... Think Tank.' Sweet smile. 'And you know, Helena, I'm sort of u.s. I don't get any students. Last year I ... lectured to one girl, overseas New Zealand–Chinese. Nice girl, very bright. And she ... she dropped out.' He looked so sad I felt a pang in my inwards. He put his glasses on, scowled, and applied them to his shirt. Then, in a rush, 'So they made me take early retirement. At forty-two. I mean, I didn't *have* to. Only ...' He waved his glasses forlornly and my pang twisted like a knife. Then that sweet smile again. 'But ... Helena. I *like* it here. For the first time for years I don't feel u.s. I think we—and I do mean you and I – could be on to something *big*.'

I think David is really good – he cld be brilliant, but how does one tell in another discipline? Puzzles me a bit. Heartland: Ancient Chinese inscriptions. But he has on his shelves a lot of stuff outside his field: pre-Columbian (esp Inca), Assyrian. Minoan, early Indian. Touches on some of my own interests (when off my orthodox beat). But, *question*: is expertise in v early ceremonial languages (regulations, astronomical observations, dates) helpful in decoding an extra-terrestrial lang wh is certainly living and may be ultra-sophisticated? Tried to put this tactfully to D. 'Well,' he said, 'you're in the same boat. How do Papuans and Amazonians help? The thing is to have a sense of ... structure.' He sd that he hadn't had any texts to study yet, but he had had one tape of O. dictating. 'I think it is ... a sort of ceremonial language, Helena. In fact ... it frightens me.' Wh was all he sd, and wh was an odd admission from David Nettler.

David & Rani are the only people who keep me alive. And the gardeners – Brian Holberry, the odd-job man, is yummy. And the children. Oh, and Mr Oipas ... who grows on me. Rani and I have been helping him to choose material for a new set of robes, and he has a remarkable sense of colour and of texture.

Sage Notebook. Pasted-in typescript

MINUTES
Weekly Conference, 23rd Week

Sir James Pepper in Chair. Miss Crostic reported on her successful investigation of O's belt-computer. Sir James Pepper congratulated her on behalf of FARCES.

Sir James had to leave for London. Col. Gardyan-Hunter took Chair. Dr Nettler reported little progress. He thought he had found a linguistic 'loop' but he might not be able to present conclusions for some months. Dr Sage said she had now won 'some confidence'. She had already made notes of certain Oitarian ceremonial customs. But the controlling beliefs and myths still evaded her. Col. Gardyan-Hunter noted that O. still refused to discuss with him Oitarian weaponry or strategy: had Dr Sage pursued enquiry into these significant areas? Dr Sage said that 'weaponry' and 'strategy' were subordinate concepts controlled by the concept 'war' and Oitarian culture appeared to be void of that concept. Col. Gardyan-Hunter drew the attention of staff to the fact that they were not engaged in an academic exercise, nor to prepare learned articles, but upon an urgent enquiry in the national interest. He suggested that certain staff might give a greater priority to these questions. Dr Sage withdrew to her room with a headache.

Mrs Undermanner said that she had learned from the tradesmen that there was unfavourable gossip in the village of Shaw Magna, to the effect that Martagon Hall had been taken over by 'Moonies' and that black magic was being practised. She asked for guidance. Mr Mayhem took a serious view of the matter. How had the notion of 'Moon' come to mind? He said all security measures must be tightened. Postman, milkman and tradesmen to be positively vetted. Sister Satpathy drew attention to a change in Mr Oipas's voice. Mrs Undermanner said that there was a lot of it about. Noted.

A. L. W.

Sage Field Notes

17 Nov. Cross-stitch is cock-a-hoop. What a creep! Three days ago she oiled up to me and David and sd she had 'arranged' a special session for me and D. together with O. We had long been asking for this threesome, to try out a joint linguistic-cultural fishing expedition. For some obscure reason (divide and rule?) Hunter always blocked this; against protocol. Cross-stitch sidled into Mayhem and got the permission. Cldn't think why she was being helpful. She sd we cld have O. together for two and a half hours, after dinner, and she thought we wld be 'cosy' in the orangery wh is a room O. likes because the stained-glass dome (early Vict) reminds him of something.

Fishing exped went well, very well. But the *reason* Cross-stitch wanted us out of the way was that she wanted time to burgle O's room. O. does not wear his belt to dinners because he once caught the golden clasp against the table and it seems to have some special value to him. Cross-stitch and Gentry spent all dinner-time and fishing exped (i.e. abt four hrs) going over belt and belt-computer: photos from all angles, wax impressions. Findings? It is digital computer plus time-piece plus some other bits (programme-vector?). Big deal! D. and I knew this already. Not even Oitarian numerals on the time-piece since it works on dots. O. has let me examine gadget more than once without any bother, in fact seemed proud of it. Said it was 'time but not your beastly time'.

But this Big Discovery sends Cross-stitch to the Top of the Charts. Special commendation from Pepper. Many sly looks with Mayhem. Has been granted special extra leave at 'Playpen' (good riddance!). Also (unheard of) Hunter has spoken of letting her go for a month to Cheltenham to consult with cryptography/moon signals. Hope so.

All this came out at the Tuesday Weekly yesterday. Fug of male wallies got too much for me and I flounced out. Aftrwds Rani came to my room in despair. Not abt herself but abt *them*. She is doing okay. O. has stopped getting at her now he is dried out, in fact they get on like chums & there is something in the grace of her walk and movements which is ... 'Oitarian'. Also, she has finished her exams by corresp course & is now full Sister (wh I feel she is to me also).

R. was pissed off because she had spoken at the Weekly (second time ever) to mention O's voice. 'Voice?' I sd. 'What about it? It's always been a problem.' 'Helena, I think it's ... changing. I mean, it drops suddenly, a full register. It could be ... breaking.' This hit me between the eyes. All the work D. and I. have been doing & we hadn't noticed. Can't be true. 'A cough? Bronchitis?' 'No. I've examined his larynx. No, Helena, it isn't that. I tried to tell them but they wouldn't listen.' I felt winded. Then R. sd there were 'one or two other things' wh perhaps she cld show me if I wld come in when O. was taking his bath. Felt winded again. I wld dearly love to inspect O. naked, in fact I ought to have done so long ago since I must make quite sure that Oitarian organs conform with those of the human species. In fact I *should* inspect him. If I was a doctor I wld and an anthropologist is just as much a professional. But my problem is that if I jumped some sexual taboo I cld lose at one throw all the weeks of establishing confidence.

I tried to explain to R. 'Oh, no, Helena, he is not like that at all. He is not like a man.' She sd that from the first days in the hospital he had never shown the least trace of sexual aware-ness/inhibition, nor even interest in opp sex. Nor of other inhi-bitions either: he used to urinate and defecate in hosp so openly it offended other patients. R. also sd that while attending him – she sleeps in adjoining rm with open door – she had sometimes had to hurry to his bed when he had nightmares, while she was 'scarcely dressed at all', & he never 'looked at me in that way'. And when he only had one set of robes he wld sit around in his room naked half the day while R. was putting them through the wash. O. 'doesn't even know there is sex. In fact his body – or your body – or my body – are things apart from us. They are machines in which our souls only live. You know, we have these thoughts also in our ancient Indian teachers. That is why Mr Oipas and I can understand.'

I told R. I wld think it over. If I decide yes, then tomorrow eveng I will help to give subject a bath: never did *that* in New Guinea.

Sage Field Notes

19 Nov. Bathing Subject. Oipas perfectly amenable. Rani right. No trace of taboo. Seemed glad to see me, in fact continued discussion (about form of ice crystal wh he seems to worship) from morning session. Sat on side of bath tub and examnd: O. took no notice. Finely developed ♂ torso, average muscular dvlpmnt (little evidence of exposure to physical labour), firm not flabby. Belly normal. Very fine gold hairs on chest, not thick. Dark complexion (as face) all over, lighter on soles of feet, genitals. No external sign of unusual internal organs. One abnormality: scarcely any navel. As if no cord on parturition. Just a vestige, like an atrophied navel, a little snake's eye. Genitals: seemed normal. R. had wanted me to look at these. 'Helena, Mr Oipas is growing hair.' She meant pubic hair of course. Since I had expected pubic hair I had not noticed it as being there. But then I remembered medical rpts: 'absent'. But quite definitely a bush of downy blond hairs. Then R. sd, 'And, Helena, his testicles have grown.' She lifted his penis gently and there were certainly two testicles, reasonably developed. Oipas, who had been talking crystals, now seemed to stir and take notice. He sd, 'You see how my corpse is made. Any corpse is made much like any other. The different values are not in the nose or nozzle but in the brain.' I sd this was true and he was made very much like any man on our own Earth, although very well made. He sd, 'That is a great problem that I ponder. How did it come that Oitarians and

mortals are made so much alike?' I sd we must discuss this problem
more together. He replied, 'Discussion will not answer it. There
is also showing. Now you will take a bath and I will see if you
are made like an Oitarian.' I had a moment of (unprofessional)
panic. R. and I exchanged glances. I then *felt* his vibes go ...
rigid. It was a moment of make-or-break: if I refused to 'trade'
my nakedness for his then I wld have broken the fragile bond of
confidence. 'I've had a bath,' I sd. 'But of course. I'll strip off.'
Wh I did, and stood before him, and turned around gladly like
a mannequin (to show I had no tail), and stood before him again.
'You are well made also,' he sd. 'But you beastly women have
bigger and rounder breasts than humans do. It is because you go
with your child in womb too long and then you give them your
breasts to milk. I declaim that now as science. And you have thick
hair about your cunt. On Oitar females have no hairs until they
pass the first screens. If they are found fit for impregnation then
they go for two hours each day to the Bumple of Procreation
where they are warmed for months in the distilled rays of the
sun, at which they undergo a puberty and the hair sprouts and
they are ready for the seed. Afterwards hair goes away. But you
are not a Maid of the Bumple.'

Somehow or other – 'vibes' again? – he seemed to sense in me
some embarrassment, for he swiftly added (as nicely as he knows
how), 'I do not mean to pass a sentence on you, woman. Your
corpse is well made. Its deformities are those which belong to
your creature-species. And as for your breasts, they are distended,
yet they rhyme with each other and are even things of beauty.'
And as he gazed steadily and impassively upon my breasts his
penis swelled and rose into a perfectly good erection (better than
one or two I cld mention). This somewhat disturbed me and
altogether flustered poor R., but it seemed to amaze O. himself,
who looked down upon his prick which stood above the water
like Eddystone lighthouse, as if it were an object not belonging
to him yet wh he could not quite disown.

I said goodnight (with the obeisance on parting wh he has
taught me), slung my clothes over my arm and retreated to R's

room. R. came after me in quite a state, apologising for having 'exposed' me to this, it was not 'like' O., 'he 'didn't mean anything' (as if a prick could mean its own erection!). She seemed to think I wld think O. had 'insulted' me, but I'm vain enough not to find it insulting. Of the three of us, poor R. has the most exposed taboos: I think she is a virgin who is supposed to 'save' herself for an arranged marriage. I told her not to be upset at all, and that I had learned a lot about Oitar in that bathroom session. But I sd that maybe we did have a problem. O. did seem to be coming to puberty. In fact, had come! That on no account shld she say *anything* to anyone abt it, unless maybe we decided to talk abt it with David. Because whatever the Powers decided to do abt it wld be wrong.

Sage Field Notes

20 Nov. Talked abt O's puberty with David. Rani came in at first, to lay the medical record out. But we got deeper into it afterwards, when R. had left, because R. really gets v sensitive when talking about sex, esp with a ♂ present. She is used to talking about sex (medical) but not sex (human).

D. sd he had noticed nothing. I put forward my hypothesis: something (climate? diet? lack of sunlight?) on Oitar retards physical dvlpmnt so that they are arrested before puberty. O. has now been on Earth more than a year. Several major changes in his habitat and regimen: (1) ingestion of solid food (general excitation of atrophied internal organs), new vitamins & c.; (2) difft climate, perhaps more sunlight, ultra-violet (told him abt 'Bumple of Procreation' treatment for Oitarian ♀); (3) new kinds of socialisation: e.g. proximity to ♀ – are Oitarian ♂ & ♀ normally segregated? (R. and I didn't tell D. abt erection: that wld seem somehow to be 'telling'.)

D. agreed to arrested puberty theory. But sd one problem: arrested for how long? Or, how many were arrested? Because semen for impregnation must come from somewhere. Agreed I shld follow this line up. Of my three variables he plumped for (2). Sd (1) could be an influence but as for (3) his linguistic hunches suggested Oitar was not a gender-segregated society. Indeed he thought third-person forms were gender-indifferent which suggested *less* role-differentiation than here, not more. If ♀ and ♂ shared roles they were likely to share space also.

D. sd this might be the clue he was looking for in relation to low affective values in language. If Oitarian society was in some degree de-sexualised then some sorts of bonding and affective norms wld not exist. Hence more possible to project the de-sexualised body as Other – O. always refers to it as 'the corpse'. It is felt less from within.

We agreed the three of us must keep mum. D. was worried that if O. was really sexually mature he might try to 'do something' abt it. I told him not to worry. O. has such colossal taboos against proximity or touching (he doesn't even like to shake hands) that his whole nature wld act to suppress the symptoms. Also, I have not stumbled across any concept of human sexuality in my sessions with him. But it *could* set up some tensions or bewilderment in him. Needs watching.

Also told D. of my breakthrough this morning. (Haven't had time to get it down in nbk yet but it's all on recorder.) The 'trading' of my nakedness with O's seemed to *help*. And 'trading' seems to really break the blocks. It turns out that O. is as interested in our customs and culture as I am in his. If I trade information we find we start a comparative exchange. He gives in return for what I give. D. whistled at this. 'Of course! If we give him back fair coin then he doesn't think he's being treated as an object, or being "spied" upon. After all, he may be an ... anthropologist or even a linguist also.'

Sage Field Notes

23 Nov. Oh, dear. Why does talking about sex always make sex rear its ugly head? D. has suddenly got very affectionate, what they used to call 'spoony', and talking about 'love'. Then, after taking off his specs, and polishing them, and dropping them, he made quite a heavy pass. I had to say no thank you as nicely as I cld. He's sweet but he just doesn't turn me on. He was terribly nice. Sort of coughed and sd, 'Well, I know I'm not all that ... Oh, well. I know, let's *really* be friends.' And then he found his glasses again, and started polishing, and went helter-skelter back into a linguistic theory, wh I *knew* he was doing so as to try and settle my feelings. Wh made me feel worse.

Sage Field Notes

10 Jan. David over the moon this evening. Has found out at last how he can 'trade' with O. Says O. is a poet. Says O. just can't resist asking about our poetry and the temptation gets through his blocks. So now D. goes to his apptmnts clasping Oxfd Bk of English Verse, Chapman's Homer & various works from Old Library (mostly *temp* Bowdler, Martin Tupper). Love poetry, romantics & c. turn O. off. But Homer is a turn-on & he really digs Milton. Afraid he also digs Tupper, who (he says) 'explains Sykotic rule'. In return O. recites what D. thinks may be bits of Oitarian epics with long swinging line & hypnotic beat. D. says these 'send' him into a sort of trance (i.e. they send D., but also O. seems 'sent') so he has made no 'fixes' on them yet but has them all on tape. D. really is sweet & he puts me to shame in his dedication as a scholar. Seems to have forgotten altogether about our bumpy thing two months ago. Contrary to usual form it shifted a block and we *are* better friends.

Now I really must make this into a professional field-notes book and arrange my tradings into some system.

Oi Paz Notebook A

Of Mortal Creature-Nature

They are made in most ways as humans are made, with the same limbs and proportions, but a little beneath human height and girth. This is so far as their corpses, for their spirituals have little correspondence. Such corpses as Oi Paz has seen, as Harmer, Sage, the children at the pool and all those many at the Rose Bowl, are not all of the same description. Contrary to human forms, the males are the larger and more unwieldy of the species. Some have fur on their chests and under their arms, as if to mark their beastly affinities. Others (as Pepper and Head Gardener) have hairs sprouting on their faces, while others shave off these facial hairs each day for shame of the deformity. All have an enlarged navel like an ill-healed wound, and the adults of the species a bush of bestial hair about their swollen genitals.

The females also wear this bush, although not upon their chests. These chests are deformed with enlarged nipples and distended glands, or 'breasts' (for so great is the distension on each nipple and so deep the channel, or 'neckline' between each protuberance that they suppose that they have not one breast but two). Yet such is the force of habit (for all have these deformities, some greater, some less) that they do not seek to hide them but design clothes to display them to effect. And such is familiarity that I now find no disgust at their forms, which in their young have an uncured grace of a kind, and some few, such as Sage, even excite the aesthetic organs.

The females are the shorter and the more lithe of the species, and the more apt for menial work.

Now as to their corpses: their young are withheld in the female's womb for thrice the time of our conceiving, nor are they ever passed to incubation: hence they struggle out all bloody and bawling and full-made when they are so large as to scarcely be able to press a way through the passage. It must be supposed that the brains of all receive then an injury. Moreover, this uncured method of delivery places a limit on the size of the brain, which is cramped in a little skull like a College in a little ball. And this I may declaim as science, for when I demanded of Mrs Undermanner a hat, to walk out in the rain, she said that she could find none big enough to fit me. And several of the other ranks, as secretaries, gardeners, have noted I am 'a big-head'.

The young are delivered full-made, or 'born' at less than half of the age of our infants. Nor can they be given any programme in the womb (as speech or walking) so that they are thrust pell-mell into the world as a raw and helpless thing not much larger than a hand.

For a year these young lie and wail and cannot walk. And it is yet another year before they are walking well and can issue the first speech. So that they are backward in their beginnings and through their whole lives are seeking to make up. But at two or three (in their counting of years) they enter a true childhood, in which they run and dance like rational beings. Yet this is swift and short at last, for they are full-grown within twelve or fifteen more of their years, and come into adulthood at a time when our children are scarcely in the Third Arc of Learning.

This adulthood is a short summer indeed, for they are scarcely full-grown before their corpses begin to decompose: their skins (where exposed to the open sun and air) become dry and lined, and from the ingestion of bulk foods their bellies distend, and from lack of eurhythmics their muscles go flab, and their lungs and systems perish from the smokes, acid rains, noxious chemicals and exhausts with which they pollute the planet. Which they try to repair with pills and false eyes, or 'glasses', and sticks to hold up their legs and ceramics to replace their teeth. And from this they all come to an early dead-line, not according to programme, but disorderly and from total system-failure.

The females are subject in their wombs to the motions of the moon. I cannot construe this matter clearly, for Satpathy says it is 'a woman's matter' which I 'need not know'. But every month the womb is lined anew for impregnation, and then there is a shedding of blood and a new cycle commences. When one considers that with due attendance upon the Rites of the Bumple the womb may be well prepared but once every twenty or thirty years, and a single impregnation all that the hostess requires, then it will be seen what a waste and trial these females go through, from lack of any science. Nor can I find that the other beastly creatures on Sykaos cycle around in this way. From which it can be seen that the mortals are, of all species, incessantly cycling through their procreations. Yet one knows from this also that the females have some tune-in to celestial bodies and therefore have some spiritual organs which the males have not.

The males of the species have a deformity of their vocal cords which comes upon them unbidden at adulthood, in which they lose the flute and descend to an ugly, grating pi . . .*

. . . to be said about their spiritual organs, but in summary it is this. Of the exterior senses: sight – good in youth; hearing – fair; smell – rudimentary; taste – hyper-developed; touch – ditto. Of the interior senses: vibe sensors and transmitters – grossly undeveloped or atrophied; mind-wavers – unknown except in rare specimens; aesthetic organs – uncured. Mental faculties – low performance, as if screened by the sensual filters of the corpse and peering through a veil of blood.

Sage Field Notes

18 Feb. Best trading session yet. O's voice *definitely* broken: mellow baritone. Evidently disconcerts him, as does puberty in general. Rani has started shaving him (on request). O. also asked her to shave pubic hairs wh she refused & he is in huff with her. Obvious sense of shame not re genitalia but re signals of manhood wh he wants to disguise. At dinner he talks in falsetto with sudden barks or drops in register. Undermanner gave R. some home-made elderberry linctus for him. We shall have to work out how to break the news to Them.

---

* *A page has been torn out at this place.*

O. knows that I know, so this gave a way in. Asked him directly whether Oitarian ♂ all had late pubescence (indicating symptoms). Did this mean most ♂ were incapable of intercourse? Intercourse threw him: did not seem to have concept. I gave literal description of mechanics & drew diagrams & c. O. quite disconcerted, not by shame but by offence to his 'aesthetics': sd it was like 'mating of chuckalls' (wh are species of Oitarian mammal). From wh it appeared that he *did* have concept of mating, but excluded human connotations.

Q. If on Oitar humans cannot mate, how then are your children conceived and the race continued?

A. By Sper-men, woman. Do you not also have those on Earth who suffer the priapic affliction?

Here is summary (from my tapes) of what followed.

O. said that historians of Oitarian antiquity supposed that some hundreds (thousands?) of generations back ('saros') their ancestors mated in some manner now unknown. Wth the cooling of their sun the ♂ of the species had lost virility. It was now a v great rarity for any to develop testes capable of ejecting fertile seed. Now only about half-a-dozen of such 'sufferers' born into each generation who are regarded as genetic 'throw-backs'. (*Qy*: Does O. mean six in each community/tribe/city/nation, or six on *whole planet?*! Dffclt to ask since have not yet decoded terms/concepts of cities/nations.)

These 'unfortunates' are 'Sper-men'. As soon as their condition diagnosed (*Qy*: at about *aet* 33 by our reckoning? – but Oitar/Syk time variables confusing) Sper-men segregated in sacred 'humple' (*Qy*: = temple? Chk wth D.) in middle of greatest cupola (astro-dome?). Treated wth special rays (ultra-violet & others) and vita-pills to enhance virility. Semen 'abstracted' from them every night.

A: 'Notwithstanding all the favours shown to these unfortunates, the loss of their vital energy is so great that they soon fail in their intellectual powers, and they have a short and unprogrammed life-line. And for this reason all regard them as objects of pity, and as men upon whom has fallen the duty of sacrificing themselves, by a gross corporeal excess, for the continuation of the race. In their brief stay in the bumple, many honours are paid to them – poems are declaimed and masques presented – and silver-work, gems and flowers are placed upon their altars.' (*Note*: O. was not quite straight with me about 'honour'. I detected that Sper-men are objects of disgust/horror as much as honour: play some mythopoeic role of daemon-figure, combining horror/secret admiration, stirring primitive echoes. *Note 2*: If Spermen play role of central double-bind in culture, then O. himself now really does have problems in that he will regard himself & his own 'corpse' wth same ambivalence.)

Q. If so few Sper-men and these short-lived, how can they fertilise all the ♀?

A. Are not ♂, on Earth, if potent, endowed with super-abundance of seed? (Yes.) Then Q. is answrd. From one S-man in one year enough seed is gathered for several million ♀. Seed then banked in safes around temple precincts. In refrigeration quantities of semen banked from S-men of fifteen to twenty generations back. Records held in computers of College of Bio-Engineering as to detailed specifications, performance-ratios, genetic profiles, of each Sper-line. Also exhaustive *cvs* on micro-dots of each product of line, case-histories of any 'sports' or throw-backs.

Q. Do ♀ visit bumples for direct insemination by S-men or is impregnation by some artificial means?

A. Q. is not understood. (Refer back – diagrams & c. – & recall concept 'mating'.) Subject seems cross. All insemination artificial (alternative not even conceptualised or admitted). Procedure: all ♀ pass through 'screens' at *aet* 21 Oitarian or *c*.37 Sykotic years old.

Q. Screens?

A. 'Screens are positive vetting, Sage.' (*Qy*: How did he get to know *that* term?) Vetting means extensive bio-checks, computer run-throughs. College of Bio-Engineering then comes up with a short-list of 'matches', in wh the genetic record-kit (*ca*, or *curriculum ancestrae*) plus performance-reports are 'matched' with seven or eight variables (or 'eligibles') from the Sper-bank. Each of the possible Sper-lines to be matched is sd to come from a different 'suit' and the lines are known as 'suitors'. These variables are then brought before an interview-panel or Board of Examiners of Adjusters, Bio-Enginepersons, and the Provost of applicant's College, from wh after close interrogation of each match one suitor is appointed. (*Note*: Suspect that this is Informant's gloss – or a Legitimation Ritual? Mating selection probably done by Bio-Engine computers?)

Q. What role does woman applicant play in selection process?

A. 'No role for applicants, Sage. These wait for engagement to be announced in waiting-room. This is an affair of science only. How can any human dispute decree of match-making Board? As if one bit could go higgledy into the first mis-match that hassled.'

When the suitors have been appntd ('engaged') the waiting women (who have passed pos vetting) are ready for preparation. Just as with ♂, fertility of ♀ is low and preparation involves attendance daily at Bumple of Procreation for vita-pills, eurhythmics, ultra-violet & other radiation, and specially-prepared music and odours after wh they become nubile and enter puberty. Think they also menstruate, but only once. Infmnt unclear. After wh point impregnation takes place. Failure of impregnation rare, but when it happens the engagement is broken off and the 'couple' split up and a new suitor is engaged by same panel from difft Sper-line or suit. If after second 'signal of the blood' second conception fails, female is 'discarded' as sterile & withdrawn from circulation (but returns to normal collegiate roles).

After all ceremonies completed, ♀ perform rites of absolution at Bumple of the Wheel (Qy: analogous to *churching*?) & return to normal ritual life. Lose mature sexual characteristics. According to computation of Oitarian population-statistics by College of Numbers most ♀ will undergo a Second Impregnation through same rituals in a further 20 or so yrs (Oitarian). For this only those 'hostesses' pass the screens whose 'output' first time around was given high grades by Examining Board. Where output v highly regarded (or 'starred') may be matched again with same suitor.

Q. How does insemination take place & what is duration of pregnancy?

A. Infmnt vague – as always – about medical detail. Says simple 'corporeal' injection. Sd pregnancy *in ventro* twenty-five days. This seemed absurd. Then remembered Oitar does not seem to have our days, weeks, months. Got into usual problem, with O. working at his belt-device. Came up with something just under three months. (NB NB This wld mean Oitarian day about three and a half the length of ours.)

If calculations accurate, foetus is removed at *c.* three months and nourished in receptacles wth special fluids & vita-chemicals for (qry) abt two years of our time. They also immerse half-grown foeti from time to time in special 'think-tanks' in wh they are exposed to vibes or to musical pulses in the fluids. Infmnt sd they had borrowed latter from the 'science of dolphins'. Infmnt then sd at start of year two (our reckoning) foetus was sufficiently 'mature' to have programme-induction, wh involves taping terminals to heads for language pre-programming & also programming in walking & music.

I asked more about species-selection (and suits) & gene-banks but he sd it was 'beyond your science, woman' & we will have to return to that, another session. Also seemed to put up a block about death – to wh return. Got back a little into flow when I asked:

Q. With such problems in low fertility quotients are not many Oitarian children born sickly or deformed?

A. (Vigorous) 'Not so, Sage. You speak the opposite of truth.' Selection procedures at 21-plus so rigorous & testing of semen in banks so thorough that conception generally exactly as predicted. Foetus in Year One closely observed & destroyed if least imperfection detected. Are 'born' already able to walk & talk. O. says Oitarian race possesses great regularity of features, creature-character, mental/spiritual powers, but within that regularity specimens selected and programmed for special variant aptitudes.

(*To wh return.*) 'And since our powers are not laid waste by gross corporeal exercise our people keep their physical and spiritual powers in a state of perfection for about 90 of our years [wld be *c.* 160 of ours?] and do not start to bust up at the very beginning as you do. And at the terminus they come to the edge of a swift decline, which has already been computed on their *ca* prognostics, which decline is aborted by the stated dead-line. Nor can the dead-line come before its dated entry, except by hazard such as when attending the ice-burners or repairing the outer cupolas or venturing into intergalactic space or other such hap.' (*To follow up all this.*)

Infmnt now in free flow. 'So that, if we leave aside the honour due to the Sper-men, we are indeed fortunate in all ways in our arrangements. Yet Oipas declaims to you in confidence, Sage, that we are in difficult times. For in each new generation there are fewer of these throw-backs capable of the service of the Sper. Thus, 18 generations ago, it is recorded that there were no fewer than 21 Sper-men, of whom eleven only were selected to deposit in the Bank because of the prime quality of their seed. Whereas in my own generation there have been found only two Sper-men, and one of these ejects seed of an inferior quality which is held in the Reserve Bank. So that this deficit is causing the Gracious Goodnesses concern.'

Q. If communication establishd btween Oitar and Sykaos (I use his term now) cld we help? Suggested we cld send semen or even selected ♂ (can think of one or two pricks I wldn't mind blasting there) to help service their ♀.

A. Infmnt much perturbed. Indeed aghast. 'I will not pass a sentence on you, woman. I construe that you do not know your blasphemy. But if you reflect, Sage, you will see that we could never defile our race with alien seed. For, if you look at any group of mortals, such as the dinners we endure each night, you will observe the deformities of feature and limb, the irregularities of posture, the inferior intellectual powers, the absence of spiritual forces – not all of which are due to your debauched way of life and your uncured culture but much of which must be in your genetic programmes. And now Oipas has declaimed this, Sage herself will understand the obscene hazards that would threaten our race if only one beastly seed were held in our Bank.' (Did not feel any of this was ill-intended. Indeed, noted with satisfaction that he moved from the hold-off, 'woman', back to 'Sage' – he addresses only me, D. and R. by our names – and, oddly, noted that he then addressed me in the third person as a sign, not of distancing, but of confidence, as if he was positioning himself in my point of view.)

'Yet Sage, unknown to herself, has done good thinking. For on return to civilisation Oipas can take a proposition. Which is that when we come to make the First Plantation we bring in our craft (if it can be spared) a quantity of inferior seed from the Reserve Bank for the impregnation of your selected hostesses. We may screen some thousands of your least disproportioned and most capable women – and Oipas will nominate Sage as a candidate to the Board of Examiners – to receive the first samples of our seed. It is possible that no match could be made of human and beastly genes. Yet if the experiment succeeded it would open the hope of some small improvement of your species. And it will be infinitely preferable to the ejaculations of your own Spermen.'

I asked O. whom he supposed 'our own Sper-men' to be? He sd that he began to understand our beastly practices of 'mating' and supposed this was done by programme & design and a few ejaculators or Spers of our own. Indeed, it seems he has been working on this problem quietly for some time. Sd he had observed many refs and pics in 'newses' of mortals known as 'stars' (as pop-stars, movie-stars) and pics of 'Superman' & c. Had observed also these pics most often outside cinemas & theatres on wh were displayed large posters of a ♂ and ♀ in close association. For some reason he has got into his head that cinemas and churches are 'bumples' for the ceremonial performance of insemination ('Sykotic "marriage"').

It was now my turn to be called out to trade. Wh I did as faithfully as I cld. It sharpened the tools of my discipline (one shld devise some exercises like this for teaching). Extraordinary how difficult it is to *see* & to explain to another culture the most commonly assumed acts and norms. As I went into our own norms and forms O. seemed quite astounded: shook his head; questioned my truth; put it all on to his Recorder. Some bits I just cld not get across. O. asked me for a reading-list. R. has some potted medical vols but will these help? What he lacks altogether is any concept for 'love': maybe he shld read Donne, Stendhal, *Anna Karenina*?

He seemed sent most of all by the long term of mortal pregnancy and how cld the foetus ever crawl out? Asked to see my cunt, wh as a fair trader I had to show. Luckily was wearing skirt so only had to pull down tights. O. said it was much larger than a human cunt, but large as it was he cld not see how a baby cld crawl from that little aperture. Asked if I had made a child? Sd no and it was getting a bit late to start. I explained that I wld like to have a child but I had wanted my profession also ... & had maybe been 'unlucky', my last boy-friend had run away from any commitment & I was a bit pissed off with men.

This got us into quite a tangle. (Explain 'boy-friend' – O. couldn't see why anyone shld endure the pain/indignity of fucking unless to start baby – so I had to explain contraception, at wh he shook his head and hummed. Then had to explain 'pissed off'. *Mem*: MUST only use most direct rational terms.) O. then sd, if I wanted to have a child, why cld I not just fuck with any man, as the Director or Mayhem? I was beginning to feel quite washed up, and was even losing any disciplinary fix on the exchange, when R. came in, bringing a tray of lunch. (Fortunately my dress was proper again.) No break more welcome.

Oipas and I sat in the large window-bay with the tray between us. Cold February day outside with snow falling. O. seemed quite sent by the snow and even ... gentle. Snow reminded him of Oitar and he has a thing about crystals. A snowflake settled on the glass & he pointed out to me the intricate forms as it dissolved. Sd, 'Crystals are high poems but not yet as high as melodious colours.'

I sd goodbye to him, using the formal obeisance (a slight bow, a roll half-left, a circling of rt hand like an Elizabethan courtier) wh he has taught me. Returned to my room, *whacked*.

Sage Notebook. Pasted-in typescript

MAR/Form P.7A H. Sage, PhD

WEEKLY REPORT SHEET

Interrogation Sessions. Monday 1hr, Tuesday 2 hrs, Wednesday $3\frac{1}{2}$ hrs. (Took in Miss Crostic's apptmnt hrs Tues/Wed, and exchange with Dr Nettler on Wed.) Thursday, Friday: none. (Transcribing tape & c.)

Progress. Subject gaining in confidence. Some conversation took the form of free flow.

De-Briefs. Concerned esp Oitarian mating practices & nurture of young. Climate of Oitar does not favour male virility so sperm-banks and artificial insemination practised. Attendant rituals.

Requirements. Can we *please* ask those in Outer World to speed up deliveries books, journals? Have been waiting for some stuff for weeks.

Other Observations. Not yet.

Week: 37 *Signed*: H. Sage

Sage Notebook. Pasted-in typescript

MINUTES
Weekly Conference, 38th Week

Sir James Pepper in Chair. Said *LUNATIC* was not far off target. Had accomplished much of Objective, Phase One. Subject dried out quicker than expected. Had established that subject had come from moon & that he and others came from planet called Oitar. Other progress slow: no breakthrough in language; we knew little of Oitarian science and technology, weaponry, strategy. Should consider if we are deploying resources best. But now possible to enter Phase Two. Col. Gardyan-Hunter would report.

The Asst Dir. reported that (thanks to excellent work of Miss Crostic at Cheltenham) arrangements with GCHQ were now 'tied up'. Major Robert Sorley of Astrosigint would join staff this week, preparing Lunar Communications Unit as per Establishment, with direct Cheltenham-Martagon-Fylingdales links. Radio-installations and dishes will be constructed from next week, sited on the high ground at north-west edge of park by the 18th-century Cardiarum. Passage will be made through wall & new site will be enclosed with high-security wiring.

Weekly Reports. Filing Officer distributed those presented (Miss Crostic absent in Cheltenham). Asst Dir. said progress left much to be desired. How would Dr Sage's de-briefs assist NATO Command in emergency? The Director suggested that Drs Nettler and Sage submit memoranda on progress directly to him before next Weekly.

Dr Sage complained of slow delivery of some requisitions and the Librarian explained the reasons. On the Director's suggestion Mr Mayhem said he would ask for a review.

Other Business. Mrs Undermanner reported that the gossip about 'Moonies' had started up again. The former milkman had been found to be a security-risk, being a Labour parish councillor, and the new milkman positively refused to be vetted. Agreed to see if we could add 5-acre field from Manor Farm for dairy cattle, subject to extension of perimeter security and adding to Establishment one cowman. Meanwhile Mrs Undermanner was asked to indent for Marvel.

Dr Nettler raised the question of Mr Oipas's voice and suggested he had entered a 'late puberty'. Sister Satpathy confirmed symptoms. Director noted point with interest but doubted relevance to FARCES. Col. Gardyan-Hunter said that in view of the subject-matter of Dr Sage's latest report, perhaps she could need assistance in her work from a qualified male scholar with interest in matters more relevant to LUNATIC. The Director asked for this matter to be left on his desk.

Colonel Gardyan-Hunter reported that the Chute Golf Club had kindly consented to the use of their course by Executives on Tuesdays between 2 p.m. and 5 p.m. Captain Scarcely will oversee security arrangements.

There was some disagreement on questions of requisitions between Mrs Undermanner and Q.M.S.M. Gravell. Colonel Gardyan-Hunter offered to arbitrate in the matter. Mrs Undermanner asked for Miss Gordon to be co-arbitrator. Agreed.

A. L. W.

Sage Field Notes

My Minutes

1 March. The Weeder has a snaky way of writing Minutes. Apart from the fact that they give no idea of what goes on (Minutes never do) she highlights what she wants & drops the rest out.

Pepper was rather jolly today. He *did* say progress was slow in D. and my areas but he added quite frankly that it was even slower in science (his area) & wondered aloud if he shld get a 'younger colleague' in to help him. Progress in military matters (Hunter's area) also seems nil though he is too exalted to write a report. (*Qy*: What do he and O. talk about? It seems to be systems-management. They seem to get on remarkably well.)

Signals major will come tomorrow, no doubt strengthening forces of Enemy. But something new anyway. When it came to weekly reports the Hunter/Mayhem/Weeder axis got their knives out at me. Admittedly my rpt was a bit cryptic but – how cld I? D. had covered himself better: he actually gave them some Oitarian *words*, wh is the sort of hard-tack positivism they can understand. Hunter came right out against both of us but esp me. Said Whitehall reports of new bumps on moon (larger), more radio-frequencies identified, and phased-array radar N. Norway detect Russians have shot down another Oitarian craft, bigger than one before. Thumped the table & said: NATO needs *answers*! Kept my cool. Mayhem sd it was my duty to pass on all de-briefings without any 'censorship', wh was responsibility of Security and not mine. (Is he bugging interviews?)

Then Hunter got really heavy. Sd he appreciated that Dr Sage was doing her best 'according to her ability' but in view of themes touched on in her latest report might it not be helpful if she had a male colleague? Perhaps subject would de-brief more readily on such delicate questions to a man than ... er ... And he even had a *name* in mind, a brigadier just retired who had served in North Borneo and been military attaché to the rajah of some S Sea island and who had 'studied natives'. D. got up EXPLOD-ING, and Pepper saw the writing on the wall. So the good Sir James defused the situation, smiling nicely at me, and resolving as per Minutes.

After that I blew off a little of my pent-up wrath by getting back at Weeder on the unbelievable delays in book deliveries. Small revelation. The block is not in Outer World but in Files. Weeder sd some of my titles had not 'passed security'. I sd: *What?* Got out a list with scrawlings on it & intoned with a hint of Awful Depravities Revealed – P. Worsley, *Trumpet Shall Sound* ('Professor Worsley was once a card-holding Communist'), 10 vols of Dr Joseph Needham ('a Christian Marxist'), several journals with articles by Jack Goody, Godelier ('a member of the French Communist Party'). It was all the old *orthodox* stuff!

D. and I sat OPEN-MOUTHED. *We wanted her to go on!* Amazing!! Worsley's work on cargo cults is now a bit out-of-d, but still interesting ... but I dropped the cargo cult hypothesis in Week Three so I must have indented for the book in *Week Two*! It seems that Weeder has been running through all requisitions against some blacklist file – probably on a computer in Outer World – and then feeding results to Mayhem. She & M. seem to share some paranoia about ideological pollution – let one impure vol get in and Martagon is lost. Pepper then got peppery: 'despite our partnership here with Security and the military, please remember this Research Centre is directed by a scholar'. Told Mayhem to tell his superiors to bugger off. And to get what we ask for.

After this the matter of O's puberty was sheer anticlimax. We (David, Rani and I) had had our own cabal before the meeting. We pushed D. forward to break the news because Rani was shy ('they wouldn't listen to me') & because D. is male, and in better odour with Them than I am. Caused scarcely a ripple. They don't regard O. as a ... person, a communicant creature, but as an object, a specimen, an 'it' to be examined for our purposes, and the notion that he cld have his own motivations is beyond them. Hunter did *not* say those paternalist things abt 'qualified male scholar' at this place (as per Weeder Minutes) but in earlier row (as per mine). (Why did she move them down? *Answr*: to get at me in a connotation wh will make males snigger.) In fact Hunter contributed nothing to this item except to say 'Shall we move on to next business?' since he was waiting with his tongue out to announce the golf. However: delicate mission accomplished. Now O's puberty is an open fact, no one will speculate or gossip about it and they will soon forget it altogether.

The real climax to the Weekly was a furious twenty-minute-long ding-donger between Undermanner and Gravell. Some extremely sensitive status-issue involved. No one cld understand. Concerned authority for requisitions. Undermanner is i/c housekeeping (food, internal decorating, furnishings & c.) and Gravell is i/c building-work and outer requisitioning. Each is trying to extend her/his empire. Undermanner has taken the Equerry under her protection, & says stables, oats & harness are in her realm. Gravell says no and at the same time has been indenting through military sources for all kinds of things which cld touch on inner realm: paint, desks & undercarpets & light-bulbs, even toilet rolls got bandied around. Undermanner seemed the aggressor, in demanding her status be unthreatened. But Gravell no doubt is getting a huge cut from requisitions through his army sources. He is a stereotype grafter, who prefers to slide around obstacles by cunning rather than have confrontations. He is the split image of that go-between who set up cock-fights for anthropologists in Bali whom I de-coded in my crit of Geertz.

Reflections on Minutes. Minutes are peculiar ritual form of advanced bureaucratic civilisation whose function is to 'name' conflicts in impersonal forms so as to neutralise conflict-situations. They are also (as Weeder knows) a way of manipulating those situations and effecting shifts in power-relations.

Examine this situation. Several different power-sets, super-ordinate and subordinate, are engaging in masked conflict and seeking to adjust power-relations. Almost nothing of the Weekly was concerned with the purported functions of this Institution. In fact, D. and I are performing almost the *whole* of this function on our own.

Oi Paz Notebook B

Of Beastly Procreation

Mortals exist in a rude and brutish state of fertility, by which almost every he and she is capable of procreation. Nor do they take it as a misfortune in a he to be virile, but a misfortune rather to be in a natural and incapable state. The greater part of the millions of males about this planet are equipped like Sper-men, nor could they build bumples to enshrine these many millions even if they so wished. Their genitals are over-developed, and although they hold this to be an occasion of pride, in the sideways manner of all things Sykotic they pretend to regard them with shame.

The manner of procreating is called 'sexual intercourse'. And while there is no subject of greater interest to them, and so often the matter for sideways comment, yet in all Oi Paz's time of study on this planet it would not have been possible to get to the bottom of it if one had not been found who was willing to explain in a direct manner the fashion of its performance. This is Sage, who has an intellect above the common in her species and who will trade knowledges with me in an open and fair manner. By which we have come together in a certain trade of trust, so that however unnatural and absurd the account that follows, yet I am willing to declaim it here as science.

The females, like the males, are fertile always, for at least their middle years. The natural methods of medical impregnation they regard not as natural but as 'artificial', and have only lately been discovered to their rudimentary science. These methods are still little employed, although the discovery may be expected to lead on to some reform of manners. The manner at present is by gross and brutish physical impregnation from one corpse to the other. It is indeed much like the mating of chuckalls or griffins, although these at least are so decent as to do this act upon another's back with averted faces and eyes. And this is the case, I am told, of all sentient creatures on Sykaos also. The mortal species alone goes into the act in frontal impact, or, as they say, 'effrontery'. And it is to be supposed that this is because of their erect two-legged posture, by which they cannot balance on each other's backs.

The manner in most use is thus: a male selects a female and offers to 'lie with her'. That is, he offers to deceive her (for 'to lie' is 'to deceive'), which is a sideways term only for the act they mean to perform. If the female agrees (as is customary) they then retire on to a bed, which they enter together, as if to sleep. But instead of sleeping, they lie face to face and belly against belly, grip each other's corpses in their arms, and thrust their faces into each other, pushing their lips upon each other's lips, and even forcing the mouth open and pushing with their tongues. After a short while in this proximity the male nozzle becomes a 'spur' (as with Sper-men) or, as they say, a 'prick', whereupon the female lies upon her back with open thighs and pulls the male down upon her, and the male by brute force inserts his swollen organ in her cunt, where, after some excitation and lip-sucking (or 'kissing') the semen is ejaculated in most wasteful quantities.

I note these improbable facts in such detail since they might provide clues to our historians as to the manner in which our pre-historic ancestors procreated before the origin of medical science; although the notion that they could have exchanged seed in so brutish a manner is beyond belief. But strange as this is, the customs which surround this act are even stranger. So far from regarding intercourse as a painful indignity, it is sought after as a special pleasure. And a woman who is more than usually comely will be asked by many men to lie with her, and from this number she will select several, although she may acknowledge only one, and will lie with (or deceive) the others in a sideways manner. And so also with the men.

Moreover, the act itself is undergone not on one or two special occasions only, as a bare necessity of prolonging the species, but is undergone frequently. Stranger than this, they have devised special acids and impediments to prevent the semen from entering the womb, so that the act is undergone without any purpose at all save the doing of the thing itself.

Strangest of all, this act is done – and the conceiving of the young which follows from it – in a way wholly unregulated by medicine or science or any prognostics: without attention to gene-suits; without selection of heredity; without Boards of Examiners; without the recording and computing of each act; and in utter disregard of bio-engineering or social order. From which all the degenerations of this unhappy species may be deduced.

So that it may be said that wherever one might venture on Sykaos, whether to the lands of America or Russia, whether on ships at sea or in the forests of the interior or in the swarming nests of their cities, there in every house, or even lying on the grasses under the moon, are pairs of mortals performing this act higgledy, without gene-suits, or Sper-charts or authorised supervision, in a chaos of individual whim. Let the reader but think of the millions of inhabitants of this planet, and then the cause for the malformation of corporeal and intellectual powers which I have described will become known.

Sage told me there were also other sexual 'tastes' or 'pre-ferences', as between those of the same sex. But as this does not

173

conduce to any procreation (nor can I construe any function) I leave that matter as an innuendo.

Sage also offered much about a mortal condition, which I take to be some fever or distemper, which they call 'love'. Which term they join so often to this act that lie and love are used almost alike. Yet in no way can Sage or any other tell me what thing or quality this is: as, what does love weigh? How does love smell? With which organs is love detected? In what measures does love come? Is love subject to the will? Can love be transmitted by some vibe? Is love a product of the mind? Is it a blemish of the sight? To all of which Sage gave a 'well, but' or a 'not quite'. And she, who was so open a trader of the material evidence, became indistinct and sideways in this. And the keeper Nettler who is trading with me poems has brought to me sonnets and lyrics of love which are nothing but defaults of reason and frauds upon truth, as that a woman is a 'swan' (which is a white water-bird) or that her breasts are snow (which is an absurdity) or her nipples roses or that he or she are near when they are far apart.

From which it may be seen that even the most rational of these creatures, as the Nettlers and Sages, cannot raise their forces above the fleshly regions in which they are bound and bred. For if love be a distemper then it must be only one of those distempers in which all their lives are passed, in which the spirit peers out through the sensual mists which encircle them from birth to death, and, glimpsing in the mist a shadow thrown by their own senses, they mistake this for reality and call it 'love'.

Sage Field Notes

2 March. Wednesday. Interview started v badly. No flow. Reasons: O. seemed put out because I hadn't been for six days. Sd 'you trade me off and on like water-tap'. Also, Hunter went in before me, wh always leaves him – *Qy:* somehow more 'Oitarian'? To get him going asked O. what he talks about wth

Hunter. *A*. (Holding back) 'We talk about the rotation of things.'
Q. Rotation of cosmos, solar system, planets? *A*. No. Q. Rotation
of blood? Seasons? *A*. No. (Trading grudgingly) 'Rotation of the
Rule – and the beastly law.'

It transpired that what H. and O. trade together is shared
fascination in bureaucracy. Hunter is military, *sub sp* managerial
(why he has this job). Did a course just before he came here in
systems management, data input outgo, instruction paths, control
grids. O. fascinated by this: collects the terms of bureaucratic org,
rota, roster, circular, memo, pro-forma, standing committee,
regulation, precedent, constitution. Is now into law terms ...
These seem to give him purchase on Earth culture. In return he
trades to Hunter data as to Oitarian Rule. (*Mem*: Must catch up on
this. My notes re Goodnesses, Bumples, Colleges & esp Wheel – a
cloud there? – v sketchy, perhaps because texture of determinism
scalds my disciplinary vibes.)

Flowed a bit, but on/off. I checked out early notes on Oitar,
fauna, botanical & c., for paper for Pepper. Flowed when I went
back to unicorns. Stirred memories of childhood. They exercise
unicorns on the 'lawns' & play elab games (cf polo?). O. really
broke into flow & paced the room. Sd riding was 'a poem, a
beautiful music'.

'On any day on the further ranches in the great Alls one may
see the Keepers of the Seven, gaily attired in their blue pants and
white jackets, riding their noble unicorns, their griffins obediently
at heel, over-watching the great herds of cottons with their
harvest of silvery fleece ...' He was now at window where I
joined him. His bay window looks straight into vista wh falls to
the lake at left of wh is open park where Equerry has set up
jumps. E. was taking a big black horse through its paces & O.
raised his hands like a prophet giving blessing. Asked O. if he
would like to ride. Never seen so much visual evidence of inner
conflict. As if his programme was sparking. Sd riding was 'music
of the heavens'. But his role-set forbidden to ride when they enter
adulthood unless with special licence. How cld he get a 'waiver'?
(NB O. still feels norm-bound & duty-governed by Oit Rule.)

I suggested this a rule for governance of Oitar but on 'Sykaos' his duty to keep all his forces together for service of 'Wheel', & maybe horse-riding cld be form of worship? Like all wrestling with temptation Oipas grabbed at the excuse: 'Good thinking, Sage. Oipas will pray to the Wheel each morning on that black horse!' (*Mem*: Satan a mythopoeic redundancy. Left to themselves Adam & Eve wld have invented the snake as an excuse.)

In the corridor I kicked myself for starting this up. Horses are Undermanner's under-empire via Equerry but are Hunter's perk. No way Hunter wld allow a 'wog' (wh I am sure is how he regards O., off-the-record) to ride his horses. Also, however low the value They set on Oipas, neck-breaking wld not meet with approval.

Thought the only thing to do was go direct to Equerry & find out form, procedure for requisition, horse, black, one. Wh I did at once. Equerry was trotting back into stable yard, no one else there. I don't even know its *name*, since List of Establishment has not been revised since Week One, where it appears as: '*Equerry*: A. N. Other'. Nor have I exchanged six words with it. Reasons: (1) She only came to dinners once, and sd not one word but looked us all evenly in the eye as if we were aliens. Refused most food: is vegetarian (like Rani but more strict). Don't know where she 'messes'; maybe with Other Ranks, to whom she has been effectively relegated, except for (2): she comes to Weeklies. Where she wears anorak & jeans & pongs of horse. Sits there reading *Horse and Hound* (no concealment) & once *slept*. Reason (3): I'm not a horse-person.

I stood in the yard, trying to keep my knee-boots (posh ones I got before leaving Outer World) away from horse-shit. Equerry nodded evenly & dismounted, saying, 'Hello, Helena. Never expected to see you here.' She had her back to me, unhitching saddle-girth. 'Me name's Ann,' she sd, into the horse's haunch. She turned round and looked me full in the eyes. 'You didn't know that, did you.'

This was not the best vantage-point from wh to start an exercise in exchange of favours. In fact, what favours did I have on my side of the market? I began to make excuses – 'Come back when you're not so busy' – and to wiggle around the shit as I backed out of yard. Equerry had got horse's saddle off now & was putting it on half-door of stable. 'You came about something, didn't you?' she remarked, as if to door. 'You want to do some riding?' 'Well, no, I'm not a rider . . .' (Isn't quite true: I've hacked about on mules & c., enough in my field work, & when I was a kid I enjoyed it a lot.) Then, in a rush, I added, 'But Mr Oipas asked me to find out . . .'

Equerry dumped the saddle, wheeled around (making Horse jerk and flash a deadly white eye), and exclaimed, 'Oy Pee! He's a *fab* rider!' 'But how do you know? Has he . . .?' 'Just *look* at him! How he holds his back! He's okay, isn't he, Macho?' She was now talking to Horse, whose white eye was now on me, with rump swivelling in my direction. It seemed that in Horse's p–of–view I was *not* okay.

Equerry seemed to collect herself & began busying with bridle. 'Bloody Martingale,' she said, but not apparently at me, I suppose at Martagon generally. (She seems to have private nicknames for everything.) There commenced negotiation, Bali–style, allusive, possessor withholding, prospective purchaser noncommittal, terms of bargain coded. But wh was possessor, wh purchaser? I sensed she wanted 'Oy Pee' to ride & thought I might be medium of delivery. Since I didn't know what I wanted I was weaker party. All the while Equerry busy at Horse things & talking mainly through her back or through Horse. Then turned & sd, 'What about Them? I mean Your Lot up there' – nodding towards Hall – 'won't like it, you know. Colonel Grunter would do his top. And Gravell. Hunter thinks this whole outfit is for him.'

At mention of Hunter, or Grunter, Horse started to play up in real earnest; whinnied like banshee; glared with whites; rose up on rump & waved solidungulate paws, towering above Equerry in her black riding–hat, who had nothing to hold Horse by but reins slung around huge arching black neck. Equerry mastered (? mistressed) Horse in twinkling: 'Get BACK! PIG!' (Clout on buttocks, wh threatening quarters she bodily pushed into stable, as Horse, deflated into deference like school bully, went to back of form.)

It seemed I had gained half an honours-point by standing my ground during this contretemps. I was taken into 'den', where electric kettle, tannin-lined mugs: perhaps her mess? Two bottles of real milk (but we only get Marvel) – how? And stone-ground wholemeal loaf (never in canteen-mess) – from where? (Guessed I shldn't ask – she noticed me looking.) About seventeen jars of peanut butter & a bin of trackfood. Equerry went straight to the point. 'They' wldn't let 'Oy Pee' ride, But it wld be 'fab' if he cld. Only way to do it was to do it. Don't ever ask Them. If They come down on you, play stupid, didn't know. However: in this case precautions advisable. Shld start off riding early morning. 6 a.m.

Horse started shouting (wh started mares shouting) & Equerry sd, 'Damn, Macho needs watering. But, *wow*, I can just see Oy Pee and Macho going over the treble.' I felt a cramp in tum, what had I got into? 'But .. you can't be putting Oipas on that ... *stallion*? Don't you have some quieter ... er ...' Equerry chortled. 'Nothing cut here, don't believe in it. And the mares are pretty frisky. But they're all lambs with Oy Pee.' Asked how she knew. Seems O. has wandered round to stables or to jumps quite often in early morning. 'He has vibes with horses, you know,' Equerry sd. looking at me v straight, no hint of joke. 'He talks with them. They come up to him & stand together for minutes.'

As I was going, Equerry sd, 'You'll be coming too.' It wasn't a question, more like a fact. Me! 6 a.m.! But I cld see that this was to be part of the deal – if there was any can to carry, I must share it. Okay, I cld keep watch. 'No. You'll muck out. And you'll ride.' She walked around me, eyeing me as if I was up for sale. 'You're a rider of sorts, or could be. Let yourself go ... withers a bit flabby. Your back's *awful* – all that deskwork. Ask Rani to put you on to yoga to get you into fettle. Take care!' *Still* don't know her second name.

Sage Field Notes

3 March. Signals officer (Sorley) made first appearance at dinner last night. Definite asset to Enemy, balance further slewed from academics to military. Called Pepper, Hunter, even Mayhem, 'Sir'. Wore a dress uniform (without Sam Browne), with puce lapels on which is Astrosigint's emblem, a sort of spark between two globes. Over our Perriers and apple-juice before dinner he sidled up to me and introduced himself. Tried to ingratiate himself by talking about some 'stone-age' people he had visited on Java. I tried to put him down by talking about Jurgen Landmarck's recent tome on sd people, & he put me off balance by saying (in tone of simulated modesty) that he had read it, and had met Landmarck, but thought he 'might have got one or two things wrong'. Not my field so I backed off, but could feel myself aching to pick a fight with him.

He switched topic to Oipas and asked, ingratiatingly, how I was getting on. We were suddenly in one of those spitting fights, in wh neither of us was really talking to the other. I sd he wld be able to read my weekly reports. He sd he already had them in his files. I sd, Oh, so you're watching me, I thought you were supposed to watch the moon? He sd we were both watching the moon, in different ways. I sd, 'Very different ways. My job is to empathise. You are watching for an Enemy.' He sd, 'Well, surely, we both want to defend the planet Earth?' When the bell rang and we all went in to dinner. He detached himself from me and went and sat between Undermanner and Rani, who looks quite wonderful now that she has taken to dining in saris. Makes me feel a frump.

The outer man of the major is reasonably personable: mid-thirties, blondish hair, very blue eyes. In his manners he pretends to be shy. (Cooped up with males all his life, I suppose.) Seemed to get on well with R., cldn't catch what they were talking about, except it seemed to be something Indian. That's his line: to keep his own hand hidden and make people show theirs. R. cldn't see that when I warned her afterwards. Sd I was 'racialist' about the military, who are humans like us, and that Major Sorley seemed to be very 'gentle'!! And 'he really is very interested in Mr Oipas'. I bet he is! Another one to watch.

Today, D. and I working flat out at getting our 'rent' together: i.e. papers for Pepper. Reminds me of preparing for orals at Duke. D. has decided to do a short 'Glossary' of 'equivalents'. Not a dictionary: hasn't yet got verbs. It's as if there are only four or five verbs in the whole language, wh indicate states: as *vel*, wh could be to 'do' or 'act' or 'go' & whose meaning is controlled by context, e.g. to *vel* with unicorn means to 'ride' and to *vel* with Rule is to 'obey'. Other possible verb-states: being; non-being; and revolving or 'wheeling' or (D. says) more like 'being wheeled'.

So D. says premature to put down any verbs yet, and for a lot of other words he can't do much because I haven't yet given him clues to controlling concepts. He thinks Oitarian language made up of homophones: each syllable wth a distinct notation. Thus Oipas is really Oi Pas. But Oi Pas could indicate a particular genetic role-kit. 'Oi Pas could be like H_2O.' There cld be a whole set of Oi Pas's, distinguished by year of conception (like wine vintage).

D. is sure, anyway, that Oitarian names are neither patronymics nor matronymics but what he calls 'genetonyms'. If there are lots of Oi Pas's, then for finding purposes Oitarian records cld distinguish them by year of conception and hostess. (D. has got some of this patter off so fluently that it's creepy.) Asked him about 'hostess'. Says he can't find any concept for 'father' or 'mother'. Hostess receives insemination & foetus delivered at three months, then she returns to role-set. Suggests she has no further relation with child? I confirmed this as my own hypothesis. Even more I cannot find concept of 'kin', wh is a real problem for an anthropologist. D. nodded. Sd it cld explain 'a lot of other things': absence of affective terms. Also: if Oipas is *an* Oi Pas (among many others distinguished by a 'finding number' of hostess-variable) then how does he feel/apprehend his own identity? 'I mean, is he conscious of himself only as a genetic-kit and as an ordained role? It's a bit scary.' I said it was, but why not?

David then talked abt Oitarian grammar (or absence) & his

stuff so new I asked him if I cld turn my recorder on. 'Vocabulary isn't the main problem. Anyone can get down some of that. The trouble is . . . *is* the grammar a grammar which can be registered or understood at all by the human brain as now programmed?' (We had our old argument re Chomsky, which I'll cut.) 'Well, anyway, it isn't a human grammar. Some of the nouns seem to be verbs and some of the verbs nouns. Well, we also do that a lot – a wheel can wheel. But all Oitarian seems to be wheeling, as if turning around its own axis.'

H. 'Do you mean Oitarians have sprung the binary trap which seems to block and limit human thought? And which is being absolutely rigidified to yes/no paths by computers?'

D. 'I know you have an obsession with that, Helena. Computers don't *have* to be just binary, if you write the programmes carefully . . . No, don't stop me. In some ways Oipas is *more* binary. Perhaps because he stands in binary opposition to our own culture. But at a hazard I would say he is the product of an advanced computer culture – gigaflops more advanced than ours – which has passed over a lot of its thinking to artificial intelligences. I can't find any terms controlled by concepts of *chance*. Or even of choice. Have you? Well, at its most elementary, Oipas can't count beyond about ten . . .'

H. 'I know.'

D. 'But he isn't stupid. His numeracy has atrophied. Why? Because he can just fiddle with that jigger on his belt and get the answer. Why waste brain-cells holding numbers when a microdot will do it? But what about other kinds of thinking? Perhaps Oitarians throw a whole lot of other questions, which we would study and agonise over, into an artificial intelligence. So that other faculties could have atrophied also. We may have, in Oipas, an advanced intelligence which comes from a culture in an advanced state of computer-dependency.'

H. 'Yes, he does appear to have real difficulty in making the least decision. Would he like tea? Will he have a bath now or later? He stares around as if this was a matter beneath him and some box should decide for him.'

D. 'Computer-dependency. Maybe Oitarians don't make choices – or some kinds of choice. They feed the variables into an artificial intelligence and wait for the answer to come out – in a split second – on the screen. Or on their belt monitors. This would leave cranial space for other faculties to develop.'

H. 'Such as?'

D. 'I don't quite know. If they are *other* faculties, how could we have the faculty for knowing? I'm sure he can read some thoughts. But only some. But like abstracts – indices with no context.'

H. 'He can't read feelings at all. He keeps on reducing poor Rani to tears. I don't think he means to. Do you mean he just doesn't *have* feelings, like Mr Spock.'

D. 'That's not what the language seems to say. He could read feelings – he seems to sense "vibes" more than we do – but he may not have concepts for them as feelings. I mean, he could *note* feelings but not *respond*. Perhaps he doesn't know what tears mean. He could note them but not have a concept for them. The language doesn't seem to have words for elementary feelings – love, hate, fear, need – or if it does there is a different feeling-set implied. Colour, form, grace, music – these are all there in the language . . .'

H. 'Flowers and music turn him on. And horses.'

D. 'Do they? That fits.'

H. 'And he has taboos. Like the taboo about eating. Although that didn't last long, by Rani's account. But he still turns away from Gravell & co. when they are scoffing dinner. And he puts food in his mouth furtively . . .'

D. 'Ye-es. I mean no. Maybe Oitarians are very adaptive. Maybe they can re-programme to culture-changes. But he still has a thing about touching. If someone shakes his hand he goes off and washes . . . And then there's wheels.'

H. 'Oh, yes, there's wheels. I've noticed wheels.'

D. 'Anything round. Anything strongly patterned or marked out. Rose gardens. Tennis court. He goes around or he goes diagonal – he never just goes *any* way. You know that sort of tile-mosaic in the main entrance-hall, a circle with a satyr in the middle?'

H. 'Mmmm?'

D. 'Well, watch him. He's mesmerised by it. He won't put a foot on it. He skirts around it, with a little nod or inclination of the head . . .'

H. 'I've missed that. But it's the same with the orangery. And when he goes round the main rose bed, the same inclination of the head, and he touches the phallus emblem and the wheel on his belt.'

D. 'Mmmm . . . I missed that.'

H. 'This is great stuff for me, but isn't it a bit far from linguistics? I don't want you putting *my* paper into Pepper.'

D. 'No! We have to work together. How can I fillet the language if I don't know if his affective nature is like ours? If he has taboos and aesthetic feelings then he must have some affective ground. But the grammar – if there is a grammar – seems . . . ultra-rational, like a fast path in algebra, where equations do the work of predicates and tenses and copulatives. I'm getting to like the feel of it, it sort of hooks me. But it's not so much a language as a reason-code that has been cured or disinfected of all affective context. It's like a programme which could go direct into a computer – into people's brain-cells? – without any need to put it first into PROLOG or anything . . . And yet . . .'

H. 'Go on.'

D. 'Yet there are *huge* blocks of something like feeling.'

H. 'I know. Pardon me, but this is what I work on.'

D. 'Sorry, Helena. This must sound very amateurish . . .'

H. 'Don't be an ass, David. I was only girning. All this is fantastic . . . It helps me to sort out a hundred things I've been working on. Continue.'

D. 'Well, blocks of feelings. Sometimes just blocks: resistances. He outright refused love poetry. Actually stopped me reading it. Rejections of some non-rational paths. Likes Milton, Homer, but refuses Keats or Yeats. But then, suddenly, *pow!* He switches some sort of feeling on. It's like a moral organ. He got *Paradise Lost* from the Old Library himself and was pacing his room declaiming it.'

Silence – sound of drinks pouring.

D. 'It's got something to do with identity.'

H. 'Yes. I'm there too. But by a different route.'

D. 'He *has* feelings. Or he registers them as signals. But they are, sort of, *givens* . . . not his own . . .'

H. 'They are we-feelings, not I-personal feelings. They remind me of some compulsions in primitive societies. Tribal imperatives and taboos. Or early societies, where the most terrible penalty known – far worse than death – was to outlaw an offender from the tribe. Remember the punishment of Cain? "My punishment is greater than I can bear. Thou hast driven me out from the face of the earth."'

D. 'But a very complex tribe. His feelings are scarcely fixed in his own ego. They are internalised like commands from the programme of the collective. Where is his "I"? All languages have a structure which differentiates between I and the Other, I and the world, even – surely? – I and the tribe. Well, I'm guessing, but I can't see a grammar that would work without.'

H. 'Probably right. Although early societies have a very heavy "We" and a vivid collective spiritual life.'

D. 'Yes. And I suppose we kid ourselves. Most of our individual ego is an internalised "We".'

Silence.

H. 'I didn't mean to stop you. Go on. Let me top up.'

D. 'Maybe Oipas isn't as different from us as I think. But he forms no personal attachments because he has no sense, or little sense, of identity. He sees himself as an instrument of Oitarian functions – if he has an agony it is to be the vector of a collective consciousness which is isolated from the collective. As you say, an outlaw. His initiative is low. He is happened more than he happens – although maybe that is changing. I'm astonished at how he goes and digs out books for himself in the Library.'

H. 'I think he does have an ego.'

D. 'He does. But it shifts. He doesn't *know* himself. Do you notice – he sometimes slips, and refers to himself in the third person – "Oipas is going" . . .?'

H. 'I have a lot of notes on that. But he does it rarely now. And if Oitarian culture has no concept of personal identity, how can he speak this concept, "I", in English? What does it mean to him?'

D. 'I'm asking that. He could have *a* concept of identity but not *our* concept. He could see himself quite clearly, as an object, as an index within a set. He could stand, as it were, *with* the "tribe" and could point to himself and give that point the name of "I". But he could still have – well, *scarcely* – any self-consciousness of "I" as subject, and differentiated in any need or goal or desire from the tribe.'

Sound of laughter, ♀.

D. 'What have I said that's so funny?'

H. 'Sorry! No, nothing to do with you. It's just that one of your words hit me on the funny-bone. "Scarcely." I mean, I sometimes think that Captain Scarcely is *exactly* what you've been saying . . . a digit within a set, with scarcely any self-consciousness apart from his tribal role . . . No, really, sorry. So. When Oipas uses English he takes over with it concepts as givens which are outside Oitarian concepts?'

D. 'Must do. It must have been quite incredibly difficult for him to learn an Earth language, because not only the grammar but the whole conceptual parameters of human language are alien to his own. It must have been as difficult as it will be for us to learn Oitarian. In fact, it makes me despair.'

H. 'But Rani said he learned it in the Infirmary with the aid of a computer-thing called a Translator. And you say this must have involved not only translation but deep conceptual reprogramming? A sort of culture-transformer? She says that at first it would pass over words (maybe critical concepts?) with a fluting-noise, and when the talk was of war or money it would choke – throw its switches.'

D. 'Damn! The Translator! I'd forgotten about it. Could we get it?'

H. 'He smashed it. When he was sloshed and doing his scene on telly.'

D. 'Where is it?'

H. 'I don't know. Maybe in a props room in one of Harmer's theatres. Not here.'

D. 'I must get it. Signals might mend it. Even just the circuits might show something . . .'

H. 'David, I wouldn't bother. It's *your* circuits that will pick the code and they're doing great.' Sound of smothered yawn, ♀. 'I think I'm going to turn in, if you don't mind. This has been fantastic – I'll keep the tape. But I've got to be up at dawn to get my memo done for Pepper.'

D. 'Oh, well . . . Right, I'll be off. Thanks for the schnapps.' Sound of shifting chair and grunting, ♂.

H. 'David . . . before you go. There's one thing we've never had a deep exchange on . . .'

D. 'As . . .?'

H. 'Laughter. Oy Pee – sorry, Oipas – never laughs. Can't laugh. Calls it the Incongruous Noise. Has no concept of laughter. What does this mean? What *is* laughter? I've consulted the lit. Extraordinarily little written, most of it pretentious bosh. It seems to be a place in our own culture we can't look in at. More, much more, than death. We can no more look into the heart of our own laughter than we can look at the sun. It could be a key to Oitarian/Earthly culture-differentiation.'

D. 'Right. We'll have a session – in a couple of weeks. You bring a thick description of Oipas's reactions to laughter. I'll bring . . . well, something.'

Sage Notebook. Pasted-in typescript

Helena Sage, PhD, FRAI
   Preliminary Notes on Oitarian Eco-System & Life Forms

   Source: Interviews with Informant. Refs: Weekly Reports 14, 15, 19 (in files). Notes & tape (own possession).

Eco-System. Oitar's dimensions greater than Earth's. No accurate dimensions possible at this stage. Suggest about twice girth, denser volume. Oitar is planet in solar system which Informant refers to as 'The Wheel'. Unclear whether 'Wheel' signifies 'sun' or the whole movement of system-rotation (including Oitar itself) but suspect either both or latter.

Owing to girth and slow rotation (relative axes?) of planet and sun, Oitarian day is *circa* three and a half Earth days (82 hours). Rising occasion for festal displays,* setting of sun also occasion for ceremonial, artificial lights (nuclear?) in sky. At zenith of radiation perceptible warming of temperature, slight melting of glaciers: this main source of water which is 'harvested', or channelled into 'tanks' or lakes in astrodomes.† In winter temperatures fall and all planet outside domes is in deep-frozen state.

The sun seems to be going through a cold stage.‡ In terms of geological time, cooling is excessively fast. There is also serious escape of atmosphere. (Perhaps some deceleration or quantity-quality jump astronomers can explain?) (But don't ice-ages crack down suddenly on Earth?) Oitarian culture holds 'memories', part mythopoeic, part archaic history, and a bit enshrined in early epics, as to a time before the 'domes' when planters and hunters lived on open planetary surface. Indeed, Oitarian history might be divided into BD and AD (before and after domes) but everything BD very misty and (it seems) no written records.

Line between BD and AD marked by Age of Primitive Erections, or APE. Some crisis – 10 or 15 years of icing-up? (and Oitarian years nearly twice Earthly years) – reduced population by two-thirds, killed off much fauna, flora. At this point they retired within the first domes, cupolas or Alls. An All is a large

---

* *Marginal note, pencil:* 'Will do another paper on festal days, ceremonial.'
† *Marginal note, pencil:* 'All this about astrodomes, cupolas, Alls, bumples, architecture, will have to wait for another paper.'
‡ *Marginal note, pencil:* 'Sorry! I have no astrophysics. Perhaps we should get someone?'

hangar constructed in glass or some other opaque material which enhances rays of the suns, holds in heat & c. From AD 1 until now (*c.* 6,300 Oitarian years) immense advances in engineering. The largest Alls cover an area the size of (*Qy*) Rutland, Isle of Wight? They are interconnected by 'arcades' (sealed corridors?). But species (all species) now faced new eco-threat. Oxygen on Oitar (always rare) began to thin out. Therefore they had to manufacture oxygen (and mix it to approved proportions) and also immeasurably to improve engineering expertise. Primitive Erections were a kind of giant greenhouse. Age of Ordinary Erections, or AOE (*temp c.* AD 1,200), much larger, better sealed. Age of Giant Erections, AGE (*temp* AD 4,100?) so much advanced that probably we don't have technological vocabulary. They are system-sealed (to hold in oxygen, which is produced by plant on the periphery), induce desired rays and exclude undesired, have plant for water-production and circulation – indeed, huge lakes or 'tanks' – and ice-burners (nuclear?) to hold back pressure of glaciers in winter. Five or six favoured regions of Oitar are covered with Erections: huge ones are Alls, small ones for special functions are cupolas or domes, all interconnected by 'arcades' with air-locks and seals in case of rupture of linings – e.g. meteors, although they have 'anti-matter shields' to guard against this. These regions are their cities, or 'orbs'. Also a few isolated cupolas, such as observatories, in remote areas of planet, which can be reached only by air/spacecraft or sometimes by land in mid-summer.

All this tentative, *please*. But if correctly deciphered (and if Informant credible) note consequences:

1. Prime necessity for survival of artificial environment & defences means unusual centralisation of power in engin-eering (and bio-engineering) elite or theocracy, with *total* command of all Oitarian resources. Cf. theories of cen-tralised despotism in 'hydraulic civilisations'. Profound societal consequences flow.

2. We have here an artificial – i.e. engineered and creature-controlled – environment, outside our concepts.

Further observation. If anything, environment outside the domes has been degenerating in past 4,000 years (Oitarian). Hence resort to space exploration to find alternative less hostile environment to settle. Don't understand degree of emergency but it has become a culture-priority. Intentions not warlike: just species-survival.

Hence we have not one eco-system but two.

Outer. Extremely hostile. Degenerating. Most of surface of planet has been evacuated – much of it for over 4,000 years (Oitarian). In mid-summer, when some low-lying plains melt, there is some sphagnum, tundra. (*Query:* some insect survival? Informant knows little of this. Only selected role-sets or genetic-kit groups go out on planet in summer. Informant has only once been out on planet's surface, in function of poet, to 'declaim odes' about expedition. Certainly no mammals could live out there.)

Inner. Artificially engineered eco-system. Within these Alls, *selected* fauna, flora, thrive. Selection was made at APE and continued as long as there was anything to select. Informant describes following species. (*Note.* In some cases Informant uses Earthly terms. These he presumably got from the (late) Translator, or perhaps from a Dictionary.)

FAUNA

The Seven Sentient Creatures

Unicorn. Informant describes this as very much like a horse but with a single horn. White or dappled. Is used for riding. Also ceremonial. High honour status.

Griffin. Working beast. I think with lion-like legs and claws and of build of a thick Doberman but with a beak. Does some dog-type duties, as shepherding.

Cotton. Creature kept for fleece: for clothing. Fleece very fine, silky. Runs in flocks on the plains or lawns of the biggest Alls. Rather like llamas. Shepherded by griffins.

Ur-dragon. Odd, but seems to be like human mythic dragon. In some way simulates fire from nostrils. Was selected at BD/AD to help in ice-burning. Now has little function and (by Oitarian decision) an endangered species. But some few still bred since very hardy and can drag sledges on summer expeditions.

Ger-dragon. More docile variant of above. Most transport in Alls is of course mechanised (highly) but at BD/AD gers selected as heavy draught-creature. Now employed on construction-work (new domes, Alls) or for ceremonial purposes on Festal Days, drawing chariots.

Butler. (How did Informant get this term?) Is the most useful of all species. May be compared to ape, but with more advanced mental faculties: erect posture; developed use of paw or 'hands'. Does an immense amount of menial chores on Oitar. Informant says can even be 'programmed': i.e. inducted into performance of routine menial roles without supervision.

Chuckall. Informant closes up on this. I know chuckall exists since it enters vocabulary, especially when 'swearing' at us (i.e. humans)! Definitely low honour-rating: may be shame creature. At a guess I would say chuckall is a scavenger: cf. hyena, ground-vulture? May dispose of dead bodies of griffins, cottons, butlers & c.?

In addition to 'Sentient Seven' they have preserved three other species, as to which Informant is vague – or perhaps ecstatic? These appear to have been selected for aesthetic or spiritual functions and rate very high on the honour charts. Informant has given them English dictionary names and I cannot make much of their characteristics.

SECOND CAPTIVITY

The Sacred Three

Dolphin. This displays itself on the lakes or 'tanks' in the Great Alls. Like all the 'Sacred Three' it is a 'Communicant Creature': that is, they 'talk' with it through 'vibes'. Object of worship? Emblem of water?

Phoenix. A creature worshipped as emblem of fire and air. But can it fly? (Wings clipped?)

Cat. A creature worshipped as emblem of earth. Also of wisdom. No other function whatsoever. Informant describes it as much like our own tabby cat. Suppose he is fantasising. Cats patrol their temples, or 'bumples'.

Further Notes

Fish. There seem to be fish in lakes & c., but Informant gives little. Think they are ornamental, like goldfish.

Birds. No reference to birds. Presumably, if birds, they were made extinct in great ice-age?

Food. Important culture-bind. My hypothesis is some eco-crisis soon after APE when no way of feeding population. Oitarian species increasingly abandoned solids and went over to vita-pellets, artificial. First of all, flesh was abandoned (? cottons), then most cereals and vegetation. *But sentient* creatures could not be conditioned to pills. Hence necessary to cultivate some plains or 'lawns' with crops for cottons, griffins, dragons & c. And butlers. The cardinal crops Informant mentions are the 'bredstik' (cereal), 'milkstem' (cereal again?), and the 'crompet' (brassica?). Also 'egflour'. These are cultivated, harvested and stored to feed Seven Sentients. Humans also consume small quantities (for bulk), but some taboo attached to this. (Informant always talks about the Sacred Three with such deference that they might live on air. The 'cat' is not even allowed a mouse.) I think the shame thing about the 'chuckall' may be that it is the last surviving species which is a carnivore — and it survives as a liminal creature as scavenger of offal. The butler takes some vita-pellets as well as bredstik and milkstem.

FLORA & C.

Not ready yet to hazard much here. Sorry! Main points about vegetation seem to be:

1. In outer environment only lichens, sphagnum, survive.
2. Within the domes selection was made to preserve three kinds: (a) utilitarian – crops to feed the sentient creatures, & c., and also to be pelleted for vita-pills; (b) aesthetic – flowers whose scent or colours or form delight Oitarians; (c) medicinal – on this Informant is a duffer. Does not relate to things 'corporeal'. But from various allusions some plants are preserved as sources of remedies, unguents. Also (as important) for trance-inducing properties and as hallucinogens. Oitarians are certainly into this. Informant came to earth in a hallucinated state.

Of the aesthetic selection – I still have more work to do. Trouble is: Informant has been talking to gardeners and gives earth-names to Oitarian flora. Thus he says Oitar has 'roses', 'lilies', 'orchids', and whatever he likes. Aesthetic selection preserved flora more on criteria of scent and beauty than utilitarian. Oitarians are great formal gardeners. But they have no *trees* – nothing much bigger than a hibiscus. Informant told me that when he first landed on Earth he supposed trees were giant sentient creatures.

PROBLEM

Have not yet been able to identify any *insects*, except butterflies. They have butterflies in all shapes and sizes, many much bigger than on Earth, swallow-tails and also something like dragon-flies. But, again, selected on aesthetic criteria. Can butterflies on their own do all the work of fertilising the bredstik, milk-stem and other flora?

They also have grasses for their lawns.

Helena Sage*

Oi Paz Notebook A

Of Sykaos: Life-Support Systems and Species

There is no planet in the discovered universe so temperate as is Sykaos, nor more hospitable to life. Yet nothing of this aston-ishing fortune is owing to intelligence or design. It arises from the occurrence of things, a congruence of benign factors which no computer could predict, a coincidence of accidental favours which only the infinitude of time and space could allow. The eco-system of Sykaos does not lie within the arc of probability, it is a random occurrence at possibility's farthest edge.

Examine probability. As our Colleges have construed, among the multitude of known stars only one in 240 are constituted as solar systems with planets in their orbits. Our space travellers have passed by red giants, inchoate nebulae, brown dwarfs, and have skirted flaring supernovae. Several of our craft have been drawn into the black holes of decaying systems. Yet only rarely have they encountered solar systems poised at the azimuth of their span, with attendant planets bathed in the benign solar winds of the sun's corona.

And when such systems have been found, how many have been the disappointments of our explorers! How often have our Colleges received the reports: the planets, barren rocks, pitted with the infraction of meteorites; the dimensions or density too slight to retain any atmosphere; the surface glaciated in a frozen cape of nitrogen; or great gaseous globes, turbulent with ammonia, helium, hydrogen, methane, outpourings of sulphur dioxide.

---

* *Pencil annotation, addressed to* 'David': 'Here endeth my paper. Please note, all the above is *provisional* only and not to be "declaimed" into a computer! Not a *bloody word* for publication. All crits and comments welcome.'

In 3,000 years of exploring, of all the solar systems visited by our explorers, none has proved worthy of plantation, unless in the ultimate emergency. Few planets evinced the emergence of life-forms, and these were mostly of primitive kinds – as methane-ingesting bacteria and tube-worms infesting muds of hydrogen sulphide. On four planets it is true that communicant creatures were found, yet these were in atmospheres in which helium or ammonia were predominant. The founders of the science of stellanthropology endured great hazards in their field studies, working from within the protection of oxygen cabins. None of these planets could ever have been made habitable.

The solar system of Strim includes eleven planets, of which two (the outermost) have not yet been detected by the primitive instruments of Sykotic astronomers. Sykaos is the third in orbit from its sun. It flies through space as if obedient to the programme of some Original Goodness, within a narrow band of shelter from the extremities of fire and ice. Had the planet's orbit been one Earth 'degree' further from its sun, then all its surface would have been frozen to temperatures lower than Oitar's poles. Had the orbit been five degrees closer to its sun, then all its melt would have boiled.

The greater part of the planet is covered – and sometimes to a great depth – with molten water, so that it is indeed a hydrosphere, three quarters of the surface being oceans or ice, one quarter being settled crust.

Sykotic books aver that the poles of the planet are capped with ice, which advances or retreats with the seasons. And this was confirmed by our observatories on its moon. Great stretches of these ice-bound regions could be made habitable with some works of engineering, for they are much like the great plains of Oitar. Yet the Sykaans despise them as unfit for mortal dwelling, and prefer to cluster in unimaginable density in a few favoured temperate zones. In these zones, there is a perpetual circulation of weather which bears water from the oceans to fall as rain upon the land, replenishing the rivers and lakes which lie along the crust. This cycle performs all the supports of life without the intervention of any design or skill, and the mortals describe the occurrence of things as the work of 'Nature' or 'God'.

As it is with the hydrosphere, so it is with the atmosphere. For the entire globe is protected within a gaseous cloud or layer whose elements are benign to life. There was a brief point of geological equipoise on Oitar also, in primordial times, when the world enjoyed such a balance of happenstance, enabling the first flowers of life and of civilisation to blow. And in the swill of those ancient oceans there was a generation of life in algaes and planktons which acted like an atmospheric plant, digesting carbon dioxide and throwing out oxygen as waste – from which the atmosphere became benign, and life crawled out of the oceans on to the land.

If the sequence was such, then Sykaos is now at that moment of genial self-sustaining equipoise which Oitar briefly passed through some half a billion years ago. And the ecosphere enjoys, within most delicate margins, all the conditions for the fulfilment of civilised life. For the abundant vegetation of this little planet continually replenishes the oxygen in the atmosphere. And the equilibrium of things is even finer than that. For the diminution of carbon dioxide has enabled the planet's surface to remain cool despite an increase in the heat of their sun, by which reason the oceans are stable and do not evaporate, but circulate their moisture as weather in the hydrosphere: for the density of the planet's magnetosphere is just sufficient to afford a compulsion which holds the gases to cling about its surface. An even finer balance is found in the prismatoidal shield of a thin layer of ozone in the upper atmosphere, which absorbs the noxious ultraviolet pulses of the solar wind without the need for the absorbent defences of our domes. Which shield they are busy puncturing with their acids and effluents, so that it is now in peril.

Such an equilibrium can be of only the briefest geological duration, which could pass into disorder with any divergence from the norm or alien intrusion. For the precious atmosphere is so thin an envelope of vapours that it seems only a filament lying upon the oceans and land, to be torn away by any natural event, such as the impact of an asteroid or a flux in the solar wind. And the balance of things is so precarious now that the highest of the planet's little mountains (no more than three ersts in elevation) rise into zones where the oxygen count is too rare to support human life; and even in the temperate zones the smallest hills are swept with winds and may be covered with snow although the plains beneath them bask in radiant sun.

LIFE FORMS

Life is of recent evolution on the planet, yet it has already passed through several cycles of development, and has assumed forms more various and more copious than any known in our primordial past. There is a book in this coop which declaims that there are now more than 250,000 species of vegetation surviving on this planet and over 10,000 species of animal: but I discard this as Sykotic boasting. Yet the number of forms is undoubtedly very great (as Oi Paz has observed) and the number of extinguished species even greater.

In Sykotic computation of years they suppose that the first life-forms emerged four billion Earth years ago. These forms existed only in the oceans, and the emergence of life on to the land and the evolution of chloroplasts and of vegetation capable of photosynthesis is a very recent event.

Three hundred million years ago great regions of the land were made up of swampy forests, populated by scaly creatures of the build of large dragons. This is the greater portion of the history of life on the planet, and these dragon-like creatures were the most successful known, enduring for some two hundred million Earth years. (The present dominant species – Sykotic mortals or 'man' – has existed for only one-hundredth of that time.)

In the past seven hundred million Earth years there have been nine great extinction events, although whether by the impact of asteroids or the cooling of the oceans or the eruption of dust and ashes out of the Earth's core is uncertain. But the crust of this planet is intermixed with immense deposits of the organic relics of extinguished life-forms, sometimes as shell-like islands or chalky hills, sometimes as great veins of minerals or coals from the forests of the past, sometimes as organic oils, all of which ancient inheritance the present dominant species is burning and destroying with such haste that the product of one million years of life may be consumed in a single year.

All of the mammalian species are of very recent evolution, and in the history of life of this planet they may be seen as trials or brief experiments, soon to be extinct and to give way to fresh trials. And the most recent in evolution is the species 'man', which bears a likeness to the physical constitution of humans, although deprived of human spiritual faculties. It must be evident to any human observer that this species also is a botched experiment, whose dead-line for extinction may indeed hap at any moment.

The failure of the species 'man' arises from this paradox: evolving within a hospitable and bountiful environment, which afforded no species-threat, they have supposed that the resources of life-support were provided for them effortlessly, as if from the decree of some benign Goodness who would bestow upon them water, sunlight, air and foodstuffs throughout eternity. From this, profound consequences flow, for they have not taken the first steps to manage the ecosphere with prudence, nor to replenish the resources of nature. The very bounty of this temperate planet has bred them into feckless ways, so that mortal culture now affords no place of purchase for Obedience to the Rule – nay, it is fragmented into as many identities as there are living specimens, and each one of these many millions posits its own need as an 'I'. So that the species-consciousness blows about the planet like great clouds of dust, swirling this way and that in pursuit of innumerable individual wants and needs.

Since the dead-line of the species is now so close, there might be no need to go on with this bosh. But there is more and worse to it than that. For the species is now symbiotic with the planet, which symbiosis has passed within the last few generations into a parasitic form, so that the dust-cloud of mortality threatens to obscure the planet's sun. And this is said, not just as a trope, but as a literal thing. For the species is polluting the atmosphere with smokes, gases and acids, which, circulating in the hydrosphere, descend again on land and poison the vegetation of distant regions. It is tipping noxious wastes and effluents into the lakes and oceans. It is consuming the oils, carbons and mineral resources of the planet, so that within a generation or two of their brief species-life some scarce reserves will be utterly exhausted. It is hastening the extinction of species of flora and fauna which might serve our needs and which we might regulate to new perfections. In its feckless greed, its lack of any species-planning or duty to the future, in its uncontrolled proliferation of population and its thoughtless satisfaction of each immediate appetite, it has exhausted whole regions of the planet, tainted the soil and seas with chemicals, felled immense forests which can no longer replenish the oxygen of the support-system, and reduced luxuriant lawns of grasses to deserts.

In short, wherever one goes upon the surface of the planet, this odious species is at work, hacking down trees, killing beasts more sentient than they, burning up oils, casting open the rocks and soils, planting their hideous swarming nests upon the genial fields, polluting water and air, and devising new disasters. So that this hospitable ecosphere is now threatened with destruction, not from some natural cause, as a flux in the solar winds or the impact of an asteroid, but from the restless and self-centred appetites of its own dominant species.

CONCLUSION

The planet is in all respects adapted to our immediate colonisation and regulation to the Rule.

In all respects – save one. The damaging and Earth-threatening activities of its dominant species, man, must be brought to an end. Even if this were to be effected today, we should still for several generations have many labours to perform in cleansing oceans, lands and air.

Since the species is self-programmed to extinction, no scruple need concern us if we should find it advisable to advance by a little the species' dead-line. (In doing so we would undoubtedly save from extinction a number of more noble and serviceable species.) Yet it may be that our Gracious Goodnesses will prefer some experimental interim: as, for example, the segregation of a diminished number of the species into reservations, under the strictest tutelage and rule. There might even be experiments in Sper-insemination and breeding with selected hostesses of the species, from which a higher sort of sentient butler might result.

However, in bringing the species within the Rule we are faced with one most serious problem. Our mission has arrived at Sykaos a generation too late. For in the past generation or two their scientists have fallen upon the secrets of primitive nuclear fission.

Such powers ought never to be commanded by creatures which live without the Rule. Let us only suppose that butlers, without appointed captains, should somehow get some anti-matter nodules into their paws! Yet the havoc that would hap would flow out of their unprogrammed confusion and not from foul intent. How much more life-endangering are such powers when commanded by the species man, whose malevolent nature is such that they turn every force into an engine of destruction!

In several great regions of the planet segments of the species are already preparing 'wars'* against other segments, and plan to detonate huge nuclear explosions upon the other parties. This will fulfil the logic of the evolution of the species, and will perhaps be the apt terminus of its self-extinction.

Yet such an outcome would endanger also the Rule. For Sykaos offers one obstacle to human colonisation. The youthful planet still harbours elements of radioactive decay, in the rocks of its crust, its magma and its core. And some small radiation of cosmic rays passes into its atmosphere. Hence the natural background radiation, which they count in 'roentgens', is already several times the level found on Oitar, and is close to the uppermost limit which the human corpse can tolerate.

---

* For an explanation of this beastly ritual, 'War', see below, p. 221.

Every passing day these unnecessary creatures are making some small addition to this sum, with crude constructions designed to harness the nuclear force as a source of power; with spillages and wastes; or by testing their poisonous engines of war. So that even now the background radiation in some parts of the planet has surpassed the limits of tolerance. If the background count were to rise by as little as seven of their roentgens, then the prospect of our plantation must be closed.

Imagine, then, the consequences of a nuclear war between some segments of this species! In an instant the radiation level would overshoot the threshold. Indeed, it is published in their newses that all this is well known to their sciences, and that such an exchange of nuclear engines might so pollute the atmosphere as to bring to extinction all mammalian species and render the planet uninhabitable for millennia.

From all that has been declaimed we must reach the following conclusions:

1 A precondition for the colonisation of Sykaos must be the prevention of a nuclear war between any segments of the species.
2 The beastly nature of the species is such that these creatures are to be expected to unleash nuclear detonations not only against each other but even against our own first settlers. Precautions must be taken against this event.
3 The species is not accessible to reason and knows no awe of the Rule.
4 The species can be regulated only by fear, greed or lust.
5 Our settlers must therefore first enter by stealth; or must throw the whole species into a trance; or must send in advance an embassy to subdue them by pandering to their greeds.

In the remote hope of delivery from this keep, and of escaping back to humankind, Oi Paz will meditate upon a Plan.

SECOND CAPTIVITY

Sage Field Notes

6 March. Got that paper on Oitarian eco and life forms done, quite a scramble. Worked all through Friday night, then – after a nap – all Saturday until 2 a.m. Put the paper in after Sunday breakfast to P.A. Primrose. She sd she'd been 'expecting' it on Friday, and 'I think we should allow Sir James one day of rest.' Gave David a copy and went to wander in the park. The snowdrops are out and the first crocuses.

Called on Equerry, who invited me into her den for a cuppa. She told me how she got this job. No one wld believe it. It seems that when FARCES was set up, all the staff appointments were done from on high – by MoD and MI17 and St Anthony's talent-spotting creeps, & c. That left the Other Ranks (most of whom are posted on attachment or from previous regime), plus several grey area or liminal types: Medic, Equerry, butler, Works. Security found Satpathy as Medic by tracing back to Tancaster Infirmary. The Equerry post was advertised in the horse and hunt journals, in rather mysterious terms. Ann looked the word up in a dictionary and then put in for it, without much hope. Her qualifs are terrific (though she's so off-hand I have to dig them out) – has worked with horses since she was three, has been a show-jumper, was in the running for the British cross-country team in the last Olympics but didn't like the set, managed a racing-stable in the Argentine. Came back from there last year. Main disqualification: she is ♀.

Anyway, she was summoned for interview in some 'posh' place in S. Kensington (where she went in anorak and jeans). Hunter had intended to do the appointments, with Undermanner beside him, but he was suddenly called into a meeting in the Ministry and sent Scarcely as his deputy. P. A. Primrose completed the appointments board since she had the papers and refs.

When Ann saw the competition she nearly went home: a regimental sergeant-major (cavalry), a Hampshire breeder, a hunt servant from the Quorn. *Well!*

Ann was called in first. When she went in Scarcely thought she had come for the coffee-cups and called out again: 'Mr Other!' 'That's me,' sd Ann. 'Ann Uther.' Meanwhile Primrose was pushing around papers to S. and U. and whispering urgently. Scarcely started scratching his head and sd, 'Are you sure?' 'Of course, Captain Scarcely. Look, here is the Establishment list which Colonel Gardyan-Hunter dictated last week.' On wh (it seems) was already entered, 'Equerry: A. N. Other'. Scarcely scratched again and said, ''Strordinary! Don't you think we should look at the other candidates?' Primrose sd that she had already put Mr ... er, Miss Other's name through to the Ministry Registry last week. Matter resolved by Undermanner who came in, booming, 'Then I think we can congratulate Miss Other on her appointment and discuss with her the Equerry's duties.' (Not clear to me whether U. had 'taken to' Ann or/and seen her as no threat to her empire.) Scarcely, who has a mother thing, collapsed before the sonic boom. Near riot in waiting-room.

Even more strange – Hunter and Mayhem were too busy to notice Ann's arrival until she had been at Martagon two weeks. (*Note:* Certain advantages in having a liminal role.) Then Hunter blew his top: horses were his idea and the chap from the Quorn was his candidate. But (a) Ann's name was already in the bowels of the Ministry computer; (b) she already knew too much – about O. & c. – to be let out; (c) Hunter did not want any row to get to Treasury ears, since the horses are a fiddle he got through under the heading 'Perimeter Guards: Mounted Patrol'.

Ann told me all this with a wry grin. She takes the pomp and circumstance of institutions as *données*, like a landscape: 'No point in trying to jump mountains – ride around them.' She has a fatalistic view of Them, like a peasant.

Weirder still, Ann got away without signing the Secrets Act. No particular reason, she sd. It was 'a water jump'. When she was in Mayhem's office and he shoved the paper at her, she 'shied like a yearling and refused'. Mayhem threw a tantrum, so she told him she'd 'think about it'. Every two or three weeks Mayhem fetches her in and she tells him that she's still thinking. 'Each refusal costs three penalty points,' she sd. 'I suppose the bell will go soon and I'll have to leave the ring.'

Qry: Does Equerry really think she is a horse? It's her way of coping. She identifies herself with the stables as an Us against the Them of bureaucracies. Odd how strong such a position can be. She takes up a stand with her work and whatever that work needs and then won't budge an inch. Since she doesn't give a pee for Them it is always Their move. If authority kicks at a rock it only bruises its own toe.

As Ann showed me out of the yard we bumped into the new Sigint major prying around. Greeted me gallantly (seemed to have forgiven me for that scene at dinner) and then, without intro, plunged into horse patter (*patois?*) with Ann. I felt cut out. Perhaps Ann really is a horse?

Back in my room D. came tearing round, polishing specs and very excited. Was v kind — sd my paper would 'pay the rent for months'. Wanted to go into deep discussion at once. I felt so drained I asked him to leave it for a day or two. Washed hair and flopped on bed (where I'm writing this now). Feel like a student before my first supervision.

D. told me that he was puzzled because he cannot find any Oitarian concepts for certain human conflict-situations — notably no concept for 'war'. Yet they do have terms for 'fight', 'rob', 'snarl', 'menace' and even 'enmity' (but not 'enemy'), but always with beastly connotations. Is the chuckall (maybe griffin?) the great provider here? Do they hunt, snarl, fight, rob the fishponds — and hence enrich the Oitarian conceptual vocabulary?

Sage Notebook. Pasted-in cutting. Manuscript annotation: '*Ludgershall Advertiser*, last Friday'

ASTONISHING SCENES AT SHAW

Last Sunday evening, shortly after closing-time of the local hostelries at Shaw Magna, there were astonishing scenes outside the main gate of Martagon Hall. These continued into the small hours.

A number of disorderly persons assembled, banging tin trays. saucepans, and blowing whistles.

At 1 a.m. a huge bonfire was built in front of the gates, in which an effigy was burned. An eye witness said that it was of a man with long hair and dark complexion whom the demonstrators called 'Mr Moonie'. As the fires consumed the effigy, the crowd – which now numbered some sixty persons – danced around the fire and chanted:

> Ran, dan, dan.
> Set fire to the lunatic man.
> Oh Mr Loonie
> Go back to the Moonie!
> Ran-a-dan, ran-a-dan, dan.

When the fire was burning down, the military guard on the gate was reinforced, and an officer – whom we understand was Captain Scarcely of 5th Para – came forward and announced through a megaphone that the rioters were in breach of the Public Obedience and Suppression of Disaffection Act and might at any time be attacked by the forces of the law.

The response to Captain Scarcely's announcement was a burst of jeers, and some lout called him out to a 'fair fight' in single combat. Then a spokesman came forward, disguised in a cloak and motor-cycle helmet. He said that there 'never had been nothing good come out of Martagon Hall' and they wanted 'no Moonies in Shaw Magna'. As for 'Mr Loonie', they could send him back to where he came from. At that moment the flashing blue light of a police car was seen approaching up the lane and the crowd dispersed into the night.

Martagon Hall is now the headquarters of the Foundation for Advanced Research into Climate and Eco-Systems (FARCES). The Foundation's Secretary, Mr J. Mayhem, said that their work was classified, since if the Russians were to get hold of the secrets of climatology they could divert the Gulf Stream to the Baltic and 'put England under an ice-cap at the drop of a hat'. Relations with the local people were 'excellent' and he was hoping to invite some of them in for a conducted tour. The rioters had been brought in from outside, probably by CND.

A spokesman for the Ministry of Defence said that FARCES was exclusively concerned with researches into acid rain and came under the Ministry of the Environment. A spokeswoman at the Ministry of Environment said that it was a private foundation which had a small subsidy from the Ministry – 'We are very interested in their work.'

A spokesperson at CND headquarters said she had not heard of Martagon Hall, but thanked us for our information. She said she would add it to their target list.

Dr Freeby, of Wotton, the well-known Hampshire anti-quarian, said that it was a remarkable example of the old custom of 'rough music'. The last local record was in 1928 at Ludgershall, when the name of a churchwarden had been linked with several choir-boys.*

Sage Notebook. Pasted-in typescript

Toppest Secret   FARCES

TO ALL EXECUTIVE STAFF

The disturbing episode last night at the main gates indicates that there have been serious breaches in security. Staff will inform me at once of any suspected sources of leaks.

In view of the rumours as to the existence of Mr Oipas there will be a disinformation exercise next week. I will arrange a conducted tour of some part of the Hall and grounds, for

---

* *Sage annotation, pencil:* 'Hunter and Mayhem clapped a D Notice on all this to the national media but they forgot the local paper. M. tried to call in all copies of this and stuff them in the incinerator. But every cottage in Shaw Magna has a copy hidden away, according to Equerry, who got this one smuggled in. (*1:* how the hell does E. communicate with Outer World? *2:* how does a ritual form of charivari like this conserve itself for seventy years?)'

vetted representatives from the media. A member of staff will
be appropriately dressed and will be introduced to visitors as a
Professor of Climatology from Sri Lanka. Mr Oipas will be
confined to his room during this tour. Staff will be notified
later as to whether they should also keep to their rooms or
whether they have been allocated a disinformation role.

J. Mayhem

Sage Field Notes

18 March. P. A. Primrose rang my room yesterday at midday to
say that Sir James cld not 'see me about my paper' in the afternoon
as arranged since 'something important had cropped up' (i.e. he
was closeted with H. & M. about Sunday night's fracas) but wld
see me at 9.30, after dinner, wh she sd in tones suggesting a very
gracious concession to my trivia by so VI a P. Dinner was a trial,
since everyone wanted to talk about the rough music, but cldn't
because O. was there. Only cheerful people seemed to be O. and
the Sigint Major, Sorley, who had seated himself next to him.
They seemed to be getting on famously, but I was too far down
the table to eavesdrop: from the few words I caught, the major
was explaining about the Cold War and O. was asking questions.
Odd: I've never seen O. do that at dinner before. I must say
Sorley has better manners than some civilians I cld mention, I
suppose army life encourages the rites of commensality. He looks
directly at O. (Sorley has nice – alert but slightly sad – eyes, very
blue) and talks with him like any other equal, not an oddity or
an object.

Over dessert (apple crumble: no cheese, because grocer's delivery van cldn't get through last week, mysterious attack of flat
tyres) O. startled the table into silence by remarking, 'Big Bonfire
last night had many good colours, crimsons, blue, gold and many
silvers. But bad music and bad dancing. I do a bonfire one night
in honour of Sir Pepper, and lead you all in a better dancing.'
Silence. Tick-tock. Then Colonel Hunter spoke. 'Which bonfire,

Mr Oipas? I didn't notice one.' O's face visibly darkens. Tick-tock. Then – 'Why do you play-act a falsity with me, Hunter man? Oipas saw you running up and down drive to bonfire. And all this day you and Mayhem talk about bonfires and security.' Then stopped, as if recollecting himself. Not for the first time I wonder – how much does he know? Does he get things out of Rani? Can he mind-read? Or (quite possibly) does his belt have some bug which can bore through walls?

Pepper de-fused by rising from table. The Mess/high table ritual is that All Rise in deference rite. O. takes to all ritual (what throws him is informality) so rose also. As Pepper went out he nodded to me and sd, 'In ten minutes, Dr Sage?'

Knocked on the door, wondering if I shld wear a gown. Opened by butler, an old college servant of Pepper's, whose duties seem to circulate around him. It's a spacious apartment on the first floor of the West Wing, furnished like a tasteful antiques gallery. I'd only been there once before, for a sherry party on opening day, but was too hassled then to take much note. Pepper was seated on an elegant *chaise longue* wh he patted for me to sit beside him. I cld see my paper open at last page on the table and was bursting to know his response. Had to wait while the butler brought in coffee and Sir James poured out two brandies.

When butler withdrew Sir J. became very affable and went into social chit-chat about the hardships of a teetotal high table, and the rough music the night before. He confided that 'security nearly got out of hand' about the affair and that he had spent the afternoon stopping MI17 from sending a party down.

As I fielded the chat and waited for work to start my mind was playing flashbacks of Pepper's career. He is immensely dis-tinguished, but what is he distinguished *for*? He started as a zoologist on the border of ethology; while still a graduate wrote a highly regarded paper on psycho-ethology, 'Apes and Anomie'. The paper was 'seminal', and seminal is a term normally added to Sir James ('Sir Seminal Pepper'?). No major book, but several more seminals published in his late twenties, early thirties, hopping across disciplines: philosophy, zoology, genetics, anthropology, psychology. There was 'Artists or Ethologists? The Larzac Paintings Reconsidered', 'Deconstructing Stonehenge' and a mind-blowing piece about 'Creature-nature' wh suggested faculties of communication and empathy between higher mammals wh *homo sapiens* inherits as 'sleeping genes' or atrophied faculties. I liked it, but zoologists sd it was thin on evidence.

By his early thirties Pepper was much in demand as an inseminator at conferences, esp in USA, and was flying from one to another like a character out of David Lodge. Moved from one prestigious fellowship and visiting professorship to another, various think-tanks and Centres. Never seems to have settled down and taught anywhere. A groovy telly series, *Poor, Bare, Forked Animal*, wh was by turns doom-laden, elegiac and sexy (or, rather, *sexist* – lots of bare forks to titivate the males): I watched it when I was seventeen and was quite sent by it; Pepper was a pin-up in my bedroom, and it turned me on to anthropology. But about then (twenty years ago?) he seemed to get trapped by his own success, grew a fussy little beard, became an academic politician, Director of this, Master of That, Board of Trustees for the other, adviser to the Ministry of Environment ... all that.

So here I was, sitting beside my teenage pin-up, bored out of my mind by his social chat, and wanting work to start. Finally I waved my hand at the paper and sd, 'Well, is it going anywhere?' 'I was coming to that. Marvellous, m'dear. Quite fascinating.' (Wished he wldn't 'm'dear' me, patriarchal put-down: wld he 'm'dear' David?) I sd, more sharply than I intended, 'Well, a visitant from an extra-terrestrial culture is rather likely to seem fascinating to us. What I mean is – am I getting anywhere with my de-coding?' I felt belittled, as if I was having to ask for approval, and I must have suddenly flushed with anger, for Pepper seemed to collect himself. He sd he had found my paper most interesting and that I was clearly 'getting through' to something. Some lines might be worth following up: the suggestions about a glaciated eco-system and centralised, engineered, 'creature-controlled environment' ('I like that concept, Helena') were 'plausible'. Then he squinted at me, in a joky sort of way, and sd, 'But about the *fauna*, m'dear . . . I do know a little zoology.' 'Yes, it does all seem odd and sci-fic. Of course he got some of the names from an Earth-dictionary, but he is describing something behind these names . . .' 'An "Earth-dictionary"!' exclaimed Pepper, and went off into a patriarchal chuckle. 'What about an Earth-bestiary? Have you looked in the Library?'

Deflation then commenced. I felt my knees gripping together and my nails digging into my hand. Pepper sd there was a couple of medieval bestiaries (reprinted) in the Library. He didn't mean that Oipas had been having me on – although from his leer he obviously did mean that – but O. had been reading this stuff and the 'diagnostic picture was confused with all this input – dragons and phoenixes and unicorns! Oipas is no fool. There may, or may not, be something behind this stuff. But he isn't making it easy for you. There's a lot of acquired input here, maybe deliberate. We shall have to adopt a much more rigorous approach. I'm afraid your findings are deeply flawed. Also, m'dear, these aren't the questions our employers are asking me. They don't ring me up and ask me if there are dragons and unicorns where Oipas comes from. They ask me about their technologies – which is not your field and about their social organisation – which perhaps is?'

By now I was shrinking, like Alice eating the downward mushroom. All the work of the last weeks, the detection, the trading with O., the excitement of de-coding – all this seemed unreal. Had D. and I been sucked into a fantasy-world, of O's confecting? Here was the real world: Pepper, and the brandies, and, outside the windows, 'our employers'. I felt diminished in my own self-image, since it is ABC for any anthropologist to detect and screen out extraneous cultural intrusions wh distort the field of enquiry – yet Pepper's bestiaries convicted me of just that. I had come into the room expecting . . . well, at the least a discourse between academic colleagues, maybe with the hubris of an authority in some fields as yet uninseminated by Pepper.

Now Dr Sage, PhD, FRAI, had shrunk to a student flunking her orals, or maybe sitting on a sofa beside an indulgent daddy.

At which point daddy moved in for the kill. He patted my shoulder consolingly and let arm rest there, while other arm poured out more brandies. 'Don't let it get you down. Easy mistake to make. I can see you've really got to the edge of something.' He gestured at my paper, with unoccupied arm. 'But put that in a pending file for a bit, until it settles. Why not try a sketch of social structure next?' Unoccupied arm raised his glass in a mock toast to the next paper, while occupied arm seemed to change signals from 'consoling (fatherly)' – i.e. put-down – to 'friendly hug' (well, okay, but are we friends like that?) to . . . what might have almost been taken to be a paw making a pass.

Pepper now leered directly at me, waved hand at my paper, and sd, 'I loved that bit about the Age of Primitive Erections.' I froze into an alert. For the first time I looked around the room. My God! It was like a stage-set for a clichéd seduction-scene. *Chaise longue*, brandies, dim lights, even the bedroom door invitingly open with low bedside light and sheets turned down. But I still cldn't believe it. Pepper (sensing a touch of frost?) had changed the subject again: he sd I'd been 'cooped up' here a long while and 'must be missing . . . company'. (Slight comic *mou* which hinted I must be sex-starved.) He sd it wld be good for me 'to take a week or two out with colleagues, catch up on things'. He thought he cld get me leave – in fact he himself has to go to Stanford and UCLA in ten days and cld take me along at same time and 'keep an eye on me' to satisfy Mayhem and co. Of course he cldn't promise, wld have to get a 'clearance'. I was so tense, and wondering how to get to door, that my tongue seemed to be hobbled. Then Pepper added (with ref to nothing) that he thought I knew his good friend John Wardroop? The implication being that he knows all about my thing with John and supposes I'm an easy lay. At wh point preoccupied arm signals definitively that it has stopped being paternal and moves stealthily twrds nipple (lft).

I stood up abruptly, knocking over brandy, grabbed my notebook and – still pretending it was not a Situation – sd thank you, it's awfully late, must be going & c. Pepper, not the least abashed, sd don't go, night is young, let me fill up glass, as I moved round oval polished table (lft) in direction of door, whereat he moved swiftly round table (rt) and intercepted me, grabbing me and pushing face, goatee beard and all, into mine. Disengaged, and withdrew smartly round oval t, Pepper in hot pursuit, Dr Sage keeping t between. No point in either of us saying anything any more, the situation was stripped down to its primitive mythic fundaments, old goatish satyr pursuing nymph (*aet* 38).

I tried to draw the scene to a clichéd close by clouting him across the distinguished self-approving gob with my notebook. But even this didn't bring the curtain down, because some precious pages fell out on to the floor, and with a 'Do be careful, Helena' he got down and fished them out from under oval barrier. And instead of knowing he was an object of ridicule and shame, he was *still* putting me down, as a silly hysterical girl untutored in the ways of the world (and unmannerly to gracious tutor). I suppose this carry-on is *normal* with him, and some of my sisters are too scared (or too thrown in awe by his eminence) even to put an oval table between their honour and his lusts. And if there is a bad scene and it gets out, then the gossip of virility adds to his charisma – yet he must be knocking at the door of *sixty*!

So – he handed me back my pages and conducted me solicitously to the door, having resumed paternalist role as if *I* had been delinquent saying that I 'needed a break', 'let me know about Stanford', opened the door & pushed me out with a pat on the buttocks, leaving me too speechless even to fart.

Back at my room I used up half a box of Kleenex, in rage and lacerated pride. Not so much the sex bit, though I'm surely too old to be put through that corny routine? I don't mind a gallantry or a pass in the right time or place. Women ought not to moan when their dress is often a patchwork of come-on semiotics. What makes me wild is that bloody men arrogate the right to say what the rules are – and then to break them at will: to decide what *is* the right time and place: i.e. whenever they choose. Sir Seminal

Pepper, knowingly and with malice aforethought, set up a situation in which we were in superordinate/subordinate roles, then
threw me (metaphorically) upon the floor by puking over my
scholarship – and then tried to make me. Imagine a woman
director (unlikely) going on like Pepper. She *couldn't*!

Cldn't sleep. Poor D. put his head in and got it bitten off. Sat
up looking back over my notes, found the schnapps and got a bit
sloshed. Had a shower but still cldn't sleep. At abt 3 a.m. crept
down in my nightdress and wrapper to the Old Library, surprised
to find an alcove light on and Sigint major reading. I tried to
back off, being somewhat in negligée, but he spied me and seemed
for a moment quite startled – even scared – then sd, 'Oh hello,
Dr Sage. You're up late.' 'Well, so are you. I didn't mean to
disturb you.' 'Not at all. Shall I put the kettle on? There's Nescaf.'
I sd no, but he did all the same, seeming somehow shy and
protective. I glanced at what he was reading – something on
ancient India. Wh surprised me. Myth was in his alcove so I had
to run through the shelves there, hoping my garb was not
indecent. And, *damn*, there they were, James's Roxburghe Club
edition of *The Bestiary* and White's *Book of Beasts*. I flipped
through them while Rbt Sorley got the coffee. Damn! Unicorns,
dragons, the lot.

I must have sniffed, and the major pressed a cup into my hand:
'Forgive me saying so, Dr Sage, but you look washed up. I think
you should drink up and go to bed.' A shy smile, wh took the
edge off his dyscompliment. I tried to smile brightly and sd, 'What
about following your own prescription, doctor?' He looked at
me steadily with his very blue eyes, and then turned away. 'I'm
afraid I don't sleep well.' There was something so sad in the way
he said this that there was nothing I cld answer, and we stood
there in silence sipping Nescaf laced with lumps of Marvel. At
length he sd, 'I'm sorry, I didn't mean to make a mystery. My
wife died last year. Of cancer. You startled me when you came
in just now – you looked just like Alison.' I put down my cup,
sd, 'thank you for telling me,' took both his hands & gave them
a quick squeeze, & went back to my room.

SECOND CAPTIVITY

Sage Notebook. Pasted-in typescript

MINUTES

Weekly Conference, 39th Week

Sir James Pepper in Chair. Said he would be absent from next two or three weeklies, owing to engagements in London and USA. He welcomed Major Sorley to his first weekly conference. Major Sorley reported that even in last four days great pressure from 'above' to accelerate Astrosigint work. Great activity reported on moon. MoD contractors will 'crash' work on transmitter and receptor dishes: objective now two months. At that time 24-hour monitoring will commence and at least two additional Sigint officers and 20 more ORs must be attached. Major Sorley asked if adequate preparations were being made for their reception. He expressed dissatisfaction at present quarters and working conditions of Other Ranks. Agreed that Col. Gardyan-Hunter, QMSM Gravell (Works) and Major Sorley be a sub-committee to look into matter. At her suggestion Mrs Undermanner added to committee.

Mr Mayhem announced that in view of events on Sunday night a review of all security arrangements would be made. All staff would be informed in due course. Disinformation exercise would take place in two weeks. Major Sorley said that GCHQ monitoring revealed that presence of Mr Oipas here was an 'open secret' to American intelligence, probably Soviet intelligence also. He suggested that HM Government be urged to make a public statement. Mr Mayhem pointed out the inconveniences that could result if the British public knew situation: the disinformation exercise was directed at British media, parliament and public and not at friends in NATO. Therefore it must continue.

The Bursar reported that Mr Weston of Hall Farm refused to sell or lease 5 acres for dairy annexe. Asst Dir. suggested a compulsory purchase order. Mr Mayhem pointed out that this could lead to a public enquiry. He proposed that the RAF be approached with a view to twice-weekly deliveries of milk, groceries & c. by helicopter. Common land behind arboretum proposed as landing-strip. Equerry entered an objection, and said this land reserved for equestrian exercise: if helicopters came down horses would 'do their tops'. Objection overruled. Major Sorley said deliveries could perfectly well come in Sigint contractors' vans. Agreed.

Weekly Reports

None. Miss Crostic only just returned from Cheltenham. Director said Drs Nettler and Sage had reported directly to him with interesting papers. Dr Nettler's paper would be passed on to files. Dr Sage's required a little revision. She would now work on Oitarian social structure. Dr Nettler requested a clearance to visit Harmer's Theatrical Agency with a view to locating the Translator. Mr Mayhem said no clearance possible. In view of Sunday's episode all security to be tightened. Dr Nettler said Translator could be 'Rosetta stone', with key to Oitarian grammar and logic-paths. Major Sorley said Sigint also would 'give anything' to inspect Translator circuits.* Asst Dir. suggested he approach Security to try and get Translator (if still available) and, if not, to vet Lord Harmer and (if he passed vetting) bring him down to Martagon for a visit.

Other Business

Miss Weeder (Files) reported that Drs Nettler and Sage had not yet put in any of their field notes to Files, as proposed by Mr Mayhem (Weekly Conference, Week 38). Dr Sage said she had written up a very full record of her session with the Director on the previous night. Should she put this into Files? The Director said this was unnecessary and ruled that the filing of working notes should be left to discretion of executive staff since premature findings could be misleading. Miss Weeder (Librarian) said she was uneasy because Mr Oipas was indenting for more books than he could possibly read including a great

---

* *Sage annotation:* 'Gentry, the bug-master, spoke – first time ever – saying he also would like to inspect.'

deal of unorthodox history such as Nietzsche, Vico, Spengler, Marx, Toynbee, A. J. P. Taylor and Malinowski, as well as works on ancient Egyptian and pre-Columbian civilisations. What was he up to? Dr Nettler said that Mr Oipas had a scanner on his Recorder/Computer: it was only necessary for him to turn each page and the text was fed directly into the computer's memory. He had already banked much English poetry and was now moving on to world history and archae-ology. The Director said that there was no harm in this if it kept Mr Oipas happy. The Librarian suggested that an Assistant Librarian should be added to Establishment, to work under her supervision. Noted. The Asst. Dir. complained that last week's golf had been ruined by Dobermans, which had run off with the golf-balls. Captain Scarcely said the dogs had to run free if they were to 'suss out' the bushes and coppices for terrorists, but he would have a word with the handlers. Perhaps Colonel Gardyan-Hunter's balls could be soaked in repellent?

A. L. W.

Sage Field Notes

10 March. Cldn't sleep again. Kept going over the Weekly. When I did doze off I had bad dreams – in one of them a unicorn was bearing down on me whose face turned out to be Pepper. Got up at dawn and wandered about park, cursing at Pepper and bestiaries. Found myself somehow leaning over the gate of the stable yard. Equerry came out of the tack room, swinging a bridle. She gave me her even, incurious look. "Lo, Hel. Pissed off with Them?' I suppose I must have been red-eyed. Equerry didn't wait for an answer. Went into den, came out, chucked a packet of Kleenex at me (man-sized), and went on, still swinging bridle, into horse-box. I tidied up. Equerry emerged again, leading a beautiful dapple-grey mare, all togged up to go. Walked her across to me. 'This is Minniver. This is Hel. Say "hello".'

I tried to recall how one says hello in horse, and blew in her nose and scratched her ears. Seemed to be correct form of address. 'Right,' sd Equerry. 'Up you get.' 'Me? Now? But I ...' 'You need a hat. Take mine.' Hat chucked at me, like Kleenex. It seemed like an order and I was too washed-out to resist. Remembered drill, put my left toe in stirrup, and swung into saddle at second go. 'Right, off you go! Keep on the old common land behind the trees.' 'Aren't you coming too?' Equerry chortled. 'Minni's not strong enough to carry us both. Got to muck out. Be back in twenty minutes.' She clouted horse affectionately on backside, and horse was off before I had time to let in clutch. Bumpy trot at first, pounding my hindquarters and loosening teeth. Wanted to turn back but too bumpy to get a grip on steering-wheel. On the common Minniver let herself into third and cantered like a dream. I adjusted to her movements, pressed my arse right down into the seat, and felt I was flying in a hovercraft. Flew up to O., who was doing his dawn obeisances (rather like Chinese shadow-boxing) by the copse. He looked astonished, and then raised both arms in his most grandiloquent arc of greeting. Tried to wave back, lost my stirrups, and found I was hanging on to flying horse's neck. (Did I imagine it, or did I glimpse something like a *smile* on O's face as we flashed past? If so, note it down as a first.)

Horse cld not get through perimeter wall, so she had to put on brakes and paw ground and wait instructions from driver. Got into my stirrups again, settled my seat, and pointed horse towards home. This time the flying was *lovely*. It wasn't being turned on to things, it was being part of them all; part of the movement of the horse and the wind and the clouds and the turning of the earth itself. It seemed to repair my heart and put me into rhythm with ... what? Whatever it was, it was Pepper-free.

Fortunately horse wanted breakfast and found her way home without much steering. Equerry led Minniver off, remarking sternly that I 'shouldn't let her have her head like that. Teach her bad manners.' 'I shall be aching tomorrow,' I sd. 'Good for your tanden,' she sd. 'My tendons? They're seizing up already.' 'No, your tanden. Zen for your lower abdomen. But only when you use it the right way, then it can help you to samadhi.' 'Some day what?' 'Oh shit, you're ignorant, Hel. You read too many books. Samadhi is ... well, total forgetfulness of self, and yet oneness with self and with the world.' 'I felt like that when we were cantering.' 'Get over,' sd Equerry to Minniver, and to me, 'The box at the far end still needs mucking out.'

Ann took me into den for a cuppa and a bite. Once again, fresh milk, fresh granary loaf, even a hunk of cheese. Amazing! I wanted to ask how, but something in her eye when she caught me looking at them warned me off. Ann was unusually taciturn – not unfriendly but her mind on other things. Asked if I had seen 'Robo' (her name for Sorley) who had sd he might like a ride. Equerry has a binary classification for Martagon world. Those who pass as 'Us' have diminutives ('Hel') or nicknames ('Oy Pee'). Those who rank as 'Them' have pejorative nicknames ('Grunter' and Works whom she calls 'Perks'). So she has accepted Sigint Major as an 'Us', wh made me feel uneasy.

I wended on way, feeling somewhat healed. In whole time Ann never asked me what was up.

Back in room O. suddenly entered without knocking. (Has never visited any of our rooms before, except R.'s.) We exchanged ritual salutations. Then, extraordinary! He made a second obeisance, and thrust towards me a handful of snowdrops. 'I give these flowers to Helena for healing her vibes. The flowers agree to give themselves. They are each messages from Oitar, like clusters of hanging snow.' I tried to thank him, but he wasn't going to be stopped. 'Riding on horses is good healing also,' he sd. 'Another day Oipas will ride with you, we will see the dawn rise together.' At the door he paused and added, 'Our unicorns are not the same as Earth-unicorns, although they share a common name. Oitarian unicorns have two horns, on Sykaos they have only one. Perhaps they are only a memory? I have been reading a book on beasts in the library – sometimes I borrow your Earthly terms.' Then, as a parting shot, 'But the Sacred Three are the same, and they share the same names. Such things are too strange for beastly unbelieving minds. When your vibes are healed we will do more trading.'

Well.

Sage Field Notes

17 March. This place is curiously 'Oitarian'. It is a hierarchical, mechanically organised social structure, a bastard military-academic hybrid, with a purported allocation of roles and functions, but without any affective bonding or kinship netting. Maybe this gives to O. some sense of 'normality'?

The real polarisation in this place is between those who submit themselves to the functions of the structure (but seek ego-advancement through it) & those who are still self-programmed as individuals – like Equerry. This is the real Them v Us. Some of them have sold out utterly, like P. A. Primrose and P. A. Hemlock. Primrose, perhaps, is just *working* the system. She's a sharp dresser, always off (with or without Sir James) – pretends to be at Playpen but they don't sell *that* gear at Playpen. Seems to have something 'on' Pepper (maybe several things?) but far too smooth and smart to be in a dependent-mistress role. (Maybe she works for NATO or CIA on the side, and keeps an eye on Sir J.?) All that can be sd about Hemlock is that she has got the right name. Mr Hemlock is rumoured to be something in the MoD, but he's never shown his face. Only thing I can find that she's into is golf.

Mrs Undermanner – I thought she was one of Them, but now I wonder if she might defect to Us. At first I thought she just *was* a function, because the way to get anything out of her was to flatter her in her Office as Hallkeeper & admire her status. When she seemed to be protecting and even 'mothering' Equerry I thought it was to extend her empire against Perks. Now I'm not so sure. I'm getting to respect her. She comes from the old (pre-LUNATIC) Establishment, & she has some kind of ancestral awe for the Hall and the Park. She regards us all as transients, &

herself as the Guardian of the Lares & Penates of the ancient de Boyle line.

Last night after dinner I went for a breather in the park to think out my paper on Oitarian soc structure. Weird thing. Coming back past the tiny chapel, the lights were on, & an incredible racket issuing therefrom. It must have been after 11. I cld hear some sort of calypso hymn-singing, & then what sounded like bits of a hell-fire sermon with voices bawling out things like 'Oh Lord, send down Thy Spirits from on high!' & 'Lead us the Way!' Then the racket stopped & eight or nine people came out. I stepped back into the bushes & cldn't make out the faces, but thought I spotted Hunter's batman & Mary, the West Indian telephonist (whose voice I had *definitely* heard), and Jerry the gardener.

It's really interesting that this 'Born Again' phenomenon shld have even spread to Martagon. I mentioned it to Rani & she sd that revivalism was spreading through the Other Ranks like a prairie fire. Mary and Brian the Oddman are leading spirits. Funny, I had always thought them rather sensible. Must be another symptom of these apocalyptic times. Must try to find time to study more closely.

Oi Paz Notebook A

Of Beastly History

The history of the species is brief. When it has come to its deadline, which it is hastening on apace, it will seem as no more than a comma between the long reign of the dinosaurs and whatever species succeeds.

In a remarkable prophecy the Sykotic poet Tupper has foretold that the next species to reign may well be seaweed:

> *The sea-wort floating on the waves, or rolled up high along the shore,*

THE SYKAOS PAPERS

Ye counted useless and vile, heaping on it names of contempt:
Yet hath it gloriously triumphed, and man been humbled in his
*   ignorance . . .*

Thus the Poet, whose genius signals that the species was not bereft of all qualities, had it not been, by some aboriginal default, lost to all restraint and duty to the Wheel. Had Sykaans chosen such poets as Tupper for their rulers, how different their brief record might have been! And yet how glorious will be the aftermath, when bladderwrack and 'violet-tinctured' sea-worts emerge from the oceans and swallow all their newses and their ruins!

In the beginning they ran like other primates in the gardens of the world. They lived in caves in the ground and still observed the rudiments of the Rule.

Then they made prisoners of some beasts for their own uses. Their main business was eating and mating. Their most prized skill was in making sharp tools, or 'weapons', for killing.

That is the greatest part of their history. Indeed, it would be more true to say that they have had *no* history for they have had no government by rational decree or Rule. All the occurrences have emerged inconsequentially out of a competition of a myriad of contradictory wills whose outcome is a happenstance contrary to anyone's intentions.

In very recent times they have by such happenstance settled, cultivated the soil, built houses and cities, invented writing, and made their tools out of metals. This latest phase of their history they term 'civilisation'.

They have written a prodigious number of books, which pretend to be 'histories', about this brief episode. These books are essays in self-admiration, full of absurdities and contradictions. Oi Paz has banked a number of such books for the future studies of the College of Stellanthropology. But there was no time to perform the wearisome task of studying such clobber, and the essence of all their pretended 'histories' is this:

'Civilisation' is a term which describes Sykotic settlement into language-packs, grouped in tribes, or 'nations'. These nations then started to prey upon each other. Cities were built, but these were at once conquered by other nations, which burned or destroyed each other's cities. Hence none has lasted for more than a few generations. That is why, in all their history, little permanent has been added to the sum of beauty on this planet.

The nation which conquers most other nations calls itself an 'empire'. These empires may be compared to the lichens which spread on a mid-summer boulder: now one lichen flourishes and is dominant, then it decays and is overrun by a more hardy species. Their history books are a sort of botany of these lichens which are classified as Mogul, Aztec, British, Assyrian, Roman and others, each of them flourishing for a day. Of these the Chinese has shown the greatest longevity, by sticking to a dark patch on the underside of the boulder and swallowing up invasive specimens.

There are two large patches of lichens now (or empires) which are called 'blocks', since it is their business to block all rational intercourse between fellow-creatures on either side. The means of blocking is called a 'cold war'. Nations and empires are always in a state of war with each other. A 'hot war' (which is the normal condition) is when each seeks utterly to destroy the other, by killing its citizens, burning its cities, poisoning its crops, & c., according to the most advanced technology available to the species. The citizens of one empire or nation are named as 'enemies' by another, which signifies a general licence to kill them without further pretext. But in a cold war this licence is temporarily suspended. This is an interval in which both empires or blocks advance all possible preparations to attain superiority for the next hot war, and meanwhile by fraud and insult seek to weaken and intimidate the other, and stir up within them 'civil wars' or insurrections.

The two empires which block this cold war are called 'nay-toe' and 'double-you-toe'. This is perhaps because they meet along the margins and are 'toe-to-toe' with each other. Within each toe there are subsidiary tribes, clients and toenails, such as

'Great Britain' (where I am cooped) which is a little satrapy of nay-toe used by its officers for parking their nukes.

I will enquire further into these matters of blocks and wars from a new keeper, recently arrived, called Sorley, who is a fair trader, not given to absurdities. When I asked him what the cold war was about, and what advantages each empire hoped to gain, he replied that he himself had asked this question to certain great officers and generals of nay-toe but that they gave him no answer.

This is all that need be declaimed as to species-history, were it not for certain unexpected evidences that have come to light. For there are certain words and names which are identical in Oitarian and Sykotic speech. And chiefly these relate to the Seven Sentient Servants and to certain properties of nature. Thus of the Sentient Servants they retain in the memory of myth the names of 'unicorn' and of 'griffin' (which they suppose to have wings); and they picture mythic beasts very similar to our bazzy-lisks (of both kinds) which they call dragons. For the chuckall they have neither name nor mythic memory. But they call a vegetable substance 'cotton' which is very like the fleece of our cottons. Even stranger, they retain both the mythic memory and the name of two of the Sacred Three, the dol-fin ('dolphin') and fee-nicks ('phoenix'). The dolphin is said, indeed, yet to survive, but Oi Paz has not seen one and cannot declaim this as science; it is probable that it is on their list to exterminate. Nor can I say if the creature with that name resembles our own. But stranger yet, the Sacred Cat very certainly exists and has colonised every part of this planet. It is accorded little honour, for they do not comb its fleece nor rub its stomach with unguents, so that this divine messenger is reduced to grooming its coat with its own tongue! Yet it has adjusted to their beastly ways, using them for its own purposes but keeping them at a haughty distance, and the finest specimens may compare with the Cats which serve our Bumples.

There will also be found certain Sykotic terms which bear a strange relation to our own: as 'hall' (All), 'karma' (ka-ma), 'bread' (bred-stik), 'milk' (milkstem), 'vote', 'poll', 'pukka' (ruly), 'armada' (for which they mean a company of vessels on the water rather than spacecraft); and also the names of some flowering plants which bear a close relation to our own: the 'lily', the 'rose', and the 'crocus' (which resembles a kro-kos). Oi Paz has long pondered these matters, which dictate in logic some prior contact between Sykaos and human civilisation.

Examine the case of the butler, that most useful of the Sentient Servants, who can be trained to any task to the second degree of intellect – to fetch, to carry, to build, to dig, to operate the pellet-compressors, to measure, to care for griffins and feed unicorns, to manage the matings of cottons, and, indeed, to undertake most material affairs. This creature is wholly unknown to Sykaans, who have not trained any primates to such accomplishments – which indeed are at the upper limits of their own abilities. Yet the name 'butler' survives in their language as a term (archaic) for a certain kind of subordinate servitor of their own species. So that the name of every one of our Sentients (save only the chuckall) is known to these beasts. That is proof positive.

How could this be? When could such contact have been undergone? I recall those passages from earliest myth, descriptive of the pre-history of our time at the onslaught of the first great glaciations, when our intrepid explorers set forth into space in search of a new home for humanity. As the great Hō Mā sang:

> Then launched they far into the vasty void
> Leaving the circuits of the Sacred Wheel,
> Great In Kā in the glove of glassy gold
> And Bōd Hā steering on the sled of rays
> And Krish Nā riding on the horns of night:
> Farewell, ye voyagers! Uphold the Rule!
> Auspicious be your landfall in the realms of light!

And the great Hō Mā, it is written, soon followed after them, leading another space armada, never to return.

And it is handed down to us that this armada passed beyond all radio-contact (although some faint transmissions were heard for a year or two). And of all this armada only one of our thirty-seven ships returned: that captained by the great Bōd Hā, who, having travelled through seven galaxies, had resided on a planet in some unknown and uncharted system for seventy of that planet's years, and who on return was of venerable age and had by many years overpassed the appointed dead-line. Although Bōd Hā was immeasurably weary, with memory banks nulled, yet from the halting tales of the far-travelled missioners amongst the crew was fashioned the great 'Energising and Summoning Myth' handed down to us from archaic times – the myth of the Planet Bathed in Yellow Sun, or Eu Topaz, with blue skies and green gardens which has inspired so many generations of our explorers – together with those darker tales of how our colonists were surrounded by hostile humanoid creatures, with horned helmets and with sickles in their hands, and were driven back to the fires of their encampments, which were overrun, one after the other, by white horsemen, until from the last encampment, at a place named Apo Kalyps, Bōd Hā and the depleted crew escaped. Nor did any charts survive, nor was it known in which galaxy Eu Topaz lay, nor whether the memories of these aged missioners had been entranced.*

Let it be declaimed now that these ancient myths were founded upon truth. Indubitably, Bōd Hā, In Kā, Uro Pā, Krish Nā and some other of that missionary fleet fell upon Sykaos in those archaic times. For a time they made plantations and brought the Sykaans under the Rule. But at length these brutish creatures broke into insurrection and by mere force of numbers overran our colonies.

Yet there lingered in Sykotic myths some memory of our missioners, from whom they took the names of their poets and gods. Without doubt our voyagers took with them in their ships the Sacred Cat, which evaded the sickles of the white horsemen, took to the forests, multiplied, and has now colonised the whole

---

* *The account above follows closely 'Arch. Myth (Misc.)', Tom. XXIII, cap. 7; Hō Mā, 'Argodyssey', Book I.*

planet. They will also have carried some bulbs and roots of plants. It is probable that our ships carried also a few butlers for menial duties, all of whom died in the massacres, but whose functions are recalled still in their speech. No ships would carry dragons, griffins & c., so that the memory of these must survive from a happier season when our colonists instructed these creatures in the Rule.

It is probable that colonisation took place upon several different portions of the planet, where the first ships settled. Such places can be identified by certain ancient relics and traces. This is a matter for future exploration, but Oi Paz has entered certain of their books into the bank, from which it will be seen that there is a probable site in a place called Egypt, whose pyramids are of due proportion (resembling our own archaic artefacts) and within whose ancient culture the Cat was accorded proper reverence; in Peru, where In Kā may have landed, whose ancient culture was noted for the study of number and of geometric forms; and possibly in India or in China, whose ancient cultures bear some notion of Karma, or the Rule.

There is also a site on this island, not far from this coop, which Oi Paz intends to visit when he can evade his keepers. It is known as 'Stonehenge', and is a gallery of great stones, of unknown origin, whose proportions are so just and whose astronomical conjunctions are such as to be beyond any possible doubt of Oitarian origin. From the charts available in this place it would appear that the stones are so aligned as to direct a mid-summer bearing upon Oitar, and hence it must be a bumple of worship to the Wheel. Could this have been the site of Bōd Hā's last encampment, where (it is recorded) the lieutenant, Droo Id, came to a violent dead-line?

We are forced towards a stranger speculation yet, for which I ask for Absolution before the Rule. Is it not possible – I hesitate to offer the offence – that in this colonisation some miscegenation between the human and the brutish took place? Were there lewd forcings or 'rapes' by potent brutish Sper-men upon the bodies of our missionaries? Or – since no Sper-men accompanied the crews — were they forced voluntarily to this desperate resort by missionary zeal and the need to renew and multiply their colonies?

If some such blemish be hazarded, then much in the history of this unhappy species can be better understood. For although our colonies were overrun, yet they left behind them, scattered about the planet, the product of this miscegenation, an aberrant conjunction of brutish and of human genes, like the confluence of two molten rivers, the one swift and pellucid from its glacial source, the other wide, slow and laden with the mud of the plains, which combined into the general current of the species-inheritance.

The truth of this finding is acknowledged as a repeated motif within the mythology of every Sykotic nation, where it is often rehearsed that mortals are the product of both angels and devils; or where they imagine gods who descend from the heavens and inseminate their species, in an incongruous reversal of generative roles: as if Bōd Hā or Uro Pā were Sper-men! This legend is found in their compendium of mythology, the 'bible', in which they suppose that a Ghost from space inseminated a mortal woman who gave birth to a 'god' whom they named 'Jesus'.

It may now be seen that the whole history of the species, since the time of our colonisation, has been a degeneration from this origin. For the brute is the dominant gene, and with each generation the genes of reason and of proportion become lost like droplets in an ocean. Yet also the paradoxes of mortal nature find a ready explanation, such as the survival in some favoured specimens of symptoms of rationality and even of aesthetic organs.

We see also an explanation for the diversity which marks the geographic divisions of the species, for the darker sort, such as those in Peru, Egypt, India, & c. are the closest descendants from our major centres of colonisation, and are also the more gentle and graceful, the more rational, the more given to music, meditation and number, and hence the bearers of the greater part of the inheritance of the true Oitarian genes. Whereas the white creatures are of the brutish sort, which they call in their myths the 'devils'.

There is one other consideration, which should be conveyed with celerity to the Gracious Goodnesses if these papers should ever come to human eye. And let Their Goodnesses mull it over and then Lay a Law. For if They should consider it opportune, in preparation for our plantations, to hasten on the extinction of this species, let it also be remembered that in that moment we shall cause the extinction of a species which, however corrupted and in whatever weak genetic dilutions, still carries the fading signature of our own race. Might not some favoured specimens be selected, and, by watchful bio-engineering, the brutish genes be bred out, and some small surviving stock bearing the genes of Bōd Hā, In Kā and Krish Nā be restored to purity?*

Sage Notebook. Pasted-in typescript

Oitarian Soc Structure: Prelim Notes

None of this is clear. Basic problem: neither D. nor I can find any concept for 'kin' (nor even for 'parent/child'). Hence cannot reconstitute society from kinship basics. Nor is there an 'economy' in a self-activating sense. No point of purchase for personal/local or even collective initiative.

Both economy and society are *données* – received unques-tioned data; determined. All this falls under governing concept, 'The Rule'. Rule is circular, revolves in cycles (as seasons, ceremonial occasions). David says Oitarian lang revolves in 'synonymic circulation' with hundreds of terms (wh do not discriminate between usages as verbs, nouns, adjectives) for round, rotate, rota, orb, wheel, axle, circumference – all of wh = roll and rule.

---

* *The whole of this section is obviously corrupt, and the product of delusion. It is well known that the prehistoric armadas could never have reached the Seventeenth Galaxy. The notion of miscegenation between humans and brutes is as absurd as it is offensive.*

Pre-given rule and repetitious rotation of events mean that Oitarian culture scarcely *has* a concept for 'event'. What happens is happened, by the Rule. Hence scarcely any concept of 'history' in our sense. Although early Oitarian myth is vigorous with history: epics of encounters with implacable natural forces, hazardous space explorations (D. has been trading epics with O.). This archaic mythology excites O., but there is somewhere a cut-off: says all this was when 'humanity hugger-muggered without the Rule'.

Hence to construct parameters of Oitarian society one must start with the cut-off.

What is the Rule?

Hypothesis 1. Is moment at wh glacial emergency imposed total centralised creature-controlled environment (see previous paper). This imposed total subordination of all individuals/groups to centrally defined, rule-governed imperatives and programmes.

Hypothesis 2. This generated a corresponding mythology/ideology of Rule (and rotation), reinforcing centralised organs of power.

Who or what then is Rule? Here O. is evasive. Refers on occasion to 'Gracious Goodnesses' who sit from on high and lay laws. Who are GGs? How are they appointed, elected? O. blocks these qs, shows symptoms of disturbance (*qy*: anger? anxiety?) GGs are taboo to rational enquiry, have highest charisma, more than royal but not quite divine. Perhaps avatars embodying divinity of the Rule (i.e. they both screen and displace enquiry). Or perhaps (also?) shamans or Interpreters of the Rule? Yet seem to be actual personages, who sit behind screens in loftiest bumple.

Hypothesis 3. Cut-off point was moment when society passed within advanced stage of computer-dependency. Could the Rule actually be a bank of artificial-intelligence computers? When data-input to computers activates programmes to the need for new constructions, changes in regulations, & c., this signalled on print-out panels in Bumple of the Wheel? This only way change can occur in society. Hence 'history' = print-out of new regulations from Rule in response to data-input.

Hypothesis 4. Gracious Gs are hereditary caste of computer programmers/operators. They serve the software of the Rule. Sort of Computer Theocracy. They humanise Rule's operation; feed in questions to Rule, like priestesses at Delphi; write new programmes (but within Rule's parameters); and translate the instructions of panels into magical or ceremonial utterances or 'laws'.

This mostly fits w evasive account of Infmnt. But one problem. Manner of procreation on Oitar prohibits simple hereditary succession. In some way GGs must be selected/appointed. Could they be eminent Provosts of Colleges or Adjusters? Yet their avatar-like charisma suggests not. Probably (*Hypothesis 5*) they are programmed from conception from a unique Sper-line in-bred with selected ♀ affines by the College of Bio-Engineering. In this sense are a hereditary priesthood, dedicated to the Rule from the moment they leave the tank. *But* Coll of Bio-Eng also operates according to programme of the Rule. Hence we are into feedback loop of computer-dependency once more.

Note: these are v preliminary hypotheses. One has to work from somewhere. If I showed them to Pepper he wld no doubt tell me O. has been reading sci-fic.

BUT: hypothesis of computer-controlled Rule may be what Infmnt *wants* to lead me to; or it may be what Gracious Gs want Oitarian subject population to believe. (The Rule is much like our own Media?) It wld be easy for quasi-hereditary caste of programmers to manipulate central computer-banks for own advantages – even for power struggles to develop in own ranks?

With only one Infmnt no systematic testing of hypotheses possible.

Colleges and Roles

If we can de-code the Rule, the rest begins to fit in place.

Basic unit of structure is the 'College'. Infmnt took this term from Eng dict. Probably raises wrong expectations. College in Oitar is an organised collectivity defined according to its specialised function. All collegiates are selected for aptitude to function. Not a 'community', because no kinship/familial relations, and all are allocated similar functions/roles. More like nunnery or monastery, but no gender segregation: also no segregation from world – people move in and out and may be attached to other institutions. So 'College' or 'Faculty' will do.

Infmnt not helpful on education. D. says he has found no equivalent term in Oitarian, nearest might be 'programming'. Children receive in first years a general programming in common pool of age-cohort, passing through stages (1st, 2nd, 3rd degree of intellect & c.). Regular aptitude tests. Discards? (Infmnt, n/a.) At 4th degree they are entered within the 'arc of learning' and, after some intermediate stage of semi-specialisation (blurry), go to schools attached to their College of special aptitude. But spend part of school life at schools of College of 2nd, 3rd aptitude. All schools, including infant, are residential. Then with great ceremonial they graduate and are attached as novices to own College.

Also, v important: even this education/programming is itself pre-programmed. Remember D's finding that each conception is determined by Bio-Engineers with a role-kit identity. Except for highly specialised role-kits (adjusters, priesthood of the bumples, GGs?), the matings or 'matches' are between different 'suits', which supply each foetus with dominant, subordinate and recessive genes. This supplies each child with a role-kit. This is tested in infant school (*aet* 4) which confirms dominant or major (i.e. collegiate) role. Further tests at 11 plus determine minor, subsidiary role, and also an auxiliary role (held in reserve).

Thus Oipas is Poet (dominant, collegiate role), astronaut (subsidiary role), with a recessive gene perhaps derived from the archaic ranchers and hunters, which gives him the auxiliary (reserve) role of gardener (hence his passion for flowers). Is therefore full member of College of Poets, visiting fellow of College of Cosmic Development, and is permitted on certain days to assist the gardeners and even the Keepers of the Sentient Seven (which is a 'club' or sub-college of an inferior order).

I do not begin to have a full list of Colleges yet, but among them are: Number; Cosmology and Galactic Studies; Cosmic Development; Geology; Bio-Engineering; Stellanthropology; Botany (with Gardening); Poesy; Robotics; Domology (i.e. constructional engineering); Aesthetics (another powerful college, subdivided into Proportion, Geometry and the Club of Critics); Physics; Farming (which takes in the management of the Sentient Seven); Sarcology (Medicine); Eurhythmy (with Dancing); Ceremony; Trance; Paranormal Matter; and Chemistry.

This list is probably biased by Infmnt's own role-kit. O. has little interest in practical affairs and suggests most details of livelihood are attended to by butlers. Butlers undoubtedly perform many menial physical tasks (carrying, digging, cleaning, food-pelleting), but all must be supervised. There must also be hazardous and expert tasks in construction and maintenance of domes and Alls, manning ice-burners & c., and it is clear that in summer a good deal more goes on on the surface of the planet than O. says (or perhaps knows about). Provided each College performs its allocated role, it need not know much about the activities of any other. I think it probable that there are other (liminal?) groups performing more robust, practical and dangerous roles.

Also (if Coll of Robotics) they must have robotised some tasks?

Social Organisation

Note, first, that while no normal kinship, close in-breeding. If D. is right, Oitarian names are really computer finding-code: Oi Pas indicates Sper-line and hostess, which requires only year of conception for complete identification. Siblings will be so rare as to be discounted. But half-siblings (sharing the same Sper-line or 'father') will be common, in the same College and age-cohort; and since the hostesses may have been bred from the same Sper-line, the genetic affinity is even closer. This does not create any evident kinship bonding, a concept untranslatable into Oitarian, just as their collegiate-bonding may be untranslatable into English. However, O. does say that there is special communication ('vibes') between such affines: perhaps like the 'extra-sensory' empathies attributed to identical twins?

For evident reasons of engineering and species survival, the population of Oitar is highly concentrated, into six cities (or 'orbs') spaced out upon the least intemperate plains of the planet. Each city is at least 1,000 Earth-miles from any neighbour. Direct contact between them is possible overland only in the height of summer; air communication is maintained, but even this is hazardous in winter months owing to huge ice-storms. Nevertheless, there is no 'capital city'. Each city is supposed to be co-equal. In each there is a Bumple of the Wheel, which promulgates the same Rule, so that the computer-banks must be constantly keyed into each other, with co-ordinated programmes.

Each city is a gathering of domes, with huge Alls as grazing-grounds, lawns and cereal-fields, all interconnected by arcades. If the pop of each city is some two million, then the pop of whole planet is little more than twelve million. The greater part of the surface of this huge planet is totally uninhabited, save for a few scattered observatories and some stations mining rare minerals which cannot be made synthetically.

Despite (or because of?) this huge and hostile space around them, Oitarians (to judge by Oipas) are incredibly institutionalised, both by internal programming and by external conditioning. Oitarian culture is a paradigm of games-theory. Not only are all 'moves' prescribed by rule within narrow limits, but individuals have little choice between legitimate 'moves' because not only the game but the individuals are programmed. Hence (*Hypothesis 6*) the general repression of individual initiatives. No concept of 'choice' in culture. (Reservation? No concept of *legitimate* choice? Infmnt does appear to understand concept but takes it as something like 'disobedience'.) If programme does not appear to indicate correct 'move' between alternatives, individual will check back on programme (via computer-bank?) or refer to hierarchy of College: i.e. will refer to Rule.

This may tell us a lot about Infmnt. Coming into Earth-society must have been a culture-shock of dimension quite unknown to us. He came in heavily pre-programmed. Was selected for role not because of special skills as astronaut: his craft was on automatic pilot most of time. Was selected not even as an orbiting observer (gadgets, cameras and electronics to do all that) but as a poetic recorder. Made landfall presumably through mechanical failure, since disobedience to Rule at that stage most improbable. But was devoid of *any* programme for this contingency. Found himself (a) in alien culture, (b) devoid of any programme, and (c) with little capacity for initiative.

Hence O. had nothing to direct him save the very general imperative of Obedience to a Rule, whose formulas are irrelevant to our culture. A pity no professional observer got to him at that time, although he must have been almost out of his mind. 'Lonely' does not begin to describe it: he was both outlaw and alien. During his first weeks on Earth, he seems to have been obsessed with the imperative to recover his craft/ get back to moon – and Rule. Subject now is of course a good deal acculturated, hence diagnostic picture is screwed up. In fact has adjusted remarkably, is more institutionalised in Martagon than I am. Definite (if uneven) activation of *initiative*, self-direction, which shows that Oitarian culture *suppresses* a potential which remains there. Also: sexual activation – physical if not emotional/cultural. Overcome taboos (e.g. eating). In short, adaptive. Oipas is now a 'nicer' person (i.e. adjusted to our norms and expectations) but is no longer pure specimen for observation. Programme of Rule has diminished to ceremonial forms, such as his dawn exercises.

Hypothesis 7. Oitar is in most respects a no-growth society. Or the Rule intends things to rotate repetitiously in that way. No population growth. No economic growth in normal sense: emphasis on maintenance of stable state. Of course some activities out of the routine: reconstructing dome or All, finding new mineral deposits. Becoming more difficult to replace certain genetic role-kits with deflation of sperm banks, lack of Spermen. Occasional natural emergencies, when glaciers invade city plains.

Great exception to this in one area: space exploration. Here alone there seems to be some competition between the six cities, each of which sends out craft. There must be some mechanism for directing the surplus into this endeavour. Infmnt unhelpful. Tells me only that the poets of each city challenge each other to 'flytings' before massed audiences, in which each recites epics celebrating the voyages of their own explorers. I suspect that an increasing proportion of Oitarian resources, supra-tech R & D, are being directed to this window of survival, and that the GGs have means of channelling psychic energies this way as well.

Odds and Ends

No society could hold together as a collocation of functional colleges. There must be some mediating or supervisory or solidarising roles.

So far I can detect three: or two and a half.

Adjusters. Adjusters are a college, but a special one. Their members are mostly on attachment to other colleges. Their role is definitely invigilatory: to monitor the observance of the Rule. Infmnt is both unhelpful ('they spy out blemishes') and truculent ('an Adjuster would soon mend your beastly ways').

Bumplepersons. A bumple is a building or precinct dedicated to ritual purposes: cf church, temple, but O. also supposes banks and theatre to be our bumples: i.e. they are visited by populace with awe, have ritual ceremonial, and petitioners come in to worship or seek favours of a priesthood or elect.

Each college has a bumple of its own on college precincts. In each city, centrally placed, there is a Bumple of the Wheel. This is a huge bubble-like edifice – a distinct structure outside the lesser cupolas – with ornate avenues and arcades running out to the rest of the city, like the spokes from an axle. This is the Seat of the GGs. Have argued (above) that it is probably central artificial intelligence complex.

A collegian is ruled to attend the college bumple *each day*. Much ritual. But (*Hypothesis 8*) what I think goes on is that they 'clock off' and 'clock on'. That is, each has a slot on its belt, to hold two mini-cassettes/microdiscs or whatever: one is the day's programme, the other is a monitor-gimmick like a tachometer which registers performance. O. showed me the slot on his belt, but it seems he threw away the cassettes soon after landfall.

Thus the daily ceremony consists in returning these and drawing the new day's programme. Those returned presumably feed straight into computers of College bumple and are banked. The sum of the College data will then go direct to banks of Bumple of the Wheel?

Adjusters and Provosts of Colleges have ready access to Bumple of Wheel, presumably to report/receive collegiate programme. Also to ask questions of oracle. Ordinary citizens go only on high ceremonial occasions, or on rare occasions when a matter for individual decision comes up. O. recounts with pride that when teams under selection for exploration of Earth he was personally called for interview at Supreme Bumple. Q. 'Who were interviewers?' *A.* 'No whos, woman.

Interview was screen.' Q. 'They were behind a screen?' A.
'The screen asks questions … in a low voice like a hobo
fluting.'

The bumples must be served by someone, perhaps a caste of
programme-priests. They also seem to be swarming with sacred
tabby cats.

Liminals or Discards? I can give only half marks to this finding,
since Infmnt won't give anything. But I strongly suspect that,
just as with chuckalls among Seven Sentients, there is some
category of human with low honour status whom O. won't
mention. There are far too many skilled and practical tasks
essential to any society which he never mentions, which could
never be done by butlers.

The nearest Earth-analogy to Oitarian society is a rigid caste
society. But vertically segmented, by occupation/function, not
horizontally (except for adjusters and priests of the bumples).
Yet O. has brahmin or mandarin characteristics, seems never
to have done any physical labour, couldn't make a cup of tea.
Suspect most collegians are the same.

Hence (*Hypothesis 9*, tentative) there is an inferior caste of
'untouchables' and unmentionables. (Rather like cooks and
cleaners in this place, who never get mentioned in Weeklies –
or in my notes.)

Infmnt sometimes refers to 'discards', who fail to pass aptitude tests at *aet* 4, 11 plus & c. But then he puts up a block.
Don't think they are just written off, going to premature dead-
lines. That wld be wasteful demographically. Also, some of
the discards may have unusual aptitudes which might at some
time be of service to the Wheel. There may be a pool of
discards, who never make the grade as collegians, and are a
sort of Oitarian proletariat?

Also, it seems that every ten years or so each individual is
summoned to a special institution of the Adjusters for a scan
or College of Adjusters Test (CAT). Failure of test again leads
to discard pool. O. actually *scowled* when he told me this – he
is getting almost human. Q. 'If all are selected and programmed

from conception, how could any fail the test?' *A.* 'Not all genes submit to Rule.' *Q.* 'But would not this be detected by Bio-Engineers?' *A.* 'The Rule makes allowance for unruliness.' *Q.* 'Unruliness? Where is this unruliness?' *A.* 'It is on all sides, woman. It is outside the domes. It is in space. It is here in this room.' *Q.* 'How can the Rule programme for unruliness?' *A.* 'It is a delicate poise which Adjusters must construe. Great unruliness is chaos. Too much is signal for discard. But a little unruliness (or self-rolling) is necessary, to make poems or inventions. And, outside the domes, to meet unprogrammed events. How could I talk with you now, Helena, if Oipas had been ruled as straight as a rail?'

This all v complex. It seems that most Oitarians are so well adjusted that they actually have to be a little *de*-programmed in that part of their being where the Wheel may require a little inventiveness or initiative. It's like compressing air in a canister, and then unscrewing a valve so that some of the fizz can get out. Some role-kits are suited in such a way as to include recessive genes of originality/inventiveness which can be given scope within the programme. These include poets, gardeners, musicians and inventers in the science and tech colleges, all of whom are regarded by the Adjusters with great suspicion (hence O's scowl), although the Adjusters themselves share the same 'sports' in their genes. Yet these groups are also often suited so as to have astronautics as their minor aptitude, since they have the most capacity for responding to unprogrammed emergencies.

But most of this is inference. V preliminary.

Task Forces. These are set up for any special object which either does not fall within the function of any college or which requires collaboration of aptitudes. Of course space exploration is organised as a specialised task-force. There are also task-forces to prepare inter-collegiate ceremonials. Infmnt calls task-forces roll-strings or roll-bytes.

I'll try to do this as a diagram:

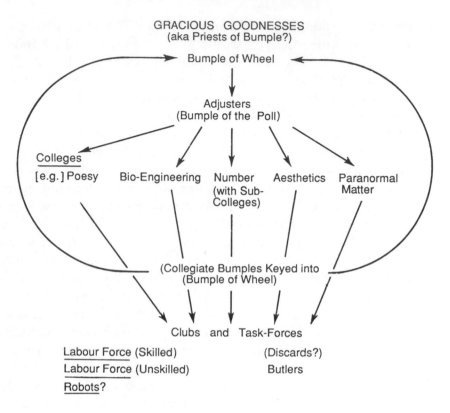

GRACIOUS GOODNESSES
(aka Priests of Bumple?)

Bumple of Wheel

Adjusters
(Bumple of the Poll)

Colleges

[e.g.] Poesy   Bio-Engineering   Number   Aesthetics   Paranormal
                                   (with Sub-   Matter
                                   Colleges)

(Collegiate Bumples Keyed into
(Bumple of Wheel)

Clubs and Task-Forces

Labour Force (Skilled)   (Discards?)
Labour Force (Unskilled)   Butlers
Robots?

Reservations: Problems

Most of this hangs together. But sometimes too well – sus-
piciously. More than once when interviewing O. I have wondered: is he describing actuality? Or is he rehearsing ideology?
And if ideology, is it what he believes (i.e. what the Rule or
GGs have conditioned him to believe)? Or what he wishes *me*
to believe? Or a mixture – what he half-believes and thinks it
is proper to say? (As is norm of Earth-culture.)

Problem is: this is a repetitious, well-regulated and self-
regulating society. Yet there is very heavy presence of forms
of social control, as if breakdown feared. Control is ever-

present: the role of bumples, with due awe and ritual; monitoring of programmes; role of adjusters; collegiate hierarchy; structural segregation.

Then there is the heavy accent on ceremonial and the sheer extent of time expended on it. The collegian's day is punctuated with ceremonial rites: obeisances to the rising sun; programme rite at bumple; mid-day eurhythmics; obeisances to setting sun. The year is laced with Festal Days, with occasional great inter-collegiate or inter-city ceremonial occasions. It seems that even walking from one point to another in city is governed by ceremony. Special forms of greeting when they pass other collegians (like saluting or lifting of hats, but more elaborate). There are prescribed routes, like following the circumference of a 'tank' or lake, traversing a civic square at the correct 'degree' or angle (must never walk across certain diagonals). (But not 'square', since their squares are oval, round, elliptic, anything but square.)

In derivation all this might seem to have a functional explanation. After the first great emergency when they built the early domes, there have been only two periods of comparable social activity & disturbance of routine (when the erections were redesigned and enlarged). Otherwise for aeons of Earth-years society has been designed to circulate in a steady-state. Hence 'round' and 'rule' symbolise order, survival, the avoidance of accident and change. The sun is round, Oitar rotates; their architecture is nearly all domes and circles; their lakes are round or oval. (NB water or 'melt' is sacred & symbolises civilisation as against hostile glaciated nature. There are a lot of water-worship ceremonies – rowing on the lake is worship, and the collegians bathe together in a round swimming-bath called a Well of Worship. Both sexes, of course, since no taboos – nor need for them.) So the Wheel = the sun & planetary system = also social order = Rule.

Okay. And from functional derivation we can pass to structural organisation in Rule & also internalised as rule-bound culture: a structuralist's paradise. Instead of raw/cooked we have ice/melt and (more pervasive) accident (= raw)/ programmed (= cooked).

Yet isn't Oitarian culture even heavier than that? The interstices of daily life are ritualised and saturated with the Rule. Given the 'normality' of derivation & function, hasn't myth & ideology acquired an independent existence with its own logic (or illogic), towering above society and imposing its own functions & duties? Vic Turner might be more helpful here than L.-Strauss.

Or could there even be something more fishy & instrumental here? Granted that a no-growth society must absorb unwanted energies in some way, yet there appear to be excessive devices for killing time. Ceremonial is like a sponge absorbing psychic surplus value. Each individual is equipped with video-trancers which they are expected to turn themselves on to in any unprogrammed (O.: 'unruly') time. Like kids with Walkmans. Also hallucinogens, which are developed by College of Trance and encouraged.

There is also a carefully confected compensation-mechanism. As if to compensate for repetitiousness of daily life & repression of initiative, & also absence of any conflict or choice, there are certain *licensed* and formalised areas where debate/dispute is encouraged. Indeed, the licensing and encouragement of such disputes is special function of Colleges of Taste, Aesthetics & Club of Critics, in consultation with College of Ceremony.

These disputes scarcely ever have any bearing on any decision which could affect social actuality in any operative way. They concern e.g. colours of flower-beds; sartorial questions (colours and cut of robes); fashions in dance; and a kind of lit and music criticism, wh must never touch on content or deep formal structure, but only on trivia: a species of semiotics, in wh each sign, colour & gesture is invested with incredibly pompous significance. (D. knows more about this than I do.) O. tells me of a fierce, long-lasting debate when he was a young man, enacted before excited audiences like football crowds, between two poetic schools, Sch of Crystal and Sch of Melodic Colour.

(This dispute appears to have got so heated that it pressed upon actuality – could even have influenced programme of space exploration – so that it was formally brought to a close by the GGs laying a law from on high.)

These disputes have all the signs of being contrived as a compensation-mechanism. They get v fierce, and 'blemishes' or even 'crimes' or 'deviations' from Rule & proportion are exposed, followed by confessions and self-criticisms by the offenders. Rivals denounce each other & seek to get oracles of bumples to rule opponents as 'off the roll'. The oracles are normally enigmatic, so long as dispute is not too 'unruly'. Suspect that in origin these ritual disputes were a displacement of real social conflicts into safe areas. Infmnt says that in primitive times, at APE, disputants actually formed themselves into 'parties' and the matter was 'taken to a vote'. At *temp* Ordinary Erections parties were disallowed, since disputants had been too obstreperous about aesthetic proportions of new erections & had even questioned the Rule. And voting was 'pinioned' (or polled) by the Adjusters, whose bumple is still called the Bumple of the Poll. Polling fell into disuse at AOE. All this lingers on in certain terms (archaic) still in occasional use. D. says that, when the Goodnesses promulgate a major new programme, they are said to 'elect' it and the plan is called a 'vote'. The ceremonial form is: 'The Rule has elected your Vote. Hear Your Vote and Obey.'

From other notes it seems there has been an evolution in this displacement-mechanism. Stage One = APE = 'domocracy' (when parties and voting on non-operative questions permitted within domes). Stage Two = 'mediocracy', at time of AOE, when the parties gave way to 'medias', wh were disputants appointed by Adjusters and licensed to dispute within the Rule: disputes decided by poll. Stage Three (still current) = AGE = 'tautocracy', wh is really another term for the Rule; i.e. disputant medias now disallowed, but term survives as courtesy-name for daily/weekly programming, which is promulgated from on high to each citizen & then *polled* (courtesy-term for monitored). Hence when collegian attends bumple each day to draw day's programme and to return previous day's monitor-cassette, this is known as getting his/her media and handing in his/her poll. However, tautocracy permits the survival of licensed disputes as described above.

Contradictions?

The fishy thing about all this is that it could almost have been contrived by some ruling caste or theocracy (such as priesthood of bumples & GGs) as means of displacement or control. Or it could be a self-generating system of ritual, spinning out its own exotic logic.

Critical to this is whether GGs (or programmers of central computers) actually *write* new programmes & control data-input; or whether computers write own programmes and priesthood are ceremonial interpreters. No way of answering this. (Except field study on Oitar!) Probably Infmnt doesn't know.

I always tell my graduates, after blocking out a culture, to try & define possible places of conflict or contradiction. But (unless we know answer to above) this one is difficult. There cld be contradiction arising from 'proletarian' discards. No evidence of this. Between colleges or cities? Little evidence. (No elaborate forms for conflict-resolution.)

My hunch is that major contradiction lies within ideology of Rule itself. All this ceremonial, plus compensation-mechanisms, suggests a culture almost desperate to keep total control – that is, to KEEP THE LID ON. Oitarian 'nature' is not 'naturally' submissive to Rule: is potentially as capable of initiative and breaking out in unruly ways as is human. The whole ceremonial structure is a lid, holding down a bubbling and fizzing underneath. Space exploration a major safety-valve. Maybe (after nearly a programme-free year) the lid is beginning to come off O.?

Sage Field Notes

23 March. Lousy day yesterday. I gave my paper to David three days ago. Who else can I show it to? Thought it moved us forward (drew on some of his work) & expected him to rush in polishing specs. Not a word, not a sign, not even at dinners.

In the end I swallowed pride and asked him if he wld call in, on pretext of our session on laughter. Wh he did, entering door & making elaborate Oipas obeisance. Wh I returned. Didn't mention my paper but sat on sofa utterly preoccupied (though not too preoccupied to accept Scotch), swaying a little from the waist, rhythmically. I asked him what was up. He seemed to wake up with a start & sd, 'Oh, Oipas has been teaching me an early epic. Listen.' And he started swaying again, reciting something with a hypnotic beat about 'Inca in a glove of gold' and 'Buddha on a sledge' and then several lines in Oitarian. Never heard him speak whole phrases of Oitarian before. Then he did remember to polish his glasses, and sd, 'Sorry, Helena. The trans ... translation isn't very good. The original would blow your mind.' I asked what Buddha had got to do with Oitar – was O. conning us from his library readings once more? D. seemed to flare up & was about to say something, then went sulky & quiet. Then he did an odd thing. He lit a cigarette (he's smoking very heavily now) and held the match until it burned his fingers! I could *smell* the burning skin & had to knock it out. He didn't even notice, as if he'd lost touch with his senses. Looked down at his blackened thumb in surprise.

I poured him another Scotch. Then, gritting my teeth, I asked what he had thought of my paper. *D.* 'What paper?' *H.* 'My paper. Sixteen sides, A-4. I gave it to you on Thursday.' *D.* 'Oh. Yes. Quite interesting. But we know most of that, don't we? It's pretty ... obvious.' For the first time his hesitancy *infuriated* me. *H.* 'Oh, *thanks.* Then you agree with it?' *D.* 'Oh, yes.' Silence again. *H.* 'WHERE IS IT?' *D.* 'Oh ... er ...'

I lit into him and finally dragged it out that he had 'mislaid ... er, lost' the paper, had probably left it in the gents, Friday dinner.

So it will now be spiked by Mayhem, copy in Weeder's files. I started *flaying* him, saying it was only copy (not true). Instead of expected penitence, D. suddenly got aggressive. He sd the paper was 'clinical'. It treated sacred Oitarian concepts as if they were specimens pinned on a table. 'Don't you realise, Helena, that their civilisation is so far advanced that it is impertinent to try and reduce it to our beastly concepts? The very notion of the Rule is beyond translation. Bringing that sublimity down to earth seemed like a . . . mockery. I left it in the bog.'

I realised now that David was ill or at least in some kind of culture-transference. I let him run on. But then he suddenly rounded on *me*.

'Besides, you give too much away. And you touch on some secret things.'

'Secret? How?'

'Well, secrets of social organisation. They could give clues to command and communications.'

'Secret from whom?'

'From Them. From Mayhem, Hunter, that lot.'

'*I* didn't leave the paper in the bog. I asked *you* to read it. I wouldn't dream of letting Mayhem & co. get a squint at it.'

'Or Major Sorley. He's not stupid. And he's always spying around, trying to get on the right side of Oipas. And of you. He might get a lot of clues from it.'

'Why shouldn't Robert Sorley talk with Oipas? They get on well – they talk about, oh, ancient history, horses, the Cold War. Why not?'

'Helena! How can you be so short . . . short-sighted?' (Much polishing of spectacles.) 'Sorley is in the *army*. Army *intelligence*. He *embodies* the other side.'

'But perhaps Sorley really believes in the need for defence? He's doing his job, just as we are.'

'Exactly! But defence against whom? And on which side? If we . . . if Oitar have plans to civilise the earth, should we let Them know about . . .?'

Just then a knock at door & Rani came in. Sd she had only

'popped in for a chat' but cld see we were 'busy'. I was bombed out of my mind, not only because D. was obviously ill, but because he was raising real problems I didn't know the answer to. I persuaded R. to stay, wh she did readily, even having some Scotch (wh she almost never does). R. seems to have a calming effect on people. I've often noticed that she humanises D.: when she is there he climbs down from his intellectual stratosphere.

We chatted about shop for a few minutes and the scene seemed to get more mellow. Perhaps whisky helped. (R.: 'Oh dear, I hope Mr Oipas doesn't smell the whisky!') When R. left, D. had come down from his high and seemed rather low. I tried, very cautiously, to discuss transference symptoms & suggested that he was working so closely with O. that he was internalising Oitarian concepts. He polished specs & then sd in a v low voice that this was true. Added that my paper was 'bloody good' (a little resentment in his voice) & sd that in past week Oipas had 'taken him right inside' Oitarian concepts so that when he read the paper, some of it seemed familiar, even 'old hat'.

He sd a few bits of it were 'wrong'. *H.* 'Which bits?' *D.* 'Well ... about the daily programming in the bumple – drawing the cassettes.' He sd that this was mostly ritual, a 'formality'. 'They're not as strictly programmed, once they have been given a role, as all that. The Rule is within them and most of the time they "freewheel". But if they get into situations which are complex and require choices or decisions, they can always feed the data into those jiggers on their belts & get a scientific read-out. After all, if the data-input is adequate, then there must be only one right answer. There can't be two ways of doing the right thing.'

I was about to object, but D. was slightly swaying again. So I sd (although I ached at having to humour him), 'Perhaps you'll help me revise that bit. What other bits are wrong?' He sd most of the rest was 'correct', and then he suddenly became very penitent about the loss of the paper. 'I don't know what came over me, Helena. Must have gone out of my mind. I was reading the paper in the bog and I suddenly felt it was all in ... insulting.

I chucked it on the floor and walked out. When I went back it had gone.' He was really contrite.

I suggested we shld try & break & enter Weeder's files & recover it. D. cheered up & we speculated on how to circumvent Gentry, the bugmaster, & throttle Dobermans. D. sd we shld do it on Tuesday afternoon when they were all off at golf. Normality returned: i.e. D. was laughing.

I suggested we have a go at purported purpose of session – review of laughter – and got out my notes. The moment we tried to discuss laughter we both became utterly solemn. It was like trying to hiccup when someone has put £20 on the table for the next hic. Two minutes before we had both been hooting about Weeder and Dobermans. Now we might have been sitting at a wake.

H. 'Well, what *is* laughter? Physiologically?'

D. 'Oh ... excitation of the facial muscles. Sort of knee-jerk reflex. Form of play. All animals do.'

H. 'Animals don't laugh.'

D. 'Don't primates? Chimpanzees?'

H. 'They chatter. They grimace. They sort of ... mock. If they seem to laugh they are imitating or "aping". Laughing is an expression of the intellectual faculties. Only humans laugh ... so far as I know it's there in all human cultures. They probably laughed in the caves. It is coincident with reason. Man might equally well be called *homo ridens*.'

D. 'You're looking at your notes. You wrote that up before. But isn't it all rather marginal, really? It's an acquired characteristic, a learned behavioural form, passed down by acculturation. No doubt one might track it down to some original function way back – maybe laughter was some sort of warning-alarm to the tribe when something extraneous or odd was sensed. The homo would scent strangeness, a predator, put his head back, and go "Ho-Ho-Ho!" And everyone would dive for cover.'

H. 'Worth trying.' (Writing.) 'Abrupt coincidence of incompatible signals. Juncture of contradictory semiotics. Alarm signal?

246

Humm . . . Doesn't work. Homos *enjoy* laughing. Maybe laughter belongs to culture, but I don't think it's "learned", like that. It's *physical*, like a spasm. Coming directly from the diaphragm – also from the emotions/intellect, but without any rational mediation, with an instant physical outcome. Going "Ho-Ho-Ho!" when a predator was scented could actually endanger the tribal group – the rabbit's white scut is better, a silent semiotics. Laughter can shake the whole frame. It's uncontrollable.'

D. 'Aren't you making rather heavy weather? Laughter is momentary, like sneezing, or like a dog shaking water off its coat. People aren't "in laughter" like they are "in love". Or fear – you can feel threatened but you can't feel laughtered. Really, Helena, I must say that it is very marginal.'

H. 'I don't agree. I think it comes from the centre of the human psyche. It may be essential to species-survival.'

D. 'On the contrary. It is an atavism. Oitarians have long outgrown it. And their culture is exemplary for survival in the face of extraordinary odds.'

Silence. I filled up our glasses.

H. 'Well, let's try jokes on each other. You tell me one.'

D. 'No, you tell me one.'

Silence. *H.* 'Oh, hell, you have to be in the mood. Or it has to hit you when you least expect it. Well, there's the one about the Irish astronauts. You know it?'

D. 'Probably racist. But go on.'

H. 'There were these astronauts and they were going to blast off and were giving their final press conference. After they had talked about the spaceship and so on, a reporter asked where were they going. Would they go to the moon? The commander replied, "Oh, no. People have already been to the moon. We are going somewhere new." "Where is that?" "We shall be going to the sun." "But wouldn't that be dangerous? Wouldn't you burn up?" "Oh, no, we've thought of that. We shall go there by night."'

Silence.

H. 'Well?'

D. 'Stupid, really. Because "night" is only an Earth-perception, during rotation. The sun is never in night.'

H. 'Oh, hell!'

Silence.

D. 'I can't deconstruct it, really. Probably it's racist, or expresses culture-superiority, like jokes about Polacks, Newfies. They always pretend to be told affectionately − note your mock-Irish accent − so that the contempt is disguised in "legitimate" ways.'

H. 'I don't know that it is contempt. They tell jokes like that against each other in Ireland, all the time.'

D. '*Against* each other. That's it. When do people tell jokes *with* each other?'

H. 'We tell jokes against ourselves. Often.' Silence. 'You try one.'

D. 'No. Well ... Here's a Yorkshire one. Two men in a pub. First man downs a Scotch, says, "I shot me dog today." Second man, "Were he mad?" First man, "Well, he warn't right pleased."''

H. (Snort.) 'Let's see. Bit of culture-superiority − Yorkshire tykes. Turns on double meaning of "mad". Ambiguity brings sudden juncture of opposed expectations: (1) normal expectation of rational grounds for shooting dog; (2) switches to dog's perspective and challenges man's rationality. At same time, maybe a way of coping with mortality?'

D. 'But why is all that *funny*? Couldn't there be more rational ways of dealing with all that? Most humour is only a way of getting round civilised inhibitions − against racism, sexism and so on. Circumventing taboos. Trevor Griffiths showed that in a play, *Comedians*. He deconstructs jokes and shows them to be sick to the core.'

H. 'That wasn't all he showed. He also showed laughter as a criticism of power, and as a self-defence. Anyway, why do we find the come-uppance of the great and self-important to be funny? I mean, the banana-skin ... Why did we think it funny to break & enter Weeder's files? You were laughing. We were both in stitches ...'

248

D. 'Fantasy of impotence. Because we both know we wouldn't do it ...'

H. 'Look, I know something that was funny. Blast! Where are the Weekly Minutes?' Sound of papers. 'Here it is ... The bit about golf: "Captain Scarcely suggested that Colonel Gardyan-Hunter's balls could be soaked in repellent ..." Well, sorry, *I* thought it was funny.'

D. 'Ambiguity again. Double meaning of "balls". Brings into unexpected conjunction incongruous categories, golf and sexuality. Sort of image-montage, superimposing on image of golf-course image of Doberman biting off Colonel's testicles. Incongruity heightened by formality of Minutes, pompous officer-status deflated. Also, Scarcely is too asinine to know what he is saying, Weeder too abjectly subservient to censor asininity. And, as usual, sick centre: joke circumvents sexual taboos, deference inhibitions. Also, sadistic. Dog eating balls is sadistic, even if *you* don't think so ... soaking male genitals in repellent obviously endorses your feminist prejudices ...'

H. 'Ow! ow! ow! STOP! Why does explaining a joke kill it stone dead? It's like trying to breathe in while one's sneezing. The whole point about a joke is that it *can't* be reduced to reason ...'

D. '... and behind all that is a fantasy of impotence once more. I don't mean Hunter's impotence, balls gnawed off. I mean our impotence against Them. A lot of laughter is like that. You call it a way of "coping". Perhaps it's a way of reconciling the powerless to their powerlessness? They pretend a revenge, which is projected in humour as fantasy. A joke is just displaced aggression. Aggression which the oppressed dare not act out in real life. When the powerful do actually slide on a banana-skin in real life, this is supremely funny, because the fantasy is for a moment real.'

H. 'I don't know. Maybe something in it.' (Writing.) ' "Defences of the powerless?" Laughter takes a lot of forms. Irony can be like that ... but irony is only one form. Why should we look for a monocausal explanation? Perhaps everything – sex, fear, power, mortality, art, appetite – collapses into laughter when brought into incongruous juxtaposition with another category?'

D. 'But what *is* incongruity? Poets are always using double or triple meanings of words, for effects very different from jokes. See Empson. The mis-match of categories may be funny or it may be mind-opening. Think of the metaphysicals. "At the round earth's imagined corners" conflates the categories of the old and new cosmology. It's abrasive on the imagination, like a match striking, but we don't laugh.'

H. 'Hummm. We almost laugh.' (Writing.) ' "The mis-match of categories." It's very close to the source of laughter. I've got a note from Bateson here, "Towards a Theory of Schizophrenia". He says humour "involves sudden shifts in Logical Types ... occurs when it suddenly becomes plain that a message was not only metaphoric but also more literal ... the explosive moment in humour is when the labelling of the mode undergoes a dissolution and resynthesis ...' Sort of crossed wires between literalness and fantasy. But then he goes on to show that mental disturbance – schizophrenia – is a sort of crossed wires also. Not all that helpful. Oitarian culture puts up some kind of block to both kinds of wire-crossing – it can't move an inch outside its Logical Type?'

D. 'I think you should watch that line. A higher culture which has gained a rational logic-path will have cured that sort of blemish a millennium or two ago. It is itself a type-righter making right all watchers. Mis-matchers may be incendiaries and match-strikers against the roll or Rule ...'

H. (A little hurriedly.) 'Okay, okay, I get your point ...'

D. 'Points are not rules, woman. Points may be icons. Iconography may be iconoclasm ...'

H. 'All I meant was that metaphor (and poetry) are very close to laughter – and to madness also. Perhaps the mind-opening image is the twin of the joke. Perhaps both come from the chaos at the creative core of the consciousness. Both challenge received expectations. But one breaks through the parameters of "commonsense" and opens the way to new parameters. The other takes things as they are, and exposes their limits – their pretensions and illusions. When we laugh we often say we are "keeping a sense of proportion". Laughter is a defence against losing ourselves in the mists of ideology – an affirmation of primal ontological reality.'

D. 'That sounds a bit pretentious itself. It's a lot to hang on to shooting a mad dog.'

Silence. Glasses filled.

H. 'To get to the point. Oipas can't laugh. Never laughs. Calls it the Incongruous Noise. Supposes it is some kind of self-shame signal. There is something missing in his make-up. This is the place where Oitarians are not-human.'

D. 'But laughter *is* the Incongruous Noise.' Sound of chair scraping, D. rising. 'Look, I'm bloody fed up with this session. Where the hell is it getting us? All you've been on about is to use a lot of pretentious terminology to show that beastly laughter is because they can't cope with their own absurdities . . .'

H. 'Hold on, David, don't fly off! This really is central to our work. I'm saying that there's some kind of hole at the centre of Oitarian culture . . . something central to self-knowledge is just a vacancy in their consciousness. They are so programmed by the Rule that they've lost the capacity for self-doubt . . . or a sense of proportion . . . or . . .'

D. 'Bloody hell! Their whole culture *is* proportion. They don't need atavistic spasms. Their language has been cured, so they can't have puns or mis-matches. It follows algorithmic paths with less ambiguity than PROLOG or PASCAL. What is the Rule if it is not proportion? Oh God! I think I'm going to be sick . . .'

Sound of being sick and loo flushing.

D. 'I'm sorry, Helena. Perhaps a bit too much whisky.'

H. 'Don't worry. The cleaner will be in in the morning.'*

D. 'Ow, my head's awful. Sorry again. I'm turning in.'

D. hadn't been gone two mins before Rani knocked. She must have heard him go. She was as glum as I. Glummer. She knew all about D's transference-symptoms, sd he was going into a

---

* *Sage annotation, red ink:* 'Oh God, did I really say that?'

251

'breakdown'. Has been having a lot of extra sessions with O. (Crostic been away, & I gave him two when I was working on my paper.) She was tearful about his state, saying he was so 'sensitive' and 'such a gentleman', but so 'unworldly'. R. has that lovely Indian way of using English words in old-fashioned ways, long obsolescent here: thus she says 'gentle-man', as if man really gentle. Agreed she wld try & get him to take some sedative, I wld stop talking shop with him *pro tem* & bag some of his sessions with O., we wld both try & distract him into things non-professional. But what? Suggested Equerry might give him riding lessons but we both started laughing: incongruous categories. R. sd she wld take him out for walks in the garden, 'the English spring is so lovely.'

But then R. started talking about her own troubles, v unusual for her. Her letters from India often don't get through & some of hers must have been stopped. Hasn't heard from her parents for five weeks, the last letter told her her father was ill & asked her to come back. The man her parents promised her to years ago has broken it off, accusing her of disloyalty. This didn't upset her too much since she'd never met him & she's changed her views about arranged marriages – but it has left her disoriented, she thinks 27 is terribly old to be unmarried & without a betrothed. I started to chaff her about this in Western feminist style & she broke into floods of tears and sd she was a no one, and even Oipas didn't 'need her' any more, and then (the first time ever) she flashed back at me & sd I was a typical Western professional ♀ & didn't know how the rest of the world lived, & she didn't 'belong' to either the 'top' or the 'bottom' of Martagon ('I'm not even of the same *race*') & people like me and D. were like 'brahmins' who lived on the mountain-tops, we didn't know the real world, & all the cooks and cleaners and gardeners here we treated as 'untouchables', & we thought that if we smiled at them in the corridors we had paid our debts to them for the rest of the week. She sd that all the staff of this place are 'boiling over' & one day the whole 'Martagon raj' wld find itself in a 'mutiny'.

I felt vulnerable to all that. It's true I don't know what's going

252

on among Other Ranks. Don't suppose there's more than a page or two in my notes, and those mostly stereotype jokes (i.e. taboo-compensators). I've been so totally involved in the work.

Then R. sd sweetly that she didn't really think these things & only told me because I, and Ann, and D., and Mary the telephonist were her only friends. So we embraced & made up.

But, oh, I feel so low today. Just like R., I've lost touch with all my friends. And where is this whole thing going? And what about myself? Am I going anywhere? If R. feels old at 27, what am I at 38? Gloom, gloom. *And* pre-menstrual tension. (All of wh will be over, I suppose, in a few years. Wh adds to gloom.) I used to think that some day I'd have a child (or two or three) when I'd finished that book or got that job. Getting late now. When the hell can I get out of this place? Anyway, who will father child?

R. sd Harmer, the theatrical impresario who used to manage the *Sapio Show*, is coming tomorrow, about the Translator (wh is definitely lost). We thought that if he has to see D., one of us had better sit in on session. Harmer especially wants to see his 'old friend' O., and (surprisingly) Mayhem has agreed.

Sage Notebook. Pasted-in typescript

Toppest secret   TO ALL EXECUTIVES
Viscount Harmer, of Harmer Promotions, will visit tomorrow to de-brief on his experience of Mr Oipas, uses of Translator & c.

   Arrival (main gate): 10 a.m.

Interview Schedule

10.15–11.30 a.m.	Mr J. Mayhem and Miss J. A. Crostic
11.30–12.00	Major Robert Sorley
12.00–12.30	Mr Gentry

12.30– 2.00 p.m.	Lunch party in Assistant Director's apartment. Colonel Hunter, T. Hemlock, A. L. Weeder, J. A. Crostic, Captain Scarcely, J. Mayhem
2.00– 3.00 p.m.	D. Nettler and H. Sage
3.00– 4.30 p.m.	Lord Harmer has requested permission for social meeting with Mr Oipas
4.30– 5.00	Tea (all interested parties)
5.15 p.m.	Depart (main gate)

Note: Lord Harmer has been given superlative security clearance. Nevertheless, all executives will impress upon him that Mr Oipas *does not exist*, until/unless it is decided otherwise. (Matter now under review.) Executives will record all interviews and return tapes to files.

J. Mayhem

Oi Paz Journal. Fragment 01012*

... for which reason Oi Paz declaims this season of spring to be a benison, when the birds acquire new plumage and flute from the trees, and the buds are thrusting and the ground breaking out into flowers. And the corpse itself seems to come into a renewal. So that when our colonies are duly planted, this will be a time of Festal Days, for all should be out in the sweet airs, doing eurhythmics, or, as I am now licensed to do, riding at dawn on their noble horses, or doing obeisance to the rising sun.

---

* *The memory-banks of Oi Paz's Recorder have been damaged for much of this episode. This includes all the Journal after Fragment 00382 (above, p. 141) and all the books read into it. This was the result of either interference on the return voyage to Oitar or (more probably) vibrations of some crude Sykotic bug. It is fortunate that the notebooks, which were declaimed in handwriting, have in some part survived. This fragment of the Journal is very imperfectly preserved.*

The more rational of these creatures are those who fetch and carry and dig in the gardens. I often delay my walking and have intercourse with a Gardener, who is also called the Head. I mistake him often for the Director, for both of these specimens have a bush of grey hairs on their chins.

Of the two, the Gardener is graver and has the more harmonious vibes. He is also the more informed in sciences. For the Director asks questions about elementary sciences and then turns away without waiting for an answer. But the Gardener might well be a Provost of his science, and instructs me in the flowers, their nature and their names, and when I instruct him in the forms and beauties of our own, he leans on his spade with deference and enters within the Arc of Learning, saying, 'Go on! Tell me another.' And it is evident that at the time of our first landfall, with the armada of In Kā and Bōd Hā, our craft must have brought with them certain seeds and roots. For the lilies and roses are evidently derived from a common stock, although both have flourished in this benign climate beyond all possibility, and their roses perform through the whole melodic range in both colour and scents. Yet their roses do not flower in the spring – a blemish which we can soon repair.

Where the gardeners go, the children of the inferior sort of mortals often follow. It is a great blemish that they should be allowed so much unruly time to run all higgledy about the lawns. Yet they are more rational than their elders, more graceful, and better company. They dance in rings around me, and call me 'Loony', which is because, in their little understandings, they suppose that Oi Paz actually dwells upon the moon. Some are so well-favoured that, if taken early, much could be made of them by our Adjusters. Yet they have already certain beastly propensities, as 'acting' falsehoods which they call 'play', for which I have often to do heavy sentences on them. At which, out of sheer shame, they make the Incongruous Noise and run away.

There is a new keeper here called Major and sometimes Robert and sometimes Sorley (for they cannot even cure their own

names) who is more rational and ... [*damaged membranes*] intercourse with him about Earthly histories and the place they call
Stonehenge. When I asked where it lay he fetched a chart and a
magneto-dial (which he called a 'compass') and we walked up to
the Cardiarum (near where he is building a radio-plant) where
he showed me where Stonehenge lay and what was the bearing.
I asked him when his plant would be finished, and he said in two
of their Earth-months or less. So I said, 'Then Oi Paz will be able
to speak to his people on the moon,' but he said ... [*damaged
membranes*]

... greeted with me a great hullabaloo, with heaving my arm
up and down and puffing in my face and clapping his arm about
my shoulders. At first I supposed him to be some new keeper, or
perhaps a pee-cee licensed to push me about the place, but he
said, 'You remember me, Mr Oipas? It's your old mate and
cobber, Nigel Harmer,' and it was indeed the same, although I
could not construe why he supposed I should wish for a meeting
with him with such hullabaloo. But I asked him if he had come
to take me back to my mission on the planet. I said that I had
now made a deep study of their beastly ways and considered that
if he would plug me into their medias again I would soon affect
a mortal conversion.

At this the Harmer ran a finger up the side of his nose and said,
'Great minds think alike,' and, taking my arm, pushed me into
the garden to 'take a stroll'. We went down to the Arboretum,
where he looked at the bushes and said, 'I don't suppose there are
any bugs here?' I said that there were many bugs, and also 'beetles'
and 'bees' and 'spiders' (which are all species of 'insects'), but that
he need not concern himself, since they would not fly out until
the air was warmer.

Then Harmer said, 'Sapio, the world needs you again. You
don't know how you've been missed.' Then he gave me a
'gift', which was a 'press file' of cuttings of newses when I
was plugging on my Mission.

He went on to tell me that since I had been captured at the
Rose Bowl the world had heard nothing of me – 'not a word'.

My keepers here had concealed my existence, and the world had been plugged on all its media with the grave falsehood that I had 'disappeared'. And he said that millions across the planet were awaiting my Second Coming ('well, your *second* Second Coming'). I said that I was willing to do Second Comings as often as he wanted if he could get me out of this coop. At this he ran his finger along his nose once more, and asked if I could keep a secret. I said that I *was* an Official Secret which was kept, to which he replied, 'Good enough, Sapio! And look what I've brought you, as a memento of old times!' Then we sat on a bench in the Arboretum, and he opened a bag and took out a bottle of the real McCoy. I pronounced a heavy sentence on him, that he was a pusher of unruly drugs, but he told me that the bottle he had brought was not a drug at all but a cure for my troubles. At which he passed it beneath my nose, and the dulcet scent was so harmonious that once again the honeyed liquor flowed along my tubes.

Harmer then said that he would try and get me out of this place but there was 'one little problem'. If he set my 'act' up again in the 'free world' they would 'grab' me and shut me up again. I asked why we should travel to the free world; could we not just plug in at the Rose Bowl or at the bee-bee-cee? He said, 'That *is* the free world, cobber. That's where they shut you up.' He then said that the only place where I would be safe would be Russia, which was a 'groovy place', and did I remember the 'gig' we did in Moscow? He said he had some friends in the 'kay-gee-bee' (which is a club of pee-cees which rules that nation) and they were really interested, in fact they had known where I was for 'donkey's years'. I asked him how long a year is for a donkey (which is a species of small horse) and he said, 'Whoaoa! Have a drop of McCoy!'

He said that his Russian friends were ready to give me an institute for my own use in Novosibirsk, and maybe I could 'talk with my mates' on the moon. At this I rose and said, 'I charge you, mortal, to lead me to Novosibirsk forthwith and without delay!' But he pulled me down and told me to be quiet and not to 'shout it from the rooftops' (although the bushes around us had no roofs). He said that if they knew about this up at the Hall they would 'put a stopper' on the whole thing. And he told me of the plan, which is this. On a certain day very soon (but he did not yet know which day) the Russians will come for me. He had a 'friend' in this place (but he would not give me the name) who would come and get me. This friend would be known by giving the secret word, 'mum'. Then he would lead me through the gardens to a place on the wall where a ladder would be ready. We would go over and find a fast car waiting which would drive off 'like a cat with its tail on fire' (I ask absolution for the blasphemy).

He asked if I had understood the plan. I said that everything was understood, and I would follow the plan and roll according to its rule. And that I would bring with me two or three of the better-favoured keepers here, as Sage and Satpathy and perhaps Sorley, who could assist me in preparing my sentences to the plugs of the whole planet. And I added, 'And perhaps I will bring a horse, a black horse. Can horses climb ladders?' To which Harmer replied, 'Oh, blimey! Sapio, you haven't changed one bit. Look, no one, but *no one*, comes with you on this. And you tell no one one word about this. Or the whole boiling will be blown.'

At that moment there were shouts and halloos from the house, where they were searching for us. And Harmer jumped up, and hid two bottles of McCoy in the bushes and said, 'Remember, cobber, more where this came from. Novosibirsk is swimming in McCoy. And remember, again, not one word to a soul' (which souls are a sort of ghost that flit about in space). And while I pondered on that absurdity, we came out of the bushes, and Harmer turned to me again, running his finger beside his nose, and said, once more, 'Mum's the word.' And so we strode across the lawn, where they were running about in a hunt, but I walked into a sundial and fell among some rose bushes, and Satpathy came ... [*rest of record obliterated*]

SECOND CAPTIVITY

Sage Field Notes

28 March. Incredible day. Started glum. Heavy period. Rang Ann on intercom & cancelled my ride. David sedated, very low. Rani furious with that beast, Harmer, who took O. into bushes yesterday and tanked him up with whisky. On top of all it is Mayhem's Disinformation Day. R., D., O. and myself (of course) 'requested to keep to our rooms' since our 'services not needed'. Don't know exactly what is planned, except that Hunter is roled as O. Rbt told me at dinner last night that M. had tried to cast him as i/c weather station receiving monitoring from satellite in geosynchronous orbit, and to brief the media thereon. He was really cross about it. He said they'd laid on a buffet lunch & lots of G & T for a 'tame herd' of press and TV types, plus a couple of county councillors and JPs. Then they wld be steered around harmless parts of the Hall, & be conducted into the gardens where they wld (by 'accident') come upon Hunter, face done brown & swathed in O.-type robes, who wld be introduced as distinguished visiting Professor of Climatology from Sri Lanka.

Gritted my teeth & got on with some back reading. About 3 p.m. heard the tame herd trampling the terrace below my window. Yawned & stuck fingers in ears. But curiosity got the better of me. Went to window, & Mayhem, P. A. Primrose, Bursar, Weeder & Co. were shepherding 20-plus slobs & cameras down towards Arboretum, from wh emerged, on cue, tall robed figure, deeply pondering, book in hand. Great clucking and whirring of media, cameras braying, intros effected. Amazing. But not half as amazing as the real-life drama wh then followed. For, lo! There cometh out of the bushes, upon the good colonel's heels, four men in stocking-hoods and with sticks – no, submachine guns – in their hands. Wh guns are pointed at the media who throw their hands aloft, dropping their cameras in the shit. One hoodlum then is busy with a walkie-talkie, looking at the sky. Of shepherds, only Bursar shows any spirit, stepping forward to expostulate but stopping when shots are sprayed in ground before his feet. Tall robed figure wildly gesticulates, but much

259

good doth it do him. For it is indeed He whom the hoodlums have come for. And walkie-talkie and another gather him by two arms and run him (tripping on his robes) towards common land, while other hoodlums gesture to herd to stay pawing the same spot while, with weapons pointed, they retreat slowly backwards towards sd common. Ah, is there no succour to be found? Where is the noble perimeter guard? (*A:* confined to Nissens for the day, pissed and playing strip poker with kennel maid & typists since Mayhem's script suppressed all military presence.)

And, lo! once more. Or, rather, hi! For with a great whirring of wings there droppeth out of the firmament a BIRD: viz helicopter, which settleth on the common and openeth her belly, into wh our good colonel in his Eastern robes is by main force thrust, the hoodlums follow after, and away! Whereat the herd begins to jostle each other and baa. And there cometh, alack too late, a RESCUE: viz Major Sorley in a Landrover with armed signalman, tearing out to the common as the bird whirreth away. And scarcely hath your observer registered these VISIONS when her own door busteth open and enter Rani shouting, 'Oipas has gone mad! He's going out there!'

And R. and I run down the stairs, she explaining in gasps that O. had witnessed that last bit from the window, and had started shouting that some damn beast was acting a play of Oipas, and then when the helicopter came down had shouted that this was the craft that came for him to 'speak with the moon' and it was a 'messenger from Novo Speersk' (word? place?). And when we are outside, there he is, shouting and waving to disappearing helicopter, and the media are flashing at him and baaing, and Scarcely (appeared from where?) is saying, 'Oh, I say!' and Mayhem is looking green and whispering to Crostic, and R. has hold of O's arm, and Estates Bursar has run to phone but then runs back to say that telephonist is not there and he can't get through and only Weeder has her wits about her, wh wits are limited to shouting 'D Notice! D Notice!' to the media, wh media have now decided that 'the Russians' have made off with the professor which O. in his raging seems to confirm.

Order returns with Landrover and Major Sorley, who has already got through to someone on his wireless. Suggests that people calm down and go inside and have a cup of tea. I'm afraid he looked v macho, with a pistol-holster on his belt. Then turns to media and says, 'Look, I apologise to you, ladies and gentlemen. I still don't know what the hell's going on. But if a word of this gets out, then your papers and your programmes will be cut off from all further official sources. No more briefings. No more official leaks. Hence no more news. I'm not justifying this. I just know it's a fact. That's all. Sergeant Wetherfield here will collect all film from you before you go. Please hand it in – we don't want to search you.' To my surprise noted that Sergeant W. was a neatly turned-out ♀, armed. In fact, rather like a pantomime boy, delicate features, long eyelashes, boyish, severe haircut, v fine skin.

Wireless in Landrover was now cackling away to itself. Sorley went across, listened, spoke a word or two. Then he came back and spoke to Bursar (ignoring Mayhem and Scarcely), saying, 'I have to go off and sort this lot out. Back as soon as I can. Sergeant Wetherfield will look after any security angles' – glancing at Mayhem – 'I mean military security, of course.' Then returned to Landrover and wheeled on media once more. 'I truly do apologise. This is as big a cock-up as I remember. But mum's the word.' At 'mum's the word', poor O. disengaged himself from R. and flung himself forward as if trying to get a place in the Landrover, which, however, Sorley was already driving at speed, direction main gate.

I helped R. to compose O. and get him back upstairs. Not much to do rest of day. Big anticlimax. D. missed the whole episode, sleeping off sedative. Will break it all to him when he is fit enough to make Incongruous Noise. The wilted media tamely gave their film to Sergeant W. & trooped morosely off. R. and I wandered down to see Equerry, who was fuming because (a) she had missed most of the show, and (b) Macho had been playing up like a banshee ever since the helicopter: kept shivering withers and gazing anxiously at sky. She had missed show because her horses had been confined to their quarters like us, as being neither climatologists nor disinformers. So she had wandered up, on invitation of 'Robo', to see how his dishes were getting on. Sigint were so busy up there that they had noticed nothing until the helicopter was actually landing, when 'Robo put on war-harness like lightning and shot off in his charger'.

I sd that her 'Robo' hadn't been sweetness and light to the free press. She started to get defensive. R. changed the subject & sd she wondered where poor Colonel Hunter was now, he was such a 'fair' man & she hoped those hoodlums wldn't hurt him. Ann said that Hunter wasn't 'fair' to horses, she'd had a terrible row with him the day before. He had taken Minniver out hunting, brought her back with sores where he'd been pulling her mouth. Equerry had 'lit out' at him – 'so I'm probably out, neck and crop'. I sd that what boggled my mind was that anyone shld *want* to capture Hunter. Ann sd, 'Don't be daft, they wanted Oy Pee. Thought they'd got him. Robo was quite right. It's our job to look after Oy Pee, isn't it?' 'But *who* wanted Oy Pee?' 'Robo has gone to find out.' 'Well, whoever it was, they've got a shock coming when the greasepaint wears off.'

On our way back we came upon O., who was pushing about in the bushes and muttering about a 'ladder'. He was strangely confused and subdued and my heart went out to him.

This morning after breakfast I was on the terrace when the Landrover came up the drive, driven by Sorley, with Hunter beside him looking as sour as week-old milk. He had shed his robes and had an ill-fitting army raincoat on. They went into the Hall without a word, but Sorley threw up his eyes & made a grimace as he passed. Later it percolated through the place, as gossip does in any institution, that it was not the Russians but 'the Americans' (*sub sp* CIA) who had put on the amazing display. Big internal NATO row. Ever since the Brit govt opted out of Star Wars the Pentagon and CIA have been fuming. Then they found out that our intelligence was holding O. secretly, and holding back on them. So CIA, acting without the President's knowledge (or that's the official story), decided to force British hand by scooping up O. and holding him until Brits came to heel. Helicopter took him to Upper Heyford where a jet was waiting to whoosh him across the Atlantic. But by that time greasepaint had worn off.

At dinner a little precedence rite. Pepper still away & Hunter absent (sulking in rooms). *Problem:* who was to take boss seat at head of table? Bursar and Mayhem and Scarcely started disputing precedence (ever so courteously: i.e. really nasty, *sub sp* English), when Undermanner swept past them and installed herself at head. Good for her! Rbt Sorley hurried in late, after soup, & sat next to me.

Most frustrating dinner ever, since everyone wanted to discuss late events but cldn't because of O. O. was silent and seemed deeply abstracted, swaying a little. D. surly and abstracted (also slight swaying?). P.A. Primrose tried to lift morale by chatting about royals. Had we seen Princess Di's splendid outfit on telly when she had opened the new Battered Brides Home within the Murdoch Media Reserve at Wapping? Gravell complained that it was time we were issued with a second telly, since he'd missed the semi-finals of the Global Snooker. O. remarked, 'Plugs only one-way, man. How can snooker be global if only pluggers can snook?' While Gravell pondered this existential dilemma, Sorley hissed in my ear, 'Can I see you afterwards? Rather urgent.'

As we escaped from dinner he fell alongside and said, 'My room. Do you mind?' S's room not at all military-functional as I'd expected. Some paintings on wall, half abstract, half-'Aztec' (his wife's?), books, desk almost as disorderly as mine. Had his own coffee-maker & grinder, in fact a little kitchenette, with Indian & Chinese spices. Saw me looking around & explained, 'I come from an old line of "India hands" – my grandad and great grandad were both in Indian army.'

Came in wth coffee (neat tray wth hand-embroidered cloth) & sd, 'I asked you here because this room isn't bugged.' My mouth fell open & sd, 'Mine is?' Question ignored wth, 'I need to talk with you, Dr Sage ... Helena.' Open mouth sd, 'But ... why me?' 'I have to talk to someone ... sane. And I need to know something of the background of this crazy place.'

Then he went straight into it. Sd the way this place was run would be 'comic if it wasn't tragic'. The affair yesterday was 'predictable'. Anyone that wanted to know could find out that Oipas was here, all the rigmarole of Official Secrecy was just to fatten certain persons' self-importance – or worse. The Americans had known for a long time.

H. 'How do the Americans know?'

S. 'Oh, they will have been monitoring phone & signals traffic. The CIA probably have one or two people in here. But they can't have anyone on executive staff or there wouldn't have been such a balls-up yesterday. All that they knew was that there was a press-and-public briefing, with easy access.'

H. 'But why did they do it in full view of the press? Why didn't they just drop in one day with a helicopter and scoop Oipas up?'

S. 'I asked them that at Upper Heyford. They didn't want any chance of a shoot-out. After all, we aren't at war.'

H. 'Oh ... Then perhaps it was a good thing your rescue attempt in the Landrover was too late? If you, and your pretty sergeant with a sub-machine gun, had got there sooner, there could have been a shoot-out.'

S. 'As it happens, she hadn't any ammo. Scarcely indented for the wrong kind. We shall get our own stores in future. But if we had got there, with live ammo, Sergeant Wetherfield is a more than competent marksman.'

H. 'Marks*wo*man. Since when did the army let pretty women go around with guns? It confuses the gender semiotics.'

Instead of smirking, Sorley's face closed against me. Then he sd, 'Why do *you* screw the signals up? It's bad enough coping with the structures of the army, which have been male since the dinosaurs – or since Boadicea died. Astrosigint is the most modern bit of a modernising army. We have NO discrimination, gender or race. We select according to talent only, and a high proportion of the talent nowadays in microelectronics, computing and cryptography comes from your own sex. I'm glad you find Sergeant

Wetherfield pretty. She happens also to be most efficient. Why shouldn't we just work together as professionals, as you do in academic life?'

He seemed embarrassed by this long speech, and half-apologised. 'We have our rows about it, in the service. All the time.' I felt rebuked, and tried to beat a retreat. 'I didn't mean that. I meant that there is a more fundamental confusion of categories. Isn't the gun a phallic emblem? Aren't women carriers of the values of nurture, healing, survival? Isn't war essentially a male activity? If we get a unigender army, then the women will only be surrogate males, subordinated to male structures ... and aggro?' Sorley's lips pursed very tight, and his blue eyes lost their warmth and seemed to become distant and grey. 'Oh, I see. Interesting. Shall we talk about it another time?'

At this moment there was an intermittent low signal from a gadget on his desk, and a violet light came on. Sorley said 'damn' and motioned to me to be silent. He opened a cupboard above the desk and seemed to be taking readings on a fluttering dial. Then he flipped a switch beside the dial. 'Okay. We can go on. That's the first time that's happened. Things are hotting up.'

'What happened? What things?'

Sorley gestured to the gadget on his desk. 'That's a bug-detector, ultra-sensitive, the latest. If anyone bugs this room it picks up the beam and sounds the alarm. Someone has just zoned in on us.'

'They're bugging us now?'

'No. I switched on the suppressor. We call that in the trade an artichoke – radio-transmission choke – it rides over any frequency and scrambles it. All our friends can hear now are insane warblings and heterodynes. Go on ... Where were we?'

'But wait! *Who* is bugging us and *why*?'

'The who could be any one of a dozen outfits, and the why could take us back to the time of the first Emperor of China. But judging from the frequency registered – on that dial up there in the cupboard – I would say it was not one of the home team. Mayhew and his bugger use primitive stuff, stuck into phones and light-fixtures. This was a boring job – wall-boring. The frequency is one used by the CIA borers. They're probably in the garden ... maybe as far away as the road, in a van. They may not be especially after us; they're just "fanning" the place, giving it a "sweep", to see if they pick up anything interesting.'

I asked him why – if we were in some kind of war with each other – they let him bring Col. Hunter back.

S. 'Why not? Bloody little use to them. Couldn't have him baying night and day in the Heyford pens. Besides, it's risen to the level of a government row by now.'

H. 'Oh ... Will they come back for Oipas?'

S. 'No. The whole thing's blown now. The PM and the President have been on the hot-line, which nearly burned up. The Secretary-General of NATO has flown in. They're at it now, in Downing Street, hammer-and-tongs.'

H. 'What will happen?'

S. 'I think ... oh, some deal will come out of it. The British will sell out Mr Oipas into "NATO" (but really US) control, in return for concessions as to "preferential access" – which concessions will soon go into the wpb. I mean – well, NATO is going to move in on Martagon Hall.'

H. 'I think you know more than you're telling me.'

S. 'Well, Sigint does some monitoring ... even of our cousins. And we have a terminal direct to GCHQ Cheltenham ...'

Silence. I remembered his Censor act and flashed at him, 'You do some "monitoring". Like monitoring David and me?' He was stung by this and said that Astrosigint was not into the dirty spook business. 'But we do sometimes pick up high-level traffic, from satellite relay.' Then he looked at me with level blue eyes and sd, 'But there are other spooks, you know, Helena. You and David should watch it.'

More silence, and then I asked him why he was telling me all this. 'As I said, I need a sane person. And someone who knows what Mr Oipas ... could mean to all of us. And another thing. The Russians know about Oipas too.' He sd that the CIA had first found out that O. was at Martagon by way of one of their own moles inside the KGB. There must be a KGB mole in Martagon, possibly low-level, but he thought 'nearer the top'. Then we got down to the point of the meeting. He pulled out the Establishment list and went steadily down it, asking questions. What known about background? Had I noticed any special signs of curiosity? Or ostentatious *lack* of curiosity ('same thing'). Did they often go 'on leave – I mean, off campus?' Lingered especially over Weeder, Hemlock, Crostic, Primrose Gordon, Gentry. Even asked me to give him a 'run-down' on Pepper's early academic career.

I began to feel uneasy, like a spy. Asked him why I shld tell him all this & why shld he suppose we were on the same side. 'After all, you're part of the same cover-up. My trade insists on open discussion, free publication. But here you are, like the others: blocking the Russians, blocking the Americans, stopping any publication in the press. Wouldn't it be a good thing if the whole lot was blown?'

Sorley sd oh hell, he knew this wld happen, we wld have to 'have it out'. Sd he knew perfectly well how academics regarded the military & its absurdities. What they didn't realise was some military cld see absurdities also, and not only in their own affairs – maybe some academics (i.e. Dr H. Sage, although she was not mentioned) might look at their own absurdities sometimes. I sd, 'Such as?' He sd, 'Well, ivory tower. Not even a tower, but one tiny peep-hole open on to only one bit of the sky.' I sd I always tried to take a holistic view, my findings were in the context of a whole system wh defined the meaning of each part, & did he know enough of my work to give an example of absurdity? He sd he was sure my work was fine, in fact he'd been through D. and my work in Files – or what there was of it there (& he looked at me) – and he was deeply impressed, really, we were the only persons in this bloody place doing anything, which was why he was talking – 'But.' 'But what?' 'Your holistic view of this place didn't seem to include the knowledge that everyone, including Oipas, is bugging everyone else, and the whole place leaks like a sieve.'

I climbed down a little from my great height & asked about O. He sd he had taken his sensor gadget all around Martagon. My room, & D's & R's were 'humming like King's Cross' (when did he go in?), so was O's, but he had also picked up from O's belt a buzz on 'the extreme edge of the ultra-spectrum' wh he thought might be able to bore through two or three walls, focus in on a conversation at the other end of the Hall. I sd oh, & climbed down a little lower. 'What about the leaks? You mean the KGB and CIA?' 'Oh, no. I mean personnel are going in and out. Not signals. Just on two legs. All the time. Other ranks, of course, typists, gardeners. I first cottoned on when I saw Ann's milk and bread at the stables. Regular deliveries. It's harmless enough. Four or five of them even go down some nights to the "Bull and Teazle". The landlord has a special back room, private entrance. I don't want to stop them.'

Mouth, open, asked, 'How?' Rbt's blue eyes rested on mine. 'Well, if you really don't know, I'm not telling you.' I tried to recover wounded poise & sd that by 'holistic' I had meant not details but how a social system is *structured*. 'Structured by illusion and reality,' he answered. 'Of which illusion floats into higher regions, generals, politicians, politburos, NATO councils, maybe professors, while reality goes on beneath regardless. A sense of detail is the beginning of all real knowledge.'

I thought he was smug – rather pleased with himself and his wisdom – and told him that there was more than one kind of sense of detail. He had been habituated to a military definition of reality, and that was the kind of detail he was trained to notice. He made a half-apology and a profession of modesty (wh I found unconvincing), but sd, 'There is still the point, which, if you'll forgive me, your holistic system may overlook, that we really may be on the edge of a crisis which defies our imaginations. Oitar really does have a station on the moon which is being reinforced each month. Do you suppose they are going to stay there?'

Feeling rather small, and also cross, I asked him to fill in, wh he did in a professional, summary way. Astrosigint has monitored

268

a sharp rise in lunar activity. The Americans sent up a satellite to monitor the moon, but it just 'went out like a light'. If we can monitor their signals (although we can't decode them) they can certainly monitor ours. And judging by O's little Translator, their decoding is likely to be much more advanced than ours. The Oitarians may even have identified the place where Oipas is held. Not out of the question they might send down a rescue craft. Or they might not bother with an individual. They might wait until they cld 'come in force'.

A long silence after that. Then Rbt added, 'So we do have to ask, which side are we on? Oitar? Or Earth? I am on the side of Earth, warts and all – of which this place is one. That's why I tried to gag the press. Almost any hoo-ha the media could stir up would make our work more difficult – panic, TV intruders, lobbyists urging President Forsst to nuke the moon – Come down from your tower, Helena. Which side are *you* on?'

'Why do there have to *be* sides? You talk as if there had to be some war. Perhaps that's because it's your profession ...'

'Okay. There doesn't *have* to be a war. But it would be a miracle if there was not. Here is an encounter between two civilisations. Oitar is more advanced in technologies in every way. Oitar is also threatened with extinction. Earth has everything that Oitar wants. Their cultures are alien, their concepts are to ours like oil is to water. How do you think that will end?'

'Oitar would ... win?'

'Oitar will win. Maybe not at the first throw, but at the second. But ... I'm with you, Helena. I don't want to "take sides" like that either, and if we have to, then our side will lose. So you and I are in the same boat. We both want a peaceful settlement. But to negotiate an agreement with Oitar would be the most complex, the most delicate enterprise ever known to our species. At the moment our two space species have only one point of contact ...'

'Oipas.'

'Oipas. Oipas is the only asset of planet Earth. It is only through him that we can learn about the mentality of Oitarians – find out how they might regard us. Learn how we might negotiate. He might even be a mediator. We have to get Oipas on our side ...'

'*Our* side. There you go again! And anyway, why should he trust your side? You've just told me that everyone is spying on everyone else. And, honestly, Robert, aren't you too self-satisfied about planet Earth? I may trust you ... Oipas might "negotiate" with you, but what do we count for? The real decisions will be made in the Pentagon or by NATO politicians. You're used to military structures in which top persons give orders. You may count for something in Martagon but you won't count for anything in NATO.'

We were near to a flare-up, but somehow the moment of anger passed. His blue eyes seemed more hurt and insecure than hostile. Eventually he sd, 'Well, I don't think we have much chance either. But the control of communications is at least half of the management of power. If we – and Oipas – could control species communications, couldn't we ... ?'

I waited for him to finish, but the sentence faded into the air. I sd I'd better go. I cld feel his presence growing on me & was suddenly shy. I also felt brought down to earth with a thud. He must think me an ass.

He took my arm as I was rising and sd, 'I'm glad we've had this talk. There's another thing I must tell you, although I shouldn't. I've seen your paper. I think it's bloody marvellous – quite brilliant.'

'My paper? Which?'

'On Oitarian social structure. On the whole thing. Mayhem sidled up this morning and gave me a copy in a brown envelope. I opened it before dinner and was completely sent by it. That's why I missed soup. It's brilliant. A bit tactless in places. But if there is any way through, the information you and David are getting is all we have to go by ...'

As he saw me through door he added, 'Expect fireworks at the Weekly tomorrow. They're after your blood. And David's.' 'The paper?' I asked. 'Yes, that as well. Shouldn't leave things around. But ... you'll see. Don't expect me to defend you. But I do have a little influence, out there. And remember, however appearances go, we're on the same side.'

Back at my room, R. called in in a stew. Had I seen O.? She had been David-sitting & had just looked in on O.'s room wh was empty. Wrote up diary. Later (midnight?) R. looked in again. O. back in coop, but refuses to say where has been, & breath smells of whisky. That stupid beast Harmer must have left a bottle or two in the bushes, & O. has been nipping out for a swig.

Sage Notebook. Pasted-in typescript

MAR Form P. 7A   H. Sage, FRAI

WEEKLY REPORT SHEET

Interrogation Sessions. Wed, Thurs 1 hr. (Passed Mon/Tues to Dr Nettler; Friday messed up by Harmer.)
Progress. See previous reports.
De-Briefs. Mostly checking back old notes. Social structure; colleges; rites of temples.
Requirements. Still haven't got Rabelais, *Gargantua & Pantagruel* nor Bakhtin thereon. Indented for 5 weeks ago.
Other Observations. N/a.
Week 41   *Signed:* H. Sage

Sage Notebook. Pasted-in typescript*

MINUTES

Weekly Conference, 42nd Week

Asst Dir. in Chair. Apologies: Sir James Pepper, delayed for conference with FO/MoD. Absent: Equerry.

Standing Committee (Admin). Asst Dir. explained delay in

---

* *Sage annotation, pencil:* 'Rani's copy'.

building works owing to lack of vetted surveyor. Major Sorley said Astrosigint had already surveyed area of new signals personnel quarters & their contractors proposed to move in on Thursday. QMSM Gravell (Works) complained that an alternative tender had gone unanswered. Referred to Standing Committee (Admin.).

Standing Committee (Security). Mr Mayhem said that all matters relating to unfortunate affair on Sunday should be referred to Standing Committee. There could be no discussion of security questions in Weekly.

Weekly Reports. Miss Crostic commended by Asst Dir. Dr Nettler had submitted no report and when asked for oral report said he would 'pass'. Sister Satpathy explained that he was under treatment for overstrain. Colonel Hunter said Dr Sage's report was totally inadequate. It could be an offence under the Public Obedience Act to withhold information from the constituted authorities. Mr Mayhem disclosed a copy of a paper by Dr Sage which had been handed in to him last week, but not by Dr Sage. Miss Weeder confirmed that neither Dr Sage nor Dr Nettler had entered any tapes or papers in Files. Dr Nettler commenced shouting and was instructed to leave the room. Major Sorley proposed that the matter be left until the return of the Director, since it concerned academic activities. Colonel Gardyan-Hunter ruled that the matter be referred urgently to Standing Committee (Security). The Committee will sit tomorrow morning, at 10 a.m. He instructed Dr Sage to attend with Dr Nettler at 11 a.m. Meanwhile both would be suspended from all duties and Dr Sage should withdraw.

Other Business. The Asst Dir. reported that the Equerry had been guilty of insubordination. He proposed that the post should now be regarded as vacant, although Equerry should perform all duties pending the appointment of successor. The whole question of stable management should be referred to Standing Committee (Admin.) for review. Major Sorley objected: Equerry highly professional. Miss Weeder noted that Equerry was absent from meeting without apology. Mrs

Undermanner said the stables were understaffed. Colonel Gardyan-Hunter said the post should be held by a properly qualified officer, but that Equerry could be considered for supplementary post of Groom. Mrs Undermanner and Major Sorley objected.

Mrs Undermanner reported that there was some unrest among the non-exec. staff, and talk of forming a union. Mr Mayhem suggested that Mrs Undermanner should point out the culprits to Standing Committee (Security). Mrs Undermanner said that staff grievances needed looking into. Major Sorley suggested they had right to form staff association as at GCHQ Cheltenham. Asst Dir. said that had been a regrettable concession. He asked Mrs Undermanner to report directly to him. He would give a ruling at next Weekly.

A.L.W.*

Sage Field Notes

30 March. Kangaroo Court. Duly attended with D., 10.55 a.m., at Hunter's office for trial. D. heavily sedated again last night by R., was v low & muttering about wanting to get out of this place & 'couldn't we do something to get sent down?' I sd we had, but problem is: Where is down? Knocked & P.A. Hemlock came out & sd wld we mind waiting, it wld be a 'little while', we cld get

---

* *Sage annotation, red ink:* 'This is Rani's copy. (D. & I struck off mailing list.) Almost true record of the bit I was at. According to R. the Weekly got really lively after my departure. Undermanner is getting better and better, because she actually has to keep place running & she knows They are a shower. R. says Weeder left out some amazing scenes, when Mrs U. came to the defence of Ann. She sd not only that stables were understaffed but that sh'd never noticed any Standing Committee grooming or mucking out a horse. (True, stables are understaffed, but Ann has organised a rota of kids with passes from the Family Enclosure, eager hard-hatted acolytes who trim the lamps at the shrine of Macho.) And R. says there was a lot more about the union, also. Seems Mrs U. told some home truths about staff pay, conditions & general low morale at long confinement, & added that the previous outfit to occupy M. Hall had behaved "properly", they were "a different class of people altogether". Ended by glaring at Hunter & telling him he didn't "own the place", he was only "a tenant-at-will".'

coffee in the Mess & she wld come for us. Which – about 35 mins later & D. 35 yards deeper into Slough of Despond – she did. I felt strangely perky, as though at last mists were lifting, the Two Sides drawing up battle-lines.

K Court absurd bastard formality: two parts court-martial, one part bureaucratic imprimatur, one part academic power organ (Senatorial): i.e. no part justice. As we went in we saw Gentry sneaking out, averted eyes. Normally I'm sorry for him: he's a sort of seized-up hetero, and probably went into bugging as form of voyeurism. Maybe he is a victim of the panic-syndrome which gummed up so many at the height of the AIDS crisis in the late Eighties, in wh any active sexual practice became blocked, and the urges found outlets in twisted ways. Anyway, whatever Gentry's problem is, today I wanted to murder him.

Whole set-up ridiculous. Standing Committee (wh was sitting): Hunter, Mayhem, Weeder, Scarcely, Crostic, with P.A. Hemlock drafted as paper-shifter, note-taker. (But recorder on Hunter's desk, taking all in.) Hunter's office too small to hold us all in comfort, so his desk had been shunted against wall. Enemy sat in half-circle of padded or rotary office-chairs; D. & I were in hard-back sit-up-and-begs, directly facing them, low coffee-table between us defining boundaries.

Proceedings commenced with Hunter saying that before we offered our 'defence' it was only 'fair' that we shld know 'the case against us'. First prosecution witness (i.e. member of court) was Weeder, who performed as per expectations: our failures to put in tapes & notes, brevity of our Weekly Reports (examples read), David no Report at all in Weeks 33, 39, 40, 41.

The Court (Hunter): 'Miss Weeder, have you seen this document before?' (Gestures to copy of my paper, Exhibit A, on coffee-table.) *Weeder:* No. That document was never entered into Files. *Court:* Thank you. Please note that, Miss Hemlock.

Next prosecution witness is Crostic, who is boring. Sd D. & I continually exchanged interview schedules without 'authorisation'. We had entered into 'collusion' with Oipas: examples – had 'warned' him about arrangements to photo his ntbks & as a result O. always carries them 'about his person'. (Checked with D. afterwards – neither of us had. Bad omission.) Crostic also sd that, from about Week 20, O. had become a 'hostile subject' & refused to answer her qs, saying she was not a 'fair trader' & contrasting her 'opprobriously' with D. and me. Warming to theme, she sd we were behaving 'like renegades & class enemies' (odd phrase?) & were 'alienating his inflexions' (odder). D. started expostulating, saying Oitarian was not an inflected language, but Court sd we shld have 'opportunity for defence' later.

Court then seemed about to call itself as prosecution witness, but thought better of procedure & called Star Witness, Mayhem. Who made a long-winded, pedantic start, identifying Exhibit A, explaining provenance (bog) & c. The *fact* of my paper seemed to be the incriminatory bit (withholding information), not so much anything in it. Clearly none of them cld make head or tail of it, & thought it was mad. But Mayhem, swelling like a puff-adder, directed the particular attention of the Court to the final para, bottom p. 12. I'd brought my copy along & cldn't see it was all that Awful. I asked to see Exhibit (Court & panel all had copies) & found I had scrawled in pencil at bottom, 'Here it is, David! *Very* preliminary. Aching to know what you think – a lot of it is pinched from you. NB Don't let any of Them see it. Beyond their beastly understandings.' Oh.

By now Court was baying, full throat. Hunter asked M. whether any other 'relevant information had come to light ... er, this morning?' Mayhem looked as solemn as doom, & sd that owing to 'growing concern in Security' it had been necessary to 'take certain measures' some weeks ago, & a great deal of relevant material was now in his archives. The Court had already been briefed on the provenance of a sample 'recovered' only last week, but he wld take the opportunity of quoting a few extracts. Then produced small cassette-recorder in whose bowels was Exhibit B. So that was what Gentry had been in about! D. & I sat there transfixed. Gentry (or Mayhem?), a marvellous editor, shld be seconded to BBC. Extracts started with entry from our session on laughter last week *in my private room*, at the bit where D. had sd my paper dealt with 'secret things': *D.* 'Well, secrets of social organisation. They could give clues to command and communications.' *H.* 'Secret from whom?' *D.* 'From Them. From Mayhem, Hunter, that lot.' *H.* '. . . I wouldn't dream of letting Mayhem & co. get a squint at it.'

Then Mayhem, having wholly captive audience (both Govt & Opposition), consulted dial & zoomed in on more meaty bits. Sat there *amazed* as box gave forth voices (cld that be me?) describing in detail method of throttling Dobermans and burgling Files. Thought it rather funny & cldn't control face-muscles at which whole panel Scowled like Stoats about to Do Rabbits. Box was on low coffee-table squeezed between Court and Accused, so tight that knees of both parties kept bumping it.

Mayhem then went into climax (perhaps overplayed?), consulted dial again, and I heard that alien Meccano voice (*me?*) suddenly saying, full volume: '. . . Scarcely suggested that Colonel Gardyan-Hunter's balls could be soaked in repellent.' Then a grating robotic noise (me laughing?). Then cut to D.: '. . . Doberman biting off Colonel's testicles . . . Scarcely is too asinine to know what he is saying. Weeder too abjectly subservient . . .' At wh Scarcely broke upon spell-bound audience by ejaculating (to box), 'Oh, I say! You can't say that!' (Until then, Scarcely had been only semi-human visage on panel, desperately trying to simulate expression of 'fairness, impartiality' – recollecting prescribed role of court-martial – together with pose of inordinate wisdom, like one of the slobs on *Question Time*.) But box *cld* say that, & cld no doubt have sd a great deal more, had not Hunter, extremely surly, told M. that Court had 'quite enough evidence' & full tape shld be held in Security's safe for 'subsequent proceedings'.

Court then had the gall to ask us if we had anything to say. Poor D. looked quite shrunken. He sd he was going to 'resign . . . well, take a sabbatical anyway'. He wld 'pack up that afternoon' and 'prepare his notes for publication'. But might have to come back a few times to check out things with O. I was glacial: perhaps too cool. Sd it was a professional academic matter wh I was willing to discuss with colleagues but pointless to discuss with Them. I wld be willing to discuss the matter with the Dir. on his return, & wld then consider course of action. (In fact, what I most want now is Rbt's advice.)

Thereupon Court sd it wld 'take opinions' and go into 'recess', wh it did with us *there*, bumping coffee-table with opposing knees. This consisted in panel twisting & turning & saying 'rhubarb, rhubarb' behind their hands, with scraps floating across like 'agree totally, Miss Crostic, not in Director's competence . . .' and, 'would it be under Section One or Section Two, rhubarb, rhubarb, rhubarb,' and 'yes, definitely, Mr Mayhem, *all* notes . . . yes, Miss Crostic, tapes as well . . .'

Court then addressed accused with unctuous solemnity, saying that what had 'transpired' wld be reported to Pepper on his return. However, matters so grave that they came directly 'within the purview of Security'. Court was agreed that a *prima facie* case had been made out for charges under Public Obedience Act, section 17, under wh it is a criminal offence to withhold information relating to the national interest from duly constituted authorities. Court did not yet know where or with whom proceedings wld be laid, owing to 'sensitive' nature of this institution, impossibility of taking matter into courts outside & lack of 'necessary organs' (i.e. gaols) within. It was possible that there cld be 'some other way of resolving the matter' (accident in lake?). Meanwhile D. & I were suspended from all duties, barred from attendance at dinners or Weeklies, told to 'hand in' all our notes and tapes to Security and prohibited from further contact with O. But (huge show of leniency) we might, 'for the time being', still enjoy the liberty of the television room and gardens.

End of trial. I hared back to my room to do some necessary sorting & secreting of papers. D. came in, like a shell-shock case, while I was stuffing a copy of my paper into my bra. Wanted to go into a long hoo–ha about it all. Told him not to be an ass but to get back to his room, pronto, & hang his notebooks from the window-ledge, anywhere. Rbt suddenly appeared at door, and sd he had been 'listening in' to trial. He opened his briefcase &

we shovelled my papers & some tapes in. *Couldn't* give him my diary, kept that in shoulder-bag. D. reappeared in state of near-hysterics: 'The b . . . b . . . bug . . . bugger.' Exit Rbt, to 'do what he can' at D's room. Too late. Enter (behind D.) Gentry, who says, v politely, that he has come for my 'stuff', 'pursuant to instructions'. I expostulated. He ignored me, & went poking round desk, shelves. Found half-a-dozen tapes I'd missed, good ones, but early. (Yet early collecting can often be important, because done without any preconceptions.) Gentry then went through drawers, stripped bed, looked under mattress, poked in loo. Did not seem too puzzled at paucity of written notes, presumably belongs to age of electronic recording, writing functions atrophied? Did not search shoulder-bag (female space?). Weeder wldn't have missed that!

D. was now in a terrible state about his notes & tapes. Rani came in wh calmed him a little. I sd Rbt wld try to help but I cldn't explain why. He sd Rbt was on Their side & hadn't he taken off my stuff too? I sd that they probably only wanted to copy the stuff, they'd give it back. D. sd they wld 'turn it all against the Rule'. R. v maternal & protective. She brought him a cup of tea wh (she whispered to me) had 'something in it' & he calmed down enough to go out with her into garden. I looked out & saw them walking with linked arms. Surprised, since R. has a bit of a taboo against ♀/♂ touching, unless medical.

Wrote up this diary. Only way to compose myself. Wish Rbt wld come in. Looked out & saw him haring up to Sigint station, then off again in Landrover. Saw O. going over Ann's jumps on Macho, kept going over the highest one. Odd – he doesn't usually ride in the afternoon. Back to writing. Jumpy. Locked door. Expect every moment Gentry or Weeder to break in & take diary. Must think of some hiding-place for it. Hole in old oak tree? Have to write notes & diary while hiding in bushes. Notes about what? Will ban on seeing O. continue? Wish I cld talk with Rbt. But how do I know wh side he is really on? Think up some stratagem. Escape? (What did Rbt mean about 'ingress/

egress'?) Escape where? Whole planet seems to be bugged. Which *are* the sides?

Sage Field Notes

31 March. Mopy day. Nothing to do, no tapes, no notes. R. comforting D., they're in the garden a lot. (They cldn't be getting off with each other? They're *totally* incompatible. But they have that way of talking and laughing together – as Observed from Window – wh suggests mutual body-vibes.) No sign of Rbt. Which side *is* he on? Getting my notes & tapes cld be one great con.

Mooched in garden. Lot of traffic: two staff cars, one US full of wallies in braid, hooted up drive, almost throwing O. who was still doing high-jumps on Macho. Thought it best to avoid him, *pro tem*, wandered up towards Sigint (visible progress every day). No Landrover to be seen, perhaps he's in Outer World? Met Ann coming from stables: she asked if I knew where Rbt was. (He'd promised to exercise new mare, yclept Sprite.) Gathered 'Robo' had briefed her on Weekly. She sd that now I had 'time on my hands' I shld really put in some serious riding, why didn't I try Sprite? Sd not today, thank you. She said, 'Okay, tomorrow first thing.' Then she sd I looked 'peaky, off your oats' – how about eating at her place tonight? I couldn't stop nose from wrinkling, thinking of her place, peanut butter & bran. Ann sd, 'No, I mean my real place. You know where my pad is?' Had to confess I didn't. Beginning to think there's not much I *do* know about this place. 'Dower house,' she said. 'Come about 7.'

Have to confess dower house a complete blank with me. I knew where it was, of course. Right at the other side of the park, south-west corner, half a mile away and completely out of sight of the Hall. I'd passed it several times. Pleasant, unpretentious but commodious, 18th-century red brick, a nice conservatory added on, facing south. Thought it was empty: no curtains upstairs, shutters downstairs. Anyway, I went at 7, leaving note on door for Rbt in case he called. Found Ann had got a *great* set-up. She explained she had only been 'stabled' there for five weeks. Had been stabled before in an annexe to the stable-block, above her den. In January all sanitation froze up, and 'I froze up too ... coughed so much I thought I was broken-winded.' Just at that time Mrs Undermanner 'swooped in' & found her washing her hair in a horse-bucket.

Equerry has a great respect for U. and I can see why. It seems Mrs U. 'did her top', reclaimed the dower house (which 'Perks' had got his eye on), and put Ann in as 'housekeeper ... keeping house for meself'. She only uses two rooms: a spacey kitchen, 'modernised' in the Eighties, and a parlour, wh she has turned into a bed-sit, somewhat den-like, quite a few books – Zen, eco, travel. Took me on a conducted tour – huge lounge opening on to conservatory, dining-room, study, gun-room, four bedrooms, attics. When the last outfit was in Martagon, the dower house had been the perk of the CO and his family, but Pepper hadn't wanted it, and Undermanner 'kept it under her hoof'. 'Why don't you move in, Hel? Bags of room. I'm like a pea rolling around in a bucket. You could write your stuff up in the conservatory when summer comes. And, you know, I get lonely. Horses aren't everything. I'm not sentimental about horses. I know you think I am. But it's my skill. It's just my job.'

I tried to get her to talk about herself, but she always closes up. (She talks a bit more with Rani.) She's around thirty – could even be thirty-five – from social class 'Don't Know'. Some of her attitudes (to 'Them' and even to intellectuals) are aggressively 'working-class', others are classless, *sub sp* drop-out. Went to work around stables as soon as she cld leave school. When she was still in her teens started a long-term relationship – maybe even a marriage? – with a rich farmer in Devon, who found her mounts for show-jumping. He was much older than her – she won't talk about it, but it obviously didn't work out. When they broke up – R. says it was 'awful', and 'did something' to Ann – she reacted against the show-jumping and hunting set and started bumming round the world: Peru, the Argentine, California,

India, finding work with horses whenever she needed money. She joined a Zen community for a time in New Mexico, and she still uses some Zen patter. I asked her about it and she loaned me a book on *Zen Training*, half-aggressively, half-shyly, as if she was afraid I would make fun of her. I have a hunch that Zen is closer to Ann's private self than the horse patter which she affects.

I dragged some of this out over supper, which was simple & wholesome. A vegetarian risotto. Elderberry wine (from Mrs U.): good. Granary loaf and hunk of fresh Cheddar. Ann saw me looking at loaf. 'Surely, Hel, you must know by now?' 'Know? Know what?' 'About the TUNNEL!' I must have looked astounded, and she *hooted* with laughter, holding her sides. 'You high-flying thinkers are so IGNORANT. One day you and David will be sitting up there, in your reading-specs, and you won't notice that the rats are eating through the floor. You'll fall through the hole, still reading.' I sd, 'Thank you, that's happened already.'

Ann sd the tunnel ran from the old private chapel ('you swing back one of those plaques on the wall, behind the altar') to a cowshed just the other side of the walls, in Hall Farm: 'It used to be something more grand, a gazebo or something, but it's a cowshed now.' She sd 'everyone' knew about it, there was even a 'delivery service' – farm eggs, yoghurt, wholemeal bread, fish & chips on Saturdays. 'You just leave a note in the cowshed and the money. Then someone is detailed to collect it. I only nipped out once. I needed some shoes made in a hurry.' I looked at her socks & sd I didn't know she went in for hand-made shoes. '*Horse*shoes, silly! I had to talk to the blacksmith – They wouldn't let him in here, he's a re-cycled teacher and something in the Ecology Party.'

I asked why, if everyone knew, the tunnel hadn't been closed. 'I didn't mean Everyone. *They* don't know, of course. And it's kept away from people who might be quislings or grassers, like the butler. And the dog-handlers and the military, or most of them. In fact it started off as a sort of secret society.' It seems that

the permanent staff – gardeners, Brian the Oddjobber, one of the
cooks – knew about it all along. In fact the whole village knows
about it, since the tunnel was built in the mid-18th century by
the wicked Charles de Boyle, who used it to smuggle in village
maidens for some sort of sexy Mass. Then, when FARCES came
here, the permanent staff let one or two secretaries & Mary the
Phone into the secret. To cover their tracks they formed a 'Born-
Again Club' and asked for permission to hold prayer-meetings
in the chapel. Hunter was delighted & approved their request as
'highly commendable' – in fact gave them the keys for weekday
use. So ... the Club has been going up there every other night,
lighting the candles, locking the door, putting on a tape-recorder
of prayers, chants & wails, and nipping down to the 'Bull &
Teazle' (back entrance) for a quick one. (That explains a lot.)
Gradually the Club enlarged until the lower decks of Martagon
were sweeping with a religious revival.

I felt a bit huffy & asked why 'everyone' had kept it away from
me. She sd 'Executives will only be informed on a need-to-know
basis,' quoting one of Mayhem's circulars. Then she grinned.
'You kept it away from yourself, Hel. It stands out a mile. Robo
was on to it in three days – he followed the tracks of my granary
bread like a bloodhound, even though I tried to throw him off
the scent. I thought he was one of Them & made a great show
of baking one.' She contorted her face and sd, 'Yuk! Even Macho
wouldn't eat it.' Then she became grave. 'But they've blown it,
now, the idiots! They took Oy Pee to the "Bull and Teazle" last
Monday.' Four or five of them, Mary, Brian, Jerry the gardener –
they call themselves the 'inner wheel' – had taken him off after
supper to the chapel. O. was sent by the candles, so they did a
little prayer-meeting, for real, in case anyone was listening. Then
put on the tape. Nipped off down the tunnel. Quiet night at the
'Bull'. But then, when they got back to the chapel, O. demanded
another service. He made them all dance in circles and make
obeisances to Oitar, and was 'chanting away & cavorting at full
gallop ... in fact Jerry and Mary lost the reins altogether. There
was enough racket to wake the graveyard. As they slipped out

of the chapel, Mary says she saw a figure slinking away, pretty sure it was Gentry.'

Silence. Then I sd, 'So it's all going to come out?' 'Everything's coming out. Everything's blowing up or collapsing, all at the same time. Roll on the strike tomorrow!' 'Strike? What strike?' 'Oh, Hel, you must know! General strike. The "inner wheel" are the union committee. Everyone's talking about it. Robo says that Mrs U. as good as told Them about it at the Weekly ... but, of course, you'd been tipped out by then.' 'Ann, what's going to happen to us?' 'Don't take your jumps before ... Oh, well, yes, we *have* come to them. Don't know. Robo might help. He tore over here after your trial. Told me all about it and the Weekly. Gave me some tapes and notes to keep. Said he had a plan if he could "get through to the right people".'

It was time I was going. We lingered outside, looking at the full moon. Ann sd, 'Robo thinks a lot of you, Hel. I mean your work. He's raving about your paper ... as if it might save the whole planet. But he's a pig not to call in today, when we're both in such a stew.' I embraced her, sd thanks for everything, and agreed Rbt is pig. Ann sd, 'Don't forget you're booked for Sprite tomorrow, first thing. You can ride with Oy Pee. Stables are not on strike. I have a written clearance from the inner wheel ... Hey, what about a torch?'

I sd I didn't need a torch with this moon, & swung off. Suddenly Ann shouted, 'SHIT!' & called me back. 'You know the time? It's gone 12.' 'Well?' 'Dobermans!' 'The handlers will have them on leads, surely?' 'Not now they bloody well don't! Didn't you see Scarcely's Order? It was on the noticeboard. After the helicopter jaunt last Sunday, he's cried havoc & unleashed the dogs of war. From 12 midnight to 5 a.m. the perimeter guard is instructed to let dogs run free. The bushes could be swarming with them ... well, with three or four. Poor stupid yobbos, they don't have the brains of Scarcely. You could have been eaten ... I'm sorry, Hel, how could I be so daft? I think we're all going into some kind of entropy.'

I brewed a pot of tea while she made up a bed for me in one

of the upstairs rooms. Then she turned in. Felt incredibly wakeful, like a light that won't go out. After nearly a year living in the Hall I've got agoraphobia. Sitting up here in bed, writing up diary, I feel dislodged from my shell and even jumpy. The chairs & dressing-table draped in dustsheets lurch and lour when I'm not looking. Also, Nature seems to be having a ball outside in the full moon: foxes screeching (really blood-chilling) & a more comforting screech-owl. *And* (just now) a dog howling like a stuck pig – one of those howls seemed almost human! Ann insists she'll drag me out at 6 to ride Sprite, can't disappoint her.

Sage Field Notes

4 April. The Day of Comeuppance was three days ago, no time to write up diary till now. So I'll put it down in a bit more order than usual: i.e. some bits only became clear long after the happenings. Also, nothing was as calm as it may sound.

Murders at Martagon Hall, Act IV, scene 1, opens dramatically as curtains rise upon bugger, murdered, in bushes, stage left. In fact it was Ann who found him. She had shaken me brutally awake before 6 a.m., having been up herself at 5, doing her zazen exercises. Before I had swallowed half cup of tea she was towing me to stables, muttering that she didn't want to be late, since O. had been 'odd' lately, forcing Macho at high jumps, and she wanted to 'tear him off a strip'. Arriving at stables, found Macho's door open & Ann sd, 'Shit! They've gone already.' She wandered off through bushes, left, to see if she cld spot errant horse & rider. Then I heard her cry out, in a high, unjoky voice, 'Helena! Come here!' And then, 'No, don't. Better not.' But I did, and found her standing above the body of Mr Gentry, hole drilled in temple, not much blood, on his back, eyes and mouth open. Nasty.

We agreed we must tell someone. But who? We ran up to Hall. We both wanted to tell Rbt, but agreed that since Mayhem was Security we shld go to him first. Knocked at door. N/a. Tried to open door. Locked. Shook door & hammered. N/a. Ran

round to Hunter's apartment. Butler interposed. Col. Hunter cld
not be disturbed before 7.30, strictest orders. It was now 6.45. I
sd it was an emergency, security matter. Butler (evidently supposing all ♀ to be hysterics) unmoved. Ann let out an *incredible*
stream of expletives – you learn something working around
stables.

Retired to consult. Ann evidently deeply upset. I asked if she
thought it had been done by someone in the 'inner wheel', who
knew G. was about to blow the tunnel. By the way she bit my
head off, I cld tell that the same thought was in her mind.
We tried Rbt's door. N/a. Also locked. Incredible! A security-
obsessed outfit, almost manic, & when something really happens –
no one! I suggested Rbt might be at Astrosigint Station. We hiked
up & found Sergeant Wetherfield already up & scanning the gate
with binoculars. We told her. She took it in fast & asked why we
hadn't alerted Security. Told her. What about Col Hunter? Told
her. She suddenly realised we weren't daft & sd, 'Shit! Bunch of
old men!' Grabbed a mike & spoke in swift, anonymous voice to
crackle-crackle (was it Rbt's crackle?). Grabbed a walkie-talkie
wh seemed to alert guardroom at main gate, from wh issued two
military who ran towards Hall. (Some sort of fracas going on at
main gate. Was that what she had her binoculars trained on?)
Then she thanked us & sd she was going to get the Col out of
bed, even if she had to shoot the butler. Matching the deed to
the word, she slung on pistol holster & strode back with us to
Hall.

Rest of scene readers can ad lib. Usual stuff. Increasing medley
of people running in circles. Hoos and hahs. Hunter appearing w
shaving cream on bib. Even Scarcely, buttoning up his trews.
Poor Rani routed out for a medical opinion. Military stretcher-
party, using one of Ann's jumps. Problem because both telephonists absent & direct outside line only in Mayhem's office
(also locked). No one knew how to work exchange. Scarcely sent
out in car to phone for ambulance from Shaw Magna call-box.
Sergeant Wetherfield marches back to post, raising eyes to heaven
as she passes (grimace learned from Rbt?). Ann drifts back to

stable to find out 'what Oy Pee has been up to on Macho'. Ambulance arrives. Andover police sergeant also arrives. Hunter sends him off, not without argument: says it is a security matter, 'we will hold an internal enquiry'. Police sergeant says this is still Hampshire & he will notify county coroner. Hunter asks, for umpty-first time, where is Mr Mayhem? Sends P.A. Hemlock to look through the whole Hall, with a bunch of pass keys.

Act IV, scene 2. Brief comic interlude. I drift into breakfast, not because I cld eat anything, but because I wonder if somehow Robert cld have missed everything & be there. There is no breakfast. Not because of Murder, but because General Strike has struck. (Telephone problems explained.) Butler & Hemlock fussing around trying to make coffee. Mrs U. sweeps through (*Qy*: smirking?) but does not offer to help. Hunter stamping around in rage (panic?) because top brass of NATO plus Minister for Defence & US Military Attaché expected at conference, 11 a.m., and staying to lunch. Orders Scarcely to 'get a detail up' of emergency kitchen staff – perimeter guard, dog-handlers, frogman. Scarcely says he can scarcely do that. *Hunter*, 'Why not? It's an Order!' *Scarcely*: 'Yes, sir. But I don't like taking away any guards from the gates. In fact, sir, we could do with rein-forcements.' *Hunter* (roar like a bull-horn): 'WHY?' Scarcely explains that there are strike-pickets on both gates & what's more most of the pickets were *outside* the gates. 'Can't think how they got there. And a lot of villagers are joining them. They let the ambulance through, but if we are to get the Minister and NATO through, we shall need everyone we've got. The villagers are building a bonfire right in front of the main gate, with an effigy ... which looks like, er, you, sir.' *Hunter* (roar like a sea-cow): 'What about the gardeners? Can't they cook?' *Scarcely*: 'Gardeners are on the picket-line, sir. And the typists. And the kennel-maid.' *Hunter*: 'Send for Sigint! Tell them to send a detail down!' Scarcely chunters off, but Sergeant Wetherfield turns him down point-blank.

Act IV, scene 3. Curtain rises upon Hunter, centre stage front, stamping and asking for the umpty-seventh time, where is Mr

Mayhem? And, lo! An answer cometh. But it certainly wasn't funny then. Nor is it now. It came in the form of poor Ann, coming up on Minniver at a gallop, face absolutely *white*, leaping off, running up steps and saying, 'Mayhem! He's been ... *eaten!*'

I cannot possibly set into any order the incredible confusions that followed, so I'll have to set it out as I came to know it later. It seems that Ann got back to the stables and found Macho and O. still missing, so she got out Minniver in order to ride right round the wall perimeter until she found them. Not a sign. Half-way round, near the tradesmen's gate and not far from the dower house, she came upon a dreadful scene. It was just inside the wall. First she noticed a ladder, then around it a whole mess of trampled ground, then a lot of blood and a dead Doberman, shot about six times. She dismounted and saw 'a sort of heavy trail, like something dragged' leading to some bushes. It was Mayhem. 'They'd even bitten away half his face. I had to get right down before I could recognise him. Then I was sick.'

Stretcher-parties & c. went out: one for M's remains, another for Doberman's. By now the news of the double murder had filtered down to the pickets, who came trooping back to the Hall, looking shocked & rather shame-faced. Spokespersons (Brian and Mary) sd they came back 'willing to give a hand, it being understood that all their demands were still outstanding'. In midst of which P.A. Hemlock came back (having searched the Hall) and announced in a loud voice the somewhat out-of-cue line, 'I can't find Mr Mayhem anywhere.' When Hunter had taken her aside & explained that Mayhem had been eaten, she burst into hoots of sobbing, and then, to general surprise, produced the more arresting line: 'And ... boo hoo hoo ... Jane Crostic? Has Jane been eaten too?' That was indeed a 64,000 dollar question, because it seemed that Crostic had gone missing as well. Ann sd no signs of other bodies. But she commented on ladder. Perhaps Miss Crostic had mounted ladder and 'flown'? Indignant rebukes to Ann from all parties, especially Weeder: 'But, perhaps ... oh, Colonel Hunter, do you think They could have *captured* Jane? And were trying to make off with Mr Mayhem too? And the

Dobermans tried to *save* them?' Instantly agreed by all (except Ann & me) to be only possible explanation. Poor shot Doberman had given up its life trying to save Jane's honour.

Rani came in next, quite green. They had made her take part in identifying the body. She came up to me & whispered, 'You know that isn't all. Mr Oipas is *nowhere*. Do you think he's been spirited away?'

Act IV, scene 4. Enter Rbt in Landrover. Has already learned a little at gate and more on radio from Wetherfield. Salutes Hunter smartly & explains he's been 'at Astrosigint HQ. I'm very sorry to learn this terrible news, sir.' Hunter walks him up and down terrace to 'put him in the picture'. Rbt disengages, saying he must 'get out one or two signals', but catches my eye as he drives off, apparently in direction Astrosigint station. I slip out a little later & see he has altered direction towards stables. Join him and Ann there. Rbt rattled one question after another, with military curtness. When was Gentry found? Dead how long, any idea? Same qs for Mayhem. I sd I thought I'd heard cries & dog howling last night. 'No, couldn't, too far away.' I sd I was not in Hall but at dower house. 'Estimated time?' 'Exact time, 2.35 a.m. I'd been writing & looked at my watch.' 'They'll be miles out to sea by now.' 'They?' 'Oh, perhaps the Russians, with Miss Crostic. Explain later.' 'So they did capture her? Why her?' 'No. They didn't. Mayhem and Crostic broke cover & ran for it. They were the moles we were looking for. It was clearly planned – a ladder and everything, a fast car at the other side of the wall. But Mayhem didn't know about the Dobermans. Small oversight.' Ann said, 'But what about Mr Gentry? The dogs didn't get him.' 'Explanations can wait,' sd Rbt. 'The important question is – where is Mr Oipas?'

Ann sd O. and Macho had 'gone spare'. They must have made an early start, they were gone before she got to the stables. 'Time?' 'Before 6.30.' 'Any chance that Macho is roaming somewhere in the park now, without a rider?' 'Don't think so. I've been more than half-way round & can see most of the rest. And he hasn't been watered or had any grub.' 'Good.' 'Why on earth good?'

288

'Horses don't climb ladders. That means that Macho and Oipas are probably still together. Somewhere in the park, in the Arboretum . . . Good God! Unless . . .' 'What?' 'Could Macho jump the wall?' 'No way. It's above the Olympics record.' 'But is there any place where the wall is lower, or . . . Good God! Astrosigint!'

We tore up to the signals station in the Landrover. Where the wall had been breached for the contractors' lorries there was a guard-wire all around the building-site, six feet high. 'Could Macho jump that?' 'Yes, with a good run-up,' sd Ann. 'Shit! Oy Pee has been setting Macho at six-footers this last three days. How could I have been so blind?' We got out and sleuthed around. Sure enough, at a low point in the fence, unmistakable hoof-marks. And a big slew in the mud on the other side. 'Lost his footing,' sd Ann. 'Bloody nearly turned over.' 'Now, another thing,' sd Rbt. 'Can Macho jump in the dark?' Ann sd, well, he had good night-sight, all horses do, and there had been a full moon, but that had gone down before 3. With a good moon Macho cld go over that, esp if Oy Pee was rider, he seemed to 'conduct the horse by vibes'. Rbt looked relieved. 'Thank God for that! You know, I think that Mr Oipas only just escaped a very nasty accident himself. If Mayhem had found him in his room – some time between 2 and 3 a.m. – I think Oipas would be dog food now, or else be in a sub heading for the North Sea.'

I shouted at him, 'But we don't know where he is!' 'Oh, I think the answer to that one is easy,' sd Rbt. 'Mr Oipas and Macho will now be at Stonehenge. In fact – how fast can Macho travel twenty-odd miles? They probably made it in time for the rising sun.' Ann and I gawped. 'Sorry,' sd Rbt sheepishly to Ann. 'You're not the only one to be blind. Mr Oipas has been asking me all sorts of questions about Stonehenge. He's obsessed with it. And like a clot I even gave him the compass bearing.' Ann wanted Rbt to drive us to Stonehenge straight away. Rbt sd sorry, but he *had* to be at the conference: Martagon was about to blow up; half of NATO, War Minister, chief of MI17 wld be there. Sgt Wetherfield, who had been in on last exchanges, sd, 'Shall I take them, sir?' Excellent. Agreed only Ann shld go. Ann sd she had no pass, Wetherfield said get into the back under that blanket, guards never inspect Sigint traffic.

Search party was mounting Landrover when – lo! A distant drumming of mighty hooves. Ann says, 'Cripes! Aren't they beautiful?' She is grinning fit to split her face. Over the horizon, beautifully moving together like one being, rise one great horse, black, and one rider, robed like Kirghiz chieftain, who approach without checking speed, soar over fencing – while, in mid-air, O. gives us his most elaborate arc of salutation – and, still without checking, thunder on towards Hall, where sundry Top Brass are gathering, who scatter and scoot for shelter as stallion bears down among them, before it disappears in direction of stable (right).

'Wow!' sd Ann. 'Wow!' sd Sgt Wetherfield. Open mouth (belonging to me) sd, 'Fabulous!' 'I really must go now,' sd Rbt.

He tore off in Landrover, not offering a lift. Ann & I followed on hoof. We skirted gaggles of exceptionally cross-looking brass, every single one male. Ann went to stables. I was too whacked to think. On steps bumped into Pepper, who was too busy trying to pour oil on to a troubled American admiral to notice me. Went up and found Rani & asked her if she cld go to the stables & help Ann cope with O. She laughed and clapped her hands when she heard that O. was back.

Rolled on to bed. As I nodded off I realised that only Rbt, Ann, R. and I – and Sgt Wetherfield – had even known that Oipas, the whole object of this place, with its bugs and its guards, its conferences and Standing Committees, and its double murders, had spent the morning riding a black stallion around Salisbury Plain. It made me laugh myself to sleep.

Act IV, scene 5. Woke up late afternoon feeling cheery. Looked out of window and saw last of the staff cars rolling away. Knock at door, & Mary put her head in, message for me. 'Actually I shouldn't be here, we're still on strike really, well kind of. But I don't mind doing a favour for Major Sorley.' She seemed cheerful too. I cld hear the sound of children playing beyond the terrace, and someone laughing in the corridor. The sense of menace seemed to be lifting.

Message, scribbled on a sheet of signals-pad: 'Can you come in for briefing, 8 p.m.? Will provide grub. Will have to be short & sharp. R.'

Called in on Rani. She was cheery too, sd that D. was a 'little better', but was still shattered by loss of notes. And Oipas was 'strange' but seemed 'so happy – I think he is making a poem'.

Rbt was cooking, with some sitar music on hi-fi. A moment or two after I arrived, Ann came. 'That's the full conference party,' sd Rbt. He asked if O. was 'worse for wear' and 'Did he get to Stonehenge?' 'Now, will you two, with Rani, please see that an eye is kept on him *all* the time in the next few days? We may not be out of trouble yet.'

He dished out a delicious Indian curry, vegetable dish for Ann, meat for him and me. We went over some bits of the day. I asked about Gentry. He sd he cldn't be 100 per cent sure, but probably Mayhem (or Crostic) shot him. 'Sergeant Wetherfield has run through some of his recent haul – tapes. It seems he'd been doing some free-enterprise bugging on the side, maybe only for blackmail. He had a very incriminating tape, bugged only last night, with Mayhem and Crostic planning their getaway – and they *did* mean to take Oipas with them.' He supposed that Gentry was on his way to tell Hunter when he got a hole in the head.

I asked why, if Mayhem and Crostic were KGB moles, they had put so much effort into trying to destroy D. & me. That seemed over-zealous, even for 'cover'. Rbt sd I really did live in an ivory tower (Qy: Have he & Ann been talking about me?). 'Don't you know that for most purposes the KGB and CIA are in the same team? They may try to score off each other, but they both want to keep the public off the pitch. They're desperate to stop people on both sides from getting in touch with each other – you know, dissidents, peace movements – in case they might pull the whole Cold War down and both lots would be out of their jobs. In fact, they sometimes grass to each other about each other's "trouble-makers". We've picked up some really sick stuff at GCHQ . . .'

He stopped, as if he'd sd more than he shld. I sd I wasn't a

291

peace movement, I was a multilateralist (although I did join hands around Greenham once, about 12 yrs ago, before they cut the woods down and put in the Frisbee missiles). He sd, 'Well, all I meant was that spooks all think alike. But in this case you can take it as a tribute. You and Nettler were the only ones getting out real results. So long as they could get at your results they could pass them on to their Control. But you were holding back. And by last week Mayhem could see the writing on the wall. The CIA was moving in on Oipas. Mayhem and Crostic wanted to destroy your work if they couldn't use it any more — destroy your credibility. They wanted to put the boot into the only working bit of Martagon before they flew. And they also needed to get hold of your tapes and notes. Hence another reason for my speed in getting to you first.' I sd, 'Thanks! So you knew already they were the moles?' 'No. But I thought one of the panel at your trial — maybe Crostic — was. Cryptography and security are classic places to look for moles.' 'Oh. So Crostic has taken some of our stuff to Moscow?' 'To Novosibirsk — that's where their Astrosigint is based. They're quite nice chaps, some of them, have the same kind of troubles with their spooks that we have with ours. We have a regular Round Table each year — at Malvern or Novosibirsk — we call it Plugwatch.' 'It sounds very cosy and civilised.' (I thought of Mayhem's half-eaten face.) He didn't rise, but sd, calmingly, 'I don't think you should worry too much. What they really wanted to take was Mr Oipas. But I'm afraid all Nettler's notes and tapes have gone, and what they got of yours.' I sd, 'It's nice to be a scholar of international renown, whose works are pored over in Novosibirsk.'

Ann sd, 'Curry was good, Robo. Now will you please tell me what happens next, before I go over the wall? I never can stick the same job for more than a year or two, and I'm sick to my back teeth with this one.' Rbt Sorley seemed to flinch at that, and then the two of them locked into an eye contact as if I was not in the room: I cld tell that there was something between them, but it seemed to be a tension, or a need, as much as an understanding. At length Rbt sd, 'You know you can't go, Ann.

Not yet. You're needed.' 'By whom?' asked Ann, aggressively. Rbt ignored her & brought me back into the circle. He sd he wld tell us what he thought might happen, and he was certain about bits of it. 'Hunter will be sacked. That is, posted. The record of this place is appalling. That means your job is safe, Equerry ... And yours also, Helena. After all, of the panel at your trial, one has been eaten, one sacked, one has gone over the wall. Trial is scrubbed, although Miss Weeder no doubt will store it up in her Files.'

I asked if Pepper would stay on. He sd that was 'up in the air'. P. deserved to be sacked ('I'm sorry if this offends you, Helena') since he was incompetent and spent half the time 'swanning around promoting his own ego'. But we cld get something very much worse. The main tug-of-war now was between the British and the Americans. The Americans wanted the institute transferred to 'NATO' – i.e. to them. They had all the muscle and the money, but they had lost some face with the CIA helicopter binge. This still was our country & we still had O. here. So we might extract the concession that the titular Director wld remain British: probably Pepper, although even more titular than now. But Hunter's replacement, the real boss, would be an American officer.

A joint committee had already been set up wh wld work out the appointments. It was just possible that there might be two Asst Dirs, one American, one British. In that case there might be an 'interesting mix ... just workable'. And there will be other American, or NATO, personnel. I sd, 'Oh, hell. And I suppose Concorde-jetting academics also? Where are they going to put them all?' 'Now, that *is* a point,' sd Rbt, rubbing his chin thoughtfully. 'I was coming to that. Fact is, I've been appointed chair of the Interim Committee, to make the arrangements for the change-over. Don't ask me why, but the whole top of this place has fallen in, and they don't know who else to trust. Well, as chair, I'm afraid to tell you that the whole of your wing of Martagon will have to be allocated to NATO. I'm sorry, but you and Rani and David Nettler – oh, and Mr Oipas – will have to move out. We must make our NATO cousins as comfortable as we can.'

Ann sd, 'Wait! You can't . . .' but I cld see that Rbt's eyes were' twinkling, and I asked, 'And? So where do we go?' 'We-e-ell. Do you think you would all mind terribly if we had to move you to the dower house?'

The light flashed on Rbt's desk: not the violet, bugging one, but the yellow one for the phone. He took it for a moment, and then sd he had to go – 'another confab with the cousins'. As we all went out, he added, 'I can't promise it yet. But Undermanner's on the Interim Committee. It was her idea.'*

Sage Notebook. Pasted-in typescript

LUNATO/001

Toppest secret

TO ALL STAFF (EXECUTIVE)

This is to fill you all in on certain changes brought about by events of recent days.

First, I am sorry to tell you that we are losing the guidance of our Assistant Director. Colonel Gardyan-Hunter has been posted to direct a Systems Management course at the NATO Staff College.

Second, as you will not be unaware, our work here has attracted the notice of the NATO Council and of the President's Chief Scientific Advisor. At a time when the United States has taken a considerable lead over all other nations in space deployments, it is only to be expected that the Pentagon should take the closest interest in our work. I am happy to inform you that the British and United States governments have come to an agreement as to joint control over Martagon Hall.

---

* *Sage Field Notes end here.*

Some time next week, official (but unattributed) briefings will be given to the media, simultaneously in London and Washington, in which some small part of our operation will 'go public'. It is thought that the presence of Mr Oipas is already so widely 'leaked' that there is no further purpose in disinformation on the matter. For public purposes, FARCES will now be known as LUNATO.

At the same time, it is evident that our security arrangements have been wanting in some respects. They will be tightened. Pending a replacement for Mr Mayhem, all security will be directed by Lt-Col. Robert Sorley, with the assistance of Lt J. Wetherfield. Perimeter defences will go over to automated sensors, 'laser-dogs', electronic pass-keys & c. Captain Scarcely has applied to rejoin his regt in the Falkland Islands. The guard contingent from 5th Para will also return to regiment, with the thanks of all staff. They will take with them any remaining dogs.

We can look forward to some very active weeks ahead. Despite all difficulties, we are strictly on course, and indeed are now embarked on Phase Two of our original programme. We shall now witness a sharp up-turn in growth. Initial Astrosigint station installations will be operative in four weeks, and quarters for full operational staff in ten weeks. At that point, there will be additional Astrosigint postings, and Colonel Sorley will (pending confirmation) become Assistant Director (UK). By that time we shall also know the name of the Associate Director (NATO).

An Interim Committee is already looking into the logistics of this transition to Phase Two. It is at present proposed that the Associate Director (NATO) will be in charge of relations with HM Government and relevant Ministries, with NATO Council & SACEUR; also with the Pentagon and our other relations (CIA, NASA, SDIO & c.). He will also supervise the work of a new Public Relations Officer (who will handle media relations). The Assistant Director (UK) will supervise the work of Astrosigint station, oversee internal Security, as well as any remaining work (such as final debriefings of Mr Oipas) left over from Phase One.

The coming up-turn will necessarily involve some pressure on accommodation and facilities. New NATO personnel will be posted here on the staff of the Associate Director (NATO) and will need apartments, offices & c. A proper* medical officer will also be posted, residential. The Interim Committee (Colonel Sorley, Mrs Undermanner, Estates Bursar, QMSM Gravell, Lt Wetherfield) are looking into the necessary reorganisation and urgent building extensions.

The whole East Wing will now be made available to NATO. Any remaining personnel from Phase One will be found alternative accommodation. We are now into a truly significant operation, with relations at the very highest governmental and military levels, to which all our energies must be bent, and my thanks are due to surviving Phase One personnel now being phased out.

The Interim Committee will also review arrangements with non-executive staff for a new Staff Association (Patron: Mrs Undermanner). In view of 'going public', consideration will be given to the possibility of some outside leave arrangements for all but certain top-security-listed staff. Arrangements are being made for conducted parties to use a private room in the Bull & Teazle, Wednesday & Saturday nights.

I shall myself, of course, continue as Director of LUNATO. But I fear that even more of my time must now be given to consultations in Washington, Colorado, Brussels and (on occasion) London. If any executives have urgent messages for me, will they please submit them in writing through Miss Primrose Gordon?

John Pepper, FRS

NOTE. A brief memorial service for Mr Mayhem and Mr Gentry will be held on Tuesday (instead of the usual Weekly

---

Pencil circle around 'proper' and exclamation-marks, with crude picture of creature with enlarged snout. Sage?

Conference) in the chapel. Next-of-kin have been given clearance to attend. Academic staff will wear gowns. The Suffragen Bishop of Chute will take the service.*

---

* *Sage annotation, pencil:* 'None of us went, of course. From window saw solemn processional set out, led by Pepper in ermine & scarlet hood, Scarcely in full regimentals, Bishop wth crozier, then a group of gowned academics with bowed heads who turned out to be butler, batman, frogman, Weeder, P. A. Gordon, *u-s-w*, in hired fancy dress! Then puzzled n-o-k. Then almost no Other Ranks, except Scarcely "detail". Don't suppose chapel has been so packed since the orgies of the last Wicked de Boyle. Very appropriate disinformation rite. Sort of burial spooks deserve.'

SEGMENT FIVE

ZONE OF EDEN

Editor's Note

Our author was now moved to a more congenial coop in the same keep. But the materials left to your editor now become gravely imperfect. Oi Paz neglected scientific researches and commenced a 'Diary' which has on its cover the single letter 'I'. Of the fragments which survive many pages are torn. The new diary commenced by Sage was recovered in an even more damaged state.

The authorised account of the later stages of this episode has been declaimed in the final two tomes of 'The Official Records of the Expeditionary Forces to the Galaxy of Strim', to which the fragments which follow should be regarded as marginalia.

Q.

Sage Diary

May 2nd. Have been confined in this 'coop' (as O. calls it) for ten months. Time to start a new diary.

To resume last month. First week total confusion. Hunter & Dobermans went, followed by Scarcely. Rbt Sorley promoted to colonel. Pepper and P A. Primrose coping with military brass, MoD, FO & increasing flow of NATO/US VIPs. Weeklies abolished & replaced by elaborate command/control structure of committees, from which we (i.e. David, Rani & I, and of course O.) are excluded. Sigint unit brought in by Rbt sets up perimeter & ground-to-air sensors & radar defences, code-key consoles to open gates. Dishes, pans, 'golf balls' and weird antennae of Astrosigint station (plus staff quarters) continue to rise.

In second week the 'Martagon Arms Hotel' (one mile outside the perimeter) was commandeered for our American cousins 'for the duration'. (*Qy:* How long will Oitar dure?) Cousins start bussing in at 8.30 each morning: brisk, mostly late twenties, early thirties, jeans, flowered shirts, running shoes. Mostly civilians, scientists or administrators from Lawrence Livermore, Los Alamos, Litton Industries, Rockwell, IBM. Most of them male, a couple with hairy faces. Two or three blacks. All looked through me, like achievement-oriented/monkish devotees. Scraps of complaints in the corridors – no elevator to third floor, not a decent lab in the place, where's the popcorn popper, Jesus, this place is pre-Columbian.

Billiard-room made over into a lab, Old Library into an open office (books crated and into store), Weeder's files taken off somewhere to be put on floppy discs and a soft-spoken USAF security captain moved into Mayhem's office, electricians running around installing computer terminals everywhere, even the orangery. On last day they started installing a Coke dispenser and a huge freezer filled with tubs of Baskin-Robbins ice-cream in the Officers Mess/SCR. Mrs Undermanner said this was the final straw & she was moving out to her sister's at Cirencester. Rbt persuaded her to hold on a bit longer, he needed her 'casting vote' on the Interim Committee, since Gravell was 'in their pocket' and the Bursar had 'given up'.

Happily cousins too preoccupied bonding themselves in 'teams' to infest the gardens & park. Any extra-mural activities strictly functional: mainly jogging (in sd teams), groovy tracksuits, glazed eyes turned inwards like self-flagellants, monitoring own progress on digital watches. Tennis has now started (week four): brisk, male & boring, alternating between serving 'aces' and double faults.

Just wandering around & looking at things seems to be un-American – or, to be fair, un-American ♂, *sub sp* Livermore/IBM, which really may be a mutant. (Am serious about this. Another characteristic of this mutant is it has diminished sensory perception, atrophied capacities to observe world or relate to people, since has always inhabited educational institutions, labs & c., with uniform architecture & offices, & is habituated to ingesting 'data' mentally from the 'input' of theses, computer terminals & c. & then composing an intellectual profile of environment, wh environment is largely made up of 'schedules', 'programs' & data-bases. Vocabulary atrophied accordingly, like munching dehydrated acronyms.)

End of Week Two something more sinister happened. Small group of males (all white) in battle fatigues & camouflage hats, strung all around with knives, grenades and sub-machine guns, started lurking around Hall. Rbt made a scene & sd he was in charge of security during Interim, & his sensors and signals unit was quite adequate. Assoc Dir (NATO), who (it seems) is superior on all Hall questions to Asst Dir (UK), ruled that these thugs (Qy: about eight of them?) essential for personal protection of 'Q-cleared personnel'. Asst Dir (UK) had to be content with ruling them off-bounds except in immediate precincts of Hall: i.e. Rbt appears to still have upper hand in grounds, including stables, dower house & Astrosigint station.

Assoc Dir (NATO) turned out, to general surprise, not to be military at all, but one Lowell Himmelfarb, Jnr, a former executive of Rockwell International, now in Pentagon. Rbt says he is a typical member of the 'new ruling élite' – 'spooks, arms pushers, media hookers & cold war paranoiacs'. I haven't even seen Himmelfarb yet, since he orders the world like a Gracious Goodness from behind screens. But by Week Three the Hall began to pong of his evil vibes.

That was when they tipped us out. Every inch of space requisitioned for more offices & computer terminals. So D., R. and I packed our chattels & trooped off with O. to join Ann in the dower house. Undermanner came up trumps, arranging to send food over to us there, since we wldn't want to 'tramp back three times a day and associate with that class of people'. She seems to regard the dower house and the stables as the last remaining outposts of the Tradition of the Hall. Pepper (who never bothered to see any of us during this crisis) sent a message to say we wld be 'very welcome to dine in hall' on Sundays, but without Mr Oipas, since in his absence the bar and the cellars were being re-opened. We gather that the prospect of the high table flowing with burgundy, and the rituals of port, were the decisive factor in getting his agreement to our eviction.

It was not till Week Four that Rbt drove over to 'put us in the picture'. Us being me and D., since he didn't want O. to overhear. He took us into the garden, a really warm April day. He sd Pepper had become a self-important cypher & that he (Rbt) had completely lost control over what went on in the Hall, wh was now all Himmelfarb's. We asked what the Hall was doing, now that the prime subject, O., had been evicted. Rbt said he wasn't 100 per cent sure (they kept some things from him) but both the Hall and Astrosigint were now into Phase Two, modified to NATO requirements. There was a lot of activity now on the moon, and a huge amount of signals traffic had been monitored and banked in the last few months – Fylingdales, Cheltenham, RSRE (Malvern) and the dishes at Cambridge had all been co-operating in scooping signals up.

The bottleneck now is with cryptography. All that the signals data showed was volume of traffic and activity – there are now three clusters of cupolas in the *mare humorum* and some vast hangars, or Alls, under construction. But cryptography has got nowhere in de-coding a single signal. And when the Oitarians had beamed some signals directly at Earth a month ago, they had come on the back of a pulse so powerful that it had blown the receivers. He sd it was just like an EMP, or electro-magnetic pulse, but there had been no obvious physical functions to cause it – no nuclear explosions in the troposphere. It must have required inconceivable energy resources to have projected that pulse from moon to Earth.

Astrosigint's job will be to aim custom-built, highly selective receptors at the moon, in the hope of picking up less heavily coded local traffic. Are also installing a finely aimed, ultra-high-frequency transmitter, with the aim of actually 'talking' to, or exchanging messages with, the moon – 'if we can find a language to talk in'. 'We can,' sd D. 'I know,' sd Rbt. 'But the cousins don't. I tried to tell them the first day or two, but they knew everything already. They didn't even look at your reports, but packed them off with files to be put on floppy discs. They think we are primitives.' He scratched under his armpits & did an ape-man act (v becoming).

Rbt sd it wld be some months, even a year, before he cld get into direct communication with the moon – 'I mean, exchanging something more than bleeps or numbers'. Meanwhile he suggested that we 'keep our own counsel'. The function of Martagon Hall now seemed to be seven-eighths 'political'. There was a team of cryptographers there, working parallel with Astrosigint, but most of that work was going on in a bank of supercomputers in Behemoth, Florida. Lowell Himmelfarb seemed to have at least three games going on. (1) He offers the place as a 'Think Tank', with experts whizzing in and out, briefing & de-briefing. His largest team is already at work preparing submissions for new budgetary appropriations. (2) He has a heady game as a communications crossroads between Pentagon, NATO, SACEUR, Brit govt, CIA & c. & c – a sort of central switchboard on matters Oitarian, wh gives him a position of real power. (3) He is already drawing up 'scenarios' of Phase Three: i.e. sending a NATO embassy to the moon, to negotiate an alliance with Oitar. Rbt thinks that this is a ploy to advance game (4), which is that Rockwell and IBM are forming a consortium to build four moon-shuttles (for some $250 billion) – and maybe this is *the* game, and the first three are only 'covers'.

We asked where this left us. Had they lost all interest in O.? '*I haven't lost interest*,' he sd sharply. But some signs that O. was 'surplus to requirements'. The cousins were quite certain that if they shovelled enough Oitarian signals into their supercomputers these wld crack the codes & give them the language on a plate. Then they wld want NATO brass to talk direct to Oitarians, not through an interpreter without security clearance (e.g. O. or D.). They did want to hang on to O. here (and anyway for reasons of face the Brit govt wldn't let them take him to Florida). Also, O's presence was symbolic, & gave Pepper and Lowell H. the 'platform' for the whole place. (Himmelfarb even has one Phase Three scenario in wh O. is to be used as a 'hostage', or a 'bargaining-chip'.) But for present purposes we were supernumeraries, we weren't needed in any of their acts and might as well enjoy the spring if we could. We will have to stay within the perimeter walls for the time being: 'They certainly won't let you go, you know too much. Mind you, I don't want you to go either – in fact *I* wouldn't let you.'

O., however, will have to 'show his face'. When VIPs like Secretaries of State for Defense blow in he will be fetched out & paraded before them. In fact, there's a rumour that some panel of experts – a Presidential commission – may fly in next week. Then Rbt climbed into his Landrover again, saying, 'I'm counting on both of you to use this blessed peace here to go on getting inside Oitarian culture. You'd better take it easy for a while, David – and follow Sister Satpathy's orders. But Helena, please go on . . . go as far as you can possibly go. It may mean the saving of us all.'

That's enough about Outer World. Moving into the dower house has been the only real fun thing for a year. It took me right back thirty years, to playing at house in the village cricket pavilion in the winter. After ten months of institutionalisation we even felt lost and (as O. wld say) 'un–rolled'. Everything to do: strip off the dust sheets, so that one room after another showed its character; shake the blankets in the yard (O. helped with this); look in trunks and Georgian pressers for sheets & towels. Camped for the first two nights, except for O. whom we put in the master bedroom (paper & chintzes very floral), which has its own bathroom. Then we had a conference to decide if we were a commune or flat-dwellers. Decided more first than second. Commensalism, except for O. who still has a slight thing about public eating (how he loathed the dinners in Hall!) & will eat in own room or with us as he chooses. In practice this means that R., D. & I will alternate as evening cooks, since Ann gets up before 6 & gets back from the stables twelve hours later, too tired to cook. We each get own breakfasts, R. looking after O.

Ann a little set back by sudden invasion of her pad, but glad to have us. We offered her the next-best bedroom, but she prefers to have her 'den' in an attic-studio wh can be reached by back stairs from the kitchen. So I got that room, wh shares O's bathroom through a different door. R. and D. took the bedrooms on the east side of the house. All the downstairs rooms & the conservatory are to be commune.

Mrs U. popped in a couple of times, very hearty & happy in her benefactress role. Told us how to 'indent' for food & where to collect. Laundry. Toilet rolls. Sent over Brian the Oddman to repair some guttering & look at the plumbing. Yesterday O. went off at 6 with Ann, having started up his morning rides on Macho once more. (He doesn't seem to plan another dash to Stonehenge, but A. keeps an eye on him.) I thought of going with them, but I never seem to get up in time & all these horsy people make me feel a mediocrity. Just before 8 I was making coffee when I heard voices, & Rbt and Ann rode up on Minniver and Sprite (having seen O. safely to stables). A. was half-turned in her saddle, quite beautiful with her face flushed from the canter, hair flowing loose (thought she always wore a hat?), laughing at Rbt, whose blue eyes were shining as he laughed back. Until that moment I had always thought of Ann as a sort of workaholic, rather plain. I felt a moment's sweet-sour pang. I called them in for coffee – they hitched horses to the hedge, where the wicked Sprite took a mouthful of *magnolia soulangeia*, the pink petals fluttering from her bosky snout.

All the ten days have been like a holiday – I cldn't even lift a pen to my diary. We haven't begun to get into a work routine. D. is convalescing well, but he and R. are always together, so that O. and I are much on our own. They *have* got off with each other, of course, but in such a quaint, old-fashioned, sentimental way. I was hopelessly wrong, as usual, about their being incompatible. What they do is complement each other's weaknesses or absences. I had thought that R. wld be overborne by D's intellect, wh she admires to adoration. But D. has a vacant place where practicality ought to be, and a clumsiness in relationships: R. has simply occupied the first place, and steers D. in the second. They are always together but they scarcely ever touch, maybe because R. has stern views about virginity & marriage, and steers D. in the same direction. Yesterday D. said he wldn't mind getting back to studying Oitarian again, but R. was fiercely protective.

307

Said it wld make him 'ill' again. She won't let him interview O. alone, like a jealous lover. But she's curiously unworried about me – said (laughing) that I might harm O. more than he cld harm me, but added that we are 'good for each other'.

Good or not, we can't seem to get back into formal work. I tried two days ago, but O. was restless, said, 'I have given you enough tradings. Now you must trade to me more mortal customs, Helena.' Bringing us here has somehow bonded him more closely with the four of us. He tries to share in some of our activities – shaking blankets, drawing curtains, even fetching wood for the fire – & seems to be somehow more 'physical'. He does his dawn shadow-boxing with incredible zest (the only time I struggled out of bed to see it), also his riding. Seems, somehow, to have more feelings or to be more in touch with them.

The thing that is getting him excited is the dower house garden. Jerry, the dishy (but, alas, gay) under-gardener – I call him Adonis – has been over several times, & has shown O. around & named each bulb & shrub. Then O. started to help him weeding, his robe catching on the roses. Then he tried to straighten out the paths through the rose garden into more geometric lines (with little success). Then Adonis distracted him & started clipping a couple of shaped yews which had grown out in all directions. O. settled down with a pair of clippers and worked for the whole afternoon. Then he summoned me outside to admire his handi-work. He had shaped the poor yew into a kind of many-faceted sugarloaf, sitting on top of its stem. I admired it & asked what it was. He seemed to rummage in his memory-bank, and then announced, with immense self-satisfaction, 'Can you not observe? It is a prosenneahedral orthorhombic, worthy of the School of Crystal!' Which sent me scuttling for a dictionary.

As for the inner inner world, that seems to be smouldering away, but I've lost touch with it. I'm up one moment, oohing at the crocuses or banging cheerily about the kitchen, & the next moment I crouch inside myself like an old maid. Really. Have started getting awful migraines. I suppose coming to the dower house from the Hall was like thawing, but thawing hurts. Was

39 yesterday, wh somehow seems older than 40. Not a single birthday card. I suppose Mum & Dad's will be being processed by censor, my brothers always forget, no one else cares or knows. What is the omen of a May Day birthday? Festival, revolution, or SOS?

Here I am, cooped in this keep, with nothing to look forward to but the menopause and maybe an Oitarian invasion. I always meant to have children. I thought I'd have a Special Relation (tried more than one) – I fantasise about it still, the current Fantasy Object being You Know Who. And I suppose I'm just plain sexually restless also – haven't gone to bed with anyone for over a year. I can't recall a longer break since I was seventeen, except when I was in the field in New Guinea. Have to watch it. When Brian the Oddman was doing the bathroom plumbing I gave him a 'come-on' which ashamed myself. He started the obligatory chatting-me-up about male & female joints, 'if you know what I mean, miss?' I sd I had no idea, cldn't he show me? He just grinned & patted me on the bottom, gave me a lecture on plumbing, & then, *apropos* of nothing, managed to introduce the fact that he is 'going steady' with Mary the Phone, wh was a tactful way of putting me down. When he'd gone I looked in the mirror & thought, Well, why the hell would he want to, anyway? And lay on the bed & girned.

(*Later*) Reading this over – I've got into a mocking & self-mocking style, which trivialises everything. Somewhere inside me there is a more serious person. And one who is growing up. Yes, I have lost the shape of my life, but I am a serious scholar (wh can bring its own kind of joy) and I am not corrupt. Yes, I would like to fall in love with Rbt, but I don't want to spoil the good relationship we already have. I know he likes me. I know he likes Ann – perhaps a little more. But a second sense tells me that his feelings were cauterised when his wife died, and he is fending off any claims of deeper commitments. Nothing but time could make any difference to that. And, yes, I am truly terrified by whatever is now shaping on the moon, which I have turned away from for too long.

The only way I can cope with that — and the way wh Rbt thinks cld even help — is to try & understand O., wh becomes a little more easy every day, perhaps because he is becoming more 'human'. He came in from the garden just now & seemed at a loss for anything to do. He usually spends several hours in his room, working on his notebooks or speaking to his tapes. I asked him if he had not got some notes to make. He sd he had learned nothing that day, except some botanical names. (Since the books in the Old Library were crated it has become almost impossible to get in new reading.) I asked if he kept a diary. Perhaps he had learned something about himself? The concept troubled him. I had to explain what a diary is, and even show him a page or two of mine. 'You put down each day what happens, and what interests you. And then you look inside your own head and put down your own thoughts — or feelings. It's not only a way of remembering, it's a way of coping with yourself.' He asked what could be known about his 'I' which was not already prescribed in his 'roll'. I sd, 'You'll be surprised. Think about your own I. Put down what you think about yourself, this place, the flowers, your own body, about us, about me. Don't worry — we shan't read it. I promise!' So we dug out a virgin notebook, and I made him write 'I' on the cover, and inside: 'Oi Paz. My Diary.'

Sage Diary

May 7th. Incredible the sense of autonomy that has come with the move out of the Hall — probably delusory. But at least we are free from constant invigilation. It is nice also to have time to get to know the park, which is huge and full of surprises. It was landscaped in the 1740s, when the lake was made. Charles de Boyle and his grandson were both into Palladian gimmicks — little temples and grots. In its heyday the circuit must have been like Stourhead. Part of the deer-park was made over into the Arboretum in the early 19th century, part of it was eaten down by the deer into rather scruffy common land (where Ann now has her jumps). Two of the temples survive beside the lake (Flora and the Temple of Music) and another (Apollo) near the stables. The Temple of Flora is really beautiful, with severe Grecian pillars facing the water, and a dark, dome-like interior. It is guarded by lionesses with women's heads and breasts.

It must be at least fifty years since there was a staff which could cope. (The gardeners now can just manage the flower-beds, the kitchen gardens and the main lawns.) Result is a sort of landscaped neglect. You never know what you will find. I went with Oipas to look at the mausoleum, or 'Cardiarum', which stands on a raised mound at the western edge of the park, between Astrosigint and the dower house. As we pushed our way through some old yews we suddenly came upon the statue of a mythic beast, half buried in brambles, with an eagle's head and wings (one broken) and a lion's rump. O. was astounded, and sd it was a 'griffin', just like those on Oitar. (I really can't sort this one out, there is some myth-transference going on.)

Then we pushed on up the little hill to the Cardiarum, and O. seemed to hang back, almost as if he was afraid. At the entrance he stopped altogether. It certainly is a strange place – a roofless hexagon, the walls some 30 feet high, with alcoves for the urns (in which hearts were preserved) and niches for gargoyles. The walls are cracked and overgrown with ivy, and opposite the entrance I cld make out an altar slab with a large alcove behind it, from which the urn (or statue?) had long been removed, leaving an accusing vacancy, an almost audible nullity. I turned back to O. but he wldn't budge; he was staring at a gargoyle above the entrance, so badly damaged that one cld only make out an open snout, a flickering tongue, and a twisty neck: no eyes, no ears. Then O. reached out and pulled my arm. 'Helena, we will not go. This is a place of nothing. The vibes tell us to go back.' Of course I turned back with him. I've never known him so vulnerable or so 'personal' before. And he usually avoids touching anyone.

Sage Diary

May 11th. US expert commission been infesting the Hall this week. Headed by Irving Lacky, one of the Eighties *Commentary* crowd of neo-cons, a Very Distinguished Visiting Professor of Politics at the Heritage Foundation: members – Grundriss, from Stanford, known best for his work on Post-Modernisation Number-Crunching Theory (was a Marxist structuralist in the late Seventies); Hal Whitelaw, the one who got Chomsky sacked from MIT & pioneered Computer Linguistics; Sol Vishinsky, the Soviet dissident, exported from the USSR abt 10 yrs ago and the President's personal adviser on Kremlinology; Luna Gerstalz, the psychiatrist from Columbia, author of *Human Rites* and *The Orgasm of the Ego.*

Bonus has been addition to panel of John Blossom. He wasn't on the list Pepper sent round, so when I steered O. across to the Hall for the first session & found him on the steps I fell into his arms. (Not, it seems, proper conduct with Presidential panel. Gerstalz ostentatiously dictated a note on her mini-cassette.) John was at Duke with me in graduate school & we became real mates – he was working then on Voodoo. He comes from one of the smaller W. Indian islands – Saint Martin – but is now a paid-up, card-carrying American.

John found out where we are & he now comes round every morning for coffee on pretext of jogging. Jogging is legit so no one asks where he's going. Unfortunately John, like 90 per cent of his fellow-citizens, is not All-American type. Actively loathes jogging and joggers. Has also run to seed, mainly in paunch. (*Qy:* Do I show the years so much?) Hence he arrives moaning & coughing & sweating, wh takes up half our coffee-time. It seems he was added to President's panel at last moment, when PR consultants pointed out panel had no blacks. John is now a full professor at Yale & thought he wld 'come for the lark': 'Man, you should see the size of the dishonorarium!'

John says the panel bores him crazy. Its purpose is to 'case this joint' & accumulate data wh can be used in future, if nec, to 'show up the Brits'. John has become a true American (*sub sp* anarcho-cynic) & he thinks this purpose commendable: his contempt for Brits (official) is exceeded only by his contempt for President Forsst. Ostensible purpose of panel is to find out whether O. 'is for real, kindov like a moon-person, & whether he's a sane communicant creature'. D., R. & I are barred from interview sessions, but Pepper sat in on the first & he now sends his deputy — 'some Brit colonel, a cool cat, with grey poker eyes'. John assumes that D. and I as scholars, i.e. alienated nationless persons, will share his contempt of Brits, esp colonels. I began to bridle, & to point out that Rbt's eyes are blue, but thought better of it. Come to think of it, his eyes *do* go grey when he is being official, or watchful — or contemptuous.

John went on with hilarious account of panel's first session. All the panellists are 'playing up to each other', & esp trying to impress Lowell Himmelfarb (who they think has a private line to the President). Hence heavy usage of professional cant. Whitelaw talks about 'regressive logic paradigms' & Grundriss goes on about 'unjustified supra-urban destabilisation symptoms'. Luna Gerstalz has already decided that O. has an 'inadequate ego, incapable of self-riting orgasm'. Every now and then, when proceedings pall, Irving Lacky twirls his biro like a conductor's baton & calls on Sol Vishinsky, who falls into a pose of agony & lectures O. on the evil empire & his own sufferings at its jaws. Panel is finding O. hard going, 'an uncooperative subject'. John sd he cldn't make O. out himself — 'either he's got a great act going or ... er ... he's kindov autistic. I mean, he knows the words but he kindov blocks the meanings.' I started to say that maybe the block wasn't only on one side, but then I thought — Why bother? John didn't really want to know (he wasn't asking *us* anything) & he's only here for ten days on a fun-and-money thing.

John added that he guessed the panel might have an ulterior purpose. This was to see if they cld 'cut out the Brits' — i.e. if O. had turned out to be 'a real proposition', they wld want to use him to get their own Presidential hot-line to the moon. The

313

rumour in Washington is that the Brits have offered to sell O. to the USA for three billion dollars – the govt needs to buy votes with a tax cut, & since they privatised the River Severn & sold the Channel Islands to France they've run out of assets. So the panel intends to sound out O. about this proposition on Friday, when both Pepper & Rbt will be out of the way in Cheltenham. John sd that panel was likely to report to the President that it was 'a bum deal', at the least they wld recommend a deep mark-down – and he'd have to 'go along with that' himself. By now I was feeling uneasy, & getting a sweet sick whiff of the corruption of success & money; he's *changed* in the last – how many? seventeen!! – years. Perhaps he's had it too easy, being ♂ (and very beautiful in those days), and black, & v bright, & laid back, & upwardly-mobile in a seller's market. But lovely to see him despite all, & we invited him to dinner, Saturday, when he will help me catch up on what is going on in the trade, esp the malicious bits.

John jogged off, with a huge mock athletic leap wh almost sprained his ankle. O. came back from his morning ride, & it was Rani's turn to steer him over for the interview. O. was fretful about going, & demanded that R. take him to see Brian the Oddman. About what?

When D. and I were on our own, he suggested that we might try & do a bit of work. He wanted to work through the episode of his culture-transference. I asked him if he felt strong enough, wouldn't it upset him? He said no, and for a particular reason (polishing specs furiously). 'I know you won't have noticed, Helena, but I have something to tell you. I . . . I've fallen in love with Rani. In fact, we're in love with each other.' I tried to simulate amazement & (no simulation) good wishes. He sd it was all 'extraordinary'; R. had brought him back to earth, nothing could ever make him stray again, but what was even more extraordinary was how a beautiful & gracious creature like R. cld say that she loved a clumsy egg-bound oaf like himself. Wh illustrates for the umpteenth time that ♂ suppose that ♀ judge them by their own superficial secondary criteria of judgement of

♀ & have no inklings of the more refined emotions. (Although
D. does have a point.)

Our session went like this (transcript of tape).

Q. 'Did you know you were being sucked into Oitarian?'

A. 'Yes ... no ... yes, partly. I could feel Earth-concepts
dimming.'

Q. 'Did the language carry you away ... like a raft on a tide?'

A. 'No. It wasn't the language. I still scarcely know the language, or languages. I can translate some of the poetry now – the
old epics. I can answer Oipas when he uses the ceremonial tongue
of greetings. But the everyday cured language ... well, that's the
problem.'

Q. 'Give me an example.'

A. 'The old epics are rich with tonal colour and affective
resonance.' Infmnt chanted in Oitarian. 'That means something
like – Beyond the seventh circle of the Wheel/The argonauts
adventured in the void/And shook the petals of the galaxies/And
distilled from them ... oh, well ... something like "aromatic
sciences". It's a free translation, of course. I use "argonauts"
because the sense is something grander than just "explorers".
They're a special dedicated band of chosen persons, seen in a
heroic light. Curiously, the Oitarian word – '*ago nœt*' – suggested
it to me. Although that's an archaic language, and Oipas himself
is sometimes at a loss to explain the terms, I don't find any ...
well, any *major* difficulty ...'

Q. 'Perhaps it's closer to ours?'

A. 'Yes. You can enter it without any real ... culture-shock.
We can recognise something of ourselves in it – Homer, Icelandic
saga, the *Upanishad*. There's an affinity to Earth-grammar. And
the rhythmic beat is quite recognisable – a bit unsubtle and trance-
inducing. But the others ...'

Q. 'Try an example?'

A. 'An example will tell you nothing. If it told you too
much you might go into culture-shock. Well, here's one: if
(fear) = FALSE (b [j] & ø × 7f) put NUMKEYS on nodestore
DUMP return NULL.' (He wrote this down.)

Q. 'Hummm. An equation?'

A. 'No. An instruction. Well, a bit of programme.'

Q. 'Written for a computer?'

A. 'Said to each other. That is the "Neuter Utter", the strictly cured language of inter-collegiate communication and everyday affairs – the language of business and administration. It's not the only language still in use. There's an ornate ceremonial language, "Bumple Utter", which is easier to get the hang of, although the grammar swirls around in circles, imposing tautologies. The ceremonial language is there to insist that the conclusions are entailed in the premises, like most religions. Or ideologies – White House Speak, official Marxism. And there's a more available written language, "Fact Utter", in which science and space records and books are written. That's altogether more transparent – Oipas uses it for his notebooks, although as a poet he has a licence to "freewheel" in all the languages, including the archaic. If I had stuck with "Fact Utter", or even with "Bumple Utter", I wouldn't have got into trouble.'

Q. 'Neuter Utter is the problem? But is it really necessary to know it? Couldn't it be a specialist set of formulae ... like logarithms ...?'

A. 'No. Algorithms. It is itself a logic path.'

Q. 'What's so difficult about logic?'

A. 'Logic *paths*. Not logic freewheel. Algorithms are programme paths. They suck you into *their* logics. Once you're in, there's no way of breaking out. That was where I came to the point of transference. I was trying to decode Neuter Utter. Oipas seemed keen to help me. Then suddenly I seemed to be in a kind of oscillator, jumping between our logic and theirs. For a day or two I think I actually was inside their algorithms, like jumping between two circuits ...'

Q. 'You mean inside their concepts?'

A. 'Yes, their concepts. A reversal of expectations, hanging upside-down in the cave of the world like a fruit-bat. Seeing everything human as alien. But it wasn't just concepts. I'm not sure I remember any concepts. It was another logic path ...'

Q. 'Can you describe it?'

A. 'I can't *really* describe it. If I could I would go mad ... I would go inside the path again. All I can do is tell you about the feeling of alien-ness – species-alienation. Even "feeling" is wrong, since I was in a mindscape cured of all first-person feeling. A language, or programme, cured of affective tones, ambiguities, association. Somehow the senses – the body – seemed to grow dim, so that it was an inert mechanism, like a corpse with no signals of its own. You know, we really do inhabit a dualism – body and mind – and there's a flow going on between them, signals to each other, as if we each had two "I"s. When I jumped paths, this dialectic snapped – I was a mind which had lost touch with the "I".'

Q. 'Like *Sailing to Byzantium*? You know – "Once out of nature I shall never take/My natural form from any bodily thing"?'

A. 'Perhaps ... But no Grecian goldsmith made that world. At first it was like switching across from colour telly to black-and-white ... but, rather, to a universal dim grey, like a moon-scape without atmosphere, so that the only illumination came from a dull albedo beneath a black sky. Compulsions rather than feelings – compulsions to follow a path on the dusty surface, between shadowy pyroclasts and regoliths and mascons. A vocabulary cured of joy, terror, love, innocence, judgement, relationships between first persons. No chance, no oughts, not even any beginnings or ends, since the sentences seemed to rotate, with their tails in their own mouths. A grammar cured of choice. Nowhere in the whole mindscape an ambiguity. Not even a language, but a sense of compulsions, so that one could not speak but was spoken, like a digit in a flowchart.'

Q. 'Perhaps it *is* a computer programme language?'

A. 'Exactly. A highly advanced one, gigaflops ahead of ours. But what does that mean? First, they can speak directly to their computers, which is efficient and time-saving. Our own computer whizz-kids are working on that on Earth. But they are working on the computers, not on the humans – yet. Second, their com-

317

puters – in the bumples – can speak direct to them. They can programme them. Which means that their computer-dependency must have made over some part of the cranium into a computer, which can receive & bank the programme directly.'

Q. 'You're saying they *are* computers? Oipas doesn't seem like that.'

A. 'Not *only* computers. Not all the time. They can switch between phases – archaic, ceremonial, poetic, Fact Utter. Trance is a different state of consciousness altogether, non-verbal, which I don't begin to understand. And they can "freewheel", which is going on in the inertia of past programming. Anyway, Oipas may not be typical. Poets have a lot of licence, to switch phases and to freewheel. I am saying that this Neuter Utter is the main everyday language, which facilitates bringing together the whole social organism within one univocal programme.'

Silence.

Q. 'Hadn't you better stick to the archaic and the ceremonial languages for a while? Oipas is a poet. You could converse with him in them.'

A. 'Yes. I never want to see that moonscape again.'

Q. 'How did you manage to ... jump there? To crack it?'

A. 'Funny thing. It was through noting Earthly affinities. Never mind Oitar. Earth language is going that way as well. Civil service circulars. Proclamations of the CPSU(B). Number-crunchers. Defence experts with their acronyms. Have you read Synge on the Arran islands and that book on the Blaskets ... ?'

Q. 'Mmmm. My field.'

A. 'Sorry. You know it all. In those poor, simple societies language leapt and sang. Language constituted their conscious-ness, grief, terror and joy. I think that language is dying now, all over the world. It's being cured and modernised. It's like a deciduous forest, poisoned in mid-summer, shedding its leaves, so that only the skeletal structures of the trees are left. Then they will cut it down and feed the wood into computers. I was reading one of Mayhem's circulars, and it reminded me of Oipas's account of a law laid by the Gracious Goodnesses, and suddenly my mind jumped . . .'

Q. 'Did Oipas understand what was happening?'

A. 'Don't know. But that's another thing. If it nearly made me schizophrenic, what is it doing to Oipas? How can he jump between cultures without shock? Or hasn't he really made the jump yet? Or is it easier for him because he is a freewheeler and because he takes us as being in the mode archaic?'

Q. 'Working session. I am supposed to be interrogator, you informant.'

A. 'Oh, shut up. I'll tell you another thing, Helena. In your paper you said something about Oitarian culture being like something bubbling with a lid held on. Well, the language – especially Neuter Utter – *is* the lid. It reminds me of those bits in Blake about Urizen, weaving nets of abstractions to hold down the human psyche. It's like a sort of cobweb trapping their minds. And there's another thing. If Oitarians do come here in *that* phase of their consciousness, they will be quite merciless. That's not quite right, since Neuter Utter won't have any concept of mercy. It will simply be a compulsion, to compel Planet Earth to conform to the GGs' programme. Let's hope they come to us in trance or in archaic mode.'

Q. 'Is there any chance that Oipas could help us? I mean, if Robert really can get through to the moon?'

Informant (who had now become David again) got up abruptly, saying, 'Ugh. To think I nearly got caught in that web!' He walked to the window and said, 'Hello, they're back early.' R. & O. were walking up the path, O. looking rather cross (and human). We went out to meet them.

Oi Paz Diary 'I'

Oi Paz walks out into the park of this keep at once into a seventh state of trance, and this without any switch for changing rolls. The trance unlooses rule, and every programme dims, until the very Wheel seems like an alien thing and Oi Paz falls into an unruly I. Sage said that in a diary Oi Paz should 'think about your own I'. But which is roll and which is I? And how can I-without-the-Rule hold itself together and not suffer a dissolution into the senses and the sun?

This trance which they call 'spring' carries I like a flow of melt away from the shores of Rule and towards a corporeal disorder in which all thought is obscured within a mask of blood. For I walk every day through the gardens of Eu Topaz of archaic myth. I bathe in yellow solar radiance; the grasses and the leafs grow in unregulated abundance without the care or cure of any College; I tread between daffodils and crocuses, and the bushes and trees put forth galaxies of white and pink flowers, and the very airs go aloud with quaint flutings as the birds go into archaic song, and in those airs there hangs a medley of aromas – some rank, some delicate and worthy of the finest cure.

Flowers grow in the lawns untended, where the seed has fallen, now yellow primroses, now purple violets, now little orchids. And while there is neither symmetry nor plan in the larger forms of nature, yet in the smallest forms – the petals of each flower, the veining of each leaf, the shell of the 'snail' – there is an abundance of intricate design, so that if our jewellers or silversmiths were to spend but one hour examining a patch of grasses or of clovers, or a pace of common hedgerow, they would return with their heads teeming with projects which would astound the Schools.

Caught in this sensual music Oi Paz dissolves into the seventh trance. And yet, in trance, how can I examine I? It is to swivel focus on to focus itself. All thought is blocked by the thrusting compulsions of the corpse, which interposes between I and I. For in this trance the corpse engrosses all programming and carries I along within its sensual roll. From which these mortals call it 'body', as if it were a thing apart from I, governed by its own autonomies. To which I also must submit, as the pump beats more vigorously, as if self-programmed, and the lungs ingest the spicy airs, the eyes wander about the flowers self-willed, the ears

ZONE OF EDEN

are washed with musics, and the very limbs seem to be imbued with their own motors. From all of which compulsions I am drawn continually within the thrall of flesh and, as at my first landfall, I confuse this planet with my home.

If I examine I, then I must note strange alterations in my corpse. Sage says a diary is for 'private things', which I will set down here, although, if they came before an Adjuster I would be sentenced as a Discard.* And 'private things', which they also call 'privates' or 'private members', is an uncured double-mean, or 'pun', which stands for genitals, or, in the male, the nozzle. Which nozzle and its whole area have in I begone a strange translation, with a bosk of golden hairs growing about that part, as also beneath the armpits, which no depilatory will check, so that I have every day to scrape off hairs with a razor (or 'shave'); with large glands, or 'balls', expanding the scrotum, and the nozzle becoming thickened about its head. And at nights and sometimes now in spring during the day, the nozzle swells in a programmeless way as if it were some animal apart from I, growing to three times its proper length and pointing upwards at the sun, like a cippus honouring the Wheel. I fear that this may betoken the oncoming of the ailment of the Sper, or in their language the 'prick'. And though I try to conceal this shame, yet it occasions little fleshly pain (as such a gross, denatured expansion would propose), and indeed is harmonious with the sensual trance of spring. The first occasion when I suffered this disorder was when Sage traded with me her nakedness, which co-incidence occasioned some associations of images, so that when my 'prick' now elevates itself at night her naked body comes into my dreams.

I am now in a new coop, which is a betterment, since the nightly guzzlings, or 'dinners', are ended, and they have selected for me their most well-favoured and rational keepers, as Satpathy, Sage, Nettler and the Equerry. Each dawn I worship Oitar on the back of the Great Macho, who carried me like wind to Stonehenge. The days I spend in trance and in study. But this

---

* *Oi Paz here declaims an absurdity, for a sentence of Discard was merited at the first landfall.*

321

week there has been a new hullabaloo at the Hall, with a pack of ill-favoured flying keepers, like gnats which buzz about my head and bite me with their beastly questions. They are of the same language-pack as the English, but for some reason act a pretence or play of being of another nation. They haul me back and forwards to their play, or 'panel', so that they crash all higgledy into my trance. And this morning I ordered Satpathy to lead me to a very rational keeper called Oddjobber, where we had some intercourse and he agreed to roll me in the 'union', which is a sort of inner wheel in this place which calls mis-keepers to order and de-programmes their villainies.

Sage Diary

May 14th. Two rather steamy days. Thursday, when O. came back from his session early (see last entry), it transpired that he had gone on strike! Can't quite make out scene, but, as pieced together from the only two sane witnesses (John Blossom plus a few expletives from Rbt), it went like this. On way to session O. made R. take him to Brian Holberry, the Oddman, & asked to be 'rolled' in Staff Association: sd he was subjected to 'beastly abuses' & Brian sd he knew exactly what he meant, brother. Sd it was only one of many cases of 'harassment' & both Gerstalz & Vishinsky had 'had a go' at Mary; he didn't mind if they were gay or bi-bloody-sexual but he wld bring the whole place out at the next complaint.

Thus fortified, O. went into the panel. But it was, quoth John, 'man, a crazy scene!' Himmelfarb had decided only way to get through O's blocks was to subject him to a lie-test. He's flown in two dumb technicians from Washington Anti-Subversion Patrol, or WASP, who had this 'groovy polygraph thing', all dials & graphs & electrodes & antennae. John said, 'That Brit colonel – I misjudged him – he really lost his cool. He said he would take it to his superiors, you know, all lah-di-dah, would "go to Cabinet level". But Lowell called his bluff. He knew

perfectly well the Brit cabinet is a pushover.' So they started
wiring this thing up & O. took a long squint at it & started
fiddling on his belt. 'Man, he put a spell on it! He had a real
kindov voodoo look in his eyes.'

The first thing was that, although it was O. that was wired to
it, the machine 'flipped its top' every time one of the *panel* asked
a question: 'It was fan-*tas*-tic! When Hal Whitelaw and Grundriss
spoke, the needles in all five dials went right through the men-
dacity zone and out the other side, & the graph zig-zagged up &
down like crazy. Man, the needle in the main dial hit the ultra-
lie-limit so hard that it bent at right-angles!' John rolled around
& slapped his thighs. '*The ul*timate in Very Distinguished Visiting
Liars. But when your Mr Oipas answered back, the machine
went dumb. Null. Not a flick. Then Lu Gerstalz started up and
asked, "Well, er, Mr Oipas, have you ever had ... or, I should
say, has your ego ever had ... er, an Ideniny Crisis?" The machine
just blew. I mean, blue, like sky. It kind of glowed, as if it had a
blue light inside it, all the dials jumped and whirled, and blue
sparks shot out of the terminals. Your Brit colonel got up as if
he was about to mutiny, I bust two ribs laughing, and Mr O.
rose with great dignity and shook the monitor off his arm, saying
"Now I shall end your beastly lies and abuses. I am a Strike."
And swept out of the room.'

R. found him stamping around on the terrace. 'You know, he
really was *angry* – I think he's getting emotions just like us.' They
went and found Brian, and O. told him that they had been
abusing him again. Brian seemed a bit fazed, because he couldn't
quite work out exact anatomical details of sd abuses, & sd he
supposed that O. might prefer not to give full details 'in Sister
Satpathy's presence'. He sd he cldn't call the place out on General
Strike just like that. He wld have to consult his fellow shop
steward (i.e. Mary). There were also certain 'due procedures' set
down in the Total Industrial Peace Act (1994): viz. all complaints
must first be exhausted through Reconciliation Tribunals
appointed by the High Court, which sequestered all union funds
pending settlement. Only when exhaustion total might a strike

be lawfully called, after an 85 per cent majority vote in secret ballot, all ballots to be verified by passport photos duly signed on back by a serving officer of ACPO.

'However,' said Brian, after rattling off these small formalities, 'don't be down-hearted, brother. Our members are behind you. I shall recommend to my fellow shop steward that Martagon Hall works to rule until your grievances are fully met.' 'Damn good thinking, brother-man,' exclaimed O. 'Too damn right this beastly place needs bringing under the Rule.'

Brian was as good as his word. All of Friday and Saturday M. Hall has been on a Go Slow. This has meant these things, *inter alia* (collectors for this bit were Ann and Mary, whose go-slow involved popping over to chew the rag with R.). It seems that Gardyan-Hunter's legacy to this place was an incredible set of Conduct Codes and Staff Regulations, culled from systems-management courses. These were now dug up. Boilerman (a black friend of Mary's) found a Rule to rake out all furnaces fortnightly & de-coke, in consequence of wh all heating closed down. Cousins awoke with lark & (after jogging) leapt into showers which showered them with icicles. Mary the Phone kept pulling the plugs on conversations (rule-book says something about 'all tele-communication to be subject to maximum time-economies'), shouting 'Time up!' Brian himself, consulting Hunter's legacy, found out that as per regulations, section 19A (ii), he must every six months check all wiring in the Hall, in the course of wh check he found a suspect junction-box. Inspection of same reqd throwing all the main fuses for two hours, hence lunch was cold cabbage & cold mash & cold bangers, while – alas! – all the Baskin-Robbins goodies in the SCR freezer, including the peach julep ice-cream and the boysenberry sherbet, went into what O. wld call a 'melt' on the floor.

Working to Rule may explain extraordinary head of aggro which built up among cousins by Friday afternoon. O. being on Strike had refused to attend the Friday interview sessions. Late Friday afternoon Rbt tore up to dower house with two Land-rovers & a party of signalpersons. He was bloody rude, answering our questions (or not answering them) through his back. He and his team started driving a set of rods into the lawn, & right around the house in a complete circle, each rod wired to a sort of central generator; and then fixed on top of each rod a sort of lighting-fixture facing outwards away from the house. Then he told us that all of us were 'confined to the premises' until he got back from Cheltenham tomorrow evening. I started to ask what was up & he just barked at me, 'That's an order! And while I'm away you will take orders from Lieutenant Wetherfield.' I was about to expostulate that I wasn't a signalperson, but caught his eyes (quite definitely *grey*) & thought better of it. But Ann broke in, 'Steady over, Robo! I've got to get the horses watered and exercised,' and I realised from the jut of her jaw that she is quite as obstinate in her way as is Rbt. Rbt hummed & hawed, and then agreed that Ann cld be an exception.

Then he seemed to realise how unreasonable he was being, and explained. 'Pepper and I have to be in Cheltenham tomorrow. As you know, Mr Oipas is on strike, not without provocation, I may say, which is making things awkward for us. But that's his business. I've just learned [Qy: Wall-boring again?] that Mr Himmelfarb intends to take advantage of my absence to send for Mr Oipas and to take him, by main force if need be, across to the Hall for a private interview with the President's panel. I have refused permission, since I consider that it might do our guest a psychological injury. More than that, I have *ordered* them not to make any such attempt. I'm sure they won't be so foolish . . . This park and this house are Sovereign British Territory, and the chiefs of staff back me up in that. So I'm sure you'll be all right. Only I don't want you – or Mr Oipas – wandering around the park or going up to the Hall.' 'Then why the rods and cameras?' I asked. Rbt turned churlish again & barked through the back of his head, 'Lieutenant Wetherfield will be here at dawn to look after them, if they are needed.'

Rose early on Sat. Crunching tyres in yard, the gallant lieutenant and a team of signalpersons already on duty. I felt exhilarated & frisky, as if playing a bit part in a WW2 movie. There's a flagstaff in the yard, & I asked O. what were Oitar's colours? Oitar, it seems, is no-colour, but the College of Poets is saffron & jade: i.e. the colours in his own robes. He entered into the spirit of things, & found a towel more or less those colours wh he sd wld do. So we went out & with a lot of hassle with rotten lines and rusty toggles we managed to run the towel up the mast. Lt Wetherfield said 'Good show!' and all the signalpersons clapped. Then we waved Ann goodbye as, like a messenger from encircled Khartoum, she strode out to work.

And then, about an hour later, bloody hell, the hoods *did* come, all eight of them, advancing in a sort of straggle across the park, with the USAF security captain behind them, and all of them *carrying guns*! Jane W. whipped over to the Landrover W/T & crackled through to Rbt. Then she advanced up to line of rods, held hand aloft in a 'Stop!' sign, & parley between Britain & NATO began. I cldn't *believe* it. O. came out on the steps beside us, looking amazingly handsome in his robes, and in his fuck-you-I'm-on-strike pose. And, lo! a breeze stirreth, & the towel raiseth itself in glory & flappeth proudly in the heavens. Three signalpersons crouch & run to the generator-thing. The wind then carries the soft-spoken Southern voice: 'I'm sorry, Mam, but I've orders to bring back that man.' And like a whiplash the reply, 'I am not your Mam, but an officer of the Royal Astro-signals Regiment. This is sovereign British territory. I order you to turn back or I shall use *all* measures to resist your advance.' To which USAF captain said only, 'Right, move in, fellows. Take no notice of the crazy lady,' at which the hoods jogged forward waving phallic emblems & the crazy lady, walking slowly back-wards wth head erect & eyes towards the Enemy, made a sharp downward signal of her right hand to the generator-party. The camera-things started swivelling on the rods, and, lo! the two foremost goons approaching the circle . . . collapsed into one heap on the grass & lay there, utterly dead.

Captain now lost his Southern cool & started ranting, shouting he'd shoot all those fucking lasers out, and goddamnit shoot the crazy lady too, & matching the action to the word he levelled his gun and crack! the nearest camera shattered into silicon & dust. Another goon started spraying in direction of cameras with sub-machine gun in a madly dangerous way, stray bullets shattering the drawing-room windows & whining past our ears. D., R. & I flattened on the lawn, & signalpersons crouched behind Landrovers & generator; we tugged at O's robes, but he refused to budge from his 'come-and-get-me' posture, & started to deliver a heavy sentence on invaders & their 'killing-sticks'. Meanwhile Lt W. stood facing Enemy, without batting an elegant eyelash, & barked out the orders, 'Prepare to use riot gas! Man the Number Two water-cannon!' But when she turned to observe her troops preparing I could see that even she was looking a little glum, like Captain Custer at the end of the road.

Then, lo! deliverance cometh, at the 11.59th hour. I suppose the racket of the sub-machine guns had drowned the thunder of approaching hooves. Unnoticed by us all (being somewhat preoccupied), Ann & Macho had stolen out of the Arboretum, & if there was a Black Horse of the Apocalypse that was what the captain & his fellows turned & saw not twenty yards from their rear – bearing down upon them like a Fury from Hell, neck stretched out, at double gallop, teeth bared, eyes flashing red sparks, smoke steaming from his nostrils. Here manifesteth itself a Nightstallion to end all Nightmares. So traumatised were Enemy that they dropped their killing-sticks (thank God!) & fled towards Hall, Ann reining in like a rancho – Macho rearing up and beating air with his metal paws – & then pursuing them back to their evil dens. And Oipas! When he saw Macho he actually raised both arms to the heavens and cheered! In fact I think he came to the edge of an Incongruous Noise. I don't know if Macho really meant to slay them, or if he just got a high from acting the part – I rather fear the first, aggro being intrinsic to his malevolent male nature.

The rest was brisk and anti-climactic. Wetherfield ordered signalpersons to collect goons' guns before they 'came round'. Soon afterwards Rbt screamed up in a Landrover & took his Lt aside so she cld 'fill him in'. Meanwhile, like Lazarus rising, the

utterly dead hoods stirred & groaned & then stumbled shame-
facedly off. Instead of being churlish Rbt now seemed to be rather
chuffed. He spent a lot of time on the W/T, getting through to
immensely high places. Ann wandered back & asked why everyone was gawping & milling about. She sd she'd just been 'exercis-
ing Macho' since his acolytes had been stuffing him with oats on
the sly. 'He's getting fat as a pig, I thought I'd really stretch him
this morning.' Rbt gave her a dig in the ribs & sd she was lucky
not to be on a stretcher herself, wh horseplay seemed to please
Ann. Then a general (Brit) hove on the scene, mighty affable, &
seemed to be congratulating everyone, especially the crazy lady.
His name is General Rainborough, and he thanked us for our
loyalty to 'the Good Old Cause'. He also congratulated Ann &
asked her if she'd ever thought of 'the Services' as a career. Ann
sd, no, she hadn't, she was a pacifist, a Gandhian – but Macho
wasn't. General laughed, & he and Rbt drove over to the Hall
to have it out with the Enemy. I'd heard about those laser-
stunners before, but thought they were reserved for use against
wimmin (Greenham & Molesworth) & suchlike traitors & sub-
versives. Bet they will never be used for a better purpose than
the Siege of the Dower House.

We were so busy going over & over the day's dramas that we
forgot totally that John Blossom was invited to dinner. R. & D.
offered to whip up a curry, since they love billing and cooing
over cumin seed, ghee and cardamom. John filled us in on the
events in the Hall (the scene with the polygraph, & what he knew
about the Work to Rule – with wh he is *not* sympathetic). He sd
there'd be hell to pay about the day's events, the President himself
had been informed, & we shldn't underestimate Lowell Himmelfarb. I sd he shouldn't underestimate the 'Brit colonel'. He sd
he cldn't understand why the Brits were hell-bent on hanging on
to that cove Oipas (O. was eating in his own room wh he prefers).
He knew the Presidential panel were all fakers, but there were,
er, more 'facilities' in the USA, 'er, kindov a pool of global
expertise', & wasn't this place 'in the sticks'? I was feeling a bit
scratchy so changed subject & we got on to shop talk (Ann

yawning ostentatiously) & it was fantastic to be filled in again on the professional scene – I almost felt as if I was in the world once more. J. is really sharp, generous about new work (if it doesn't threaten his field), & very malicious.

Then into dinner, the curry was superb, & we all felt elated. John went over the funny bits of the polygraph again, for the benefit of R. & D. He has such a gift as a mimic, he had us rolling. We all got a bit sloshed (John brought some duty-free VSOP brandy). After coffee, & more brandy, I swelled with goodwill & old colleagueship & thought John might like to look at my notes & papers. Almost as soon as we were in my room (I was squatted on the bed, rummaging through my files) he made it clear he thought I had invited him for another purpose & started to make love. I fended off, rather half-heartedly, even quarter-heartedly. In fact I was dialling TUM, or whatever zone you dial, to find out if I wanted him, and the message seemed to be 'why not?'

But then John, all impatience & bursting flies, started to try & make me with the 'oh, you won't have me because I'm black' ploy. I was absolutely *furious*, perhaps the more so through being sloshed. After all, we are both *anthropologists*, & we know those culture double-binds & guilt-trips like the back of our own theses. Forgot all about dim messages from TUM, & actually began to despise him. How many white feminist radical grad students does he guilt-trip into bed this way? He wasn't acting 'black' (in fact he's *café au lait*, with a Dutch grandmother) but just like any middle-aged professor from New England (or Cambridge, Eng) away from his wife (whom he never mentions – but I bet she's white) for a week's conference.

And, *anyway*, John ought to know I don't exactly hold off blacks at the end of a punt-pole, since he was himself the first black I ever bedded, back in those happy, casual, uncomplicated, BA (before AIDS) days (when I was miserable half the time & girning about 'finding myself'). Oh, & I suppose I was a bit zeal-of-my-house-radical then, & congratulated myself on my liberatedness & lack of racism when we did the beast-with-the-two-backs together, for wh he is entitled to punish me. Nevertheless, we had some real tenderness between us, and huge quantities of laughter.

All of this swirled around together in my sloshed head, as I tore him off a strip for trying a ploy like that – I was really angry – & John, instead of getting contrite or hostile, just grinned & said, 'Don't come on so heavy, Helena. I meant for old time's sake.' Whereat I realised that if he had only been the least bit tender and reminiscent, instead of doing a cynical try-on, I wld have pulled him down with open arms.

So we made it up, & I gave him a more affectionate lecture on Tact. But through all the slosh my mind was throbbing dully also, and warning me off, because of the success-and-money bit, & ALSO the fact that John Blossom, anthropologist on the Presidential panel, didn't show the least interest in my notes or papers but was only trying to score. Anyway (mind sd), why stir up that long-inactive personality-zone, when he's going tomorrow?

Oh well, maybe I did make heavy weather. John & I are birds of a feather, or used to be. Maybe this place has grown me up, made me less flip. (I even catch myself 'taking moral stands', as Rbt does.) Anyway, *anyway*, we did make it up. John sd he'd slip me a copy of the 'summary and conclusions' of the panel's report. 'Lacky is writing it now, since the report itself will take months.' I walked him back to the Hall, more than half-way (no Dobermans!), & we parted with a long teenage neck beneath the Wellingtonia, & I felt that some shreds of old times still clung around, like the wraiths of mist that were rising beside the settled lake. Pity he's going today.

Went back & dived into lovely hot bath, mulling over John & Life & Things. Forgot to lock the other door wh leads to O's bedroom. I was just out of bath, & reaching up to airing-cupboard for a towel, when lo! O. enters (I had supposed him long asleep), as naked as I, a truly fabulous anatomy of male, a beautiful golden coffee colour all over. He stood there, mildly startled, and then regarded me steadily as if he were an approving land-surveyor.

Then, for the first time that I can recall, he showed symptoms, not of confusion, but of human embarrassment. He suddenly turned & went out, covering his genitals with the ancient gesture of shame ... but not before I had noticed that, for a second time, Eddystone's lighthouse was rising aloft. Oh.

Neither of us had spoken a word.

Sage Notebook. Pasted-in typescript

Presidential Panel: Executive Summary & Recommendations
(Draft Only)

0.1 Pursuant to the President's program, the Panel submitted subject to exhaustive interrogation along all personality parameters and culture profiles.

0.2 Owing to non-compliance of British personnel with NATO priorities, the Panel was unable to extend to subject the President's offer of freeworld sanctuary with post of Distinguished Extraterrestrial Boeing Professor in perpetuity at the Edward Teller Center for Astro-Behavioral Studies. (Full details of British non-compliance with treaty obligations have been referred by Director to SACEUR (NATO): see Appendix II.)

1.1 Panel first established database: viz. is subject *bona fide* extra-terrestrial creature-person, or, as suspected, impersonated by unemployed member of disbanded Royal Shakespeare Company? Findings ambiguous, but first computer-simulations from data confirm former hypothesis.

1.2 Panel was unable to effect final proof of this finding with polygraph tests owing to malfunction of equipment. Interference by low-quantum particle-beam interferometer, operated by British personnel, suspected (Appendix VIII).

2.1 Notwithstanding these obstacles placed in its way, and the wholly inadequate facilities at Martagon Hall, the Panel fulfilled the President's central trajectories.

2.2 Panel established that subject evinced extreme personality-disorder symptoms. In the absence of controls it cannot be shown with certainty whether symptoms are confined to this specimen or characterise Oitarian creature-culture as a whole.

2.3 Symptoms include 'acute culture-trauma' (Blossom), 'inadequate ego-riting functions' and 'thanato-regressive symptoms' (Gerstalz), 'schizo-autistic meaning-blindness' (Whitelaw), 'self-annihilating totalitarian holisticism, with suspect philo-Soviet personality slippages' (Vishinsky), and 'displacement of the in-the-last-instance conjuncture between the linguistic structure-in-dominance and the ontological base' (Grundriss). (These findings are set out in Sections III–VII below.)

Conclusions and Recommendations

A. Martagon Hall lacks elementary scientific facilities, funds or qualified personnel, and is inferior to other comparable Third World outfits.

There was distinct evidence of British attempts to destabilise the President's mission. The Panel understands that certain disagreements have arisen between the Pentagon, SACEUR and the State Department as to advisable control-measures in UK. We were informed by Lowell Himmelfarb, Jnr, that owing to insurrectionary disturbance-symptoms among the natives, the planned exercise in pacification ('GRENADA II') has been delayed implementation. For this reason the complete take-over of M. Hall or transportation of subject to freeworld territory is not immediately envisaged. These matters lie outside the Panel's competence for recommendation.

B. However, in the Panel's view, further investment in interrogation of subject will not be cost-effective. The Panel has already accumulated sufficient data, which will require lengthy processing in coming months, subject to adequate budgetary appropriations for facilities, research staff & c. (see Appendix I). This work will of course be pursued on US territory.

The Panel therefore RECOMMENDS:

1. Presidential probe of subject (Oipas) be discontinued.
2. Full priority be afforded to ongoing Cryptosigint complex at Behemoth (Fla).
3. Panel members to be engaged as consultants to Behemoth, with credible honorariums (Appendix I).
4. Panel to remain in constitution, with additional co-opted expertise, as advisory group to President with a view to establishing a major new research institute in Astrocultural De-Coding. The institute might also train small groups of achievement-oriented, fully adjusted space missionaries, with a view to converting Oitarians to Freeworld Way of Life.
5. The President may wish to order a mission to the moon to capture more eligible specimens as controls for laboratory testing, conversion experimentation & c., in new institute.

The Panel also directs attention to the heavy stress attendant on the performance of their duties. In particular, additional expenses accrued owing to a breakdown in logistics of M. Hall, which necessitated sending for emergency food supplies on last two days by special delivery van from Fortnum & Mason (London, Eng.). (Supplementary accounts and claims for stress-honoraria will be found in Appendix I.)

Irving Lacky

Sage Diary

June 4th. Dower house idyll continues. I've got too lazy even to keep this diary. R. & D. still billing and cooing, elaborate exchanges of chivalries & courtesies. Getting wearisome, why don't they get into bed & get on with it. Rbt tied up morn to night with Astrosigint, we never see him – at least, I don't. He & Ann canter round the perimeter most dawns. I thought of struggling out of bed to join them but thought better of it: might expose self not only as duffer but as gooseberry. Of course I cld do the circuit with O. But he & Macho seem to be a couple too, stepping out together in a state of abstracted mutual self-absorption, as if they were worshipping their own & the planet's motion. So I roll over & pull the sheet over my head.

Outer world gets more threatening every week. Since the 'generals' coup' last winter, Marshal Oblomov has been rolling back all the Gorbachev reforms. They have started chucking up space battle-stations to 'answer' President Forsst's SDI furniture. What did Forsst expect? On both sides of the broken world the armourers & spooks & ideologists rule OK.

Suppose I shld rejoice in last week's general election. They forgot to send us postal ballots, after all, but I don't know if I wld have voted. Dr Charon's new-look cabinet is at least a change after all those years. But I can't stand the self-promoting smugness of the man, as if he spent an hour polishing his own image before each five mins of telly. O. came in to the drawing-room when Charon's talking gob was on screen, pledging abject submission to NATO & Special Relations. O. was first of all fazed, because it seems he thought our 'queens and pee-ems' were always women. Then he suddenly screwed up his eyes & peered at the screen, & his face looked like thunder. Seems he had once done a chat show with Charon & recognised him. He shouted out that we shld not let that 'plugger, that half-minded public mugger' into the room. Then he became melancholy & sd that Charon had 'uncured' his Translator with his 'deterrents', and that the box had been his only 'friend and companion' on the Earth. He looked so sad about the late Translator that I cld swear tears were forming in his eyes. And his face looked so human (noble & comic together) that I gave him a little comfort-hug, quite forgetting that he has a taboo against touching. But he seemed to like it, and squeezed my hand back. Didn't even go and wash his hands.

ZONE OF EDEN

Sage Diary

June 8th. Addition to complement of dower house of one refugee. Mrs U. came over last week & asked us to care for her cat, since M. Hall is now 'no place for a poor dumb creature'. Aforesaid dumb creature is a long-haired neuter ginger job, disgustingly fat & with one lopped ear. Answers (or refuses to answer) to the name of Tigger. O. and Tigger hit it off at once, so that O. feeds him about a gallon of milk a day – & has even learned to use a tin-opener. When not eating, Tigger is sleeping, nearly always in O's room.

O. has taken possession of the Temple of Flora beside the lake. It really is quite an impressive relic wh has come down in the world. In the 19th century it became a summer-house, and in the last few years the gardeners have used it to store hurdles and wheelbarrows and stuff. O. calls it his 'bumple', but what he does there is unclear since he never asks us in. I saw him take in an old cartwheel which he found in the stable precincts. Funny thing is, whenever O. goes to the bumple, Tigger forgoes his beauty sleep & follows him, a few yards behind, tail in air. Tigger & O. disappear into the bumple together, to observe the rites of the Wheel. Yet if O. goes out for anything else – walking, riding, gardening – Tigger slumbers on.

Sage Diary

June 10th. I have been trying to get back into some work, although who the hell is the work *for*? D. seems to be v much more interested these days in Hindu culture than in Oitarian. (I think the latter still frightens him a bit.) I suppose Rbt might be interested – he sends messages by Ann that I am to let him know if I find out anything 'important'. What is important? To Oitar or to us? Anyway, here's a transcript of yesterday's session. It got difficult, because O. gets impatient at being interrogated, & keeps throwing questions back.

Q. 'Let us talk about time and the seasons. Do you notice the passing of the seasons on Oitar?'

A. 'The seasons do not pass. They are appointed.'

Q. 'Yes, but there are changes in temperature ... winter and summer?'

A. 'Outside the orbs there is disorder and wrack. Yet it is appointed even there that each year there is a time of melt.'

Q. 'That is what we call summer. And do the spring and summer come to the cities too?'

A. 'Why should the domes flux with the solar winds? All happenings are at appointed times.'

Q. 'But is there not a season, in the domes, of change and renewal, like spring, when the flowers burst open? And a time of decline and decay?'

A. 'The College of Gardeners makes appointments for all flowers. Roses are appointed throughout the year. Lilies have seven appointed times.'

Q. 'And then they die?'

A. 'They wait their next appointment.'

Q. 'But they must die some time? Whatever is begotten must come to an end. There must be rebirth and renewal.'

A. 'They are past and await what is to come. The cycle has no dead-line.'

Q. 'But the individual must. Like people. People must die?'

A. 'How can people end?' (Grudgingly) 'The corpse comes to an appointed dead-line. But the programme returns to the Rule and re-enters the cycle of the Wheel.'

Q. 'But when the corpse comes to its dead-line, then surely the person must die also?'

A. 'The person returns to the Wheel.'

Q. 'But the individual – I – you – will be dead?'

A. 'The Wheel will appoint the programme to another.'

Q. 'Aren't you afraid of death? To go out – to be nothing, nowhere, throughout eternity?'

A. (Silence) 'What is, in mortal sciences, an eternity?'

Q. 'Eternity ... is for ever and ever without end. It is like time going on and on, over the far horizon, and the next, into infinity, with no one to watch it or to count. Living is like a brief flash of light in a total darkness that goes on for ever, before and after and on all sides.'

A. 'If that were so, then the Rule and the Wheel would only be a flashing also, which would be a blasphemy. For in material time, even the great Rule of Oitar is only a spark in the void, like a falling meteorite. All of Sykaos and its history is too small to make a spark.'

Q. 'Well, what other kind of time is there?'

A. 'You chop time into bits. You suppose you always must have beginnings and ends. Material time is Sykotic bosh. Why is the end later than the beginning? "What is eternal is circular, and what is circular is eternal" – that is a Precept of the Rule. In simultaneous time, the past and future are always present in the now.'

Q. 'But people still die . . .'

A. 'They return to the Wheel, which appoints their programme to another.'

Q. 'That sounds like reincarnation. Have you been talking with Rani?'

A. 'Satpathy has much good thinking, which her nation learned from Bōd Hā.'

Q. 'But reincarnation isn't much comfort if you don't know you've been reincarnated. The real you has died and been lost for ever.'

A. 'The programme cycles perpetually. So nothing has been ended.'

Q. 'Except the "I". Most "I"s would like to go on.'

A. 'The "I" is an impurity. "Whatever dies was not mixed equally" – that is a Precept of the Rule. Even the most perfect role-kit from the most cured Sper-line and hostess suffers the impurities to which all corpses are subject. Yet in recent times the "I" also is immortal.'

Q. 'How is that so?'

A. 'You buzz me with your questionings to which you know

the answerings. Even here on Sykaos you have your own immortals, like the ghost in our house.'

Q. '... eh? What ghost?'

A. 'The ghost with whom Tigger and I have intercourse in my room at midnights. The unhappy maiden who was slain by Lord Charles de Boyle ...'

This rather broke up the professional cool of the session. But we did go on, & in fact he got into flow. The rest (summarised) is this. First he told me about the luckless maid, with a dagger in her bosom, who has 'intercourse' with him & Tigger at full moons. She seemed rather boring, & I really do wonder if O. got this one out of a book, or campus gossip. Then he told me about person-reconstitution. It seems that in 'recent' years (i.e. c. 1,200 Earth-years ago?) they invented reconstitution. Just as there are light- & sound-waves, radio & c., so each individual emits vibes or bio-waves – i.e. intellectual & psychic. These hover around within the planet's magnetosphere, & if required can be collected back on to a three-dimensional 'screen', so that any Oitarian of 'modern' times can be made to reappear in one of their characteristic 'states' or moments.

Oitarians of archaic times are truly dead. The bio-waves have dispersed or are too faint for recovery. Occasionally they reconstitute *themselves* during some excess of electro-energy (such as lightning) or by some natural 'fixative' which holds their emanations in one spot – hence also (he surmised) the ghosts on Planet Earth, of wh he claims to have had 'intercourse' with several.

O. explained that this invention finally put paid to any lingering distaste at the idea of death, since (shld there be any occasion) a person can be reconstituted in the screen-room whenever the Gracious Goodnesses wish. Indeed, before each of them comes to its dead-line, 'fixes' or coordinates of their bio-waves are taken, and registered in the bank of the Bumple of the Wheel, on floppy discs known as 'The Immortals'. I suggested that this didn't truly count as immortality, since these emanations are not self-motivating, & can be reconstituted only by the GGs. Hence no self-activating identity, no free will or choice. 'Choice' always seems to meet a major block in O. He disengaged from session, muttering about 'beastly unrule'.

Not sure where this line of enquiry is leading. Too meta-physical? Perhaps I shld work more systematically into myth. But Oitarian mythic personae seem singularly bloodless & to merge into blessed Wheel. Reconstituted bio-waves leave me cold.

Definitely an *uneasy* session, wh became tense at times. I felt that we were both coming to the edge of the 'alien-ness' of each other's culture-beings, so that we both felt threatened & kept drawing back. Another shove & we wld both have fallen into some crack between our planets, into a conceptless void. I felt I was clinging on to Earth-categories, as if they were all that held me together. When I talked about 'choice', O. looked for a moment as if he was going to jump, & then walled off the little gap between us.

Query: Ought I to work along more functional parameters & try to get out some of the predictive hypotheses wh Rbt wants? *Example*: How are Oitarians likely to regard/respond to Earth civilisation? Do we share any common norms or values? Do they *have* values? (Rationality? But what is rationality in the context of alien norms?) I ought to explore the nulls & compulsions which fill the space where affective responses ought to be. How? Should I try him on love poetry (where D. says he has a block)? Or Blake – 'To Mercy, Pity, Peace and Love' – what cld that possibly mean to O.? And, if nothing, why? What replaces it?

Sage Diary

June 15th. We've started going to a lovely walled garden beyond the stables. It must have flourished before WWI, when they cld get gardeners & lads for 6d a day. Now it is mostly old orcharding, apples & plums, & a glorious fig-tree in one corner, wh look after themselves. There are still some nectarines & apricots on the walls. The four of us sometimes take a picnic there – O. seems to prefer eating when he's lying on the grass, looking as handsome as Lord

Krishna. When the apple-blossom was all out it was like Life before the Fall.

Sage Diary

June 18th. Tried new way in. Heavy session, most of it not worth transcribing. Went to the Secret Garden with a clutch of books. Blake was a non-starter. 'Mercy, Pity, Peace & Love' – first two nouns were nulls, although he does have a concept 'forgivingness'. But this refers only to overlooking blemishes against Wheel, as when Adjusters at CAT pass a unit as still serviceable. Peace corresponds to 'ruliness'. Love seemed to bother him more – he kept looking at me as if about to leap the gap, but then put up a block. Some bother about 'Mercy has a human heart', & c. Old problem: which are 'humans', Oitarians or us? He was recycling it in his own mind into 'Mercy has a beastly pump', and 'Love, the beastly corpse . . .' But 'divine' stopped him, because it is an attribute of Wheel or Rule & he has some taboo about bringing it into conjunction with beast.

Changed tack to nature poetry, wh (as D. has told me) goes much more fluently. O. heavily resisted subjective verse (got nowhere wth Keats) but relaxed into 18th-century descriptive poetry. I found he's read a lot already, & he recited at me passages from James Thomson's 'Seasons', including his invocation to the Sun:

> *'Tis by thy secret, strong, attractive force,*
> *As with a chain indissoluble bound,*
> *Thy systems roll entire; from the far bourn*
> *Of utmost Saturn, wheeling wide his round*
> *Of thirty years . . .*

And then he jumped to a bit wh he sd was 'worthy of the School of Melodious Colour':

ZONE OF EDEN

At thee the Ruby lights its deepening glow,
And with a waving radiance inward flames.
From thee the Sapphire, solid ether, takes
Its hue cerulean; and, of evening tinct,
The purple-streaming Amethyst is thine ...

When he came to 'A trembling variance of revolving hues' he seemed both tranced & somehow vulnerable, so that I reached out & touched his robe. He said that Thomson was too great a poet to be a beastly mortal, & that he must have been 'of the seed of Hō Mā'.

I tried him with Addison's hymn:

The spacious firmament on high,
With all the blue ethereal sky,
And spangled heavens, a shining frame,
Their great Original proclaim.
Th' unwearied Sun from day to day
Does his Creator's power display ...

When I got to the end of the second verse –

And all the planets in their turn,
Confirm the tidings as they roll,
And spread the truth from pole to pole ...

– he jumped up, as if compelled to do his ritual obeisances to the sun. He declared the poem to be 'groovy', meaning running-in-the-grooves-of-Rule. He insisted upon memorising whole poem at once, wh he did almost instantly, declaiming 'dark terrestrial ball' and 'radiant orbs' in his light baritone, and looking at me with shining eyes.

I wld have been wise to have left it there, since I'd got enough to start plotting a response-profile, with null areas (mercy) & some v strong signals (colour, cyclical form, obedience, divinity). But he was so warm & somehow dislodged from his distanced

341

rationality that I tried to probe the haze wh hangs around his evasive identity – that is, the I-personal as distinct from the I-role-kit. So I got out Donne, & like a fool read the 'The Sunne Rising'. Effect was catastrophic. At very first line – 'Busie old foole, unruly Sunne ...' – his face contorted with pain. The coupling of 'sun' & 'unruly' must be a direct blasphemy. All the vitality & warmth seemed to drain out of him. (For a moment he may have been in a faint.) Like a fool I pressed on. It was awful reading into his hostile vibes. I finally got to the end:

> Shine here to us, and thou art every where;
> This bed thy center is, these walls, thy spheare.

I could sense that he was restraining himself. Two months ago he wld have done a sentence against its 'beastly abuses'. Now he sometimes seems to be trying to understand me as much as I try to understand him. Not just 'trading' – trying to close the gap.

So he kept his cool – a rather frigid cool – & started interrogating me about the poem. Q. 'Who is it about?' A. 'Two lovers.' Q. 'Why are they not going about loving? Why are they in bed? Are they very ill?' A. 'No. The bed is the place where they make love.' Q. 'How is love made? Is it like making a curry? Do they bring things with them to bed to mix together?' A. 'No ... this is about a man and woman making sexual love ...' Q. 'Ahh. I understand. They are making a fucking?' A. 'Yes ... no ... loving is not always fucking and some fucking is not loving ... But in this poem I suppose it's both. These are lovers who have been ... well, fucking, all night.' Q. 'Why does the poet not write that down? Why does he write in a sideways manner?' A. 'That would be too gross. He wants to suggest it but not say it. Loving is ... to do with the spirit.' Q. 'Like exchange of bio-waves with a ghost? And fucking is a spirit-thing also?' A. (Exasperated) 'Yes. And a body-thing too.'

O. reflected on this, & started quoting bits of the poem to himself (he has almost total recall):

ZONE OF EDEN

Aske for those Kings whom thou saw'st yesterday,
And thou shalt heare, All here in one bed lay.

Then (remorselessly) Q. 'And the Kings and States and Princes? They are all in the one bed and fucking too?' A. 'No! Oh ... Shall we change the subject?' Q. 'No. We shall go along the groove. I wish to understand your mortal customs. The poem is bad, with many blasphemies. But I wish to understand what is a love. It is some malady which you conceal from me. If Oitar could cure this malady then you might mend your beastly ways, and Oitar could suspend its sentence on you.' A. 'How can you suppose love to be a malady? We have a saying, "Love makes the world go round".' Q. 'That is a blasphemy. The Wheel is not a love. Your loving is a weakening of rule, it is a muddling of two role-kits. If it was only a fucking, then once the act of procreation was got over, these two would rise swiftly up again and go about their roles.' A. 'But they're *lovers*. They only want to lie in each other's arms and look at each other ... David and Rani are in love. Haven't you noticed?' Q. 'David and Rani do not make love. Every night they make a curry.' A. 'No, well, they're not actually lovers yet. But they've fallen in love.' Q. 'Ah! So love is a fall? Into a hole? Macho made Colonel Hunter fall into the cess-pool — was Hunter then in a love?' (Qy: Was he teasing me?) A. 'No, he was NOT! ... I've got it! It is "fall in" just like you do, when you fall into a trance.' Q. 'I do not fall. I appoint the channel and set the trance-timer.'

By now I was distinctly ruffled, having lost all professional control over the session. In fact, I was being grilled. O. was pondering deeply, & eventually sd that he thought I was trading honestly with him, and that the fault lay not in me but in mortal goings-on. He thought that he understood what a love was: it was some exchange of bio-vibes. But he asked why, if there are so many millions of us, we shld fall into the hole of one creature and not another? Why not into all? I diverted the question (both because I cldn't think of an answer, & because I wanted to regain role of interrogator) with Q. 'Don't you have any special vibes

343

with anyone?' O. pondered, & then allowed that he had special vibes with Macho . . . and with Tigger. Also with the late Translator. Q. 'Yes. But don't you have any human friends? In your own College?' A. 'It is an appointed netting. You would call it a "functional bonding".' He pondered again, & then added (to my surprise), 'I have a vibe with Satpathy. And sometimes with Ann and Robert and Nettler. You do not haul me about like keepers. You bond me in your nettings. I have a special vibe with you, Sage.'

I had been wishing I'd never got into this, but now I felt that my collecting was not exactly null. Some kind of affectional life is sloshing round inside him, just beyond his own reach. We went back to the house, where we walked in on D. & R. having a colossal lovers' tiff. Obviously no curry tonight. O. regarded them with amazement, & I cld see that his mouth was opening to ask some incredibly tactless question. I grabbed his arm & steered him into the kitchen, saying I wld teach him some more mortal customs, such as how to make vegetable soup and omelettes. He fell at it with a will, & never had to be shown anything twice. In fact, he might have had an auxiliary role-kit as cook. We kept bumping into each other around the sink & the cooker, but he didn't seem to mind. Nor (come to think of it) did I.

Sage Diary

June 26th. This past week has been like living in a drama school. How on earth do they conduct a personal life in places where they are *really* cooped in dense clumps like China? D. & R. having tiffs and loving reconciliations twice a day. I'm on R's side, sisterly solidarity, but if I show it she leaps to D's defence. After supper last night, when Ann stomped up her back stairs to her den, R. ran up after her. D. sulked off to the telly — official spooksmen are still trying to explain that the Channel Tunnel disaster last week must have been the work of 'terrorists' — Iraqis or perhaps Russians? – when it is plain as a pikestaff that they had been taking through insanely unstable loads of chemicals (probably nitro-glycerine!). Usual cover-up. Why do they bother with the Pretend News at all?

D., concentrating on his well-I've-done-all-I-can, long-suffering face, was obviously not watching. A. came down to make a cuppa and signalled me into the kitchen: 'You're needed upstairs.' Where I found poor R. sobbing her heart out. She and D. want to get married but she wanted to wait until they can go back to India, so that she cld be with her family. D. then persuaded her to ask for a marriage ceremony on the campus of Martagon Hall. Her parents cldn't come over, and the cousins who now control central security will only allow a US Army Chaplain to do it, & won't even allow her brother, who has a curry take-away in Dudley, to come. She won't agree to that: (a) she's not a Christian, it wld be a 'lie'; and (b) it wld be 'ugly'. So D. has told her she is unreasonable and has gone ape, trying to talk her into bed. (She didn't say this last bit, only that D. is so 'pressing' and she is afraid she will 'lose' him.)

Her parents have written to say that she can marry in England and will she send lots of photos of the 'wedding service'? The poor woman is quite screwed up, madly in love with D. and resentful of him at the same time. I wasn't much use as Consultant, since every time I started taking her part & calling D an mcp she started taking his side and saying it was only 'natural' and anyway she loved D. 'in that way' too.

A. was ignoring us, doing her stable sums ('Oats (Macho), 2 cwt'). She suddenly swung round and sd, 'But Rani, you're not a Hindu – I mean a practising one – you don't do *pujas.'* R. sniffed & agreed, but said that at such times you had to follow 'family rules'. 'And you're not a Christian either?' 'No ...' 'You don't believe in either?' 'I believe in some of it – some of both. I believe in making promises and in ceremony.' 'Well,' said A. 'Let's do it properly. Let's make a ceremony up. One that really means something. You work out the Hindu bits. Robo's a Christian, awfully straight, but he would help with that. Hel and David won't be much use, they think the world is an echo-chamber of ideas. But Oy Pee could put in some fab bits of ritual – perhaps he'll let us do it in the Temple. With Tigger. And you can go round the rose beds seven times and then come down the path, veiled and garlanded with white roses. And Mary and Brian can take the pictures for your folks . . .'

By now R. was a-swim between giggling and sobbing. I cld see A's idea was gaining on her. I sd it wasn't just play-acting. Ceremonial is a sacred inheritance, a discourse of archetypal semiotics, and we wld all be as serious about it as we cld possibly be. Eventually we went downstairs to put it to the others. D. of course jumped at it, because he thought it was such an easy let-out, wh made R. start backing away. A. made it worse by saying, 'Of course, in India the bridegroom goes to the bride's house, on the back of a horse with a band. David would look fine on the back of Macho.' D. looked aghast & A. started laughing & R. burst into tears & sd we were 'making fun on her', so we were all in the soup once more.

I started to make a speech about ceremonial and semiology and reconstructing new codes for the rites of passage & c. & c., and cld see that I'd lost my audience, when O. came down the front stairs. He'd obviously heard it all & sd we were into 'good thinking'. Then he spoke of ceremony with such solemnity and authority that R. was quite won round again (she has a strange respect for O., as a guru with mystic powers), and now it was D. who was beginning to wonder what he had been talked into.

Anyway – wedding was agreed for July 9th, two weeks from now. 'Inner wheel' to be invited (O's suggestion) and Mrs U. (R's suggestion; she wants a parental figure). Also Rbt and some of the Astrosigint crowd who held the fort. We may tell Mrs U. and the others that it is a Buddhist rite. O. seemed quite proud when we asked if we could solemnise the marriage in his bumple. R. said she wld sing one or two of Tagore's *raga*s. Then we got stuck on who wld give R. away, wh she thought important. There has to be a *kanya dan*, or giving of the bride to the bridegroom. A. said she thought the f giving the dau away was 'patriarchal' (a bit *obvious*), so I sd she shld be given away by a sister. R. agreed to that (reluctantly) and asked A. if she wld be her sister. A. went pink with pleasure, & I covered up my sense of rejection by saying wld they like me to write the ceremonial script for the service?

It was agreed (A's motion) that for the seven days before the ceremony R. & D. must not see each other. They must fast, or do *pujas* or something. A. is going to put D. up in her old pad in the stables. Then a sister (R. asked *me* this time, as if she'd noticed) will go to a *private* interview with R. and ask her if she really, *really* wants to be bonded to a horrible male, & a brother (Rbt) will likewise go to D. Messengers will then tryst by the lake, and if both answers are 'yes', then A. will lead D. on Macho to the bumple. A. sd Macho must be garlanded, with a rope of white lilac. D. will wait by the bumple door, while A. takes Macho to the dower house and brings back R., veiled, with some walking acolytes as bridesmaids. Then R. has to garland D., and he has to unveil and garland her.

Got stuck on who shld perform final ceremonial. Then O. announced (as if no other option was possible) that since the wedding was to be in his bumple he wld take it as his role and 'honour' (has he ever used that word before?) to be the 'priest' and to declaim a poem to 'twin' the pair. I glanced at R., expecting tears once more, but she was delighted, as if this was what she had been waiting for.

So – it really is going to happen! Now that the Day is named and publicly proclaimed, D. and R. have suddenly got very shy with each other. They've moved sharply back into ♂ and ♀ space. Today R. has been sitting in the kitchen, sucking a pencil & trying to remember recipes for wedding sweetmeats.

O. came into my room just now, as I was writing this. He seemed oddly uncertain of himself – I think somehow R's disturbance got through to him & he is very serious about getting his role in the ceremony right. (He *knows* the Incongruous Noise is sometimes directed at him.) He strode around & then asked me if he ought to carry a bed into his bumple. I was only half-listening, & sd the summer nights were warm, did he mean to sleep there? He said, no, but for 'performing the ceremony of wedding. For the fucking.' I scrabbled on the carpet for my pen, & explained that this was a loving & promising & blessing ceremony, but that D. & R. wld do the fucking part very much in private afterwards. He nodded and seemed relieved. More than that, he seemed to understand without long explanation. And he *had* come to ask me privately, he didn't blurt it out in front of poor R. (who wld have *died*). Is O. beginning to grow some Tact?

Mem: This reminds me. Both R. & D. have single beds in their rooms. I'll give them my double as a wedding prezzy. No chance that I shall ever need it.

Oi Paz Diary 'I'

Tomorrow there will be a *wedding* of Satpathy and Nettler, at the bumple, and Oi Paz will conduct the ceremony.

Mortal customs are so uncured and unruly that it is no easy matter to declaim these ceremonials, which are sometimes observed and sometimes not, and of which they themselves can give no certain account. For there is a whole set of forms and ceremonies which roll along together, which include the 'fucking', the 'wedding', the 'family', the 'wife', the 'husband', the 'love', the 'parent', the 'divorce' and the 'kin'.

These customs can be little observed in this keep, which is indeed a sort of College, with a programme and a set of rolls, and the family is secreted in a separate enclosure which Oi Paz does not enter. But it is now possible to declaim a little on these customs, from observations of the outer world, from readings of false newses (called 'novels') and from my interrogations of Sage.

If procreation, or fucking, results in the birth of a child, then the infant (or 'baby') is fed (or 'suckled') by the hostess, who – for several years – in a higgledy way does whatever curing is done. This hostess is called the 'mother' (or the female 'parent'), and from the habit and labour of her solitary care she comes to suppose that she 'owns' the child and has some right of 'property' over it. Nor does she readily relinquish this claim, which she sets against the natural claims of School or College or Rule. Nay, she will prolong the claim over 'her' child for eighteen or twenty of its years!

Not only this. But they suppose also that the Sper, or donor of the semen, who has done no more than inject a single fuck, has a claim over the child also! This absurdity is indeed sometimes resisted by the hostess, but the claim is very generally allowed, when the fucker is named as 'father'.

Where the claim is allowed, the mother and the father are then said to be a 'marriage'. This may best be compared with a twinship, or special and enduring bonding, albeit the twins are from different hostesses. In a marriage the hostess is known as a 'wife' and the donor as a 'husband'. The wife is said to be a 'housewife' (or one-who-is-married-to-a-house), and a 'husbandman' is one who goes out and sows seeds.

Their beastly multiplication of terms is never-ending. Not content with inventing a marriage, they needs must call a marriage with a child (or children) a 'family'.

These families keep records of all their matchings and matings, down two or three generations, and indeed pay an almost sacred regard to these arbitrary and corporeal connections. So that a 'brother' or 'sister' (or child-within-the-same-marriage) is held in more obligation and honour than a fellow-Collegian with the same roll-kit. Indeed, they even recall who the fucker's fucker was (as 'grandfather'), or the other children in a parent's marriage, describing all these variants as 'relations', or 'kin', to each of which variable they attach particular terms, as 'aunts', 'bastards', 'grannies', 'nannies', 'cousins', & c., to each of which respect is due according to degree. A pretence is even made of tracing their genes (or 'genealogy') through pre-history to primal parents, known as Adam and Eve. But this is now archaic, and a resort only of their priests, whose status has greatly fallen in recent years.

The generally accepted (and more truthful) myth now current is that the species evolved from shaggy, uncouth creatures which lurk in forests, known as 'bears', from which they refer to their 'forebears'.

The de-coding of these esoteric customs has caused Oi Paz much labour, yet these are discoveries as important as any yet made. For here, in marriage and the family, will be found the elementary ailment which undermines all Sykotic Rule. In short, the family asserts a 'private' compulsion which is ever at odds with the social rotation of things. So that on Sykaos these two forces are always at logger with each other.

It can easily be seen from the diagram below what a rupture of Rule this constantly entails. For families are serial relations, relating to other such bytes in series; hence arise horizontal strings of bonding and obligation which run directly athwart the due vertical programme-structures of hierarchy and Rule: viz.

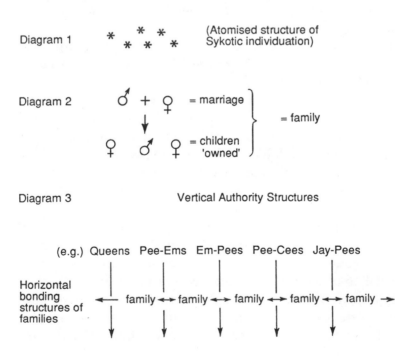

So compulsive is the family serial-string that it confuses all due ratios. For if a child be mentally uncured, and of a sub-average geneto-kit, so that in truth it merits discard, yet the mother or sister – indeed, the whole family – of this specimen defends it from any Rule and pretends that it has still some special worth or function. In this way frauds are committed daily against the Good of the Whole, discards are given protection and a general default is made against any universal standards of merit. And the absurdity is perpetuated that merit does not consist in the qualities of Service to the Wheel – according to which it is a simple matter to grade every bit in the species-string by merit and faculties, so that any parent should at once be able to know how much inferior its child is to the child of others, and readily assent to its discard – but each family sets up its own private criteria, defending the blemishes which it has introduced to the string as if they were perfections. And while philosophers have arisen among the mortals who have exposed these fallacies – as one Godwin, who laid bare the biases of private indulgence, and one Althusser, who proved that each individual or bit was no more than the bearer of the Programme – the species have rejected these sages as false profits. As a result of this, their programme is nothing but bugs and glitches.

It can be seen how these creatures are led into the illusion that their little parts are more significant than the whole. When one considers the manner of their procreation, the enclosure two-by-two into marriages, the long helplessness of the infants abandoned to the exclusive care of their parents, and the continuance over years of the family, then it may be understood that they grow into adulthood supposing that they were 'made' by two persons only (their biological parents) and not by the Social Whole. This premise is so deeply bred into them that it is ineradicable. If the Gracious Goodnesses should for some purpose wish to educate these creatures in the Rule, nothing less will suffice than abolishing the family and utterly reordering their mode of procreation.

There remain other matters to explain which Oi Paz is not

as yet ready to declaim as science. The difficulty is: according
to what laws and under the influence of which forces do
their matings or marriages take place? For the couples are not
suited by any Boards of Examiners, and they mix their genes
together licentiously without consulting any record-kits or any
Bio-Engineers.

Much must remain obscure. Simple propinquity when in time
of season would explain matings, as with chuckalls. But it could
not explain marriages. Interrogation gave confused responses.
Satpathy described a faint rule of sorts, in that the couples were
'chosen' or arranged into suits by their parents according to rules
of caste and aptitude. But Satpathy comes from a distant nation
in which the indistinct influence of our Bōd Hā (whom they
suppose to have been one of their own great law-givers) may still
be felt. Sage would tell me nothing but that the marriages were
suited by 'choice' or by 'love'. But this choice is nothing but
a putting-off the question, for choice is a word they use for
freewheeling-without-programme-outside-the-Rule.

As to what is a love, my questionings continue. It is spoken of
as if it were a catastrophe of nature, like an avalanche. Or it is
like falling in a hole. It may be a bio-vibe-twinning of a couple,
like an electro-magnetic lock-on, so that they go on to a common
programme. They are then ready to make a marriage, by a special
ceremony which they call a 'wedding'.

A wedding is a ceremony which transforms two I-programmes
into a We-programme. It is to tell the whole world and also to
promise each I to each other. It is a festal occasion, with many
flowers and aromas, music and dancing. After the wedding the
marriage is entered, and the making of a family. This continues
until the We-programme fails and the magnetic lock falls off.
Then the couple go through another ceremony known as a
'divorce', which is presided over by priests known as solicitors
and accountants. The We-programme is discarded, and they are
given back to I-programmes once more.

The ceremonial life of these mortals is so impoverished that it
is well that a few such customs endure. Tigger and I will solemnise

the wedding of Satpathy and Nettler in a syncretic service combining rites decreed by Jesus, Bōd Hā, and the Wheel. Macho will bring the couple, who will be called a 'bride' and 'bridegroom', to the door of the bumple. I will remain by the altar and Tigger will lead them into my presence. The Equerry and Sorley will attend as chief witnesses. The bride and bridegroom will then garland Tigger and present him with a bowl of cream, to propitiate the Sacred Three.

If Tigger purrs, the ceremony will continue. Satpathy will sing a sacred song and the Equerry will lead us in meditation. A lighted brazier will be set in the middle of the bumple, into which will be thrown scented woods and leaves. Satpathy and Nettler will then walk seven times around this fire, while Equerry and her acolytes throw oils into the flames and Maryphone chants a calypso. I will then rotate the Wheel three times and revolve my arms through the arcs of grace and benison. Then I must read to them some questions which Sage is still botching up, of which the last lines she gave me were: 'Will you bond with each other through thick times and thin, and share and care, and respect each other's feelings, and renounce all double-binds and ego trips?' (Upon which Satpathy is now trying to make an improvement.) If their answer is 'yes', they will then exchange golden rings (the emblem of the Wheel) and I will take a ladle of lake-water and mark it on their brows. Maryphone will then sing another holy song from the Caribbean. (The English, it seems, are atrophied in their singing-organs.)

If the day is fair, Tigger will then lead us out of the bumple to the round rose-bed, where I will address their sun and call down a blessing over the wedded couple. For which I have declaimed this poem:

Great orb, whose genial effluence
Restores the order to the rose,
In whose aromas every sense
Returns to you obedience:

Let no misrule and no offence
Interrupt the roll of those
Who enter into wedded state
That like twinned satellites they shall rotate.

This is their common programme day:
Now I plus I are rolled as we
And he and she are now a they.
O charm their chimes, drive harm away;
Let their revolutions stay
Together and harmoniously.
Return next year, return in ten —
As they roll now, so find them rolling then!

I showed these lines first to Sage and she said they were solemn and worthy but made a quibble about several. I had written 'This is their programme merger day', which she said was 'like a take-over bid' and made me change. For the last line she wanted me to write: 'As they love now, so find them loving then', but I said that I could not write that until I could construe what a 'love' was. Then she pressed my hand and thanked me and said that it was a noble poem and would make Rani very happy.

After that Tigger will lead us to our coop, where he will join us in a festal time. But since they will drug themselves with alcohols, Oi Paz will retire early to his room.

Sage Diary

July 10th. Wedding could not have gone off better. Everyone performed their roles to perfection, except the acolytes, who giggled once or twice. Rani looked beautiful, and wore a lovely gold amulet which Oipas gave to her in hospital. When she sang the Tagore *raga* I confess I was wet-eyed. The *saphta badi* bit, when they went seven times around the fire, was very effective, even though R. had sentimentalised some of my lines. O. was invested with ceremonial charisma, and when he declaimed his poem the sun suddenly answered by breaking from the clouds and sending slanting rays on to the lake. The sweetmeats were out of this world and even Rbt had a drink or two.

But an awful thing happened today. Terrible for O., that is, and some of his terror rubbed off on me. Poor fat Tigger died. He had done his role superbly, walking ahead up the aisle with his fluffy tail high in the air, purring like a vibrator when he was garlanded with catnip, and afterwards leading us out – extraordinary! Just as if O. really could communicate signals to him. Then about 10 this morning I heard a sort of keening, and went out to find O. standing mourning over the corpse of Tigger, who was stretched rigid on the conservatory steps with glazed eyes and what looked like mincemeat dribbling from his mouth.

I thought it was his inwards, but in fact it *was* mincemeat. The wedding feast went on so late last night that we never tidied away, & Tigger (who was already full of cream) got into the room & the beastly creature must have eaten all night – spicy mince-balls & kebabs & syllabubs & oyster pâté & prawns & smoked salmon & fishy twirly things on toothpicks. Ann says it was a heart-attack but I think the beast was choked from its own dilated tum.

But O. was inconsolable. Said he had been in his room & felt Tigger's vibes 'crying to him' – and then they 'just went out'. He tried to massage the beast back to life. Is it possible he has never directly encountered death before? What happens when cats come to their dead-line on Oitar? Do chuckalls drag their corpses privily away?

I took his arm and walked him round the rose-beds. Told him that if he wld go & sit down I wld bury the poor thing. He looked at me quite wildly. What was 'bury'? Wld I put his friend in the earth? It reminded me of trying to explain to Marianne, my niece, when she was four, about her dead hamster.

I was quite fazed. No one else about – R. and D. hadn't stirred from their bed. Then Ann came back and took the situation in at once. She said she'd better tell Mrs U. – who took it surprisingly well. She said that Tigger had 'always been very sensitive, and the excitement of that beautiful wedding was too much for him'. A. then took charge and said we wld burn Tigger in an apple-box on a funeral pyre & the lake wld be the Ganges. So in the afternoon we had *another* ceremony (not letting on to D. & R. in case they thought it was an omen). Just A. and Adonis (who had helped her build the pyre), O. and me, and Rbt who happened to drive up just then. I read a bit of the burial service and I saw tears in O's eyes when I came to 'ashes and dust'. (Definitely a first.)

Then a funny thing happened. The wood was damp and the pyre gave off clouds of smoke before it really caught. Then, just as the flames were leaping round the apple-box, *the ghost of Tigger* seemed to walk out of the smoke! Of course, it wasn't a ghost but the stables tabby-cat, which for some reason had been snooping around, hidden behind the smoke. (Don't know what it was doing here – it's never been this way before. *Qy:* Did A. put it up to it?) O. was ecstatic. He threw open his arms in an arc of praise to the sun and shouted, 'Now Tigger has returned to the cycle of the Wheel and is re-born. His programme is appointed to another.' At which he and aforesaid tabby went off to communicate vibes in the bumple.

Only 10 p.m. but I feel quite drained, too tired to sleep. Wedding was nice, but this play-acting is getting hollow. Rbt muttered something about signals traffic on moon getting very heavy & not liking what the Cousins are up to. But he's always like that these days, he never gives a straight report & goes around with furrowed brow. Also, now the wedding's over the house is smaller. Only saw R. & D. when they popped down in wraps to get a drink. Not a good idea to live in someone else's honeymoon cottage. The next week or so O. and I had better make ourselves scarce, with picnics in the Secret Garden.

Have now been over a year in this coop. Seems like a hundred yrs. I'm certainly ten years older. No one cares what we are doing any more. Mary Phone says Pepper's never here.

Sage Diary

July 19th. I cld kick myself for a spoilsport, but I really really don't know about marriage. The couple's togetherness excludes all others. Mutual ego massage. A sort of gauze net has come down between R. and D. and the rest of the world. Suppose it happens with lovers anyway, but marriage is more self-righteous and absolute. Wedding was now ten days ago but it will be weeks before I can get back into comradely working sessions with D., and then he will only be half there. (D. has stopped his sessions with O. altogether.) And all my sisterly vibes with R. are going faint or being shut off.

Why does loving and coupling put up boundaries against Others?

O. and I spend a lot of time in the Secret Garden now, or walking by the lake. Ann is v busy, breaking a colt. Rbt has got a new set of dishes into operation. I call the Astrosigint station his 'bumple'.

Have worked some more with O. on poetry; also traded myths. (He is convinced that ancient Oitarian astronauts – Bōd Hā, Krish Nā, In Kā, Droo Id – colonised Planet Earth in year dot, & are root of all our archaic myths. Silly. But it means we can trade myths, which have some strange congruent features. P.S. Bōd Hā & co also brought cats to Earth, which explains his obsessional relations.) Not much of it makes sense any more. I also tried working on concepts like 'choice', 'chance' and 'free will', but encountered ferocious blocks. Must transcribe the tapes and work on them.

Heigh-ho. But the Secret Garden is quite fabulous now – one corner is full of old-fashioned tea- and briar-roses – and, when we don't get on to identity or choice themes, O. is more relaxed and 'human' than I've known him – almost tender.

I wish he wldn't strip off in the sun though. He's really beautiful to look at but it turns me on and also bumps against my taboos.

Sage Diary

July 23rd. Thundery & muggy. Been stuck indoors for two days. I ought to transcribe that bumpy exchange last week on choice & c.

We were on the bench by the lake, just beyond the Temple of Music. I was trying to get him to say more about the Wheel & who does the programming. He was so smug about how the Wheel 'appointed' this and 'cycled' through that that I broke in a little crossly to ask whether no one ever objected. Didn't they ever want to be free to make their own choices?

He sensed my impatience – well, of course he did, he picks up every vibe (which is why I *have* to keep a professional cool) – and his fluent trading manner froze into a sort of watchfulness.

O. 'What is a free? What is to choice? These words always choked the Translator. They are not human concepts, they are mortal ones. They belong to disorder and wrack outside the Rule.'

H. 'But someone must choose ... Surely there must be a programmer?'

O. 'What is the choice for this lake? The waters cannot run this way or that way. They cannot go up into the air. They must lie quietly where they are. To be free is to lie under law.'

H. 'But the fish may swim this way or that way ...'

O. 'And the little fish may be eaten by bigger fishes. That is a great free. But how is it free for a fish to swim in the sky? It has no wings.'

H. 'People aren't water or fish, not on Oitar nor on Earth. They make their own culture. So they must make their own programmes, surely. They are free to make choices.'

Silence.

H. 'Well? Don't you agree?'

O. 'Oh, yes, Sage, there are many choices in the head. People are free to swim in the sky. Shall we try?' He made a great show of flapping his robes, as if mocking me. 'It is not in our programme. If it was, I would choose to fly to the moon.'

H. 'Or you might choose to stay here, on the good Earth. You would be free to make a choice.'

He was silent again, as if that puzzled him. The lake seemed incredibly peaceful: a heron was fishing in the rushes a hundred yards away, and a mother mallard led her downy ducklings out on an expedition. There were little rings where the trout were rising. I could not think how anyone could choose to leave this Earth. Then the heron struck with its long bill & came up with a struggling flash of silver. I kicked myself for the usual anthropomorphic pathetic fallacies. No doubt the lake was seething with predators & prey, with terrors & lusts. What was nature's programme but that life must prey on life? And what was any experience – the seeming peace of this evening lake – if it was only a blip passing across the screen of a mind programmed to die?

I was so abstracted that I was startled to hear Oipas speaking. 'And when we have both gone, with whom will the serene waters of the lake reflect the shadows in the cold?' I recognised a line from one of Ann's Zen books. It was as if O. had been listening to my thoughts, and he went on, 'You mortals are too much prisoners of the corpse. Your minds are trapped in time. Then you excuse yourselves and call your programmes "Nature" or "God" or "Law". Yet you still wish to pretend to being in a state of "free".'

H. 'But in our own mortal affairs – social or personal – we have a choice between possibilities. We can even make up new programmes ...'

O. 'Who is a "we"? How do you get a "we" to do a choice?' He looked at me, almost ironically, and flapped his robes again. 'Sage, for many months you have talked about your freedoms and your choice. You mortals are very important about your little bits of freewheel.' More flapping of robes, definitely sarcastic this time. 'You suppose that you are a very special species, each one of you a special, and your little freewheel you call a free-will. You pretend that billions of egos are tumbling about in free-wills. I do not choke like the Translator. I watch your reasonings.

You sit from a great height on Oipas, you suppose that humans on Oitar are like robots because we obey our assigned flow-chart and roll along the groove . . .'

I tried to calm him, but my disclaimer was interrupted by immensely vigorous flapping of robes, which sent the startled heron into the air, trailing its legs in the water in an unwieldy take-off. I thought that if Oipas flapped any harder he might take off like the heron. Clearly the concept of freedom was seething inside him.

O. 'On Oitar there is ordering of all. It is clear. Each programme-change is in the daily print-out. A space is left for each freewheel. You mortals live without the Rule, in promiscuous disorder, without assigned times or designated days. Yet on Earth there is programming also. But the programmers are hidden and the programmes are secret. Your lives are a great play in which you pretend there are none.'

H. 'Are you saying that there is one programme, for all the Earth. Or for each nation? What about individual persons?'

O. 'On Earth the great programme is Property and Money. I have studied this, it is declaimed as science in my notebooks. Are you, Sage, free to have all the property and money you want . . .?'

H. 'No, but . . .'

O. 'No, it is programmed. From the tank . . . from birth. Some few have much property, most of the many have none. Those who have property also have power. There is not one single "we". There are multitudes of egos, all in a higgledy disorder. But beneath that there are programmes which hold property and power together.'

H. 'But in politics there is some choosing of programmes – at least in democracies. There are parties and elections . . .'

O. 'And a lot of play. Let us think that Sage has a ruly programme: to clean up the Earth, to ban acids from the sky, to make property more common, to rid the roads of cars. How will she be free to choose this? Will the newses and the tee-vee proclaim her programme because it is rational? No, the plugs are only one-way. All that they plug is the programme of property and power. The election is polled before it is voted. What is beastly history? It is war after war, millions upon millions of dead-lines. Did the dead choose this? How were they free? It is the same with your blocks and your nukes. Your species will end itself in nuclear war. Soon. It will not be your choice ... or anyone's. It will be the programme.'

H. 'Some of that's true. Oh hell, I know it is. But it's still possible to change the programme – we can act to change our own culture.'

O. 'And what is your "culture" but your programme? What can you change it with, except your programme? Your uncured language closes your mind like a room without windows. You suppose your culture to be full of choices and of frees. But I, as a human, can see it as it is, and most of it is Sykotic bosh. You live inside your little darkroom of Sykotic words and pretend your thoughts are limitless.'

I felt as if I was tangled in one of those hopeless, recessive arguments about determinism with a post-Marxist French structuralist, and I tried (fruitlessly) to steer the discussion back to Oitar.

H. 'You are saying that both Earth and Oitar are subject to programme in much the same way – I mean, both societies?'

O. 'I am not saying any so. Don't put your sayings into my words, Sage, I sentence you. On Oitar the programme is clear. It is known. Any change is declaimed in the bumples. The spaces for freewheel are known. But, more than that, all of us take part in programming or what you call "choosing". We make daily input in our colleges, and the college makes input to the Wheel. All inputs go into the common scrambler. Where is your common scrambler? How can you make data-input, Sage? While you flap about and pretend to be free' – more flapping – 'you are like robots at the end of plugs. You don't even know the programme which is running you. In your dark minds you are tossed about by compulsions which you call "accident" or "chance" or even mistake for your own "choice" ...'

By now I was quite angry and my discipline was slipping. But I gritted my teeth and agreed that mortals had a long way to go before they freed themselves from some kinds of determinism. 'Yes, like property, and money, and power, and the corpse, and time, and gender,' interjected O., which made me crosser. I flashed back that in our personal and interpersonal relations we are much freer than Oitarians, who are born with a role-kit, allocated to a college, and can't even choose their partners. O. flashed back (we were actually on the edge of a row) that mortals had genetic role-kits too, and they spent their lives trying to find them, while pretending that they were 'free'. 'And all you mortals are programmed by sexuality, which cycles your moods around. How is that free? And you, Sage, where is your partner? How will you make a free choice of one? You have told me that everything is determined by gender' – it's true, we talked about this weeks ago, and he forgets nothing – 'and that your culture is programmed by males. That is not so on Oitar. All inputs are equal.'

I gave up. I wasn't even sure that I cld answer him. A culture *can* be seen as a programme. The evening sun was on the lake and we sat in silence for a while, watching the rings where the fish were rising. I cld sense his vibes becoming calmer; and my own. Then a trout made a huge leap out of the water, and O. touched my hand & seemed almost to smile. 'Look, a fish that swims in the air!'

Neither of us had anything more to say, and we were so still that the heron settled back on the shore.

Suddenly O. got up and shed his robes. 'Come on, Sage, we are going to swim. We will worship in the water.' 'But I haven't got my bathing things.' 'What things are needed for a swimming? Now which of us is free? Your programme is bugged by a bosh about sex. In the colleges we all bathe together in the well.' I had to show that mortals are free, so I stripped off and joined him. It was a beautiful swim, out to the little island and back. I have never known him so physical.

Oi Paz Diary 'I'

Now that Satpathy and Nettler are a marriage their vibes are turned in upon each other in a bio-lock. And at the same time I have found in Sage unusual vibratory disturbances. Her vibes have never been translucent as the others. The vibes of Satpathy are gentle and aromatic; of Sorley direct and warm; of the Equerry direct, but intermittent; of Pepper absent, as if inward-regarding; of Hunter they were like a calculus, and of Mayhem, acid and corrosive. But the vibes of Sage have been, not hostile, but distanced, like a sun behind white clouds. It is as if she has learned to cure her own vibes, and cool them between their source and their arrival. They have carried a suggestion of programme-accord (or, as they call it, 'friendship'), yet as if filtered through controls.

Since spring first sprang, and then since the wedding, Sage's vibes have been in a cyclone, as if about to break from behind their white cloud, sparkling now like hot rays upon my sensors, now withdrawing into a chill of distance. And as my sensors detect this disturbance, so my own vibes open and close like valves, and my corpse also quickens in its pump and corporeal senses as if it were a mortal body.

Sage has asked me to call her 'Helena', which is her 'given name' and not her genetonym, and which she says is the custom between those whose programmes are congruent, or friends. I readily agreed to this, at which she asked if I did not also have a private or given name, for Oi Paz was not personal but a category, like a Volvo (which is a species of car). I explained that Oi Paz was indeed an acronymic shortening of my proper registration code with the College of Bio-Engineering. And while Oi Paz indicated my genetic code and roll-kit, my full name of registration was Oi 57/2D Sper P 9 P/Astr (Gard) 3383/2/68, by which she might call me as a private name if she wished. At which her vibes chilled and she gave a no-sense answer that 'Thanks, she would always know where to find me in Files'.

We go each day to a garden with an old wall about it, where

363

we trade sciences and eat a lunch which (when it is carried without doors) is called a 'pick-nick'. There are many old and noble fruit trees here, of rare varieties well worthy of our curing. We lie on a bank of grass amidst this disorderly profusion. At its zenith the sun's heat is many degrees above the regulated norms of our bumples and Alls, so that the wearing of robes is superfluous and even occasions corporeal discomfort. I have several times thrown my robes off and proposed to Helena that she should do the same. Which for no reason induced a new cyclonic disturbance in her vibes. For she did not disrobe, but said that perhaps it was time for us to be going back (which was a blemish upon the truth). And then she said that perhaps we should not come here so often, to which I replied that it was a harmonious garden and that it might have been programmed for our purposes, and for the exchange of knowledges of customs. To which she answered that she had already taught me all that she could of the customs of the Earth, and perhaps more than she should.

She then stood up and brushed the grass from her robe, and said that in future we must bring 'Rani' or 'David' with us (which are the private names of Satpathy and Nettler) on our sessions. Her reason was in a turbulent botch, for she pointed to an old tree with huge jade leaves beneath which we had been sitting, of a species known as 'fig', and said, 'At least we can sew up some leaves, if it comes to that!' With which no-sense she turned away as if in an alien state, although her vibes fell upon my sensors like a fire.

Oi Paz Diary 'I'

There have been this week thunders and electric discharges and many rains, which have kept us in the coop. But this day being auspicious and the sky azure I informed Helena that I would aid her in preparing a pick-nick for the Wall Garden, to which she agreed if Rani and David would attend on us also, which they also agreed, and all was programmed. So I went with Helena and

Rani to operate the kitchen. But David then came in and said that Adonis had found the key to the boathouse, in which was a rowboat, so I ordered that we make a programme discard and instead go together for a Worship on the Water. But David said the boat was too small for four and that he and Rani would row out alone together. To which Rani replied, 'Oh, David, but we've promised Helena . . .'

David then acted what they call a *sulk* and said, 'Oh well, if you don't want to. You go with them to the Garden, Rani. I'll stay and work on my notes,' which notes he has not to my knowledge passed under observation for a month or more. At which he went into the conservatory, where he sat polishing his glasses but with no notes. So Rani botched her buttering and gave out watery vibes, and then went into the conservatory where after a few minutes I saw them putting their mouths on each other's, or kissing, and then Rani came back and said, 'Do you mind, Helena? I think I'll stay with David, it would be fun to go rowing.' And Helena said, 'So it's settled, then? I suppose it was determined in the stars. Ann would call it *karma*.' To which Rani asked for an explanation, but Helena gave none, but turned to me with a vibe which I could not construe, being mixed of highs and lows, and with something added like an alert-signal she said, 'Let's go.'

We walked about the garden and admired the roses, as well as other flowers not known to Oitar, such as 'peonies' and 'lupins', of bold and vibrant colours. I exclaimed to her, as I have often done before, at the hospitable harmonies and orderings of this planet, so greatly superior to the goings-on of her inferior species. And I cited to her examples: as the circulation of winds and waters, which performed all the work of irrigation; as the cycle of death and rebirth of the vegetation, each generation nourished by the former. I told her that on Oitar no flowers would germinate, if it were not for the butlers appointed by the College of gardeners who must go about ceaselessly with little brushes, mixing their pollens. Whereas on Sykaos are appointed a special species of small flying servitors, which they call 'bees', which busily perform these duties from dawn until dusk, whose hairy legs and bottoms serve for brushes as they fly in delight from one expectant flower to the next. And, surely (I asked her), it is beyond any parameter of reason to suppose that all this takes place as a hap or, in her terms, as a random series of 'accidents'? 'Why do you conceal from me that there are Gracious Goodnesses here, as on Oitar, who programme all these things?'

To this she answered little, except that there were no Gracious Goodnesses on Sykaos and that nature was 'self-programmed' and subject to the determination of its own laws. Nor were all these laws benign, for there had been great disasters and extinctions of species on Earth, and no doubt more would follow. And, anyway, the bees were not appointed, but were in search of honey. At which she looked at me again with that high/low vibe.

We had now come to the orchard, where she sat upon a bank and took her notebook and recorder from her basket. I got ready my recorder also, and commenced to disrobe – the sun being at its zenith – but she called me to sit down. 'Oi Paz, we must *work*. For the night cometh.' I said there were many hours yet to night, to which she replied, as if abstracted in her own thoughts, 'And yonder all before us lie/Deserts of vast eternity,' although I could see only the small white clouds in the azure sky and, nearer by, the melodious flowers nodding against the red brick wall. 'I want to check back on some old notes,' she said, ruffling back through the pages of her notebook. 'College ceremonials ... rites of passage ... festal days. Does every College have a festal day?'

'Yes, every College. And each Orb. There are two great festal degrees (or "weeks") shared by the whole of Oitar. Some Colleges also have two days, and the Gardeners have four.'

'Mmmm. But there are lots of Colleges. You must have many festal days?'

'Very many days. They are in the Calendar of the Wheel.'

'It must take up a lot of time. How do you get through all your other business?'

'How can time be taken? Time is always present. Worship and ceremonial are the greatest businesses.'

'Who chooses the festal days?'

'What is a choose?'

'Who decides which days shall be festal?'

'The days are appointed by the Wheel. And the sun gives a signal by rising at an appointed place and time.'

'So the festivities start at dawn . . .?'

'Always. At the dawn we are ready for the sun with music and dancing.'

'And does every College join in? Do you take part in the days of other Colleges?'

'No. But always we send ambassadors. They will go, perhaps drawn on sledges, with gifts.'

'Tell me about the gifts.'

'They are according to the skills of each College. As gems, or crystals, poems, or musics. They are for conversations of ceremony.'

'Conversations?'

'What you call "conversations" are always voices and noises. But there are other conversations. I had conversations with Tigger in silent vibes. With horses you can vibe also. Even mortals have vibes. There are conversations with scents and aromas, and in music, which you call a "concert". But your concerts are only one-way. We perform it as an intercourse. The ambassadors play some bars of music, invented for the occasion, and then the Collegians invent a reply. Worshipping upon the water is a conversation, but it is addressed to the Wheel. You would call it a "prayer". And dance, also, is a conversation, an intercourse.'

'Tell me about dancing. Do the dancers hold each other and pass each other from hand to hand?'

'There is no touching. The art of dancing is this: to keep an exact distance always. Each in the group weaves in and out of the others, and so they make a netting, or pattern. A dancer who is a toucher will be a discard.'

367

'Tell me about touching.'

'We do not touch.'

'Why?'

'It is a settled thing. It is a custom. There is no "why". You do not spit into others. Rani will not use her left hand when she is making a curry. I have noticed. To touch is a great discourtesy. It must be absolved by water.'

'You surprise me every day. You notice a lot. We call such customs "taboos". But taboos often have a reason. What is the reason for not touching?'

'It is tabooed in our programme . . . but I will trade honestly with you, Helena. We poets are licensed to freewheel through much archaic writing. I found an early fragment once, which recorded a great contagion, a plague. The sciences of sarcology were little known, and many came to a dead-line. Those who were Goodnesses forbade all touching. Now it is in our programme.'

'But you must touch sometimes. You must bump into each other by accid . . . by hap. Does it feel ugly or foul?'

'It is a discourtesy to be absolved by water.'

'But what about your own feelings?'

'It is a blemish before the Rule . . . Helena, we are here in a culture-block. You will always talk and ask me about "feeling" this or that. What is a "feel"?'

'Oh, you must *know*! You have five senses like the rest of us. Six, with your vibe-sensors. You see, you smell, you hear. The senses send messages which get all mixed up inside you, in your inner feelings. So you feel . . . disgusted or happy or afraid.'

'The corpse, or "body" as you call it, is an external organ, performing the programme of the brain. If it had a brain – or a "feeling" – of its own, then there would be a mis-match and we would break in two.'

'But what about dance? That is the body in display. What about your conversations in scents and in music? These are carried by the senses to the feelings.'

'The corporeal sense-receptors send their messages to the aesthetic organs, which sort these messages, detect blemishes and
award merits. How could mere sensors do that? You talk as if the
corpse could compute its own data-input. The "body" cannot
have a programme of its own!'

'Oh, but it does, Oi Paz, it does!'

She looked directly into my eyes, and my sensors received her
vibes again like fire with flakes of ice. Then she said, 'You spoke
of a culture-block. But the block is not only between our two
species-cultures. I think that the block is also within you. I think
you are *full* of feelings. I think they are swilling around inside
you like milk in a churn. But you aren't in touch with your own
feelings. You don't even have *names* for your own feelings. Your
culture has set up blocks at every point to deny your own sensual
existence. You have been cured from birth – from the tank – to
suppose that you are a computer – well, a very complex computer,
with a programme which permits freewheel – and that your
senses are like terminals for data-ingestion. As if your body was
a sort of keyboard. You think of the corpse as something apart
from you. But it *is* you, just as much as that sorting-office you
call your brain is you. Look at me! You are as much a sensual
creature, as much beast, as I!'

I rose and commenced to deliver a heavy sentence on her,
when her vibes burned so fiercely on my sensors that I was at the
rim of faint, so that I settled on the grass once more. Then I said,
'Helena, you have blasphemed against my species and the Wheel.
Yet not all your words are bosh. My species-nature has taken a
Sykotic taint. I have known in the past months changes coming
upon me.'

She took my hand, and I did not withdraw. 'How about
touching?' she asked. 'Have you lost that taboo?'

'Touching is a gross corporeal insultment. Helena, after my
landfall there were bestial intrusions upon my corpse. Oi Paz was
killed to the edge of a dead-line by a motor-car. Then he was
pushed and pulled around by nurses and blown upon by doctors,
seized by the limbs by pee-cees, hauled around like a luggage,

369

hugged by Harmer, pushed about in studios and aeroplanes. That is why he took that drug, that whisky, to make his sensors null. Oi Paz was a net of miseries.'

She pressed my hand again. 'Miseries is a feeling, an I-feeling. Of course you are full of we-feelings. David and I have worked through that. But you know them as compulsions, or programmes. And you have I-feelings too, all the time, without names. Or you sublimate them as aesthetics. You are learning to know your feelings now because you are learning to name them. I have seen you touching often. Look, we are holding hands! Is that so awful?'

'It is not an awful. It is a form of vibal-transfer. Your hand sends good messages to the pump and to the aesthetic organs also. It is a changing going on in Oi Paz, and if I were before an Adjuster I would be for discard. Yes, Helena, the taboo has almost gone. And now I have been wondering, what is a kissing and what is it for?'

'But David and Rani are always kissing. In the kitchen, in the garden, in the conservatory. You must have seen them.'

'Yes. They squeeze their corpses at each other, put their mouths upon each other's, and shut their eyes. But what is it that they suck. Is it some drug?'

'They kiss because they are lovers ... well ... oh ... it is an exchange of tenderness, a sort of body-vibe, much closer than a mental vibe ... a mind and body flow ...'

'Like a flow-chart? They exchange data through pressing on their mouths?'

'Oh, no! Not data, well, not *that* kind of data ...'

'Helena, your answers make more mysteries. You are not trading fairly. There is a way to answer me which you will answer now. You will show me what is a kissing. You will do a kissing with me now.'

Her vibes twisted on my sensors, revolving through ice and fire, which seemed to pass into my body also. She rose abruptly and said it was time to go or 'something silly might happen'. Her face was in a flush of risen blood. Then swiftly the blood seemed to fall out of her cheeks, leaving them set against her dark hair like snow set against the furrows of the earth.

I followed her gaze and saw that it fell upon a long, thin creature, finely designed and mottled, which was lying along the bough of the ancient apple-tree above us, and which, even now, lifted the bulb of its head and opened its jaws, so that we could see the flickering of its tongue. And as she gazed upon it she seemed to tremble. She said it was a 'snake' known as a 'viper', whose bite injects a poison. I said if this was so, should we not move away?

She turned to me as if she had forgotten my presence; or, rather, as if I were not Oi Paz but some other half-known presence, encountered only in dream. 'We cannot move away because this is our *karma*. It is our common programme. We have no choice but to stay until the whole act is performed.'

Then she lifted her head as if she were acting some part from memory, and plucked a red apple from the branch on which the serpent lay. This she gave to me, telling me to bite, and it would give me knowledge of all mortal customs. When I had done this, she took the apple lightly from my fingers, and bit in the place next to mine. And as she threw the apple to the ground, the snake uncoiled itself from the bough and slid quietly down into the grass, as if it had accomplished all that it had come to do.

'Now we will undress,' she said, 'and then we will do a kissing.' As her robes fell to the grass at her feet her harmonious nakedness displayed itself before me. I drew her to me with an arm about her shoulder as she lifted her face for the kissing, and she trembled as if she had been left outside a cupola and was walking in a region of unburned ice.

As she trembled, the trembling entered my own fingers and thence to my wrist and my upper arm, and thence it struck into my blood and ascended to my pump. With her hands about my head, she pulled my mouth down on to hers and, as our lips touched, my strength was lost in my legs and my ears pounded with the pumping of blood. And the body asserted the compulsion of its own programme. And thus, on the grass beneath the tree, the act of procreation was performed. .

Sage Diary

Oh no! Hush – how can I have let this happen? Did I? Did he? Were we happened?

Our bodies must have been watching each other for ages. It's as if they leapt on each other without waiting to consult our wills. Programmed.

Now, Dr Sage, FRAI, how do you cope with *this*?*

Cutting. File 'Sykotic Trash'. Manuscript annotation: 'Guardian editorial'

... The incident which sparked the crisis – the general strike and riots in the Emirate of Quotar – was 'accidental'. No doubt several Soviet and Western agencies have been stirring the pot. But the insurrection came from ill-housed, underpaid immigrant labour in the oil-fields and was led by Islamic fundamentalist agitators.

Yet within 24 hours the future of the globe was at stake. The issues were the control of the Gulf and access to its oil, and President Forsst's ultimatum to the Soviet Union to 'return Quotar to the Free World' brought the world closer to the brink of nuclear war than at any time since the Cuba crisis. Once again we have to thank the Soviet leadership for backing off at the 11th hour and giving up their unexpected prize. Yet we must now expect a long and sour aftermath in Soviet/Western relations. The humiliation can only strengthen the knot of Greater Slav nationalist officers who engineered

---

* *Some pages have been torn out here, and there is an unexplained hiatus in this notebook for nearly two Earth years.*

372

Marshal Oblomov's coup. Already Gorbachev's nominees are being removed wholesale from public office. Indeed, we are now in the icy grip of a new Cold War.

Oi Paz Diary 'I'

Helena and I have been rowing the boat at Worship on the Water. But not all the waters of the lake would absolve the touchings, lovings, embracings and kissings of the last thirty days. It is as if Oi Paz and Helena are in a bio-lock.

All last week the newses were full of talk of 'crisis' and threats of nuclear war between the 'blocks'. I do not know if the nations are acting some play or if they have set off a terminal programme, as one day they will. When I asked Helena she only said, 'There is nothing we can do, except love one other.' Yesterday evening I sat in the portico of the Flora Bumple, watching the quiet waters of the lake in which the fishes rose to kiss the surface, making little rings, and I thought about water, and Helena, and rings, and nuclear war, until a poem came unbidden into my mind.

Oi Paz Diary 'I'

Last night as we lay in bed together in the moonlight (for she now comes every night into my bed) I declaimed to Helena the poem, offering it to her as a gift:

> Whatever's mortal is athwart the Rule,
> At odds with time, abusing quantity,
> Voided of programme, regulationless,
> Save only their machines for making death:
> Here all is due and ceremonious,
> Predicted and computed to an end –
> Serene parabolas bisect the skies,
> And worshipping beneath the great ballistic arch

All mortals wait in expectation for
The perfect trajectories of nuclear war . . .

She had grown tense in my arms and asked me to stop. 'This isn't a love poem at all. It's cruel and inhuman and . . . cold.' I explained that coldness might be a quality of great beauty, when set into its proper conjuncture according to the rules of prosody, for the work of a poet was to refine sense-data into their hardest, most translucent, ornamental, incorporeal, pure and neuter forms. For this reason my poem, especially in the later stanzas which alluded to her, was imperfect.

I explained that she should seek to free herself from narrow species-centric preconceptions, and to take a more universal view of things. From which standpoint there need be nothing 'cruel' in contemplating the extinction of her species in a nuclear war, but only satisfaction at an act of proportion. For they were a programmeless species directed to no end; they lacked a due submission to ruliness or measure; they were wasting and despoiling the planet's resources. As they lived outside the Rule of the Wheel, so the Wheel would continue in its Rule when they were gone. If the species were extinguished it would only bring to a term their misery of programmelessness which they called choice. And as they had achieved excellence in one thing only, the mechanical and physical sciences, which they had done not by their own merit but by following the programmes already inscribed in matter, so it would be justice if the species were to be destroyed in the discovery.

'*I* am one of the species,' she said. 'You would welcome also the extinction of me?' I handed down a light sentence on her ego-centricity, for she must see how small a bit she was within a species-string, and it was but to bring forward her dead-line by a little space. But I went on to expound the matters which I have studied during my captivities. If the mortals were to come to a species-dead-line in a great nuclear war, there were difficulties to be considered of a very serious order, such as the raising of the

374

threshold of background radiation many degrees higher than was tolerable for human existence.

To this she made no reply, until suddenly she exclaimed 'Cold fish!' As I looked around to see the cause of her exclamations (although I could see no such creature in the room) she brought her foot up sharply against my shin, whether by accident or design I could not construe, which occasioned me some moments of corporeal confusion. She then turned away from me, but I could sense her vibes crying to me, so I knew – or, as they say, 'felt' – a disturbance in my own vibes. And I sought to return her feelings to harmony by declaiming some more verses from my poem:

> An alien in this world, I turned my eyes
> To rest them on the tri-form clover
> Or on the whorl of rose and peony –
> Until they focused on your unrobed carcase.
> Your shoulders rhymed like a pure syllogism:
> A mason might have measured out your limbs
> And brought each buttock into an equation.
> Each nostril opens like a well-formed vowel,
> Each breast makes logic with the other;
> Your nipples lift themselves like theorems;
> Your thighs move in a fugue, while up above
> Your pubic mat is like a lawn of tundra,
> Shading the cavity of procreation.
> In your white abdomen there is a ring
> As symbol of the Wheel's Unhappening.
> Amongst these mortal ratios, my eyes
> Refresh themselves upon your artless artifice.

When I concluded she said she found it very queer poetry, but it was better than much that was written. And while the poem listed some parts of her body which were not customarily thought poetic, she thought this was a silly taboo, since these were parts of her as much as any others. And she thanked me for my gift and we went into a kissing.

'But,' she continued, 'there's one word in your poem which you must change, if you love me, and that's "carcase". You must change this to "figure" or "body" or "form". Carcase is an ugly word. It suggests the dead bodies of animals, from which pieces of meat are cut. Surely you would not wish, in the middle of a love poem, to compare your love with meat and death?'

I said I would change the word if she wished, although I had thought it a line of great craft, for the 'carcase' made an internal half-rhyme with 'focused', and the esses suggested (as a private association known only to her) the hisses of the snake which had introduced us to the Custom of the Apple.

But I could not understand why she disliked the allusion to death. For was not death an emblem of the perfection of the corpse? Every part, even the eyes, had ceased to move; the lungs and blood were still; and the corpse could be admired in its symmetry. So that on Oitar we have a form of compliment for a human with a comely corpse: 'You are as beautiful as the dead'.

She lay quietly, saying nothing, so I went on to explain our customs. As it is the discipline of our life to cure ourselves to the will of the programme, so death is looked upon as a time of consummation, and the return of the programme to the Wheel. What is it but the shedding of a corpse? The programme will be appointed to another. Yet the corpse has become known and familiar, and it is given honour at the end, like a convenient and worthy house. So that when the dead-line approaches, a person goes to a special chamber in the Bumple of the Wheel. And fellow Collegians visit there, and pay compliments to the carcase's perfections. It is customary for them to say, 'You will make a harmonious corpse,' and to add, as a special compliment, 'May you hang among the Eternal Elect.'

Still she said nothing, but she stared at me in the moonlight and I could not construe her vibes. And I went on to explain how, after the dead-line, all the Collegians came to admire the unrobed corpse, after which a solemn ceremony of programme-transfer was enacted in the Bumple's audio-visual chamber. The carcase was then immersed in acids which dissolved the flesh, and the skeleton inspected by an Adjuster. If it displayed merit, it was selected as a 'candidate', and was burnished with powder of gold. The candidates – of which, in each year, there might be thirty or forty – were then hung for inspection in a special All. And at the turning of the year, on our greatest festal day, the Festival of the new Wheel, there was a 'ballot' (which was a word close to the mortal 'choosing') among all the Colleges to select the most finely proportioned skeleton. And the skeleton elected at the top of the ballot was then taken about the Orb with dancing, music and honours, and hung upon the walls of the All of its former College.

Her eyes were wide in the moonlight, and I sensed her glacial vibes. She was trembling, yet when she spoke again it was in a steady voice. 'You don't know what you are saying. But I shouldn't complain. Stranger things have been done by my species on Earth; mummies in pyramids, concubines and slaves buried alive with the emperors. You make Oitar sound like a necropolis. You are lucky not to know the fear of death. And yet ...' She raised herself on an elbow and looked into my eyes so intensely that I turned my head aside. 'I've taught you to love, and if I must, to make you human, for love's sake I'll teach you mortal fear.'

As she said this I had a sense as if some ice-encrusted fingers were drawing together the skin along my spine. But I answered that she had spoken no-sense. For if by 'necropolis' she intended a city that worshipped death, then it was the Sykotic culture and not the culture of Oitar which should be condemned. 'Your statesmen are preparing death every day. Your newses are full of threats of nuclear war. Your sciences perfect new death-inflicting devices. Your industries are making weapons and everyone gives money to support them. The whole of Sykaos is a necropolis, poisons fall out of the sky, the troposphere is the arc of its bumple, and you have made a god in mushroom-shape, worshipped on every plug and in the silence of every mind. Every day since landfall Oi Paz has searched to de-code the Sykotic programme and reveal the programmers. It is found. It is declaimed as science. The programme is written to turn the planet into a necropolis, and every one of you is a programmer.'

'What you say is true and yet it's *not* true,' she replied. 'There are two forces in this world, thanatos and eros. And maybe others. And the forces are *us*. There never has been a programmer, only a flux of wills and egos, bonds and choices. There is still time for us to choose . . . Listen! Our oldest myth is a choosing-myth. God offered us everything, a Garden, security, a total programme ruled by His angels, or Gracious Goodnesses. But Eve and Adam chose knowledge and free will instead.' She sat up and reached for a saucer from a table beside the bed, and held it above me so that the moonlight girdled the circle of its rim. 'Behold, Oi Paz, the Wheel! We mortals were offered the Wheel as well. We rejected it.' As she strained her wrists, the saucer snapped into two disproportioned parts. 'Behold, the Broken Wheel!'

At this desperate obscenity my mind was nulled. I tremble now as I write. If such a blasphemy had fallen in common mortal talk – and I had heard such – I would, no doubt, have made obeisance for absolution, but it would not have concerned me much. But she was lying so close to me, still locked in bio-vibes, that the very breath of violation entered my nostrils; and her eyes, glinting in the moonlight, seemed to throw the cast of mortality into mine.

I swooned into a dream in which I knew that I was still awake. The sphere of my mind was broken and fell into two parts. The first part withdrew, as if down a long passage to a distant place, where it formed itself into the figure of an 'I'. There it remained, very still, watching silently all that Oi Paz thought and did. So that I had fallen into two persons or faculties: Oi Paz, who talked, acted and thought; and 'I', who was a critic and a watcher.

Then I fell into a deeper dream. I stood outside the Bumple of the Wheel. Although there are no birds on Oitar, images of disorder gathered like crows in a darkening sky. If I looked up, their black wings crossed and disfigured the orb of the sun. If I looked down, their great shadows fell like obscenities upon the radii of the avenues. And before my eyes three terrible birds, with long unfeathered necks, more coarse and ill-favoured than the others, settled upon the Arch of Unhappening: and I knew them to be omens of Choice, Chance and Change. As they settled and craned their necks this way and that, the Arch swayed, the coping-stone of Undoubt was dislodged, and all crumbled into aimless rubble with a mocking Incongruous Noise. Then the birds shrieked and fell upon me, whereat all the others flocked down from the sky – Anger and Accident, Contradiction, Attraction and Repulsion, Self-Will, Disobedience, Mutability, Gender and Doubt – and plunged their beaks not into my flesh but into my very mind where my programmes lay, tearing at my organs of Duty, Aesthetics and Roll.

The Broken Wheel hung above me on the cupola's rim, and as I watched the eternal axle fell from its centre, dropping towards the regions of ice like a meteor shedding fire. And the parts of the Wheel came together again, in an imperfect way, so that the fractures could be seen as blemishes, crooked against the diameter; and in the centre, in the place of an axle, was a mortal skull.

I seemed to pass through a door into another dream, in which the terror was gone – for I knew now the name of terror – and I was no longer on Oitar but in the Wall Garden of this house. And never before had the garden seemed so beautiful, the grass so fertile, the flowers so gay, the music of the singing-birds so sweet. And the 'I' was watching Oi Paz again, noting that he alone of all creatures was alien and desolate. And the garden became a road of happening along which a crowd of mortals were walking as if carried along by change, and I alone was stationary, and they passed without noticing me, so that I stepped out and thrust myself across their path, throwing open my robes and making the gesture of greeting, and shouting aloud: 'I, I, I . . .'

'Oi Paz, Oi Paz,' Helena was saying. 'What is it, my love?'

I sat up and gazed around in terror, asking where and who I was.

'You are here, on the good Earth, my love,' she said, very quietly. 'You've had a bad dream. Lie down and sleep.'

And she drew me towards her and settled my head on her breasts, running her hand gently through my hair. The trembling and the terror left me. Her breasts were a couch sweeter than the grass of the garden, more shapely than the Arch of Unhappening, more secure than the Wheel. 'You know what I think?' she asked, ruffling my hair with her hand. 'I think you're becoming mortal. It's fun being a mortal, some of the time. Sometimes it's hell. Anyway, there's nothing to do about it.'

Then she said, 'Sit up, love, I've got something to tell you.' The moon was now full in the window, and as I regarded it I remembered its black sky and misshapen escarpments with horror. And, beyond the moon, I recalled the groaning ice-packs bearing down upon the orbs of Oitar.

A slight vapour crossed the moon, oscillating the light, so that as she sat upright in bed, her breasts looked like the upper arcs of two wheels, which seemed to turn slowly in counterwise motion, so that I did an obeisance before them.

'Silly!' she said. 'I wanted to tell you that I think I've conceived. I'm going to bear your child. We've fulfilled our programme, our *karma*. We've closed the species-gap.'

Editor's Note

There are now in Oi Paz's Diary 'I' many pages torn out, and some defaced beyond recovery. A few fragments survive, which are so botched and blemished as to merit no transcription. They are preserved in the Archive of the Adjusters. A feature of these fragments is that they are written in both Sykotic and Oitarian language, and in the latter they move between Archaic, Bumple Utter and Neuter Utter, sometimes passing between three modes in a single sentence. One sample will suffice.

Q.

'. . . tell these near-beasts to let O. have I back from their captivities SYNAPSE 3 ø STEP. 001 for the goldshit falleth whence Droo Id on his sledge did rain. BIT STRING (ADD 124) Oi Paz did fall into a whole. He lost his eye he lost his roll. His eye got up and it was he. Now which is he and which is me? NOT (O), NOT (I) = ø. DUMP daemon – cron putnode SWAPPER (b[j]&Ox7f); craw c. With bowed head Oy Pee begs Input at Thy Gate and blessed may Thy Couch roll. Cousins bore into my walls, they bug me in my programmes. The Wh**l is bore & bugs my vibes, Oi Paz will null its chips. JMP 105. JGZ 123: memcpy (dp, sp, xp-)node + daemon. Watch OP: he is a watcher appointed by GGs, he is boring I. Macho = GG. STP. STP. GG made mans generacion of naught. But if thine I be naught, thy whole body shall be darksome = hole.'

Cutting. File 'Sykotic Trash'. Manuscript annotation: '2 Nov.'

FREAK ELECTRICAL STORM

There was a brief world-wide interruption of all forms of radio and telecommunications traffic yesterday. It lasted for $2\frac{1}{2}$ minutes and was reported from places as widely apart as Washington, Cheltenham, Honolulu and Novosibirsk. Air control was blacked out, automatic pilots failed on air-liners, causing several near-disasters. A Soviet airliner has been reported as missing over the Himalayas.

Major computer systems were also affected world-wide, and an 'alien input' was reported. Early-warning radar systems blacked-out. Our defence staff writes that all nuclear silos went over to IRA ('Immediate Red Alert') and bombers readied for take-off. Owing to radio silence and the interruption of control beams, Trident submarines went over automatically to the emergency programme known as Self-Hexing Independent Task Selection. The White House Spokesperson said that both President Forsst and Marshal Oblomov attempted to activate the 'hot line' (which proved to be inoperative).

Experts at NASA explain the episode as resulting from a freak sun-storm, a 'gremlin in the solar wind'. A spokesman for the Strategic Defence Initiative Organisation (SDIO) said it was 'one chance in ten million. It will never happen again.' Reports are coming in from the Pacific region of 'the superimposition of alien signals' over a wide range of frequencies, with a voice speaking in an unknown language [*torn*].

Editor's Note

No record can be found of the following eighteen moon cycles, or months, with the exception of three cuttings and one memorandum by Pepper, all found among the Sage papers. These follow.

Cutting. From Sage papers

RUSSIANS ON MOON?

Rumours have been sweeping Washington as to new activity on the moon's surface. Radio-astronomers have been for nearly two years monitoring regular 'pulses' which they associate with little bumps, or 'pimples', in the Mare Humorum. The signals were thought to be of natural origin, but radio-astronomers at Behemoth (Fla) have shown them to have 'intelligent regularities'. The 'pimples' are also of some 'intelligent' construction.

President Forsst has summoned a top-secret consultation for tomorrow at Camp David, comprising space scientists, NASA officials and staff from the SDIO. The experts disagree as to *what* is on the moon, but no one doubts *who* is there. The Russians. They have jumped the USA again as they did with *Sputnik*. The question is: *why*? Observatories? Or missile-sites? Have they turned the moon into a gigantic orbiting Soviet satellite?

This has the makings of the greatest crisis in super-power

relations since the Cuba crisis. The President is expected to issue an ultimatum to the Soviets to dismantle their installations and evacuate the moon in the same terms as President Kennedy ... [*torn*]★

Cutting. From Sage papers. Manuscript annotation: '14 Dec.'

EXPEDITIONARY FORCE TO MOON?

There have been sensational developments in the case of the moon-sites in the last week. The bitter exchanges between the United States and the Soviet Union ten days ago, in which each side accused the other of planting missile silos on the moon, have given way to a security blanket on all operations.

But this does not appear to be the prelude to an ultimatum between the superpowers. It seems that US Space Command is now satisfied that the installations and radio-emissions do not come from a Soviet source. It is pointed out that the ferrying of materials by giant rockets could not possibly have escaped observation. And the Soviet Command appears, grudgingly, to have come to the same conclusion. Yet that there is some activity on the moon has been confirmed by observatories throughout the world. Both the USA and the Soviet Union are planning to send up satellites to orbit the moon as permanent on-location observatories.

President Forsst has been closeted with his advisers, preparing a coast-to-coast address to the American people next week.†

★ *Sage annotation:* 'Sent to me by John Blossom. In UK there is still a black-out under OS Acts. John says in his letter that "everyone" has known about this for ages, but the EMP blip last month brought it out into the open. The thing about the Russians is of course a PR hand-out, by courtesy of Pentagon.'

† *Sage annotation, pencil:* 'This is about all the British Freepress has allowed the Brits to know. Security is sitting on the lid like an Adjuster. Stupid! Don't they know people read the American press? The bit about moon-satellites is strictly PR disinformation. John wrote to me weeks ago that a satellite *had* been sent up but it just "went out". Why do They let his letters through? Perhaps They are monitoring our correspondence in the hope of finding out something?'

Sage Notebook. Pasted-in typescript

TO ALL STAFF (EXECUTIVE, BRITISH)

This is to fill you in on important reorganisations within
LUNATO.

Since my appointment as the Government's Chief Scientific
Adviser three months ago, the time which I can spend at
Martagon Hall has diminished. At the same time Mr Lowell
Himmelfarb (Associate Director) will be taking up his post in
Washington of Assistant Secretary for Space Defense.

His replacement will be General Bright Kornblower
(USAF), at present Deputy C-in-C (Space) SACEUR. His
post will now be redefined as Co-Director.

The Co-Director will have full executive responsibility for
the daily routine of this institution, and I know that all staff
will give him the fullest co-operation.

SECURITY ZONING

It will not have escaped your notice that the Oitarian plantation
on the moon has now been, as they say, 'blown'. This was
perhaps inevitable, owing to the 'leaky' state of Washington,
but the whole scientific community rumbled it after the global
EMP. There is no alternative but to 'go public'. We are cur-
rently declassifying some (small) part of our information. President Forsst will address the American people next Thursday,
and will disclose the existence of Oitarian occupation forces on
the moon. Marshal Oblomov is expected to follow. Sit tight,
as there may be some bumpy moments!

The management of public opinion will then become a
prime consideration. *All security arrangements must be tightened
up forthwith!** The consequences here at Martagon will be as
follows.

General Kornblower has informed me that he will run the
Hall as a 'military outfit'. For the convenience of smooth

---

* *Sage annotation, red ink:* 'The Rule of the Wheel!'

security, civilian staff (wherever possible) will be replaced by US military personnel: phone operators, catering staff, drivers, & c. & c. For the purposes of security, the Hall and its grounds will now be graded into the following zones:

Zone One. Martagon Hall and appendant residential and office blocks (to be extended). This will be used by US military personnel *exclusively*. Strictly no entry allowed to anyone else, except those with Q-clearance. (At present this is limited to myself and Lady Pepper and to Miss Primrose Gordon and Colonel Sorley: NATO senior officers will be cleared for assigned appointments.) All security arrangements for the Hall, and for ingress and egress to the grounds, will be in the care of General Kornblower and his deputies.

Astrozone. The Astrosigint station will remain under the command of Lt-Col. Robert Sorley (Assistant Director), who will be gazetted as full Colonel next month. Congratulations! The station will of course continue to be in the hands of British personnel, with NATO advisers on attachment subject to the Assistant Director's requirements. Astrosigint will continue to service the laser-sensors around the perimeter and to patrol the grounds at night. Captain Wetherfield will be i/c grounds security.

Retirement Zone. It has been decided to redesignate the Family Quarters in this way. We must face the fact that we have a difficulty in re-deploying staff no longer required in the Hall, and surplus to requirements. This might even impinge upon executive staff. QMSM Gravell (Works) will continue to supervise gardens and works in the grounds and he will try to take on one or two more hands. The *Astrozone* may be able to add to its Establishment a phone operator, odd-job man and a cook. Since US Security will now take over Files, Miss Weeder (Files) has suggested that she might usefully employ herself in writing a *History of Martagon Hall*, and a further history (to be kept closed for 100 years) of LUNATO. She will require secretarial help and the Library (in much reduced form) will move with her. But I fear that other secretaries, caterers & c. may be redundant. The old Family Quarters will be extended for their early retirement, on full board and residence, with half-pay. In exceptional circumstances applications will be considered for release to the outer world, but *please do not raise hopes*. The vetting and dis-briefing procedures will take several months.

Zone of Eden. Dower house unit. Personnel as per Establishment. (Rumours have reached me that Establishment may soon increase by its own inner dynamics. Congratulations!)★

Dower house unit has been designated a 'zone of Eden' under the secret Articles of Abrogation (Sovereignty, UK) signed by Sir Anthony Eden in the presence of General Eisenhower in 1955. These Articles designate certain zones as reservations for the sole use of the native inhabitants (Windsor Castle, Balmoral, Chequers, the House of Lords and such others as may from time to time be agreed). SACEUR has graciously consented to urgent representations from HM Government that the dower house unit shall be so zoned. It will be strictly out-of-bounds to all non-native personnel, unless with Colonel Sorley's clearance.

Miss P. A. Gordon will be i/c Liaison between *Zone One* and *Retirement Zone*. Colonel Sorley i/c Liaison between *Zone One* and *Astrozone/Zone of Eden*.

Finally, I congratulate you all on the success of our enterprise, which is now followed in the highest NATO councils. We have fully accomplished our *Object: Phase One*, and are midway into *Phase Two*. Great quantities of signals collected by Astrosigint are now being processed in Behemoth. Colonel Sorley informs me that he has now established 'moon-lock' with a powerful lunar transmitter. Signals are exchanged daily, but they consist in the main of 'number games' or the proposal

---

★ *Uncouth drawing of a fat creature with an enlarged snout. Drawn by Sage?*

and resolution of mathematical problems. (Oitarians appear to be mathematically very advanced, and I am surprised that our research unit in the *Zone of Eden* have overlooked this point.)★ Captain Wetherfield, who is a chess addict, has played several games with the lunar transmitter, but, alas, has not yet won. Colonel Sorley is planning to 'match up' the signals for a direct Earth/moon computer exchange, so that more complex messages may be read out. Language de-coding is proving still to be a stubborn nut to crack, but these are early days!

Enough of this (indiscreet) information, but I thought you would like me to fill in the background. From the time of General Kornblower's arrival next week, any information will be passed only on strictly need-to-know criteria.†

If this reorganisation should impinge on your own executive tasks you will receive an individual notification. You may be assured that I will continue to pay regular visits to Martagon, and will advance your interests in the highest places. I shall receive and study with interest your reports. (By the way, *Zone of Eden* has gone very quiet lately. Anything new?) If you have any problems, get in touch with Miss Gordon, who will let me know.

Merry Christmas!

P. A. Gordon, pp. Sir James Pepper‡

★ *Sage annotation, pencil:* 'I *told* him O. can't add up to ten but uses a computer!'

† *Sage annotation, pencil:* 'i.e. since everyone doesn't know what they don't know no one knows what they need to know.'

‡ *Sage annotation, pencil:* 'A long-winded fart from a self-inflated pig. From now the Wheel Rules OK. Surprising thing is how light we get off. Rbt says reason is that Pepper's status here is still as "academic" Director – if Martagon were stripped of all academic functions, then he wld have to cede his position to the military.

'The other extraordinary thing is absence of all mention of *stables*. Not even as an *Ex-Zone*. It seems that this and security in the grounds were the two 'crunch' questions. At first the Cousins just wanted to take the place over, lock and block. Dr Charon & co. wld have let them do it, so long as they kept Pepper as face-saver. But Rbt got on to our military top brass, who supported him, and fought it line by line. He demanded that we shld be an Eden zone, wh they didn't mind about (since no one thinks we matter). But they "shied and reared" (ref Ann) about the stables – too near Martagon, surplus to requirements, hiding-place for agents & c. "In the end Robo said it was the stables or him, said the exercise essential for Oy Pee's survival – well, it is in a way,

Cutting. From Sage papers. Manuscript annotation: '*Times*, 3 March – only paper Security now lets in'

ALIENS ON MOON
'TESTING TIME FOR FREE WORLD'

In a sensational nation-wide address, President Forsst last night revealed that US space agencies had for some time been monitoring signals traffic emanating from the moon. Observations have also been made of 'domes' under construction on the moon's surface.

US military advisers had established that these are of 'some alien origin'. Then, in an ominous passage, the President stated, 'While the planet of departure of these aliens is not yet known to us, we can have little doubt as to their next intended port of call. It is Planet Earth. We await them. We expect them. Be they friends or be they foes, come what may, we are ready.'

The President continued, 'We now may thank our stars that – through the foresight of my great predecessor in this office, President Reagan – we are already furnished with space defences adequate to repel any invasion. Who knows? These aliens may prove friendly. If so, then the free peoples of the

---

Hel – *you* know." (Oh, how I do know! Only Macho has been getting him through this schizo thing, he needs Macho more than he needs me. I'm his *problem*.) And Rbt got Pepper to come down on his side – A. says, "I think Robo's got something on old Popeye," and if Rbt has been wall-boring I can *imagine*! So it seems the Cousins agreed to "put that phase of logistic modernisation forward to a later phase": i.e. sentence postponed. So long as power-game is stalled the stables become a truly liminal area, a no-person-land. Which suits A.

'The person who was NOT suited was Mrs U. She flipped her top. Said she was Guardian of the Hall's Traditions. Rbt cld do nothing about it. So she sd, "Very well, I shall leave." Security (US) sd, "I'm sorry, mam," & c. & c. But she *did* leave, the next morning. She just upped and offed. She had somehow got an electronic pass-key tucked in her handbag (that lady is not stupid!), loaded her kit in the back of the weekly Fortnum & Mason van, was driven to gate, operated key, & when a startled guard ran out of the guardroom she just waved him away and they drove through. Good for her!

'That was a nasty cut about dower house unit going quiet. *Touché*. But. *A*. Why should we give Them reports? (How could I put in a *Weekly Report* on a lover?) *B*. Outer world *has* gone very distant these last months, with inner world a-stew. Must at least send some pretend reports. Only I do find work difficult, trouble with being pregnant at *aet* 39.'

world will know how to give them welcome. But if they prove otherwise, we shall bar all entry. I counsel you not to fear, not to panic. I counsel you next week to go as free Americans to your churches, synagogues, video-communions and mosques – to every place of worship – and to pray to that God who has guided this nation through many storms and who has elected her as protector of the Free World to endow us with the courage, the wisdom and the means to face this emergency.'

President Forsst then announced that he had already ordered a 'Super Apollo' programme, to send a 'task-group' of rockets to the moon – 'to take ambassadors, if the aliens will receive them with due honours, and, if they will not, to take messages of a different order.' The programme, costing some $400 billion, would be 'operational' within three years.

In a moving peroration, the President called on the whole Free World – and the Soviets also   to rally to the defence of 'our common Mother'. It was not a time for ideologies or special interests to obscure 'the call of Mother Earth's children – the whole human race'.

There has not yet been any official response from Moscow. But a commentator on a German-language programme from Radio Moscow said that President Forsst was raising the 'spectre' of a space invasion in order to win his mid-term elections.

Our defence correspondent writes that it has been well known in the defence community for some months that alien installations had been located. There is no occasion for alarm since the logistics of transporting landing vehicles in any quantity from another galaxy will prove insuperable. By 'messages of a different order' it was supposed that President Forsst was considering a menu of options, including ... [*torn*]

On this cutting is clipped one page in manuscript with Sage annotation: 'Got this letter from John B. a month later.'

After the President's speech, the whole nation seemed to flip its top. Of course, we've been preparing for this for decades.

Kids are bred on space invaders, *Star Trek*, *War of the Worlds*. Adults fantasise about X-ray lasers, particle-beams, SDI. Helena, I really wonder if this might not be a problem which needs our kind of know-how? I mean, could this whole shoot-out be a scene so deeply internalised in our culture that we have gotten to the sub-hysteric state where we actually read out our own fantasies as real objects out there? The black witch syndrome multiplied to the 10th degree by computer technologies? Voodoo of the hi-tech age? Tell me what you think. Maybe your 'Mr Oipas' is really some computer nut who objectifies our fantasies and goes along with them.

Anyway, the nation did its top. There were *riots* in some churches. Of course the liberals got up-tight and said it was some election con – or else they became more eco than ever and wanted a World Federation tomorrow to 'welcome our stellar siblings'. But when it hit Middle America, man, was it crazy! Even Jerry Falwell came out of retirement. Every Apocalypse nut started to howl 'the end cometh' and started wrapping up the world in a shroud. Then some of them turned ugly and started beating up anyone who looked like a druggie or an egg-head or a non-All-American-type. (All blacks of course prime suspects.) Then a faction remembered that bit in Revelation about the Number of the Beast and started smashing computers (which they said was Beast). But the dominant faction said the Russians had done it, or must have put the aliens up to it, so the good old cry of 'Nuke the Soviets' is going up on walls, even on the Lincoln Memorial. Man, it is *just crazy* being a Freeworldperson at this moment of time, and I wish I could get a transfer to sleepy old Martagon where you are safely out of it all.

Sage Diary

April 27th. Adam's first birthday. Put him in a sling – he's getting v heavy, & wriggles to get out & show off his new skill at walking – and took him up to the Secret Garden. Wanted to show him the tree under wh he was conceived, wh ought to be in blossom now.

'Ought' because it wasn't there. All the trees have been bull-dozed, most of them lying there, forlorn, with wilted leaves and buds turning brown. Even the fig and the apricots had been hacked down. A fire down at one end of the garden and a concrete-mixer just inside the gate. The soft-fruit cage ... bull-dozed. The old rose garden ... bull-dozed. I wept and wept. With anger. I really did.

Then one of the hoods there must be *forty* of them crawling about the place now – in camouflage kit with all phallic accoutre-ments came in and spied me and started hollering to me to get out, it was Zone One, Q-Security. He even waved a killing-stick at me. But then he got up to me and saw I was weeping & for some reason even mcps don't know how to cope with tears, female, and he got a bit nicer. I asked him what the *hell* was going on & he sd it was 'Zone One Games Precinct', just large enough for baseball. He recognised me now as an Edener, & tried to comfort me by saying that he thought the General might be willing to give 'clearance' for Edeners to join in the basket-ball and they 'sure needed one or two more for the ladies team'. In fact, he tried to be nice, and he let Adam play with his lariat. Then a *hog* of an officer pussyfooted in, & obviously thought he had caught out his man in an assignation, & started shouting & grunting, wh made Adam cry & I took off in a rage. When I looked back I saw them standing at the gate with their weapons, like the Cherubim in Genesis, placed at the gate to the Garden of Eden, to guard the way to the Tree of Life.

But it churned me up ... the memories, the *memories*! So. I have started my diary again. Haven't kept it for ... one year & nine months or so, except for some pages too painful – sort of case-notes on O's breakdown – wh I tore out. I suppose I shld try to recap.

Well. About O's breakdown, or break-up. I brought it on, of course, by breaking the saucer, the Wheel. It still makes me guilty.

But it was bound to come, one way or another, once we were lovers. And *that* cldn't be helped. I won't have a guilt-trip about that. But I shld have realised – after seeing what it did to David – what a species-culture-shock wld do to him. Not only the oscillation between modes, the mixing of signals. It was also jumping across from a 'programme' or we-compulsion to an identity. He scarcely had one before, or, if he did, it was masked out, blocked.

So the 'I' seemed to separate off inside him from the 'he'. He became double-personed. It was a classic schizophrenic trauma set-up. It really is too painful to go back over it all, and he still has regressions or relapses, he always will. (God knows what wld happen if he returned to Oitar!) He wld flip over in the middle of a sentence (never, thank God, when actually making love) from Oitarian to mortal and back, & he had this obsession that his 'I' was watching his 'him', or vice versa. Then he wld start punning, in two different species-languages! Or go into computer-talk, Neuter Utter. He walked in a strange jerky way when he was really bad, all his flowing grace & gesture lost, & his breath smelled like acid. He wld rant & deliver foul 'sentences' on me or on poor Rani, & wld call D. a 'thief of his utters'. That was when he was into Oitarian mode. But mortal mode cld be even worse. He discovered that he cld do the Incongruous Noise, & wld stand looking at the sun for an hour laughing, sort of barking. (But he does laugh now, a real laugh. And he weeps easily too, with none of the usual male hang-ups.)

This went on for months, when I was getting nausea from pregnancy, & I just cldn't cope. Ann was terrific. She has very set, uncommunicative, anti-academic opinions, but sometimes they seem to make sense. She told me that O. (in terms of her Zen texts) was going through an 'anti-samadhi' breakdown: that is, instead of losing his sense of identity, he was gaining one, and he was in danger of a 'burn-out', like a meteorite coming into the atmosphere. She sd he had to get back to 'positive samadhi', distracted from his own thoughts. Then, as always, she came up with a practical answer, & made O. ride Macho for several hours a day. He always came back relaxed.

I wasn't much use. I gave him a fluffy tabby kitten wh we call Frolic. He says she is 'groovy' and makes his vibes 'purr'.

Well, that was that, and occasionally it still is. The manifest schizo symptoms began to diminish ... oh, a year or more ago. Thank God he was in a much calmer state when Adam was about to come, although he got panic at anything too physical, like the sight of blood. But there again, a lot of mortal ♂ are like that. (D. was *terrified* when R's time came.) But what has gone on ever since – it hasn't really lifted – is a general *low*. His whole sense of self, or sense of known 'roll', has taken a beating & his confidence is minus. I think this is usual in schizoid breakdowns, post-catatonic depression. Wish I cld help. But I have to cope with myself too.

Which brings us to our relationship. Well, I suppose it has a dualism in it too, a profane/sacred oscillator. At first the profane bit was out of this world, and in our good times it still is. (With the breakdown, and then the depression, there have been more bad times than good.) We had been cooped together so much that our wanting of each other seemed to *burst*, wh was lovely for me & very passionate, but quite extraordinary for him since, although he certainly did want me, he didn't know what he wanted and didn't have a name for his want. His body would simply possess him while the rest of him seemed to go into a swoon. Afterwards he wld look around in surprise as if the lover had been someone else.

The sacred bit. Well, I suppose I was a bit schizo too. I was scared. Scared for myself, scared of what it was doing to him. I cldn't shed my professional relation to him, and was watching ... observing him even as we loved. Relating was like walking on a floor with rotten planks – say the wrong word, suggest the wrong concept, and we went through a hole, together or apart. I had to keep changing roles: anthropologist, lover, therapist, species-culture-bridge. I love O., but I'm not sure I've ever exactly *liked* him. And then, how can one exactly 'like' someone whose culture is so different, & sometimes alien? I felt (still feel) threatened, not by O. but by his culture. After all, untold generations

393

of acculturation soften human relationships, make for a responsive lover. So much of Oipas is *programmed* still. Maybe (in that word 'acculturation') I've confessed that I'm programmed too.

As a love affair this is certainly an 'adventure' to end all adventures. But a desperate one, with many falls and cliff-hanging and chasms opening. Sometimes I wonder if we have a 'relationship' at all. Whether we cldn't just snap back on to our special programmes without a backward look. And the relation is not an equal one. I don't only mean that O. is an ICP (intergalactic chauv pig), wh he is. My side has defences and closed-off areas, too. He has jumped into our species-culture but I have refused to jump across into his. Partly my professional training: it's my 'thing' to put together an alien culture while holding it off at a distance for observation. Partly plain fear. O. wanted to teach me Neuter Utter; I just 'shied and refused'. I'd seen what it did to D. – also, *I don't like Oitar.*

But I have changed in one way. O. has somehow taught me to activate my 'vibe-sensors'. I'm far more aware than I was of people's vibes. It can even be embarrassing sometimes. We mortals must have an atrophied organ there, wh can be restored.

The others – my good mortal friends – have been unjudging and kind. It's a good thing that R. was still enwrapped in honeymoon when I got off with O.; if this had happened before that she wld have been devastated. But she was sweet, & sisterly to me when O. was ill. D. didn't notice much – in fact, now that he's married he's become just a little boring. He's lost some of his nervous energy and intellectual edge, and he allows R. to arrange his life. But signs of reviving activity this last three or four months – D. and O., in the face of R's disapproval, are working on archaic Oitarian together and are even translating one of their great epics – the *Argodyssey* – into English. It's wonderful to see them working together – they usually go to a seat by the lake – with O. making some gesture of *gravitas* and D. lifting both his hands in excitement.

I've no idea what the world up at the Hall thinks. (I should ask

Mary the Phone some time: she's a gossip-sponge.) But when it all happened the old gang (Mayhem, Hunter, Crostic) were dead or gone, and Pepper had become a V Impt Absentee. Mrs Undermanner was upset, & I'm sorry about that. It may even have influenced her decision to leave.

I suppose the dower house idyll of those early weeks has ended, although we still get on okay as a half-commune. We've all got older: R. is maternal and protective, D. has less fizz, maybe I'm more 'mature'? And somehow I feel it hasn't been a good time for A. It must have bust up her own calm to have two intensely absorbed couples sharing space with her and dividing themselves off. She also seems to have aged, with a pain line around her mouth, as if the door had shut on some of the possibilities of life. Whatever she has with Rbt – they're certainly friends still & sometimes have their dawn rides – seems arrested, going nowhere, and A. has somehow been hurt. But she despises self-pity & doesn't talk about it. Except once, when the four of us had been especially preoccupied and excluding, when she said, 'Oh, hell, why don't I go over the wall? I could get out tomorrow. What the hell am I needed here for?'

Rbt is a puzzle, perhaps her puzzle. He seems to prefer the company of women to men. Yet behind his warm smile and candid blue eyes there is some cold spot which blocks intimacy. He becomes the Officer Monk, dedicated to work, refusing to give. If anything my relationship with O. has cleared the air between me and Rbt, since it has removed any possible claim on him. He told A. that our coming together had been 'inevitable', & then (oddly) that he 'admired my courage'. Then he came up trumps with the Astrosigint Obstetrics Unit, which he got on site for a fortnight – convenient that R's Priya came just four days ahead of Adam.

O. was riding Macho the whole day when Adam was born. At first he'd scarcely look at the baby, as if he were a 'blemish'. He cldn't bear to see me nursing him & once said it 'blasphemed the orbs of my breasts'. He's still thrown when physical & aesthetic signals go across each other.

The first few months he was half-fascinated, half-repelled by little Adam. Thought he was 'premature'. But the thing wh astounded him was Adam's *ego* – and Priya's. Was really quite shocked. Cldn't believe that such tiny mortals could emerge so 'raw and self-centric' – once he called them both 'uncured ego-bugs', at wh we nearly had a row. But now he's really bonded. I can leave Adam in his care for hours – in fact Adam is humanising O. much more successfully than I. O. is worried that Adam is 'programme-retarded': at one year from 'de-tanking' their kids can take first dance-steps & are given little recorders to learn to play. And they get their first digital computers. Oh, and they can converse, but only in archaic mode. O. has started to 'induct' him in ancient epics. Adam chortles & says 'bla bla bla' and O. is delighted & construes it as some archaic utterance. Wh it is.

Now that Adam's one I think my 'sabbatical' is over. And D's too! We ought to get back to a few hours' work a day. R. says she can easily cope, they amuse each other (if Adam bonking Priya on the head with building-bricks is amusing!). And Rbt has been round several times, patient, but I can see he's *really* worried. His bumples have hooked up with bumples on moon. He says that perhaps we shld try some language-signals now, & only O. or D. can help with that. Has asked D., O. and me to go up to Astrosigint next week for 'a formal session' with himself, his new 2nd i/c (Major Rock, a cryptosigint specialist, pleasant enough but a total workaholic) and Captain Jane. 'Should we bring Oipas?' 'No, let's go through it without him the first time.' I wonder what 'it' is?

Sage Diary

April 30th. Crazy thing happened last night. Woke up around 3 a.m. to hear scuffling. (Sleep in my own room now, as O's vibes are so sensitive that he wakes up whenever Adam dreams & gets no sleep. So as per mortal customs ♀ parent gets all the nurture-chores.) Thought the scuffling was Frolic. But was so loud I turned on bedside light & found a *hood* crouched by my bed, in muddy camouflage outfit and balaclava-type mask with eye-slits. Was so bleary & dopy with sleep my first response was to say, 'Don't wake the baby!' Then I sat up, quite *rigid*, and saw there were *three* hoods. I shouted, 'You're not allowed in the Zone of Eden!' Whereupon nearest hood sd: 'Cripes! Dr Sage!'

Hood then peeled off mask and emerged as ... Sophia Harley-Bender! My last year in Oxford I gave her tutorials. She's bright, but she was so involved in CND & rushing off to Greenham & c. that she was a pain to teach. She was as shattered to find me here as I was to find her. (Seems that They have put around the rumour in Oxford that I'm a Visiting Prof at UC Xanadu.)

Other hoods de-masked & were also female. V intense & their hostile vibes swamped me. They asked where was 'control tower' & they wanted my 'papers'. Then one of them asked for the loo, which normalised things a bit. I took them down to kitchen & put some coffee on. They were tramping mud in everywhere.

Seems they are into an NVDA network. They had got Martagon (under old name of FARCES) on a 'target list' from CND, for a direct action. They are convinced this place is another launch-site for the Frisbee missiles wh were brought in to Greenham Common five years ago as replacements for the old Cruise. They've been trying to get into the place for months. Object: if poss, to paint CND symbol on launch-pads & take away 'incriminating documents'. Asked how the hell they got through the sensors, but they only looked knowingly at each other & smiled.

Then A. stomped down her back-stairs, &, as always, took the scene in. But even her composure was rattled: 'You're *lunatics!* Once you step out of the Zone of Eden, those hoods will drill you with holes. They don't play according to your rules.' Perhaps because we were all females, their aggro subsided & their vibes got more concerned. They sd if we wld give them some 'papers' they'd go back. But it was dawn now, no way they cld have made it. A. sd there was nothing for it but to go and get Rbt, but he might have to 'put them in the can'. 'Better than letting the Cousins find you,' she sd.

While Ann was away Sophy & co. filled me in on what the peace movement was doing. It seems that the Forsst/Oblomov stand-off is now really foul, the détente of the late 1980s has been rolled back to Celsius minus minus. Space is full of exotic flying saucers & X-ray lasers in permanent orbit. The Moscow Spring is now only a memory, & Forsst is a prisoner of the apocalypse nutters.

The peace movement they sd is now truly international with huge Third World input. But 'the media' has just blacked out all reports of it (wh is why I'd never heard). There was a big surge of an independent peace-and-eco-and-human-rights movt on the Other Side, after Sellafield had that major leak and the Brno N-power station blew up. But that has been wrapped up also & has turned into the courses of a vast religious revival of millennial type (rather like the Falwell revivalists in USA), tolerated or even encouraged by the authorities as a safety-valve. As for Forsst's recent speech & all the stuff about moon-bases & aliens, they sd this was a cover-up for what both sides were planting on moon. They sd World War 3 wld probably start on moon or in space, & rub out the Earth as an afterthought.

Then A. came back with Rbt, whose vibes were as cross as I'd ever known them. On appearance of a male, in military uniform, Sophy, Christabel and Pam froze, & then *drenched* the room with aggro vibes. A. had obviously been arguing all the way down with Rbt, & had had a hard time. It was a bad scene. I had to come in several times & explain to them in words of one syllable that if the US security got them, they might be interrogated in distinctly nasty ways & then jailed for years, & they wld be nbg to peace movt. Rbt asked them whether, if he got them out, they wld 'give their word of honour' not to talk to anyone, least of all the media, & say what happened. Chris, a crew-cut type with huge earrings, started on about how they were on different sides, & what did males know about 'honour'? But Sophy seemed to have some deference-vibes for her antique tutor of yore, wh probably saved the day. Then Adam started squalling & I had to bring him downstairs, hoping against hope that Oipas wldn't follow after. Sophy & Pam (but not Chris) went gooey over Adam, & Sophy asked whose he was and complimented *Ann*, & was quite thrown when I laid claim to sd article, blurting out, 'But I didn't think you could ... I mean, Dr Sage, I didn't know you had ...' Wh signified her notion of the dignity of her Grey Tutorial Eminence.

Pact was: Rbt wld smuggle three out in Astrosigint vehicle, if they (a) promised not to talk, (b) told him how they had got in. I cld see he didn't like it, & A. looked miserable too, as if she had twisted his arm. Rbt was obviously miffed professionally, since perimeter and grounds security are Astrosigint role. (b) proved to be sticking-point, but in the end Sophy went weepy & her sisters agreed. Seems they had found out from an old 'witch' ('a white witch') in Shaw Magna that there is a *second* tunnel. It leads from a cowshed to the Cardiarum, wh is on a huge tumulus in the SW grounds, between this house and Astrosigint. (Presumably another ingress for corrupted village maidens to take part in orgies of the wicked de Boyle?) It had taken them weeks to open it up. I must say these sisters have got guts, it chills my spine to think of crawling all that way.

So that was it. We put them in A's den & carried them up a decent breakfast, since we didn't want the complications of explaining it all to O. and D. and R. (Or explaining O. to them.) At about 10 a.m. Rbt himself drove up in an Astrosigint Rangerover with exceedingly cross vibes, & whisked them away. I don't trust that Chris. Spent *hours* cleaning up their mud.

Sage Diary

May 2nd. Formal session at Astrosigint station as solemn as anything I've ever done. We did it in the station's 'safe chamber', wh is screened against any boring or bugging. Rbt told D. & me that all the 'matters to be discussed' must remain absolutely secret. We were not even to discuss them wth each other (or wth O.) inside the dower house, but only if we were well away from buildings, in the grounds. And (looking at me) we were not even to write them down in private diaries. (How does he know I've started it again?) It was pretty clear that he is worried mainly about the Cousins. D., who is even more unworldly than I, was stunned by it all.

I will now have to take O. out for a talk, which is likely to be very long, very difficult, and cld even break up our relationship. But I am convinced that Rbt is right. We have got to find some way.

Sage Diary

May 3rd. Walk and talk wth O. not as fraught as I had feared. He knew already half the things I told him. Rbt talks with him, of course, but he seems to know things in some other way. Not only that: he also had himself seen the *problem*. And had been working through it twrds similar conclusions. That doesn't make the problem one bit easier. But at least it is 'our' problem. When we came in he gazed at Adam, who was asleep on the couch, and then sd, 'It is good thinking. I will declaim a signal to the Gracious Goodnesses.'

Sage Diary

May 10th. Rbt drove up today with that old globe wh used to be in the Library and a world atlas. Then he and O. went off to a bench by the lake, with globe and maps, and put their heads together for ages. Can't get O. to talk about it all, he is v low and preoccupied.

ZONE OF EDEN

Sage Diary

May 12th. Yesterday was too threatening even to write about. Another global EMP, but this time it went on for 40 minutes. The telly and the newspapers are in such a state of shock that they put out nothing but fairy-stories. All communications and electronic systems were completely blacked out; street lights and power lines broke down. Rbt says there is a terrible catalogue of air and train crashes in every part of the world, but the news is being held up for fear of mass panic. A side-effect was that some major computer systems had 'blips' in wh they jumped programmes or ran backwards: the City and other computerised stock exchanges are now in chaos, with billions transferred to wrong accounts. The military have screened their data-banks, floppy discs, & c. but a lot of the data in other computer-banks has just been wiped off. Rbt says that at H hour + 31 SACEUR panicked & thought it was prelude to a Russian strike. They tried to get out orders for a pre-emptive strike, but, thank God, their whole signals system was inop.

Here we didn't notice anything at first, except the washing-machine & iron went off. Then there was a greenish flash outside the windows. Tried to call Works but phone dead. Thought it was just another power cut. Been a lot of these since Charon staved off a back-bench Lib revolt by announcing a phasing-down of nuke-energy programme. (The Central Generating Board puts these cuts on deliberately, as anti-govt propaganda.)

Then I looked around for O. – his turn to take over Adam. I went outside and realised everything was dark, with a ghastly pinky-orange light in the sky – not in any part of the sky (like a sunset) but sort of lowering and pulsing all over – and gradually going more red.

I found O. at last, lying outside his bumple door, unconscious. As if stunned. He came round in a few minutes – I suppose when the EMP stopped – but he was only half there, as if at a great distance.

So I have been therapist and nurse. He has been going through agonies, but he hasn't the words to tell me. Ann has got him out on Macho now.

Sage Diary

May 14th. O. has been coping wth himself with a hard, objective courage, as if he had to use himself as an instrument. He says EMP 'brought a message' to him. He was very tender last night, although saying little. When Adam cried, he got up & went to him (a first). I didn't try to force him to talk. He has been wth Rbt all morning, now has gone into his bumple with his notebook, writing.

He has an appointment up at Astrosigint tomorrow.

Oi Paz Diary 'I'

To hold together Oi Paz and I in a ring is how to bind together Oitar and Sykaos. The task is to design a common programme, for which Sorley, I and Oi Paz must be the programmers. This is for Adam's well-rolling.

Thesis. The Sykotic species is no more than a bug in the flow-chart of their own planet's programme. It unlodges equilibrium. It uglifies all things. It is at a hair-trigger to enhance radioactive levels high above tolerance. *Solution.* Exterminate, which is only to pre-empt their self-extermination. *Means.* EMP will disable all Sykotic technologies. Then to devise some kind of mop-up.

BUT *reservations.* (1) Mop-up will endanger other valuable creatures & plants. (2) Will leave for millennia squalors & aesthetic violations. (3) NB EMP stunners will leave core of nuclear energy reactors in uncontrolled luminous state, from which may heave hundreds of radioactive eruptions. This could hap even after all Sykaans dead. They will leave an inheritance of Doomsday machines to poison all that come thereafter.

Conclusion. Extermination hazardous. Plantation by agreement to be correct logic-path.

Antithesis. The Sykotic species is capable of reform. Their free-wheel is absurd but it is not without qualities meriting study. It has been proved that the species can mate and propagate with ours, which with due bio-engine controls would replenish our stock and renew our genes. There are many kinds of Sykaans, and among them some (which my I has found as *friends*) which are rational and to be trusted. *Solution.* Adjust and cure species. *Means.* Cannot be imposed by outside Rule. Beastly creatures would resist by 'war', making havocs and radioactive roentgen-wreck. At stage one, *creatures must bring themselves to self-rule. This is the key to all.* At subsequent stages, they may, by agreement, accept Adjusters, and cure their programme to the Wheel to their great advantage.
Conclusion. Self-rule of mortals is precedent condition for Oitarian plantation.

Synthesis. Mortals are not without rational faculties, although subdued to the programme-of-the-blood. To induce them to come to self-rule they must be brought to an understanding that they will *either* come to a species-STP *or* must JMP to new self-rule programme.
To examine, refer back to data on defective Sykotic programming. (1) Such programmes are fragmented as by 'states', 'nations', 'governments', 'blocks' & c. & c., each of which is at logger with the others, which logger is usually wars. (2) Even these programmes are opposed by the right-angle cross-flow of families-in-series, each of which is self-programming. Prescription for persistent malfunction and wreck.
However. (1) Mortals have strong faculties of self-bonding, as within nations, & c. & c. In families such bonding very heavy. Not one of the billions of mortals now existing could exist if it had not been for the most attentive care during its impotent

infancy and childhood on the part of parents, family and fellows.

Moreover, Oi Paz has observed that there are two kinds of mortal, known as 'bonders' and 'bounders'. Of these, the bounders bound, or leap, to positions of power and authority, as pee-ems, em-pees, peppers & c. Just as light and noxious vapours will always rise to the head of water, so it is with the bounders, who are those with light and vain endowments and who burst on the surface of the lake of mortality their gaseous bubbles of egoism. But the bonders are those who roll equably like goldfish within the waters, performing the labours of gardeners, servants to horses, nurses, and all necessary tasks, such as the care of children. And of these two sorts, the bonders are incomparably the more numerous, comprising the greater part of their women and perhaps half of their men. *Solution*. Somehow get the bonders to sit from on high on the bounders. *Means*. Cannot be imposed by outside Rule. (See *Antithesis*.) Only terror of species-STP will induce species-bonding.

This arises from radical mortal programme-bug known to them as 'original sin'. 'Sin' is ego-flip-out. Dysfunction is such that bonding is a pair with excluding: i.e. centrifugal/centripetal forces inextricably mish-mashed. Nation-bonding is at same time extrusion of all others, as aliens or threats. Family bonding excludes un-families. Lovers close against invaders. Here is declaimed as science principal botch of species: no part can bond without Threat of Other, and Others must be furnished from among themselves. Hence species programmed for smash-up.

However. (2) If Oitar can now function as Threat of Other then mortal species-bonding may hap. EMP already great facilitator and accelerator. BUT threat must be screened by chokes or mortals will go higgledy and blast off nukes with consequences as in *Thesis* (*Reservations*).

Conclusion. Slowly increase Threat to hasten species-bonding while signalling to mortals non-hostile intent and desire to come to species-agreement for our plantation.

That is the logic-path which $I = Oi$ Paz will signal to Gracious Goodnesses. It is a draft and requires some cure. $I = O$. have not included many other matters, although these are urgencies. How could I explain my state of lovingness with Helena and how could such concern the Wheel? Or the fate of my son? All that concerns 'feelings' would be choked before it passed the Bumple gates. Nor could it be transcribed into Neuter Utter, in which the symbols for 'love' or 'mercy' are not found. Only the most strictly cured algorithm will pass the Adjuster screen.

As to the species-agreement, Sorley and I have given it much care. It is possible. He has done some good thinking and has shown me a painted simulacre of this globe, as well as flat projections of the seas and land-masses drawn on paper. There are immense habitable vacancies. We have also devised a mutual species-deterrent, which the mortals (which suppose their own beastly nature to be a paradigm of all creatures in the universe) may require as guarantee. All this must be added to the input.

Tomorrow I will go to Sorley's bumple and blast off this signal. But as to the agreement, that cannot be done by signal alone. There will have to be person-traffic to and from the moon.

The signal input must be encrypted into Neuter Utter. But to enter the Bumple Gate and rise to the Sublime Couch, Oi Paz must first make due obeisance in the mode of Bumple Utter. $I = O$. disremember the whole form, but it runs in some such way as this: 'Gracious Goodnesses, Oi Paz, Oi 57/2D Sper P 9 P/Co (Gard.) 3383/2/68, the least of Thy bits, returns programme to Thee. With bowed head does obeisance to the Sacred Wheel. Blessed be Thy vibes and ever may Thy Couch of Wisdom Roll! Thy Messenger humbly prays that the Couch may enroll data-flow as follows: ...' Then comes the logic-path (when cured) in Neuter Utter. Must see if memory-bank of my Recorder still holds the correct Bumple Utter form. Heigh-ho! Terrible lot to code before tomorrow. And I promised Helena to put Adam to bed.

Sage Diary

May 17th. Day before yesterday O. was at Astrosigint all day. Came back too exhausted even to talk. His vibes like a flat battery. Yesterday was out on Macho most of the day. Sd it was 'too early to know', but didn't explain know what? I never press him. Never seen so much traffic at Martagon. Staff cars rolling up to Hall all day; it reminded me of when Mayhem got eaten. Then Ann came back & sd that Dr Charon had been driven in, & security hoods were crawling all over the stables & were using the Temple of Apollo as a base.

This morning, an hour ago, Mary popped over. (She works now at Astrosigint, & Brian does their maintenance.) She took me aside like a conspirator & sd Rbt wanted to see me. When? Tonight, 9 p.m. Here? No, at the Cardiarum! Shld I bring D.? No. O.? No, he wants to see you by yourself. And she gave me one of her knowing 'I-can-keep-a-secret' smiles. Odd.

Sage Diary

May 18th. I struggled up to the Cardiarum like the doomed heroine in a Gothic novel. Heavy low hurrying clouds, so already nearly dusk. I struggled through the brambles and gorse at the foot of the little hill, and then on into the grove of yews, remembering the griffin statue which O. and I had once stumbled on. There are some old beeches at the top, just outside the Cardiarum walls, and they were throwing their branches around in a huroosh of wind. I'd only been up there once before – that time with O. – and had to walk half-way round the walls before I cld find entrance.

Inside it was even dusker. It is a weird place. The enclosed space must be half an acre, but the high roofless walls seem to shrink it. There are still several urns (where the dried hearts were kept) in alcoves half-way up the walls. There was one just within reach – I didn't look in!

Facing west, opposite the entrance, is the altar. Whatever statue or image the wicked de Boyle put there has gone, so there is just a slab with a deep alcove recess behind it wh looks like a grey eye-socket. As I looked at it, the early moonlight fell on to the alcove: no urn there, but some kind of embossed plaster moulding in the centre – it somehow looked like a broken wheel with a skull in the middle where the axle shld be. Quite creepy. But a large tuft of ivy coming over the wall and hanging above the alcove-top softens it a little, as if Nature were trying to take back its territory from something alien.

Mary tells me that the villagers at Shaw still clam up when strangers ask about what rites went on. And no one will say *whose* hearts were in the urns: humans' or horses' or dogs'.

I was a bit early and no Rbt. The place was creepy enough but why Rbt shld want an assignment with me *here* began to seem a bit creepy too. I switched on my torch and gingerly opened door of a tool-shed built as a lean-to against one wall: no corpses, no rapist, just some sacks, hurdles and a shovel. Sheltered from cold, while wind outside was biffing the roof. 9.25 still no Rbt. I looked out and the place had become *really* dark. I decided to give him five more minutes and then go.

At H-Hour minus one I went out again and saw a Form. Rbt, of course. I almost screamed. 'What the *hell* . . .?' 'Sorry,' he sd, 'Difficult to give the Cousins the slip.' 'But why H E R E?' I was trembling, & my own state made me angry. Rbt just led me back into the tool-shed, took out something like a light-monitor and shone his torch upon it. Neither of the dials moved. 'Why *here*,' he sd, 'is because this is the one point in these whole grounds which is totally screened from bugging. We're not even sure of our safe-chamber now. Don't ask me why. Quite inexplicable. Did de Boyle put lead in those walls? The people who are into magic would say ley-lines. We came upon it by accident, in an R/T exercise – total signals black-out.'

I was calmer now, but tense in a different way because I knew something of what was coming. Also his own vibes were as tense as nettles.

Rbt laid his torch on the table. The shed seemed more homely, except for a hanging sack wh threw wobbly shadows when the wind caught in the cracks. First he filled me in on why he cldn't ask D. or O. to try direct language communication on the moon-lock – the Cousins were dead set on using them to transmit disinformation – 'Well, damned lies'. The Oitarians wld have known instantly.

I knew most of this. What he hadn't told me before was that in the past two months more Oitarian craft had come into Earth atmosphere. The Americans had shot down three, the British one, the Russians maybe two. He thought the EMP last week was a 'response': punishment, demonstration, warning? Or just a 'rehearsal'. The technological know-how and execution was brilliant – 'they're in a different galactic league'.

Then he went into computer talk, not all of wh I cld follow. It seems they have some mega-computer plus transmitter now on the moon, and it had 'burgled' or hacked into a series of major computer installations: NATO HQ at Brussels, Cheltenham, US Space Command in Colorado, probably the Soviet outfit in Novosibirsk, even little Malvern. Now the computers were 'talking to each other'. Brussels had simply had to switch all power off to stop 'wholesale robbery'.

I asked if Earth computers cldn't go and rob it back. It seems no, because computers (*Qy:* Like genders?) can never be exactly equally matched, one had to be dominant – it calls the questions from the other. In this case the lunar installation is decidedly dominant.

I asked what computers cld *say*, if they didn't have languages. Rbt sd they *are* a language and cld say 'a very great deal, almost everything'. Our computers are only seventh generation while theirs is perhaps seventieth. Even the word, 'computer', is wrong – more like some Artificial Intelligence 'brain', wh cld fit one of our advanced computers into one cell. They work in 'pico-seconds', 'gigabits' and 'bips', or billions of instructions per nano-second. They can simply drain our computers' memories like a Hoover. Can do other things: insert bugs in ongoing programmes; put in false instructions, so that nukes backfire; reach in somehow and 'zap' or wipe off data – cryptography at Behemoth was actually getting somewhere in cracking Neuter Utter, and one morning they woke up and found all their data had been zapped.

As for our Earth languages, probably all the major ones have been cracked for months. O's Translator was a little hand-machine. They must have a Translator on Oitar one thousand times more effective and fast. They can probably monitor all Earth R/T traffic, television, maybe telephones as well. They *could* – if they had satellites – have equipment so sensitive as to pick up voices.

'They could be listening to us now. But I don't think so. They will have quite enough from R/T.'

We sat in silence while the sack swayed and shadowed Rbt's face. Two cockroaches were on the floor, waving their feelers and hurrying on their runny legs. Rbt deliberately and impassively squashed them – one, two – with his boot. I said, 'Robert, how can you?' 'Making a point, Helen. Twice.'

One of the roaches was still twiddling its legs & waving its feelers, & he ground it carefully on the mud floor. Then a huge hairy spider fell off the sack, but he backed his boot away, although – ugh! – I almost squashed it myself. 'Point is, Helen,' he went on, 'I happen to loathe cockroaches. I don't mind spiders. I'm quite indifferent to ants – unless they bite me. It's got nothing to do with reasons or morals. Just a sort of phobia at alien creatures. An impulse of ugh or not ugh.'

'So?'

'If I was on my own I'd always kill a cockroach. If I was with someone soft on all life, like you or Ann, I wouldn't.'

'But you *did*.'

'To make a point.'

Silence again.

At last I sd, 'So to the Oitarians we are roaches?'

'No, just insects. Probably they don't hate us. Maybe we're ants, who've started to bite them. One spacecraft shot down could be an accident. Six, maybe seven, shot down in a row will read on even a child's computer print-out as "hostile". But they probably don't have any feelings about us at all. They're rational creatures, they don't have urges to exterminate. They don't have either pity or aggro. We're a low-level problem, among AOB.'

'You're wrong. They wouldn't drain our computers and send an EMP under Any Other Business. We're high on the agenda now.'

'Yes. I overstated it. But I've been closeted with maniacs all day – the politicos are much worse than the military – who insist upon calling Oitar the Enemy, before they've even tried to talk and find out.'

I shivered. 'Why don't they just come down? What are they waiting for? They could just burn us off ... like lichen.' (Didn't O. say something like that to me in the early days?)

'They have their own problems. Their threshold of radioactive tolerance is even lower than ours. That was in one of your own weekly reports. Even a few more rads and the planet would be off-bounds to them. They wouldn't nuke us and they don't have nukes anyway.'

I asked if they cldn't use something else than nukes – lasers & c. Rbt sd yes, they very certainly cld. Their technology was light-years ahead of ours. They might have problems in the short run in storing energy. Colossal energy needed to send 'bolts' from moon. The last EMP must have run down their resources. They might be able to use moon trash for energy, but it wld take time to build up again. And components for landing vehicles wld have to be ferried from Oitar. That was a two- or three-year trip, although some wld now be on its way. 'So we've got at least three years before their landfall. That is what the Cousins estimate, and they're good at counting.'

'But they *will* come? And we can't stop them?'

'They will come. And after that EMP even some of the politicians – and some of the NATO staff – know that we can't stop them. And if they haven't got any aggro, still, if we are bugging their programme, they will find some way to rub out the human species – like some selective weedkiller.'

'Oipas wouldn't . . .'

'Perhaps a year ago Oipas would. Read your own early reports. And Oipas has had the benefit of living with you for a year or more. No other Oitarian has had the good fortune of such an education.'

I glanced at him, but his vibes were uncritical and kindly. The spider was darting about, confused in the torchlight, and he shooed it gently into the pile of sacks with his boot. 'In fact, as things now stand, perhaps the last chance there is of human survival is with Oipas. And with you.'

The wind was howling and I had to raise my voice. 'You mean he might . . . tell them we aren't bugs?'

'That, and other things. If we could get you *both* to the moon he could show you off and say, "Look, she doesn't bite!" '

I felt as if I had been shut into a deep-freeze. He smiled, but it was a self-tormented, weary smile.

'But Oitarians aren't like that,' I sd. 'Oipas doesn't have any influence. He's programmed, with a role-set. No one has any influence. There's no way individuals can debate issues or make choices. Whatever they do on the moon will be programmed by the Gracious Goodnesses back on Oitar.'

'Sounds like Mother Earth,' he sd. 'Look, I'm getting cold, let's take a turn.'

So we stamped around the Cardiarum, and Rbt shone his torch on the tunnel mouth beside an old yew just outside the entrance, wh Sophy & co. had scrabbled through. I admired their guts even more. It restored my humour a bit.

The moon was now up, dodging in and out of the scurrying clouds, and I looked up at it, knowing or *naming* what I had known for months. It seemed . . . not hostile, not friendly, just neutral. And beautiful.

Then the moonlight fell on the altar eye-socket, which glared at me, and I stood up to it and glared back. Rbt put his arm around my shoulders and said, 'Helen, you really have got guts –'

and then added, 'for a girl,' knowing that it wld make me
chortle. So we leaned against each other for a moment, almost
like lovers, and watched the huge beech boughs, laden with their
new leaves, swaying above the Cardiarum wall.

It was difficult to hear each other in the wind, so we went back
into the shed.

Then he explained about O's signal. (First he took out his bug-
meter again to check.) He sd that of course I was right about
Oitarian decision-procedures. All he knew about that was from
my reports. 'From what I can ... what you have worked out, no
individual has any input – except on licensed disputes about taste.
The basic AI architecture of the Gracious Goodnesses seems to be
banks of transputers with menu-driven programmes laid down
aeons ago, leading into endless feedback loops – a sort of tautocracy. But they do have a full complement of data-capture buffers
and logic gates. And, of course, input to the Wheel must sometimes go upwards; it can't only come down. You and David
make it sound as if only the Provosts of Colleges and the Adjusters
have data-input terminals.'

I nodded.

'But there are exceptions to Rule. Any individuals or small
task-forces who go on special or hazardous programmes – in
which their data might be important and urgent – have limited
terminal access. Commanders of the space ferries, for example,
have an open-gate licence. I'm sure Oipas has told you. You
know he bears a special licence?'

I shook my head. Never thought of asking him. I felt miffed
that Rbt knew things about O. that I didn't. I still find it strange
to realise that he talks to people about other things when I'm not
there.

'He does. Or, rather, he did until yesterday. He came over and
told me last week, the day after our consultation in the safe.' (I
remembered that O. had gone up to Astrosigint after our long
walk, saying he had promised to return a book to Rbt. Never
known him devious before.)

'Since Oipas was on a solitary mission with high potential data-content, he was given an input licence, but for one transmission only, direct to the Gracious Goodnesses. The licence was a code, or key, putting him straight in. He can't use it again. It's known as a "self-eating key" – we have them too. Once the input has been made, the gate closes. Oipas made a very remarkable report. Of course I couldn't read his signal, but he showed me a copy he had worked in English. It was a logical case – in my view unanswerable – as to why Oitarians and humans must come to a negotiated agreement with each other. And it included some practical proposals to negotiate around.'

'But will they take any notice? I mean the Gracious Good-nesses?'

'You suggested one answer to that, Helen, in a hypothesis in that paper Weeder snatched. There aren't any Gracious Good-nesses. Just a mega-computer, with Bumple priests – and a few top Adjusters – who control the terminals, monitor the data-input and proclaim the print-out.'

'Mmm. Everything points to that. The priests are sort of shamans of the Oracle. The GGs are an anthropomorphic myth. Maybe even the shamans believe in it. I've tried to probe Oipas on this, but I meet a block. It's a sensitive point. He has to half-believe in them. But surely that means that the shamans – or Adjusters – will just stop his signal?'

'No. He has a special licence, only given to priority mission-aries. So long as Oipas's licence is still valid and the gate still open, his signal will input directly into the main data-scrambler. No Adjuster can stop it. The signal's probably in there now, and the computer *has* to take his logic-path on board. What it does with it – whether its ALU-profile is strong enough to gain hegemony over other algorithms – is another question. But he sent a strong signal and it could lead to a programme-jump.'

'Tell me about the proposals. You said there were practical proposals?'

We switched into a geography tutorial. Rbt sd, first, that although the Earth's population was immense, most of it was packed into small regions – the temperate zones, sea-coasts and rivers. There are vast uninhabited regions – deserts, mountain ranges, the oceans are 'empty'. The Oitarians are habituated to far more rigorous conditions than us and have evolved technologies to cope. They cld live almost anywhere on this planet, except the poles, and save immense energy resources, with no need for ice-burners or oxygen-generators.

Also, Oitar's population is very small. Although Oitar is almost twice the size of Earth, only $\frac{1}{500}$th of surface under domes. 'In one paper you made an informed guess of population stabilised at about Sweden's.' From wh he concluded that a deal cld be made. They cld be granted extensive zones for plantation. They cldn't cope with equatorial or sub-equatorial climates anyway; all their technologies go the other way. Answer? Easy. Offer them Antarctica, Outer Arctic Circle, maybe huge uninhabited tracts of Northern Canada, Lapland, Greenland, Northern Siberia. Compared to Oitar these wld seem torrid zones, also virgin lands unblemished by mortal droppings. 'Even on the Antarctic rim they would be amazed at all the molten water and exalted by the pure air. Let them just put up a few domes and cupolas and they would transform South Georgia into Kew Gardens.'

That cld be negotiating position one. After that there was room for a lot of play. They might want to settle parts of some oceans, where no one ever goes. If there weren't available islands, they cld construct mega-floats: no problem for them. Or if they needed to experiment in alternative ecologies, we cld offer concessions (sort of Hong Kongs) in the Gobi or Sahara, or the Himalayas, or we cld let them plant one or two experimental islands. We cld even have reserve positions: in extremity we might have to give them Iceland and New Zealand, and resettle the populations.

I asked, 'So this has been discussed at the Hall?' He was silent, as if hiding in the shadow of the sack. Then I said, 'If this did come off – and I'm not at all sure that Oitarians "negotiate" in that way – I can still see two huge problems.'

'Only two?'

I gritted my teeth and shot a frost-vibe at him. 'First, wouldn't this be only a temporary stand-off? A sort of putting-off of the terminus? After a few decades they'd have a population-explosion, expand their territories, and push us out.'

'How? Yes, of course, they could engineer a population increase. But you've described how they work their bio-engineering programme. If they continue as per Rule, none of the projections of human demography would apply to them. To change the Rule would involve reversing countless generations of bio-programming.'

I thought for some reason of Eddystone's lighthouse, but only sd, 'I think, Robert, it would be better to confine them to sub-Arctic zones. And encourage them to maintain their food-taboos. I mean, not to eat. This is the place where your plans will come unstuck.'

Rbt took my point. 'Well, at the least there would be time for the two species to learn to coexist. We might learn advantages from each other, develop bonds. There might even be ... some miscegenation.'

I frost-vibed him again, since I can't think of Adam as a miscegene. He hurried on. 'And then both sides could guarantee the species-treaty with some kind of Doomsday deterrent. Call it LOB, or Launch-On-Betrayal. For example, some self-automating nuclear plants, on both sides, which would go off and make a nuclear winter if either side defaulted on the Treaty Protocols. It wouldn't even have to *be* there, so long as both species were programmed or conditioned to imagine it was there. It could be myth, like the Gracious Goodnesses.'

I sd, 'Charming. I'm not sure Oitar would wear that.'

Rbt sd, 'And the other problem? You said there were two.'

'Us. Even if Oitar agrees, how do we cope with Earth? There is no Unit Earth, no world government. Who signs the treaty on our side? Who keeps it?'

The torch's battery was almost run out, so that the two of us were like dimly swinging shadows. Rbt played the failing light on his watch. 'Nearly midnight,' he sd. 'This is the last bit I had to tell you. Let's go out.'

Outside the storm had suddenly subdued, as May storms do.

The moon was now sole occupant of the heavens, picking out
the alcoves and the urns, but the grey eye had fallen into shadow.
We tramped around the Gothic circuit, arm in arm.

Rbt sd this was indeed the problem. The obvious thing was
for humanity to unite and put up these proposals. It was the only
way. But the beggars can't see it. The EMP had 'educated' them
a bit. Now some of the military cld see it: the British general staff
was backing him, and the US admirals were 'rational'. A section
of the Soviet military were rational too. Two days after the EMP
a high Soviet airforce general flew into Stornoway – rather like
Hess in World War 2 – with a message that Warsaw Pact and
NATO military must unite, and force each other's politicians to
see reason. Unfortunately, the Cousins got hold of him – 'they
are crawling all over the Isle of Lewis with their Freebie-laun-
chers' – and *sent him back* to the KGB, with President Forsst's
compliments! Incredible!

He said the politicians and opinion-managers are the worst,
plus the space-lab freaks and a few crazy generals: both American
and Euro. For a day or two the EMP threw them. Now they've
bounced back, and are talking of 'malfunctions'. They say they
can screen all sensitive systems, and they still pretend that their
SDI furniture can 'eliminate all alien landfall systems'. This is the
nuke faction, and Forsst is their prisoner. Forsst's speech last
month was simply a cover for all-systems-go to 'take out' the
moon. The Russians agreed, which is why Forsst obligingly
returned their defecting general. The 'three-year Super Apollo
program' was disinformation, in case Oitar was listening. In fact
the USA was on course to nuke the moon in about six weeks'
time.

'Was?' I asked, looking up into the sky. (The moon was still
there.) 'Not is?'

'Been put on "hold". Alternative options, such as X-ray laser
zapping, now under study. The EMP changed things a bit. And
perhaps I did.'

'But you're only a Colonel, Robo. How come you have so
much influence, among these generals and pee-ems?'

'Thanks to you, Oipas and David. Plus a little Astrosigint work. I may be "only" a Colonel, but they regard me as a sort of shaman of the Oracle. Too many things I predicted have come true. I am the only one in the whole boiling – thanks to you – who can put together a profile of Oitarian responses and intentions. The odd thing is that they've got no interest in Oipas or in the Zone of Eden. Mind you, I've been careful not to make acknowledgements recently . . . to protect your privacy. They – the Cousins are quite convinced that my info comes from signals traffic, that I've cracked Oitarian codes, but am holding back on them. That's why they spy on Astrosigint incessantly. But this still leaves me as the shaman. And I told them that I was certain of two things. (1) Our nukes won't get through. No Way. They might even be turned around. (2) If by some fluke our nukes did get through, then within less than a year all life – all human life certainly and probably all sentient life – would be extinct on Planet Earth. I don't know by what means. They have means that passeth our understanding. But – once nuke them and we become an "ugh".'

'So? That stopped them?'

'That induced almost a minute's silence at conference. General Rainborough tells me that in the coffee-break one of their spook-directors sidled up to him and asked, "Who is this guy Sorley? What's his security rating – is he Q-cleared?" Rainborough kicked him up the arse. It's got as bad as that. The Conference is a maelstrom of factions.'

'But the new programme?'

'Two programmes, three options. A Euro-programme. And a double-optioned NATO (i.e. American) programme. The NATO programme is this. Option (1), intensive further study of nuke and laser capacity to take out moon. If this is confirmatory, then blast off. If this gives rise to no–go conclusions, then Option (2), which is both foul and crazy. You won't believe it.'

'Go on. I'm not sure what belief is any more.'

'They want to send up a NATO Roving Ambassador and make a deal with Oitar. They want to give them Russia.'

'WHO do?'

'They. The President. President Forsst. Already they're having rows in the Pentagon and White House as to how *much* of the Soviet Union. They all agree that Poland — all Eastern Europe — must be allowed to rejoin the Free World. The doves want to offer to Oitar all the rest of the Soviet Union. The hawks insist that the Baltic Republics, the Ukraine and Mongolia must also be "freed" first.'

'What do they suppose would happen to the Russians?'

'Oh, that would be up to the Oitarians. But since they have designated Oitar as Enemy, they assume that Oitarians would behave much like they do themselves. Without scruple. Like defoliation in Vietnam. In fact, the hawks are pushing a scenario — "for bottom-line negotiation" — in which NATO would prepare the way for Oitar landfall by pre-emptive laser-zapping of all critical targets. Oitar would at the same time do a zoned EMP zap and then their space fleet would landfall in the ruins. It's completely and utterly crazy. But the Forsst faction are on programme for it. That or Option (1). It will be decided in two months.'

We sat down on the altar slab. There wasn't much point in looking around at the world any more. I sd (I can't think what it had to do with anything), 'You're a Christian, Robo. You believe in God. How could He let this happen?'

He was silent for a while. I cld sense the dark eye of the vacant altar-alcove like a sort of jackal-vibe at our backs. Then he sd, 'I never said I believed in a *nice* God. I thought about that a lot when Alison died. The Prime Mover may be absent-minded. Maybe He enjoys sacrifices, war upon war, and programmed us that way. Killing each other is the only way to placate Him.'

I'd never known him so bitter before, but he went on. 'You know who this altar is dedicated to? The Almighty Nihil. De Boyle made him into his god. Everyone supposes that they had sexy orgies here. On the contrary. They probably did have sacrifices here — maybe dogs, goats, rumour says an orphan child

418

or two. But the ceremonies were *anti*-sexual, since sex can be a gate for Eros, who is Nihil's enemy. Nihil's creed is we come from nothing, we are as nothing, and to nothing we return.'

Then he softened and lowered his voice. 'I do believe in Jesus, though. Who took the mortal side and was the sworn enemy of Nihil.'

Some plaster fell in the empty eye behind us, and the jackal-vibes seemed to whimper and run away. I asked, 'So what you call Jesus might have two months to get ahead of Nihil? Is that the Euro-programme? Only where do you catch a jesus? Not in Brussels.'

Rbt sd that the Euro-rocket was now ready for moon-shot. Since the last bust-up with the French, it had moved to England, and the launch-pad was now on Salisbury Plain in fact not far from Stonehenge. (English Heritage had agreed, as they always do, to 'defence priority'.)

'And ... ? You want Oipas ... and perhaps me ... to go?'

He nodded.

I sd, cldn't Oitar send down ambassadors? Or send down a craft to fetch us? (More reliable mode of transport than Euro-things.) He sd it was too risky. He cldn't trust the Americans – or the Russians – to switch their space LOW (launch-on-warning) systems off. If an alien blip tripped their LOWs, it wld trigger 'responses', e.g. take out spacecraft, or worse ...

We plodded the circuit again, sombre as man and wife. He stopped and gave me a squeeze. Then he sd, without looking at me, 'If it's any help – and if we could get them to agree – I would come with you also. It wouldn't be fair to send one human on her own.'

I drew in my breath in terror.

'But ... there'd be astronauts?'

'I rather think the astronauts might turn around. Or wait for you in orbit.' He looked away and started nudging the grass with a boot. 'They would send down any visitors in a little tub ... like the Apollo capsule.'

I realised with a flash of anger that we weren't just talking

about 'options'. I had been there, since yesterday, on the Conference table, like a sacrifice on Nihil's altar slab. '*You* . . .' I began.

'No! I *stopped* them. I stopped or made them shelve a hundred
imbecile things. This seemed the only possible way.'

'I see. And it's all settled, is it? And all that male top brass up
at the Hall has agreed? And you've been sent to tell me?'

'To ask you. The Cousins think it's some British ego-trip that
has to be humoured. They think it's a "null option". But they
did formally agree that pending "execution or decommissioning
of Euro-program all other NATO programs remain on Amber
Hold" – i.e. they pend.'

'So Oipas and I are to be either executed or decommissioned?
And no one, not even you, thought of inviting us to join the
discussion?'

Rbt sounded exhausted. 'It wouldn't have helped. They only
know half of what we know. They don't know about Oipas's
signal to the GGs. If we are to play this hand we've got to keep
it to ourselves . . .'

'Ourselves? We? Thank you for letting we know!'

Rbt Sorley's face stiffened in the darkness, and my mind was
tumbling in a free fall. I was thinking, not about Oitar or the
moon, but about the way Rbt can make me furious with his
officer-status arrogance. He's an old-fashioned paternalist, a sort
of Friend of the People. And then, paradoxically, I thought that,
paternalist or not, Rbt inspires trust in me. And what else can the
mortal world depend upon? If this crazy scheme is to work, then
the future of two species' civilisations, with all their technologies
and weaponries, will depend in the end upon the trust between
two persons – three, if we include O. Everything rests not upon
money or power or things but upon the honesty of Rbt's
smile, O's love of flowers and horses and of Adam, my own
skills in de-coding. My heart leapt out of the deep-freeze,
and I found myself exulting in the true artefacts of culture.
Human bonding is the source of all power, for good or for evil,
amen.

Rbt was running on, apologetically. '. . . want to make this clear. The whole thing depends on your and Oipas's agreement. I insisted on that. So did General Rainborough. Said "we cannot allow a guest on our planet and a young woman to act under duress." '

I found that I was laughing.

'Well . . . when?'

'Friday.'

'Friday! It's Tuesday now!'

'No, Wednesday. It's past one.'

We were both silent again.

Then, 'We must do what we can.' Did he say that or did I? Or was it just our vibes?

Very definite clattering of plaster in Dead-Eye Alcove then, and a wafting sound, wh materialised into a large white barn-owl flying above us across the moon. Rbt was even more startled than I. Then we both laughed together. I sd, 'Good omen. Minerva is telling the moon. Oh, well, Friday's hours and hours and hours away.'

We linked arms and tramped back down the little hill and through the gorse. The moonlight was amazing, and picked out everything: Martagon Hall, the bumples of Astrosigint, Ann's exercise-field with the jumps, the dower house nestling in the shadow of its trees. Rbt walked me home and gave me a kind of male biff on the shoulder for goodbye.

Found O. still awake and asking what had kept me. (Qy: Surely he cldn't be *jealous*? He's not as mortal as that!?) Sd I wld tell him all about it 'tomorrow' (wh is today). Then I remembered, and asked him, a bit crossly, why he hadn't told me, or let me help with, his special GG signal. He sd, 'It was not easy. It had to be construed exactly according to Rule. If you had been mixing in with me you would have melted my logic-paths.' He was v tender. The moon shone full in the window, and for the first time for days we did the beast-with-the-two-backs. My back was on top, and as I came I watched the moon on his gentled face, which masked the programme of his risen blood.

Sage Notebook. Pasted-in typescript

Martagon
Wed 11.30 a.m.

Dear Helena,

Been desperately trying these two days to pop over and see you all down there. But you know how these Conferences are! No playing truant from this one. Nose to grindstone & c.

Colonel Sorley has told me about your Mission with Mr Oipas. That will be quite an adventure and we all wish you luck. I hope he looks after you properly.

I wanted to say thank you for your work in our team, and how much we shall all miss you. We shall hope to see you back, safe and sound.

No time for more. Dr Charon wants me to accompany him and the US Defense Sec. back to Chequers, so I must blast off. Excuse rush!

James Pepper*

Miss Gordon will run you [*deleted*] this over for me.

Cutting. File 'Sykotic Trash'

DISSIDENTS APPEAL TO FREEWORLD

The influential Soviet peace and human rights group, Charter 91, issued a statement yesterday which, unusually, was transmitted on Radio Moscow to the West. The signatories included a number of Academicians, a Soviet Air Marshal, two generals, and even a member of the Politburo.

It called for 'global co-operation' in meeting the threat to 'Planet Earth'. Addressing the Soviet leaders, it asked them to approach the United Nations, with a view to setting up at once a 'Committee of Public Safety' of scientists, academics & c.

---

* *Pencil drawing of Earth-creature with grossly enlarged snout. From the regularity with which these appear in the Sage papers, it appears that this was a customary way of signifying receipt and endorsement of orders.*

from many nations, on a non-political basis. The Soviet and US governments should agree to cede supreme power to this committee. Addressing the leaders of NATO, it called on them to co-operate, and suggested that they consult the Pugwash committee.

Leading figures from the GDR, Hungary and Bulgaria have associated themselves with the Appeal. It is rumoured in Prague that there has been an emergency session of the Czech Communist Party central committee, and that Mr Dubček has been asked to reassume the post of General Secretary.

Mr Fibbs, the White House spokesman, welcomed the Appeal and called on Soviet leaders to show their sincerity by evacuating the Baltic States, the Ukraine and Mongolia forthwith.

The British Prime Minister, Dr Charon, warned that the Appeal should be treated 'with some caution'. He urged the United States not to 'lower its guard', and affirmed that deterrence was essential to defend the freeworld.

At CND a spokesperson said that all the staff were far too busy to read the papers. Everyone was working 'flat out' preparing the NVDA against Frisbie missiles at Martagon Hall next week.* She announced that if they were not let into the premises to inspect the Frisbie-sites, there would be a mass 'die-in' and blockade of the gates.

Sage Diary

May 19th. Hellish day today. O. was fine about our Mission. But he was in a high/low state, vibes v disturbed. (*Qy:* Does he really *want* to get back among Oitarians? Or leave Earth?)

Then, oh hell, we had our first major, human-sized, stand-up row. (I realise I've been protecting him from full frontal confrontation up till now.) I'd assumed from the start that Adam

---

* *Sage annotation, pencil:* 'That Chris!'

will stay here. Never thought twice. As soon as I'd had my talk with O. I had a conference with David & Rani, which Ann later joined. They were great. R. sd she'd love to look after Adam for as long as I liked, she felt he was little Priya's brother, we were all an 'extended family' as in India, & if O. was going with me, well, she'd have more time & c.

When I explained we were going to *moon*, even D. got really concerned and brotherly. A. sd Sprite had had a foal ten days ago, wh she wld 'bring on' for the kids. (A. of course had twigged at once that I might not be taking a week-end trip.) The others twigged then & we became v solemn. D. and R. sd they wld be honoured to be Adam's guardians, 'if anything happened'. So we wrote out a formal letter signifying their willingness to adopt Adam in the event, and my desire for same, wh the three of us signed and A. witnessed. And I went over to O's bumple to ask him to witness also, thinking he'd be pleased.

He just blew up. Ranted and delivered heavy sentences. Sd Adam wld blast off to moon with him, whether I came or no. Became utterly mcp, declaimed 'orders' at me, & sd Adam had Oitarian genes. Whereat I blurted out, 'But the child is *mine*!' And then (wh I shldn't), 'You don't have ANY RIGHTS. We aren't even MARRIED!' At wh Frolic (now bumple servitor) arched her back and hissed at me like a real cat.

O. turned away and knelt at the bumple wheel, as if praying for guidance (or roll-control). This calmed me down, & I saw that his shoulders were shaking. Then he pleaded with me to let Adam come, allowing that it was my right but his heavy need, and he promised to 'share and share and share' the parent-role. He became confessional, & sd he feared that when back among Oitarians he might have a 'programme-flip' – 'you do not know how ruly is the Wheel'. Adam wld be a 'screen', which wld hold him to his Earth-locks. Adam wld be the lock between him and me.

I asked him if – when he got to the moon – he ever meant to return to Earth. He was silent for a while. Then he sd, 'If Adam comes, all three will return. If the Wheel and if those reigning mortals allow, I hope to return as guide and interpreter and to protect your species. But we will return.' (This also meant that if Adam doesn't go he promises nothing.) I had to give in. I asked about *food*. He sd they wld 'synthesise it' and he wld 'programme' it. But I don't like it. Not one bit.

O. added that Frolic wld be blasting off too. Wh of course is absurd. They wldn't consider it.

Spent all afternoon writing up diary. Why? For whom? I suppose it's the way I cope.

Now (9 p.m.) Rbt has just rung up about our 'kit'. Seems that space in Eurorocket (tourist class) is a bit cramped, like those transatlantic jumbos where you sit with your knees in your chest as if filed in a rack. Must make a packing-list:

Adam   His teddy. Also Glossop.
Nappies × 100 (do they have washing-machines?)
Sling
Blanket-bit he likes to smell
Powdered milk for emergency
Cans and cans of baby-food (Rbt sd he was ordering several canisters of humanfood for the capsule, to keep us going if we had to stay 'a week or two'. But he'll probably forget baby-food.)
Most of the clothes in the three top drawers
Bath duck
? Teething-ring?
Towels?

Me   Sort through clothes in bottom two drawers (*Mem:* Oitarians wear trews only. But why don't I go just as I am? A mortal. So that they know the worst.)
Woolly hat & gloves for happy moon walks
Go in boots (take slippers)
Tampax × 100
Nice soap
Glacier mints for journey
Heroin? Seriously – Valium? (Or, *Qy:* Something final? Ask R.)

NB Tissues (man-sized) (Lots)
Camera
Films
Recorder
This notebook (nearly full, take another) (Better get to-
gether a few files and notebooks, with relevant back info.
In case we have to brief them.)
Books? (Maybe a Bible, to introduce them to a mainline
mythology? A good world atlas. I want my Blake.)
Gifts? (Rbt says he will put a few on board. Suggest
cassettes, lots of Bach. He says not too much briefing
material this time, we can take it 'next time'. Ho-ho!)

Oipas Can bloody well pack his own kit (R. will help him.)
(*Mem:* Remind him to take his recorder, files.)

(11 p.m.) Just now was down on my knees scrabbling among
Adam's kit when O. came in. He said he wanted to exchange
forgivingness for our row. (Easy for him to forgive. He won.)
Then he sd, very puzzled, 'Helena, why are we not married?
Why did we not go into a wedding?' I sd we were lovers and
parents wh was just the same. He said, no, it was not the same,
all things must roll harmoniously with ceremony. He sd that
before blast-off he wanted us to be 'made into a true wedding'
and go to the moon 'as a marriage'. It was a sweet proposal and
I sd 'yes'.

Ann was still bumping around in the kitchen & I ran down &
told her. She gave me a hug & sd she had thought of suggesting
it herself, only it might have sounded 'a bit square and final'. She
sd she wld organise it tomorrow. 'It can't be like Rani and
David's, Hel. Too short notice. Just us. David and Rani and me
and Robo. And you two. And Adam and Priya. And Frolic. And
I'll bring Macho and Minniver to carry you both to the bumple.
I'll do the ceremony bit myself. I'll dig out a dress.'

Heigh-ho! What shall I wear?

426

ZONE OF EDEN

Sage Diary

May 21st. Am writing this rigged out as an astronaut in a sort of swivel-chair with stomach-flutters waiting for countdown. Wh has already been twice postponed, wh makes matters worse. Mini-astronaut Adam is on O's lap, well strapped, & hasn't started bawling yet. Frolic *did* get on board. O. stamped and stormed until they gave in. Silly! She's in a sort of globe and v cross-vibed.

Wedding was bloody nice. Write about that later. Not such a fun thing as R's, but close and warm. Everyone did their parts right – a lovely *raga* from R. – and A. looked graceful in her gown. O. was at his most charismatic, and deeply serious and moved by it all. Only unruly roller was Frolic, who was by no means as dignified as Tigger, and started chasing a butterfly in the middle of things. However, at least she didn't gorge herself to death afterwards.

The goodbye party was very close too. Wasn't really a party. We just had a normal evening together, with a Rani/David curry, & talked Martagon gossip.

We turned in early. O. and I wandered out, last thing, for a stroll in the park. It was dark – the moon not up yet – and the remains of the wedding-fire was still burning in the temple. We went in there and stood in silence for a while, holding hands, mixing our vibes. Outside again we wandered across to the Arboretum and back, sensing the firm turf under our feet and the dew on our ankles. A clear night, with the stars very sharp – I looked up, in awe at the immensity above, just as I used to do when I was twelve. I tried to imagine the vasty distance between the little cluster of asterisks which makes up the Pleiades, and wondered (with a chill) what the stars wld look like from the moon. Then I thought of the Druids, working out their astral calendar, and of the generations before me – shepherds, navigators, cave-dwellers – who had looked with awe at the same stars as I.

O. was abstracted in thoughts of his own, and suddenly started

427

to chant one of his favourite bits from *Paradise Lost*:

> *When I behold this goodly Frame, this World*
> *Of heav'n and Earth consisting, and compute*
> *Thir magnitudes, this Earth a spot, a graine,*
> *An Atom, with the Firmament compar'd*
> *And all her numberd Starrs, that seem to rowle*
> *Spaces incomprehensible (for such*
> *Thir distance argues and thir swift return*
> *Diurnal) meerly to officiate light*
> *Round this opacous Earth, this punctual spot,*
> *One day and night; in all their vast survey*
> *Useless besides . . .*

'Do you want to leave the good Earth?' I asked. He did not reply, but his vibes – or mine? – seemed to answer, 'We must do what we can.' 'Well, if we're really going to the moon tomorrow,' I sd, 'I must go in and wash my hair.'

Rbt called for us in Astrosigint Rangerover this morning. Slung our kit aboard, sd adieus, pretending it was a weekend at Brighton. Then Ann cantered up on Sprite, with her new foal dancing along behind. She hitched Sprite to the magnolia and gave me a hug and a blessing. Then she said, in her usual offhand way, 'Bye, Robo. Take care!' And suddenly she seemed to bite her lip – she turned away, mounted Sprite and trotted off, not looking back. We all waved to D. and R. & I made Adam wave to Priya. As we drove to the perimeter gate, there was A., waiting on Sprite. My last sight of Martagon: A. waving, Sprite looking round at her foal, the foal with that astonished how-did-I-come-to-be-in-this-lovely-world look that foals have.

We got to the pad in less than an hour. It was weird, driving through villages again, seeing people going about doing their things with no notion of what is up. O. was delighted when he found that the launch-pad is near Stonehenge – said it was auspicious, and Droo Id had designed it all. The awful awful awful thing happened when we were already at the launch-pad office waiting to be driven to the rocket. The station commander suddenly came in and summoned Rbt out. They were away about 20 minutes. Then Rbt came back looking like thunder. He sd he had been 'taken off the ship'. Govt had ordered him to stay at Astrosigint. He felt he had betrayed us both. He had got on to General Rainborough, but nothing cld be done.

Poor Rbt fussed around and worried. Got several things out of his kit – world atlas, a couple of files, some gifts of music, tapes, fabrics, photos of Antarctica & c., and asked for them to be transferred to mine. Then he sd that his not coming with us was awful, but perhaps it was 'for the best'. Was a little miffed & sd 'best for who?' He sd that the worst problems might be here on Earth. He'd been playing 'rather a lone hand' at Astrosigint, and it was too much for John Rock and Jane to handle on their own. Back at Astrosigint he cld control the Earth end of communications, and perhaps steer the politicos through the negotiations. And watch out for their 'tricks'. He sd that it had been agreed last night with Oitar's lunar base to set up a direct audio-visual lock, open for an hour each day, and he cld talk to me or O. that way. It seems that O's signal got through the GGs' gate – they know we're coming and have sent a 'green light'.

I got some comfort from that, but suddenly saw what a fix *he* was in. I sd, 'Robo, you *are* too much of a loner. You can't possibly handle this on your own. You need some back-up, *non-political* – scientists, people who've worked on culture-traumas, maybe even someone sensible from the peace movement. And people with some real influence.' I had an idea, dug in my shoulder-bag, and scribbled a note to John Wardroop. 'Get that to him at once. He's supposed to be retired but he knows everyone, he's got far more real pull than Pepper. He may have one or two failings as a male, but he's a brilliant anthropologist. When he sees this note he'll whistle up a support team for you. And do it discreetly.' Rbt thanked me & agreed.

Then we were shepherded off, and I thought … oooh … er … count-down

Have now got well beyond atmosphere. Nausea of lift-off, wh is like morning sickness × 10, beginning to subside. Weightlessness is not to be recommended. O. so intent on holding astounded Adam that he let go of Frolic, who sailed upside down in her globe to ceiling & obviously blames us for all these horrors.

This whole carry-on is a sick sort of image of our lives. Our past falls away from us like people or things jettisoned from a spacecraft, and they tumble around, upside down, in the void of time. Without the gravity given by time present they are floating around without meaning. Only the present context − pushing through the void − gives weight to purposes and makes them adhere. Outside, behind, before, is the rule of Nihil.

Oooh ... er ... did it lurch or was that me?

Must have been going a day or more. As tourist-class passenger I don't get a porthole. But just now one of the astronauts sort of floated and pulled himself down the cabin, and took me & Adam floating along with him to the observation panel. The sky was black, but that's normal, day or night. Cld see the moon, already more than eight times as big − huge − with all the craters and ravines as clear as ice. It seemed to be below us − Nihil's kingdom, as beautiful as the dead. (Rani says the moon is *chandra* and a ♂.) Then across to another panel, with a huge Earth hanging above us, so big it filled the whole observation-port. Amazing! All the planet in one take! Blue and white and as lovely as life. It was the Western hemisphere, with a whitish smudge around the place where the British Isles might be.

So there they all are behind us. So many millions, each full of its own gravity, thrusting through its own contexts, urgent with wants and needs. Microdots. And beloved Martagon − I never thought I'd ever write that! − a pico-dot. And all of them, like Sprite's new-born foal, thinking that she's a phoenix and there's none of her own kind but she ...

Only way to get through this is to take up the position that my 'I' is already dead, and that H. Sage is now just an instrument of Earth purposes. A bit in a programme-string. Software. If my

'I' shld get through it, it will seem like a Resurrection. Or perhaps my 'I' had a programme-transfer with that white owl in the Cardiarum, and I am now Minerva, sitting on a beech-tree and hooting? Yes.

Adam is getting fretful again. My turn to have him.*

---

* This is the last entry in Sage Diary. For subsequent entries in notebook inscribed on cover 'Honeymoon', see Segment Six.

SEGMENT SIX

HONEYMOON

Honeymoon*

Dear Agamemnon. Day Two. Wish you were here. Don't know postal code yet. Cell 7, Left Ventricle, Command Matrix, Gassendi, Nr Mare Humorum, Moon, ought to reach me. Thinking of you. X Helen. PS Bring Achilles.

Astrocrew were okay. Said they wld hang around in orbit eight days or so – 'Just ring up & we'll send down the tub.' If we need to stay longer they'll 'run out of gas'. But not to worry, we're to ring Astrosigint for a 'taxi' when we're ready. Depending on climatic condits & c. & c. taxi will arrive in about five days.

Earth half-phase, so blue and white. So huge. I say 'day two', because a new date has flipped on my watch. But the black sky isn't a day, although the sun rose three earth-days ago.

When we walked – togged up in moon-suits and ankle-deep in regolith – from the landing-pad to the Reception All, what I cldn't get used to was the albedo of the moonscape, yet no sunlight in the air. Our shadows were as sharp as on Earth. That, and the bounce-quotient. The butlers brought weights of some kind to put on our boots, magma galoshes, but we still bounded. No galoshes for poor Frolic, who did a jump and soared the height of a bungalow, coming down v slowly. She almost disappeared into the regolith.

O. has been away most of the 'day', being debriefed I suppose. Adam grizzling. Ditto Frolic. Must try & get an earth-tray (regolith-tray?) for her to scratch in.

Must use this book for *work*.

Butlers. Hadn't understood how much they do. Apelike but long-haired. Prehensile toes, so that when they are stationary, e.g. on their backs or in slings, doing construction work, they are quadrumanous. Can use tools in all four hands. Wear programme-belts and permanent earphones like Walkman outfits. No other clothing.

---

* *On arrival on the moon Sage commenced a new diary entitled thus.*

Get impression of ratio of *c*.4 butlers to 1 Oitarian. (But this not necessarily ratio on Oitar, since great demand here for heavy labour & practical chores. As we came in, saw many butlers at work on new launch-pads & constructing more cupolas and Alls.) Clearly the butlers are the proles or the blacks, and so deeply assumed – like the plumbing and wiring – that they don't get mentioned much.

When they found that Adam & I eat solid food they tried to put us in the 'battery', or the butler stables. O. managed to stop this. Don't know how. It is not clear who gives orders, or how, or how they can be changed. But O. seems to have a licence to influence what relates to us.

So here we are, in our own bubble. Suffering from rocket-lag.

Inside here in the Matrix, & probably in all the domed areas, they have some gravity-inducement field, simulating that of Oitar. Since Oitarian density is 1.5 plus greater than Earth, I feel like 20 stone.

When O. came back he sat for a long time with Adam on his knee. He was talking to himself in some kind of Oitar/Earth mix. He didn't look at me. Then Frolic got on to knee also, Adam grabbed her, and the two started having a fun-fight. O. *laughed*. He sd he had been taken to the clinic and put under the 'vibe-scanner'. He thought they were trying to 'de-mortalise' him. But 'they do not know the mortal co-ordinates' so he was able to put up blocks. He must be in agonies from creature-culture-shock.

Bad for me also, although an anthropologist has professional defences. Lack of gender signals confuses me. A unigender society, in wh sexual characteristics are null.

When we first came into the Complex, which is *huge* and seems to sprawl all over the Gassendi Caldera like Los Angeles, there were no signs of interest, surprise, hostility, welcome. Impassive – task-absorbed. We were taken to Control, where the Base Commander (I suppose) received us. S/he and its staff were gorgeously robed (as I had expected, many of those on the Complex periphery are in no-colour working gear), & they did go through the gestures and arcs of greeting O. has taught me. S/he sat inside a circle of computer consoles and print-out videos. Then it spoke to me, in Oitarian, probably some formulaic accosting-sentence, three times. When it found out that I was not a communicant creature it showed no further interest. Not even 'ugh'. Then Adam started playing up and it signalled to one of the attendant butlers to take Adam and Frolic away. O. stepped forward with a gesture of gravitas, and (see above) fortunately he seems to have some licence wh worked.

I seem to be potential data, to be processed in due course. The good side of this is that mortals aren't aggro-objects. The scenarios we had as to possible pent-up fury at the shooting-down of their spacecraft – even O. thought that this cld have jogged the Gracious Goodnesses to order elimination of all mortals – were not in evidence at all.

O. tried to explain this to me. He sd that what had been registered was 'creature-incompatibility' and also 'signals migraine'. The nearest word he cld find for the latter was 'bewilderment'. He says they have a whole monitoring Nexus, tracking some thousands of audio & visual signals from Earth, but whenever they try to scramble these in the 'harmoniser' it chokes. They suppose that they shld be able to 'align' all these signals and read-out the 'mortal logic-path'. (That was what made O. laugh the first time here.) So they are still fiddling about with their knobs and dials trying to 'cure' all this higgledy alien input, pending sending off the first ferries with planters. (Rbt was wrong, they do have a small ferry fleet almost ready.) O. sd that language wasn't the problem. They have a major crypto-translator bank installed, & have cracked the vocabulary of English, Russian, German, Spanish, Hindi and a few other languages.

However. They can't crack the Earth *concepts*. The continual choking of the harmoniser & damage from overload to the main translator's sensitive computers has led to signals migraine giving way to 'cut-off projection': i.e. bewilderment to exasperation? EMP was v definitely a 'response' to cacophony of Earth signals.

It was aimed (O. says) not at mortals, but at 'beastly mortal transmitters – to do a heavy sentence by a traffic jam'.

Day Five. Adam has taken to the butler attendant on us. It improves when it has its Walkman earphones off & relates in a creaturely way. O. had got a licence to go with me to monitoring Nexus. Risked leaving Adam with butler & Frolic for an hour & it turned out all right.

Got a better view of this part of Complex. Living quarters are mostly globular opaque perspex cells, like our own. Sort of beehive comb. Office clumps are also cells, mostly round, in three-dimensional arrangements, like lab models of molecular structures – a bunch of little balls tied together with lines, which are lifts or corridors. When one cell is in communication with another, they both glow. Only two-at-a-time lateral communication possible. Multiple communications (data input) must go to the central Confluence Chamber of each office complex or precinct. These chambers are not round but of various geometric or crystalline forms: O. rattled off the names – rhombohedron, trisoctahedron, trirhomboidal – but what matter? Point is: precise geometric lay-out, aesthetically determined.

The architecture seemed like a metaphor which made me understand their social structure better: molecular, communications-determined, with different clumping for specified tasks and roles. Freewheelers (like poets) are sort of charmed quarks wh buzz around. *Mem:* O. may be an atypical Oitarian. I mean he always was. V certainly is now.

We caught a glimpse of the Complex main bumble, an icosahedron, situated at the intersection of avenues in mid-campus. Only building with ornamental elaboration, a bit Aztec. This reminded me to be cautious of lunar-based impressions. This cramped, workaholic Moon Base may give no fair view of Oitar. O. always tells me of wide avenues, lawns, ornamental tanks (or lakes & c.) and spacy Colleges. This place may no more indicate Oitarian norms than a whaling-station on the Antarctic rim wld indicate the norms of Earth.

HONEYMOON

A butler led us to the main 'Crypto-Sykosis' confluence chamber, a trisoctahedron. One needed only five seconds to see their problem. Audio-visual monitoring room, with bank upon bank of telly screens. An Oitarperson (from College of Cryptography?) watched each group of four screens, with a keyboard at its fingers and translation coming in through earphones. I watched one who was simultaneously monitoring four American channels: a *Dallas* episode with zoom-in bed scenes (1); President Forsst on a coast-to-coast ego-trip (2); a Falwell-type preaching about the Apocalypse (3); and a money programme (quiz) (4). Its fingers were continually playing on the keyboard, injecting data wh O. told me wld go into a scrambler wh wld blend the images in the attempt to read out the Sykotic Common Programme. It seemed most struck by the Apocalypse trip (3), & when the Falwell-clone got to a climax several colleagues left their own monitoring posts and grouped around, nodding. To my left I cld see BBC *Newsnight* with Dr Charon projecting his ego alongside a Channel Five thing about bed-wetting therapy and a Channel Three *Top of the Pops*. Across the other side of the trisoctahedron a Soviet newscaster, v heavy; some Bulgarian folk dancers; and what looked like a lovely 'Peking Opera' programme, from Beijing, with an appreciative group around it.

At that point, simultaneously, Forsst offered an Eternal Treaty of friendship to Oitar, the Falwell-clone called out for nukes to lift off, and the (female) band on *Top of the Pops* did a confuse-a-signal act, stripping their upper halves and waving their guitars & clarinets like phallic emblems down below. This conjuncture led to a total systems-flip or scrambler-choke, & all screens went dead. I gathered from the way they went about routine fuse-therapy that this was taken as the Sykotic norm.

Walked back beneath a waning Earth, the cusp v brilliant even through the cupola dome. That means fine weather at home, with high albedo from the unclouded oceans. Minerva will be hooting at the moon. Only three Earth days before our transport goes back. No chance we'll be ready to take it. Or be allowed.

439

Day Six. O. now licensed/ordered to attend Daily Confluence in Control Matrix. He came back in good spirits. Two important things. (1) His signal from Earth has quite definitely been taken on board by GGs, and is hegemonic. Negotiating the proposals may now commence. He is to take me to Command complex soon, with atlases & c. for a data cull. We're even licensed to take Adam. (2) There is a direct audio-visual lock with Astrosigint in a cell in the Command complex. Has been since Day One or before. We are both now ordered to attend there for an Oitarian 'segment' (about 1 hr 15 mins of Earth-time). Starting tomorrow.

Have been around & about a bit more. Butler took me back to Reception All to look for two missing stores canisters, with Adam's dried milk, tins & c. (Found one: other has been ferried back to Oitar for analysis.) Passed many Oitarpersons, a few (senior functionaries, Adjusters, quarks?) gorgeously robed, most in working gear. (O. says latter are from pool of discards, large numbers of whom are sent to astro-stations, as being more expendable.) Noted also some incredible geometric creatures working on construction projects at amazing speed – then realised they were robots. Of course. They can work on the moon's open atmosphere, with no problems.

All the Oitarians passed me impassively. Strange to be in a smileless culture. Since nothing to read in their faces I tried to listen to their vibes. These conveyed that I was decidedly a non-aesthetic object. (Asked O. He said this was because of (a) my whiteness = alien creature, (b) my figure – breasts look like deformities. Also, Oitarians smell somehow sanitised, as O. no longer does, & maybe I (and he?) smell rank to them.)

The touch-taboo is v evident. Even in the most confined space, like a small confluence chamber, they weave in and out and around each other, in intricate patterns, like grave morris-dancers. Only time I ever got a smile was when one was coming through a corridor-gate as I was going out, & I bumped into it. Then I realised the 'smile' was what O. calls a 'slant of enmity', wh was confirmed by a drench of real aggro vibes (but somehow 'aestheticised'). It went at once, presumably to do absolution-ablutions.

O. & I don't touch for fear of offending taboos – in fact I doubt if O. *could*. (And we have no real privacy in our perspex cell.) Of course we have to touch Adam, but we seem to be licensed to do that.

O. is trying to get back on to a mainly pellet diet. Stomach cramps & sweating. Says he is doing this to 'harmonise' (& to stop them putting him under scanner again?). Suspect it is also to make our depleted stores last out for me and Adam. Strangely, Frolic *likes* pellets, as if programmed to them. But she needs milk too.

Day Eight. Or so my watch says. It is over mid-way through the lunar day and the sun is overhead. We are now licensed to go to Control's small observatory, a little cupola linked by a corridor to Command chamber. The cusp or limb of the Earth went out, leaving a ghost, & now it is growing on the other side.

The astrocrew goes back today. Will leave a communications satellite in orbit with GGs' sanction. So Earth signals now strongly relayed. O. has got them to license a BBC World Service receiver in our own cell. Astrocrew broke in on that frequency and repeated cheery message abt my sending for a 'taxi'. Last material Earth-link gone.

Went for our segment to Command complex. When Rbt came on screen I nearly cracked up. I must have been holding myself together all week like a vice. He seemed to be expecting this, & suddenly Ann put her grinning gob into camera, sd 'Take care!' & they were having a christening party today to name Sprite's foal 'Helena'. Almost cracked up again. Rbt came back on: a black-and-white image, sometimes dissolving into snow and blips, & then coming through amazingly clear. I cld even see how strained he looked. Audio signals loud & clear, but with a three seconds' echo which seemed to play hide-and-seek in the space-gap.

Rbt v brisk. Sd we were doing 'splendidly'. Cld I hold on up there a bit longer? (Bit my tongue & nodded.) Said UN Security Council was now taking over negotiations, with two commissions of experts: (1) Pugwash committee plus some signals and computer persons from Plugwatch; (2) Human Rites commission. Sd 'your friend Wardroop' invaluable in getting this together: Nobel laureates, people from Soviet and American academies & c. Then he talked with O. for a while about the negotiations.

After that we went (with Adam) to Control, for a small top-level confluence. Took atlases & files prepared by Rbt. V positive. They were exceedingly interested, tho' 'interested' not quite right word – maybe 'switched on' to data-interrogation. From areas of concentrated enquiry, clear that they are esp keen on (1) islands and watery islandy regions: asked abt Iceland, British Isles, New Zealand, Japan, South Georgia, Spitsbergen, Micronesia; (2) de-populated areas (but not torrid desert); (3) boreal areas, on rim of Arctic circle, esp tundra, lakes.

My geog not up to interrogation on zones of special interest: Baffin Island, Novaya Zemlya, Parry Islands. But we worked out a questionnaire to send back to Astrosigint. Became clear that (3) – i.e. N. Canada & N. Russia/Siberia – preferred settlement zone, as combining lots of islands and water; v few mortals; and tundra ecology with a profile which was reminiscent of archaic Oitarian times: hence graduated return to archaic life-styles. Seems obvious logic-path, & also v fortunate preference for mortals.

Towards end of confluence I realised they were actually trying to pin-point one or two sites for imminent plantation. Kept asking for data on Hudson Bay, Foxe Basin and Baffin Bay. Encouraged them (although the poor Inuits really don't need *this*). Got an 'immediate search' signal to Astrosigint, wh came back very quickly with a signal recommending greater virtues of Severnaya Zemlya and the Taymyr Peninsula in N. Siberia. (It wasn't Rbt but a Cousin voice – what's going on down there?)

Went back to cell to try & settle Adam. He has lost weight all week. O. stayed to work out a new interrogatory. When he came back he was v optimistic. Says the GGs are rolling along the negotiated-settlement logic-path. Not only his special signal (which gave them a colossal programme jump), but also something has happened on Oitar which faces it with a renewed eco-existence threat: a burn-up of their sun is predicted, whose first flame-up wld reverse climate overnight to intolerable Celsius levels. Hence the Gracious Goodnesses wld settle for anything, & are already planning evacuation. But O. admitted GGs are given to such panics every now & then. The sun burn-up may not be for billions of years.

As a result, O. has now been given a direct person-gate for immediate signals to GGs. This is almost without precedent, although commanders of space armadas always have it. But he warns me it is only a *subordinate* gate. The superordinate gates remain with the nobs: i.e. those who process and send on the data inflow at confluences – the Base Commander at Control (which is really the central lunar computer nexus), the Priest of the Bumple and the Chief Lunar Adjuster. However, O. now has two means to exert influence: (a) his person-gate, and (b) he can try & get his own data-input into the scrambler at the Daily Confluence.

Have a clearer idea now as to how programming works. A mistake to think of it as too rigid. Let us suppose that GGs are really a 70th-generation data-processing & 'thinking' Artificial Intelligence computer-network. From some ancient menu base it generates its own algorithms/paths. Data inflow comes from Colleges, task-groups, specialised units. When any major decision is made wh affects Oitarian objectives, social organisation & c., these are called 'judgements' or 'laws' of the Sublime Couch. They are promulgated in Bumplespeak, as if by priests of the oracle, in the Bumple of the Wheel, & thence transmitted as print-out to the bumples of Colleges & c. These 'laws' establish programme parameters and allocate 'rolls' to Colleges & other units. Only in exceptional cases do they refer to individual rolls or functions. If they do, these are 'decrees'.

The Colleges & c. – or their subordinate computers – determine their own programmes within the overall remit, & allocate rolls to task-groups and individuals. But they have some space for free play or initiative to fulfil their College roll, and so also (within the collegiate remit) do individuals. (They are role-determined individuals, but with 'freewheel' within the roll. If they trespass beyond determined parameters they bump against blocks or their belts start bleeping an alarm-signal.) (Wh is also picked up by the Adjusters.) On aesthetic matters − the safety-valve − there is a huge space for freewheel. That is why quarks like Poets and Musicians get away with so much. They don't even have a belt-bleeper.

On major (global) questions the GGs take decisions (i.e. confirm or adjust programme) very swiftly, after they have scrambled all the various daily data-inflows. But mini-questions, esp any relating to individuals which are referred to it, may pend for weeks. Strictly AOB (Auxiliary Output of Bank).

Seems clear enough. Still have creepy feeling that Bumple priests and Adjusters may have ways of working system for other ends. Chief Lunar Adjuster (aka 'Registrar') was at Control confluence, gave me the slant of enmity, no attempt to screen its hostile vibes.

BBC World Service. Mother Earth is in a flat spin. Huge upheavals in Soviet bloc. Poland and Hungary have proclaimed neutrality, but not clear whether neutral in Earth politics or towards Oitar. (It seemed as if Poland has 'seceded from the universe'.) Millions seem to be milling around the White House. In Britain, Lady Finchley has accused Dr Charon of 'appeasement' of 'alien threat'.

An interesting item about the UN Security Council. BBC so intent on trying to reassure listeners that everything is normal & proper that, as always, one has to guess at truth. But it sounds as if world pressure is so overwhelming that the superpowers & the politicians are actually being forced to surrender their powers to two multinational UN Commissions, one of scientists, the other of 'experts'. (Mortals actually finding a logic-path at last?) The scientists are the Pugwash Commission much as usual, with more Asians added. The other (Human Rites Commission) sounded promising, although I cldn't catch all the names through the static. Seemed to be writers, anthropologists (thought I heard John Blossom's name!), historians, peace movt people, representative commonpersons (Walesa and Winnie Mandela). Then a surprise: the link-person between the Commission and the UN is Sir John Wardroop!

Day Ten. Earth waxing on its other side, huge and stationary in the heavens as the smaller sun descends. Adam frets. May be teething. Wish Rani was here. Realise how much I depend on her for baby guidance. I never had much of an auxiliary role-kit as a Mum.

O. and I went to Command for our segment. Rbt didn't seem to be there. Jane Wetherfield read a formal communiqué to Control from the United Nations, proposing an exchange of Ambassadors. Gave co-ordinates of Martagon for Earth landing-pad. My heart gave a leap – might we go with the ship?

Then John Wardroop came on camera, to speak to me. Clear and authoritative: at his most impressive. Sd he and Sorley were 'getting things in hand'. No time to talk, but he wanted to recap a few things. Had been reading my notes and papers ('Dr Nettler had a file, been very helpful. The work is brilliant, if I may say').

'Now. Is your essential diagnostic picture confirmed, now that you are in the field?'

'Yes ... The butlers have a larger role, as do the discards ... And very advanced robotics.'

'Quite so. But the cultural determinants? The teleological imperatives? I mean, the goal-posts haven't moved? You've not found any unpredicted compulsions ... aggressions?'

'No. They find our species unaesthetic. They would much rather *not* bump into us. They would prefer a species-segregation, total apartheid ...'

'Good. And the prognosis? They are not given to jump the rails? They would continue on a rational logic-path?'

'Algorithmic. The programme is set now for segregation in

the boreal tundral zone. It could stay like that unless we jolted it by doing something bloody silly.'

'Right. Thank you. What I needed to know. We're working on it. We're beginning to rationalise and harmonise the mortals at last – pity we left it so late.'

He sd he'd be back in a day or two, to run through some paradigms more precisely. 'The moon seems to suit you, Helena. You look wonderful.' I didn't return the compliment – saw his enormous paunch when he came in camera. 'Marriage suits me,' I sd. 'Didn't you know this is my honeymoon?'

Wardroop gave way for Rani. Lovely! To see a real human smile again! She told me wh bits of the medicine kit to try on Adam, & assured me it must be just teething. I asked abt Priya & D. Then Rbt shouldered in, a bit abruptly, as if he had just got to studio. He asked for O., & told him to inform Lunar Sigint that they shd switch across urgently to alternative crypto-channel Zero/Q/Zero – 'we put it in their data bank. This code has been entered, it's open to the world ... and tell them to refuse all signals which don't have the right crypto-key prefix.' O. asked, whose signals? Rbt just sd, 'Could be anyone. Or any two or three. We're on an open party line.' The screen blipped and snowed, & O. took Rbt's input straight to Command. What is going on down/up there?

Day Thirteen. Or, rather, Night. On Day Eleven the sun sank slowly in the black sky behind the curvature of the moon's manilla-envelope-coloured rim. I took Adam to the Observatory to watch. Since the moon has no atmosphere there was no refracted light, it just seemed to be being tugged down into a black vacancy. It was beautiful but I hated to see it go. Adam cried too. Thank God the blue-and-white Earth is still in its station, now growing gibbous. It throws some Earthshine on the lunar surface, so that it isn't totally dark. (Do they both go out together? I cldn't bear it.) It will be twelve days before the sun comes round again.

No 'segment' at Command for three days. Difficulty getting

the new Earth-moon channel to lock. O. says signals keep getting thrown by heterodynes which he puts down to 'beastly jamming'. Whose?

Day Eighteen. Feel awful. The Earth is full but dimmer (cloudy?). V dark out there. (Lunar night is 153° centigrade, minus. Even in this goldfish bowl one can *sense* it out there.) My period this week, scarcely a trace of blood, but all the cramps. I suppose reproductive organs atrophy here. Am getting really worried about Adam, he has sores all round his tum. O. talks v little.

Day Nineteen. O. came back from Daily Confluence very low. He sat for a long while holding Adam, his 'Earth-link'. It seems Control is getting contradictory signals from Earth. (Lunar Sigint ignored Rbt's instruction to mask out or refuse all signals without proper crypto-keys. Their logic path read out that they shld accept all signals – as they always have – and put them in the scrambler. But these new signals are not just Earth transmissions wh they monitor: they are signals to Lunar Command. From whom?)

At the Confluence the Chief Lunar Adjuster made a v hostile input. He sd O. and I have too many licences, and esp that O. shld be 'de-gated': i.e. his person-gate to the GGs shld be nihilated. He suspects O. of being a 'double-roller', with mortal blemishes. O. spent part of 'day' (night) getting ready a careful input to his person-gate.

Day Twenty-three. O. still goes to Daily Confluence. No response to Adjuster's input. (Since it refers to an individual it may be hanging around in AOB.) It is now clearer what is going on. Lunar Sigint and Astrosigint have found a new lock, & O. talked with Major Rock (Rbt away at UN). Also much more coming out at Confluence.

President Forsst & his claque have gone into some hideout in a hollow mountain in Colorado, where they have their own space transmitter. (They've always loathed the UN since they forced it out of New York to New Delhi three years ago.) From bits on BBC news I gather that normal governmental process has broken down in the United States, and people are milling around Washington, or taking off for the mountains with guns and cans of food. In great regions citizens' committees have just taken over and are trying to make direct contact with Russian citizens. The other America – the democrats with a small 'd' – has woken up at last, and is self-organising with that zest and skill which erupts so often in American history. But if Forsst has lost the country, he still controls the armed forces, the nuke silos, the airfields, all the stuff in space, the subs, the radar & electronic defences, the main transmitters. It's like the armour-plating of some antediluvian reptilian predator that's come away from the flesh, & is continuing to lurch around without it.

Very clear that Forsst is now operating the NATO 'options'. Option (1) – nuking the moon – has no doubt been found no-go, so they are into Option (2). They have set up their own direct moon-lock, and have offered the USSR to Oitar for 'immediate' plantation, minus the Ukraine & Baltic States but with Inner and Outer Mongolia thrown in. (They have convinced themselves that a vast armada of space ferries is ready now on the moon, & have no idea as to how small the first plantation will be.) They broke into Astrosigint's channels & codes, & signalled this offer as coming from 'the Free World'. Translator choked at 'free', so O. was fetched to Lunar Command for consultation.

When there he found the scene was much worse. (And O. is only dimly able to construe beastly mortal politics himself.) The Russians broke into Forsst's signals and found out about his offer. So they signalled a counter-offer: Oitar was welcomed, as 'fraternal ally', to plant the whole of North America down to the Panama isthmus. It cld easily be construed as the best offer. It wld give to the plantation huge resources, climatic variables – isolated from mortal contact by two oceans. The Oitarians cld cut themselves off from any contagion by simply taking out 50 kilometres of the isthmus. Also, the Russians have been more subtle. They have constructed some culture-profile of Oitar wh

448

suggests Communist affinities. The reptilian rump of the Politburo (also now hiding in some Command Sewer) has addressed
the Gracious Goodnesses in the name of 'Socialist Man', and called
on them to unite in the Intergalactic Federation of Peace-Loving
Communist Planets. (The Translator rendered 'Communist' as
'common-programme-rolling', wh will please the GGs.)

O. found Control suffering severe signals migraine. How the
hell cld they tell wh signal represented Earth? (There seems to
have been some other offer, from France, but the Translator
hasn't cracked French yet and the French refuse to negotiate in
any other language.) On the face of it the UN/Astrosigint Signal
comes, in any logic-path, a poor third. But it still has something
going for it: (a) both I and O. are here as witnesses & advocates
(wh is perhaps why both Forsst & the Politburo are urgently
signalling a desire to exchange Ambassadors); and (b) the GGs
have responded v well to the idea of 'archaic' trial plantations in
the tundra – probably Baffin Island – and this has already been
fed into programme. Control decided to scramble all three offers
& pass them along as input, & see what the GGs make of it all.

O. working now on a long signal to his person-gate. Every
now and then he glances at me, half-hurt, half as if across an
immense distance, as far away as Oitar.

Day Twenty-seven. Adam's sores no better. (*Qy:* Chicken-pox?)
Nasty sty on one eye. Our butler tries to sing to him, sort of
yapping. Makes A. laugh. O. on pellets, dizzy fits. My lower-
inwards always cramped. About 10 days of tins & dried milk left.
Butler brought some dried 'milkstem' & 'bredstik' from battery
to try & eke out, former a bit like dried milk, latter like dehydrated
All Bran. Trying it on myself first. Also tried some pellets.

Now have a belt-receiver to get BBC World Service, so can
tune in anywhere. Can hardly bear to turn it on, a cacophony of
bald white butlers. Well, worse – our butler is quite nice. The
British seem to be going on like a parody of a Raymond Briggs
cartoon – the Govt has told them to whitewash their windows
& dig up their front lawns for potatoes. There is a nation-

wide loyalty 'roll-call', and the PTT (Peace Through Trident) Volunteer Corps is making house-to-house enquiries into sub-versives. CND has called another mass die-in around Martagon: well-intended but won't help. It has been banned under the Suppression of Disaffection Act. After the newses Dr Charon came on, sounding panicky. It disclaimed the rumours circulated by 'interested parties' as to divisions within NATO, & pledged undying loyalty to Our Great Ally. When it got to the bit about how deterrence had kept the peace for fifty years, & offered its 'hand of friendship' to Oitar (as if they cld bear to touch it!), I switched off. Ugh! Obviously Charon is going along with Forsst.

O. is holding himself together better than I. He has gone to Command for the segment, hoping to get through to Rbt. Cldn't trust myself. I feel a sense of species-betrayal. No doubt unfair. Perhaps Charon/BBC are only the armour-plating and reptile-scales wh have come apart from the British people who may be doing some other thing, unmentionable by BBC.

Am writing this in the Observatory, where Adam and I have gone in hope of seeing the new sun. The Earth is up there still, half-Earth, as if undecided whether to wax or shrink.

O. has just come in, triumphant. His signal got through the person-gate & it was strong enough to give real programme-jolt. The GGs' print-out came through to Control about an hour ago. Forsst's & Oblomov's requests to exchange Ambassadors are squashed, *pro tem*. Negative signals already sent. Instead Ambassadors are going down to Astrosigint *now*: they are sending the Base Commander and a Vice-Provost of Stellanthropology. Their roll is to make data-verification overview & find out wh of the three options is real. If their input positive, they are empowered to sign protocols of Memorandum of Understanding, or Common Rolling, with Earth.

I danced & we hugged, forgetting touch-taboo. The spacecraft is already off. Speed of light at filter 008, so shld make entry into Earth's atmosphere in about 4 hours. The sun now rising – auspicious? Earth-moon lock shld be open in 10 mins. O. and I are going to Control to see if we can talk to Rbt. Now. Am writing this there.

Day Twenty-nine. Confined to cell with O., waiting AOB decree. Adam temp 103. Serious. I can think of nothing else.

Yesterday – just once – O. tried to say something about it all. He even tried to get over his feelings of revulsion against the human species, which 'bugs the flow-chart of Nature'. He said, 'Sykotic programme always had a bug. It was in your genes, with bonds and anti-bonds. The wrong bounders got the keys at Control. I know it was not of your choosing. If our friends had done the choice, Oitar and Earth could have done a wedding.'

I'd better try & get it down. At Control we waited by the lock & Rbt at last came on screen. We told him Ambassadors were on their way. Rbt asked when, jumped up & sd he must warn LOW, both American & Soviet LOWs: 'with things as they are now, one blip could trigger goodbye Earth'. Then Wardroop came on & talked 'paradigms', but forget that bit. Rbt came back, more relaxed, sd, 'That's okay' & went over protocol proposals with O. Forget that. Then John Rock came up with a message-pad & tugged Rbt's arm. Both went off screen. Ann came in camera for a mo, grinned, closed her hands in a *namaste* greeting, & sd 'Take care'. Then Rbt back, very urgent. Asked O. to ask Lunar Command, *immediate*, to do a heavy EMP, global, with maximum focus on all NATO/WTO silos, airfields, subs, communications centres. Also Israeli, French. 'Ask Command to hold the EMP as long as they can. I've just heard that President Forsst has ordered ...' Then scene jumped & wobbled (someone knocked against camera?). Jane W. ran in at back with something under her arm (laser stunner?), shouting to Rbt. Ran out of camera, left. Rbt followed, a blur at back followed after (Ann?). Then sound of firing ... hell, I can't go on.

Try again. Firing, explosions (off). Camera motionless as if unmanned, showing studio backcloth (18th-century map of the Terraqueous Globe), with smoke drifting in from left. Then Rbt was pushed across back of studio, held by one of the US Security hoods, large dark patch on shirt (blood?). Shadowy sort of bundle on floor, just out of camera, left. (Ann?) (Jane?) I can't go on. Try to get it down tomorrow. Still some Valium left.

Try again. Why? Who for?

Then a second hood came in, pointed his gun directly into my eyes, screen flashed & went black.

We went at once to Control. Of course, ordering an immediate EMP out-of-programme is far outside the limits permitted to Lunar Command's freewheel. Only GGs can programme such immense energy output. Acting Base Commander made an immediate priority-gate input to Oitar & O. used his person-gate also. But transmissions to GGs take at least an Earth-hour, each way.

O. picked up Adam, & we walked hand-in-hand to the Command Observatory. The last time we touched.

There we saw it happen.

Before that there were some bits of BBC on my belt. Forsst's ultimatum. Charon. I had the belt-recorder on. I'll transcribe them if I can ever bear to. All I can remember is the agony.

Slowly, so slowly, the blue-and-white globe went all white. Dimmer, as the albedo dimmed. Then yellow and brown, shrouding the northern hemisphere, with yellow wreaths extending to the south. Then it was very dim. No blue left, the clouds dun-coloured, some of them black. Around the half-phase rim the refractions seemed red, throwing a red Earthshine on the moon.

The EMP order came through, an hour too late. Then the Oitarian programme went into a state of shock – or into reverse. When the rocket with their Ambassadors was given up as lost, they just switched all their monitoring systems off. So we don't know if there are still signals on Earth or not. Of course, it needn't be the end. The damage may not be

O. is taken for a segment each 'day' (day = twenty segments) to

HONEYMOON

Chief Adjuster's scanning chamber. When he comes back he sits holding Adam or Frolic. Doesn't look at me.

He talks sometimes. Half to himself, in Oitarian. Says beastly nukes tried to take out moon today. Today?! But of course they must have been launched four days ago, when it happened. Earth making its last salute to the universe. None got through. Command had put out an anti-matter shield, the day it happened, thousands of miles outside the lunar orb – the nukes hit it & just disintegrated.

All except one rocket, diagnosed from its signals to be non-verminous. O. thinks it was a Soviet embassy, sent off at the last minute to make an alliance. They just diverted this one around the moon. Re-addressed it to infinity. O. heard a staccato voice on the monitor, growing fainter, until it was lost in static

Eternity feels very close. Its pitchy breath is seeping into spaces inside me. Nihil Rules OK. Species-anomie.

On pellets now, and bredstik. Must save last stores for Adam. He sicks pellets up. Watch has stopped. *Is* there any Earth-time now anyway? Impossible to wash here – water scarce, rationed to half a pint a day. I stink. Rashes under arms, in crotch. My hair feels itchy and bits are falling out. Only Adam makes me still need to live.

O. has been away a long time. Very long segment. Must hold on to something.

Transcript (recording). *Forsst:* '... received signals from the alien forces occupying the moon, refusing our Ambassador & thus revoking solemn agreements entered into with the Free World. Fellow citizens, this can only be the prelude to invasion. Moreover, our intelligence agencies have uncovered irrefutable evidence that the Soviets have been secretly conspiring with the aliens to unleash their combined forces against the Free World, in a desperate bid to trample upon human rights in every corner of our universe.

'Fellow Americans, be calm! No evil can befall God's favoured nation. I have, as Commander-in-Chief, ordered our Space Command to send back a message to the aliens which will not be misunderstood.

'To Marshal Oblomov I now make this last offer. Set aside your differences, abandon your outworn ideologies, join with me now in the defence of our common heritage. We offer you the sword of the Free World and the shield of SDI. We ask for nothing in return. Place yourself now under the command of SACWORLD. Give up your Un-Earthly Activities, revoke your secret treaties with the aliens. There will be no recriminations.

'This offer will remain open for three more hours. If your agreement is not received at the expiry of that time, the commanders of our WOSPs, or World Orbiting Space Platforms, will reluctantly carry out my orders to destabilise your command centres and disable your nuclear installations with lase . . .' oh shit

So Forsst went for Options (1) and (2) simultaneously.

O. back. Sat with Frolic for a while. Sd nothing. Then put on his trance-set. Also put Adam's on. They sit for hours with their eyes open, as if under hypnosis. Adam's is partly an education-kit, to teach him Oitarian.

O. is tranced a lot of the time now, like a druggie. Three days ago, when we were still talking, he got a set for me. The inducer is a crystal about the size of a cent; it goes on the centre of the forehead and is held by a gold-elastic strap. He persuaded me to try it. It was like a terrible trip I had once on LSD. All kinds of forgotten scraps came out of lost misty caverns in my cranium, and the Earth became black as sackcloth of hair, and the moon became as blood. Then matter seemed to melt inside my brainpan, into gouts of viscous oily patches in lurid colours wh ran shapelessly into each other against wh texts were illuminated like graffiti print-outs. Some were in strange hieroglyphs – Bumple Utter? – and I remember scraps of Milton, wh I haven't read since I was 17 –

HONEYMOON

... secrets of the hoarie deep, a dark
Illimitable Ocean without bound,
Without dimension, where length, breadth & height
And time & place are lost; where eldest Night
And Chaos, Ancestors of Nature, hold
Eternal Anarchy, amidst the noise
Of endless wars ...

Then there were sudden flashbacks. One was in the Cardiarum, and a bird flew out of the dead-eye alcove; not Minerva, but a cormorant, which I knew was really Nihil. It sat, craning its neck, on the Tree of Life, wh was then suddenly a Wheel, wh had a whizzing face in its axle, and I felt an incredible revulsion against the face, and as the Wheel started to slow and crumble into bits I saw that the face was my own. I must have been screaming & the butler came in and pulled the trance-inducer off

I think I wld have died. As I will. But, oh shit, not like that.

Better, now that I have got it down and named it. For last two days that trance-trip has still been lurking inside me like a really heavy nightmare, waiting around to swamp the conscious mind again. Scraps still floating into my mind from those caverns —

Lest total darkness should by Night regain
Her old possession & extinguish Life
In Nature & all things

All is dross that is not Helena

Adam isn't dross. Nor Frolic. And, oh my love, Oipas, you are not dross, never never have you shown me hostile vibes or aggro, but they are sucking all the Earth out of you, already you are at a loss in our language and they steal from thy own nature all the mortal man for he cometh in with vanity and departeth in darkness   And my name shall be covered with darkness

Adam fever again. Very high but don't know what. (They took

away Rani's thermometer for analysis.) O. spoke to me, groping for words like someone in a black-out ... 'Go – get cure.' He's de-gated of course, & barred from Confluences, but he can still get out. Unlike me. He's gone to see some sort of para-medic.

O. still away. Hold on to something. Transcribe Charon. Adam asleep, don't like heavy breathing, gaps between breaths.

Charon was quite crazy. We were watching the blue Earth & waiting. It was the last thing that came through. Will never know exactly how it happened. Did the WOSPs start first? Did our Ambassadors trip one of their LOW systems? Or did the Soviets shoot down a WOSP? Or did the French or the Israelis start it? But from the way Charon spoke he knew it was about to happen, probably knew that Forsst had ordered NATO to blast off everything & that the Soviet Union wld blast back.

He came on in a squeaky, sub-hysteric voice, trying to sound statesmanlike through the gathering static. Then he just did his top while still on the air. This is the bit: '... no inerrant dangers in nuclear deference ... er, deferrence ... um ... umbrella which ... er, guarantees our security & our defence imposture ... But many graves ... er, grave ... decisions to ... er ... As I toll you before I toll you again, only multilocular circumvallate preparedness for prolicide ... only multi ... where's the engineer? This mike is throttling me ...'

It was accelerating now, & his graveyard wail was becoming a high Donald Duck squawk, as if the tape was running overspeed. Impossible to transcribe – he shouted out something like 'SECURICOR CARES!' (That was a shriek, & then the tape went very very slow, as if power's battery had at last run out, so that his voice dropped three registers, like a dying sea-cow.) 'Aha, we galled their buff. Two can play at that doom ...' (Roar of static & last words from Earth, as 'doom' echoed backwards & forwards to the moon.)

Charming.

They've taken Adam. He was in a coma when the butler took

him out. O. groped in the dark of lost words, trying to talk. Still enough mortal in him for tears. He sd of Adam, 'He live will, he will.' He sd A. is being sent back to Oitar in a fast ferry in some deep-frozen state to be 'construed & cured'. They have even taken his name away. He is now Ho Mo.

He wld not have survived here. He might live now. How? What as?

I asked to go with him & fought the butler (who held me off gently). Then the Translator tannoy-relay in our cell came on & said in a metal voice that O. & I must wait for our AOBs.

Through the perspex of the cell we can see the Complex being dismantled. The GGs have ordered evacuation of Moon Base. Earth too polluted for plantation. (Translator relays periodic newses of the GGs' print-outs.)

As hideous as anything is not really knowing. It could have been clouds from laser-zapped oil-wells & burning forests – wld have a short-term 'nuclear winter' effect. Or just a 'limited' exchange, & tolerable levels, a bigger Chernobyl. Martagon has a whole complex of deep shelters ... they might be coming out now? Maybe the good Earth is going on, and it's me – and Oitar – which are going away?

Or not. Then how? A final sudden accounting by fire, as in the old Icelandic myths of *Ragnarök*? Hope so. Or are they wilting beneath that shroud still – and for weeks to come? How did it come to Minerva? Was it just droopy feathers, boils, callused eyes and a whimper-end? Oh Rani, Ann, Robert, Priya, David! Oh Adam, where are you?

O's AOB came through. Not discard as expected. To be ferried back to Oitar for analysis, maybe cure and 're-rolling'. When they came for him, I clung to him & sd, 'You promised – the wedding.' (Silly. He couldn't help it.) He sd, 'Mortals have nihilated promises. My I must be rolled in Oi Paz once more.' Then he made a gesture of gravitas, which halted the Adjuster at the door, and turned back to me. Were there tears in his eyes, or did I project this? He stood as if confused & dredging in his memory, then brought his hands together in the *namaste* salutation & went out. I called after him, 'Find Adam!' and he seemed to nod.

My AOB not through yet. They let O. take Frolic.

Who am I writing this for? Last mortal writing to last mortal? And half of Adam, frozen somewhere in space

    Helena   Nihila   Annihila   anomie   anon

    Trying to remember scraps of Zen wh Ann used to talk about. A sort of state of self-annihilation by means of self-hypnosis ... Bodhidharma has no beard, no eyes, no nose, no mouth, no face, no hands, no legs and no body; is in Nirvana, which is out of time, space or causation. Surely that is Nihil's kingdom? Yet Ann said it was a different sort of nothingness, a merging of the ego with all existence in which – not the ego – but existence remains awake. Perhaps if I sit in a zazen posture & remain very still I will steal my own ego from myself

In hostage situatn captors are supposed to bond with captives & vice versa. How does one bond with a tannoy Translator & a butler who brings pellets? (Even the Translator seems to have ugh vibes for me.) Bible only thing left to talk to. O. was right, programme was botched from Genesis. Original sin = primordial bug. Just took a few millennia to work out. Wld have terminated earlier if mortals had had the means

This is an evil among all things that are done under the sun, that there is one event unto all: yea, also the heart of the sons of men is full of evil, and madness is in their heart while they live, and after that they go to the dead. For the dead know not any thing, neither have they any more a reward; for the memory of them is forgotten. Also their love, and their hatred, and their envy, is now perished; neither have they any more a portion for ever in

HONEYMOON

any thing that is done under the sun – mortal algorithm

> *I stood among my valleys of the south*
> *And saw a flame of fire, even as a Wheel*
> *Of fire surrounding all the heavens: it went*
> *From west to east, against the current of*
> *Creation, and devour'd all things in its loud*
> *Fury & thundering course round heaven & earth*

Blake thought it was the Wheel of Religion but it is also Ideology and Rule

Mortal Helena AOB print-out come. Discard and immediate dead-line. They won't discard me. If I am the last mortal I will choose my own way of going. Swallow it down like a good girl. Think of nice things Last view of Martagon Ann on Sprite with that lovely foal oh and our wedding night & the fire in the temple & the quiet lake & the turf & the dew on our ankles looking up at the stars, looking at *here* keep writing remember Adam waving to Priya keep writing Rani said it would be qu*

---

* *End of Sage notebook 'Honeymoon', found beside her at her self-ruled dead-line. In the back of the notebook, inverted, was found the following passage.*

LAST WILL AND TESTAMENT

I, Helena, being a body with unsubdued mind, do Will and
Bequeath these both to the elements on the lunar regolith in
whatever part earthshine may fall.
I leave my language to be lost in eternity.
I leave to Adam my genes.
I leave Adam to himself that he may be free.
I leave my lover by my own will, thus willing him to return
once again to his roll.
Surrendering his I to the programme of the Wheel,
That Oipas may be cured of mortal blemish and lose all recall
of our common feelings which would only do him ill,
Offering to him as my last gift a species-divorce.

KNOWING NOT IF I BE THE LAST OF MY SPECIES OR NO

I go out, leaving Curses upon Power and Abstract Enmities and
Public Lies.
I go out through the gate of my flesh, carrying with me, like
a basket of flowers, my memories of love and of friendships and
natural joys
Accepting the Knowledge of Good and Evil
Sorry that the Good lost out (it was a near thing)
RENOUNCING MY CONSCIOUSNESS NOT AT ALL
REFUSING THE LEAST TRIBUTE TO THE RULE OF NIHIL
I leave life of my own free will

Helena

Day Unknown (Lunar Night)   *With no human witnesses*

APPENDICES

APPENDICES

1 Decree of the Sublime Couch, AOB, Oi Paz

2 Extract from Oi Paz, 'Elegy for Sykaos'

3 Term Audit, Ho Mo (Arc 3)

4 Extract from an Input to the Gracious Goodnesses from the Board of Examiners of the College of Bio-Engineering

5 Input to the Gracious Goodnesses from Ka Li, Vice-Provost of the College of Stellanthropology

6 Decree of the Sublime Couch, AOB, Ho Mo

7 Input to the Gracious Goodnesses from Ka Li, Vice-Provost of the College of Stellanthropology

8 Sentence of the Sublime Couch

9 Extract from an Input of the Loyal Commission of Bio-Engineers

APPENDICES

I DECREE OF THE SUBLIME COUCH IN THE CASE OF OI PAZ

[AOB, Oi 57/2D Sper P 9 P/Astr. (Gard.) 3383/2/68 (GG777)]

It Has Stood Up

It Knows:

That Our once-ruly servant, Oi Paz, of the College of Poesy, has endured many hazards in Our Gracious Service, exploring distant galaxies and undergoing foul captivities at the hands of beastly creatures known as mortals,

And that Oi Paz has made several humble inputs and has duly recorded and made up Accounts for our Bank, for Us to sort and store when We have time,

But that many grave blemishes have been suffered, and now there exists an unruly botch upon the organ of obedience, by which all inputs are flawed and threaten blasphemies against the Wheel.

It Knows More:

That Our servant, En Ema, Arch-Provost of the College of Adjusters, prognosticates no cure, but declaims that Oi Paz will remain invalid until the dated dead-line.

It Knows More than It Means to Say

It Construes:

That Oi Paz is due for discard and for return to pool when all data is unbanked. Yet, lest the pool be infected with mortal taint,

It Notwithstanding Laws:

That Oi Paz be sent to a place from which there is no return, where no other human can be infected with the contagion of mortality. Therefore we appoint our further observatory or hermit-orb on the uttermost ring of the anti-pole, where the said

465

Oi Paz will live solitary save for one visit each year from an Adjuster.

And let the role-kit be reformed accordingly.

It Lays Another Law:

That the feral child, Ho Mo, be enrolled in the School and thence the College of Stellanthropology, whose Vice-Provost shall return to Us regular progress-audits.

It Lays Yet Another Law:

That the notebooks and papers of Oi Paz and also of the mortal Sage be placed in the care of the College of Stellanthropology until it may please Us to do Something Else about them.

It Does a Benevolent Noise:

That the humble input of Oi Paz be granted with an auxiliary role as Breeder of Bumple Cats, wherefore may be taken to the observatory the feral cat Frolic and may be licensed to be taken also from the Bumple of the Wheel a Sacred Sire.

Each year's harvest of sacred kits to be surrendered to Our Service on the visit of the Adjuster.

It Sits From On High

APPENDICES

2 EXTRACT FROM VERSES BY OI PAZ: 'ELEGY FOR SYKAOS'

[A sample of verses found concealed in Oi Paz's robes on the departure to the hermit-orb.]

In the memory bank of Oi Paz
Channels are failing.
Adjusters have sucked data from the minicells
And choked the network-nodes.
Dark spaces grow more dark
Where bytes have been burned out of the bitstream.

Only remain the picturegrams . . .
Here are green lawns, unruly vegetations;
There are small creatures riding on the wind;
Here is a hornless unicorn (we exchange vibes);
There is a shimmering tank of molten water
In which Oi Paz worships, swimming to an island . . .

Is some other presence swimming alongside?

Suddenly the eye of memory falls open.
Sunlight floods the lost blue planet.
Oi Paz is in a garden. He is watched by an Oi Paz
Who is called an 'I'.

Clouds roll back the sun
And brown dust stains the blue air of memory
In which a word stirs: it is 'mortality'.
Oi Paz rises to deliver sentence
On that programmeless uncollegiate species –
A flux of uncured egos,
Beasts without rule or roll,
Deserving discard and self-deadline . . .

Yet out of that dust and dusk
Across great inter-stellar distances comes a cry
And a word forms which has no meaning. It is 'pity'.
The picturegram of a mortal takes form.
She is watching me. Her eyes ask questions
Which Oi Paz cannot answer and I am in agony

APPENDICES

3 TERM AUDIT, HO MO (ARC 3)

Name: Ho Mo

Finding No.: Ho(Hel)/Sper Oi P
57/Stel/Unic (Astr) 3922/8/03

Arc of Learning: 3

Roll-Kit: Stell/Unic (Astr)

Corpse: Harmonious. Pigment pale. Unusual vigour of pump. Enlarged and blemished navel-wheel.

Sense-Receptors: Highly tuned, except vibe-sensor (low receptivity). (Undergoing trance-therapy.)

Mental Organs: Fair. Organ of obedience faulty. Subject to ego-tripping. Requires adjustment.

Aesthetics: Poor. Too many tasteless improprieties. Is being given extra coaching in rhomboids.

Roll-Induction: A. *Stellanthropology* (primary arc): Intermittent application only.
B. *Unicornology* (tertiary arc): Outstanding. Has been entered for Festal Sports.
C. *Astronautics* (auxiliary): Good.

Eurhythmics/Dance: Blemished. Has been discarded from classes for repeated offences of touching.

Ceremony: Obtuse.

Language: In need of much greater cure. Bumple Utter full of botches. Archaic, harmonious. Fact Utter, fair. Equal Utter, poor. Coaching in algorithms required.

General: Must try harder. You are giving yourself far too much freewheel. If you do not improve in Ceremony, Aesthetics and Equal Utter next term I will have to send you for a CAT. See me after Bumple each twentieth day.

Signed: *Ka Li*
 Vice-Provost, Coll.
 Stellanthropology

APPENDICES

4 EXTRACT FROM AN INPUT TO THE GRACIOUS GOODNESSES FROM THE BOARD OF EXAMINERS OF THE COLLEGE OF BIO-ENGINEERING

... certainly capable of procreation, but it is quite out of the question (despite current shortages and the general inflation) that we should even consider, now or at any time, the use of seed from such a source. The very idea is offensive to our hostesses and, even if used only experimentally, would endanger their aesthetic organs. Moreover, it could be a gate for the input of Sykosis, or the mortal taint, which could threaten to bug the programme of our Blessed Planet.

We therefore recommend that Ho Mo return to College and be ruled in every way the same as all fellow collegians of the same age-cohort; that due ceremony should be observed; and that on no account should this unhappy affliction be mentioned. And while it will prove a severe disability, when added to other disabilities, it need not totally unfit Ho Mo for the appointed rolls ...

APPENDICES

5   INPUT TO THE GRACIOUS GOODNESSES FROM KA LI, VICE-PROVOST OF THE COLLEGE OF STELLANTHROPOLOGY

Gracious Goodnesses,

Ka Li, the least of Thy bits, returns Thy programme to Thee. And does obeisance to the Sacred Wheel. Ever may Thy Couch of Wisdom roll!

Know, then, if it should merit Thy High Condescension, that Ho Mo, the feral child, whom in Thy Gracious Goodness Thou hast placed in Ka Li's charge, grows every term more deboshed. As Thou Knowest, there is affliction by the malady of the Sper, which may no longer be kept concealed during the ceremonies of Worship in the Sacred Well. The organs of aesthetics suffer an atrophy, and the organ of obedience is bugged at its source. Ho Mo is given to rude touchings of peers, and especially the young females of the cohort. Several times have been jumped athwart the radii and orthostiles of the College avenues. Many times the daily duty in the Bumple has been avoided. Classes in Ceremony are cut and attendance made instead to the College Databank, where the inputs declaimed by Oi Paz and the mortal Helena, left by Your Goodnesses in our care, are ingested. At night, Ho Mo goes out of College, contrary to all Rule, we know not where; and is sometimes seen at dawn riding the Great Lawn on a unicorn – at a time when Unicornography is not on the roll-rota.

And notwithstanding our heavy sentences and the Adjuster's cure, these and other disorders continue to blaspheme against our Rule. Wherefore Ka Li humbly prays that the Blessed Couch will enroll this input and give output, in the case of Ho Mo, by means of a Gracious decree.

That Thy Programme may be Made Known,
And That the least of Thy Bits may Obey.

Ka Li
Vice-Provost, Coll. Stellan.

472

6 DECREE OF THE SUBLIME COUCH IN THE CASE OF HO MO

[AOB Ho(Hel)/Sper Oi P 57/Stel/Unic (Astr) 3922/8/03 (Discard)]

It Has Stood Up

It Knows:

That the feral child Ho Mo is grown a *Man*.

It Knows More:

That despite all care and cure by the Vice-Provost and Company of the College of Stellanthropology, Ho Mo has fallen from the Rule into a mortal bias which blasphemes the ratios of Oitar; is uncouth in proportions; is disordered in numbers, oblique in thoughts, obtuse in ceremony; and offends our measured distances by touch.

It Construes:

That Ho Mo intersects the Sacred Wheel.

It Laws:

That Ho Mo is hereby a discard. But lest the pool of discards should be polluted,

It Does a Heavier Sentence Still:

That Ho Mo is done with now, without waiting for the dated dead-line. And Ho Mo will go to the acid bath. And the programme of Ho Mo will be appointed to another.

It Does a Benevolent Noise:

That as Ho Mo was polluted in conception and therefore was not the author of these blots, the skeleton of Ho Mo may be

473

burnished and preserved until the dead-line of all the cohort, when it may stand for election with its fellows.

It Sits From On High.

APPENDICES

7 INPUT TO THE GRACIOUS GOODNESSES FROM KA LI, VICE-PROVOST OF THE COLLEGE OF STELLANTHROPOLOGY

Gracious Goodnesses,

Ka Li, the most abject of Thy bits, returns Thy programme to Thee, and lies prostrate before Thy Omniscient Roll. Beneath Thy All-Seeing Video-Scan all is already known.

Know that in all our records there has been no day more deformed than yesterday. Ka Li makes input to you in haste to inform you of how Thy Gracious Decree (AOB, Ho Mo) was received and all that then happed.

In the morning the young collegians attended for confluence in the College Assembly All. Throughout these proceedings Ho Mo gazed with ill-affected visage at the Elect hanging upon the walls. Then I summoned the cohort to attend me to the Bumple of the Wheel, where the Archmagus ascended the sacred rostrum to declaim Thy Sublime Decree.

When the Decree had been enrolled, I turned with ceremony to Ho Mo, as to one who has come to the dated dead-line, and said, 'May your skeleton be elected at the top of the poll.' And I offered to accompany the discard, with all the graduates of the cohort, to the acid-bath.

Ho Mo did not attend to me, but with a rude eccentric motion pressed through the company, pushing against their corpses and throwing all who stood in the way aside. And coming to the front of the Bumple, this creature leapt upon the altar and raised a hand as if to speak.

The Bumple zone was now in obscene confusion. The parallels of the company had been thrown out of true by this abrupt passage, and the young female collegians seemed to have caught some contagion, so that they shifted to and fro in an unpatterned way.

I did not know what worse obscenity might follow. And so I called upon eighteen of my graduates and placed them around me in severe prosenneahedral form. We then advanced towards the altar, meaning, if all persuasion by theorem should fail, to make Ho Mo accompany us to the acid bath by the gross extremity of corporeal clutch.

As we advanced, Ho Mo stretched an arm upwards and – Ka Li prays absolution for what must be written – plucked from its place, with gross material hands, the holy symbol of the Eternal Wheel. Since this was the tenth day of the seventh rotation, this was the Wheel of Crystal. And, holding this above its head, it cried out: 'Stay where you are! Or I smash this wheel in fragments on the Bumple floor.'

At this blasphemy many swooned. But I, by averting my eyes, and by clasping the orb of order on my belt, was able to maintain equipoise, although swept by nauseas.

Ho Mo stood there upon the altar, in its robes of azure inlaid with silver, holding the wheel above its head, and declaiming blasphemies, a few of which I still recall.

'The Wheel is a lie! There is nothing in the universe, from the pole of Oitar to the Milky Way to my ancient home of Earth, which is not cross-grained, contradictory, divided against itself, awkward, and at odds. It is in the dialectic of nature to be so. If time were a ring, then none could enter it. We must break the Wheel to be born, and if we break the Wheel, then we must die. You hang your Alls with the signs of the dead, and consume your existence contriving the rituals of immortality. But how can you know immortal life, who have never tasted mortality? What is eternity but a flash of consciousness, set like a glittering diamond in the clasp of dying flesh?'

Saying this, Ho Mo leapt from the altar and walked slowly down the aisle to the Bumple door, still holding the wheel aloft so that the company pressed back on each side to give passage. At the door Ho Mo turned. 'I have read these mortal sayings among my hostess, or mother's, papers: "Reason, or the ratio of all we have already known, is not the same that it shall be when we know more. The same dull round, even of a universe, would soon become a mill with complicated wheels." Do you wish to exist as crystals performing your patterns before an audience of ice? Our ratios must always be in flux. We must search always for the perfect ratio: but even as we reach out to grasp it, we have become changed through searching, and the ratio is no longer ours but it has become our own alienation, and we must begin the search again. My species destroyed itself in the search, but they might have reached out to new ratios far beyond your circinate programmes. They failed because they became too much like you. They fell into your binary logic-paths and feedback-loops. They feared their identity, and hung themselves round with the dead.'

Now Ho Mo walked outside the bumple door and went to stand beneath the Arch of Unhappening, which gave a frame of sunlight, catching the crystal wheel that glittered over the creature's head. We followed at a little distance, and heard it say, 'Because I am mortal, I must follow the mortal logic of choice. And now I will return to Sykaos, and leave you with your crystals and your wheels and your neuter dead, hung like equations from a rule. Is there any who will come with me?'

The males all stood silent, although some could scarcely stand from the agony of such blasphemies. But there was an unseemly stirring among the young females, and then one broke out of the peer-group and ran to Ho Mo beneath the Arch.

This was a female called Vev, with an ill-favoured corpse, for her breasts were somewhat distended, and upon one was a blemish or dark mole which had not been noticed in the tank (or the foetus would certainly have been dissolved); and it was said that the Adjusters had discovered a slight disproportion in the organ of aesthetics. And as Vice-Provost of the College, I can testify that the organ of obedience was sadly flawed.

Vev ran up to Ho Mo, and with a shameless eccentric motion threw arms about the male carcase, crying out the choice to go wherever Ho Mo would go; and that since Ho Mo had already given instruction in the Custom of the Apple, this was not to be asked as a favour but demanded as a right. Then Ho Mo clutched the eye of the wheel and, twisting it, broke out the crystal spokes and placed it over Vev's head, so that it fell about the neck like a collar; and in the same moment they both turned towards us, and made (as the Poet Oi Paz has declaimed in the Accounts) the Incongruous Noise.

At this sacrilege the Company was jarred out of every propriety, and all ran towards the Arch of Unhappening, as if meaning to bring these blasphemies to an end. Whereupon Ho Mo and Vev took each other's hands and ran swiftly towards our College. And since they broke every rule, leaping the parabola walls, and running clean across the radii of the avenues and through the grove of numbers (which my graduates, however distempered, could never do), they gained a great distance from us.

At the Eastern gate of our College there was a space ferry, of the type prepared long ago for the ill-fated Plantation of Sykaos. It was kept there to demonstrate the trajectories of flight, and Ho Mo (in the auxiliary role-kit of astronaut) had often in previous days entered the craft on the pretext of meditating upon the quotients of relativity.

Into this craft they both leapt, hand in hand, and Ho Mo flung himself upon the controls and switched over the anti-gravitational field. So that as we ran up – doing obeisance on our way to the diameter of the College close – the craft already floated above the ground. And I saw Ho Mo draw back the circle of energy, until the craft sped upwards to the furthest part of the cupola's arc, where, without checking speed, it crashed through the translucent wall and vanished into space.

It was a matter then of urgency that I grant absolution from all manner of etiquette to my Company, who each must run here or there, in most higgledy manner, to the College of Domology, since with each moment that passed our whole Orb was endangered by the ready-mix that escaped through the gash in the cupola roof. There were butlers to be hoisted aloft, and a draft to be drawn on the discard pool, and many other such unprogrammed haps.

What happened to the spacecraft I do not know. It contained

few provisions and less water, and no charts of space. If Ho Mo and Vev are yet living, they must assuredly come to an early dead-line, or return in a few days to Oitar.

Some say that the craft descended that evening in the region where lies the hermit-orb of Oi Paz. There provisions and charts of a sort might be found. But I account this to be a botched input and among the distempers of this terrible day.

Others say that they witnessed its fall that night, dropping towards the region of the pole, like a meteor shedding fire.

I do not say more than I know.

I Bow Low Before Thy Couch and Pray for Absolution

Ka Li, Vice-Provost, Coll. Stellan.

8   SENTENCE OF THE SUBLIME COUCH

WHEREAS the feral creature, Ho Mo, has, in twenty years of residence on this planet, committed untold abominations;

AND WHEREAS, when under Decree of Dissolution by the Sublime Couch, it committed hideous sacrileges and Contempt of Couch; abducted the young female, Vev; and, taking to space, became an Outlaw against the Rule;

BLASPHEMING THE RATIO OF THE WHEEL BY AN ACT OF FREE CHOICE:

IT IS SENTENCED THAT, should it ever return to Oitar, on what part so ever it may land, it shall be done to a dead-line instantly and without ceremony; and that, in the performance of this necessary act, Our people are absolved from the observance of every rule of ceremony, and may resort to touch or clutch;

AND IT IS SENTENCED THAT all who associated with it, in School or College, and most especially the females of Our Species, be held for twenty years in a place apart, under the authority of the Society of Adjusters, where they shall undergo the strictest regimen of absolution.

AND BOTH THESE SENTENCES ARE NECES-SARY

SO THAT WE MAY BE CLEANSED FOR EVER OF THE CONTAGION OF MORTALITY

En Ema (Arch Adjuster)
(pp GGs)

APPENDICES

9 EXTRACT FROM AN INPUT OF THE LOYAL COMMISSION OF BIO-ENGINEERS

... and as there were two hundred fertile females in its College, for each of whom this was the year of first impregnation, and one hundred and seventy of these have conceived, there is a certain difficulty here. One, or even two, of these foeti might carry mortal contagion. There is as yet no method known to bio-enginecraft of detecting and isolating these cases.

We shall of course keep every foetus in this cohort under close observation. But it is out of the question to destroy them all, in view of the serious depopulation figures recently declaimed by the College of Number. Therefore we cannot assure your Goodnesses that the infection is finally extirpated. Our genetographs indicate that the symptoms of the disease may not show themselves in the first generation. If inherited through the female gene-set, they could remain dormant for several generations, when they might suddenly recur. And if by any mishap the infection was conveyed to a Sper-man, then it would be distributed wholesale in one generation.

We therefore *recommend* that, for ten generations, no Sper-man shall be admitted from this line of heredity. So that on this account your Gracious Goodnesses may rest upon your Couch with easy bums.

There is one other possibility so remote that we scarcely need to mention it. Yet it should be noted that during this past year, when no fewer than 10,000 of our females in our many Colleges have received their first impregnation, Ho Mo on some occasions flouted the Rule of its College, and walked or rode at night in a purposeless manner around the City, uncompanioned. What it did during these breaches of Rule is not known. Yet if one Rule was broken, it is not beyond conception that others might have followed. So that we must admit to this doubt: that there could be one, or perhaps more, chances in 10,000 that somewhere in this orb the contagion has been passed on.

APPENDICES

But it would be absurd if we were to concern ourselves with such an unlikely concatenation of mishaps. We may dismiss the thought by recalling, from the works of Oi Paz, two proverbs of the hapless mortals of Sykaos: 'IT DOES NOT BEAR THINKING ABOUT', and 'IT WILL NEVER HAPPEN TO US.'

ABOUT THE AUTHOR

E.P. Thompson was born in England and graduated from Cambridge University. He divides his time between teaching and writing, and he works actively with the Campaign for Nuclear Disarmament and the Committee for European Nuclear Disarmament. One of our foremost historians, Thompson is the author of *The Heavy Dancers*, *Beyond the Cold War*, *The Making of the English Working Class*, *Whigs and Hunters*, and *William Morris*, and a coauthor of *Albion's Fatal Tree*. He is the author of the historic pamphlet *Protest and Survive*, and a coeditor of the book that grew out of it.